Immortal Wounds

by Angie Barton

This is a work of fiction. Names, characters, places, and incidents are the product of the author's imagination or are used fictitiously. Any resemblance to actual persons, living or dead, events, or locales is entirely coincidental.

Copyright © 2022 by Angie Barton

All rights reserved. No part of this book may be reproduced or used in any manner without written permission of the copyright owner except for the use of quotations in a book review. For more information: angie.barton@gmail.com.

First paperback edition April 2022

ISBN 979-8-9906472-0-6

Chapter 1

November 1882

Those who live in New England recognize the early whispers of winter. Daytime diminishes, leaving the sky more dark than light and the leaves, in their thick curtains of burgundy, amber and burnt orange, seemingly drop from their branches overnight, carpet the earth, and die. Light rainfall succumbs to snow, its brilliant pallor blinding as it layers upon the frozen ground while cold air invades donning the necessity of coats, hats, and gloves for every human who steps foot outdoors. The winter season shows no mercy to anyone who takes up residence in its space. And like the dull sky that materializes overhead, an aura of gloom soon spreads like wildfire, casting a melancholy spell over the young and old alike. But for Isobel, who was rarely bothered by cold temperatures, falling snow, and brisk winds, a sense of joy would reign this season. The birth of her daughter.

The child was due in January, the coldest month of winter, but Isobel knew she would arrive in December. December 21, to be exact—the Winter Solstice. A birthdate the girl, who had been named Charlotte, would share with her mother, grandmother, and all her female ancestors. Well, at least all who had been born with a gift.

It was during one of those frigid northern gusts, the kind that howls past covered ears and sends repeated shivers down one's spine, that the shrill sound of a scream carried to the water's edge and stopped Isobel mid step. She turned away from the dim ray of twilight that illuminated the horizon. It was barely six a.m.

Her stride, once smooth and effortless and unworthy of any notice, inexplicably stiffened as the cry pierced her ears.

"Mother?" Her eyes locked in an unfocused gaze as her heart slammed in her chest.

Isobel was miles from home, but the scream sounded as if it had come from behind. An image flashed through her mind, and a hollowness formed in her gut.

"Mother?"

Her breath puffed like small clouds of smoke while her long, dark lashes, refusing to blink, combed through the predawn haze of darkness for one of only two people she couldn't imagine living without. She was alone.

Loose sand, boulders and grassy areas became a blur as Isobel propelled herself away from the coastline and toward her hometown near Ipswich, Massachusetts.

Closed signs lined the window sills of the Apothecary, General Store, and other businesses, but even if the covered walkways had been littered with customers, Isobel would have gone unnoticed as she raced up Main Street and then disappeared down a forgotten path made of dried mud and pebbles. Most of the community claimed this path led to nowhere.

Nowhere good, that was.

Long and winding, the gravelly road led Isobel far from town before abruptly coming to an end. The crisp November winds stung her nostrils as she squeezed her eyes shut, and she drew in a breath. Her mother's magic, silent. The image from her earlier vision, gone. The only noise in the eerie silence that surrounded her came from the broken metal cemetery sign swaying in the distance. A rising heat filled her body.

The sun, which had climbed into a cloudless blue sky, cast a stream of light so bright that Isobel shielded her eyes upon reopening them. She squinted over the wildly growing grasses that stretched across the open field until the tiny cobblestone cottage came into view. On the rooftop, the silhouette of a magpie stood motionless just as Isobel had expected. She travelled fast, but she couldn't compete with the bird's ability to fly. Its eyes zeroed in on hers, and as an invisible force linked the two, it pulled Isobel home in seconds.

Placing a hand on the cool raised stones of the outer wall, Isobel laced her fingers through the dormant Boston Ivy. It wouldn't be long before the vines froze like woven strands of glass, glistening in the frigid sunlight. Leaning forward, Isobel peered into the window.

The draperies were drawn but sheer enough to see through. The room—a bit unkempt with its unmade bed and scattered clothing on the floor—sat quiet and empty. Isobel's warm breath fogged the glass in front of her. She rested her forehead against the window, and the thunderous beats of her heart slowed to a more normal rate. The room on the other side belonged to Thomas and her. It was where their children would be born. And where they had planned to live out their life. Together. Forever.

Releasing the vine, Isobel moved towards the large six-pane window in the center of the house. She bent around the weathered black shutter and heavy burgundy draperies that had yet to be fully opened, and peeked in.

Their parlor, neatly arranged with its second-hand furniture and small wooden tables her mother used for displaying her favorite objects, sat as empty and silent as Isobel had left it this morning.

Odd, she thought as she examined the stack of logs in the cold cast iron firebox. Her mother always had the wood lit before sunrise. A surge of adrenaline shot through her veins. Isobel opened her mouth to call out, but a feathered shadow swept over her, warning her to stay silent.

Isobel moved toward the last window that stretched unevenly below the roofline at the edge of the house. Her husband had added it when a gap between the roof and wall unexpectedly appeared after the last rainy season. Grabbing the long rectangular ledge mounted slightly above her head, she pushed up on tip toes and eavesdropped on the shouting that had suddenly erupted from the other side. The voice belonged to a man. And one Isobel didn't recognize. She looked through the bottom of the pane.

There were no drapes hanging, nothing to obstruct her view—just clear glass that allowed her to see across the room from the cast iron stove to the icebox to the shelf lined with mismatched jars of dried herbs from the garden. It was there, on the floor below the shelves, that she witnessed the unimaginable. Cold spread from her chest to fingertips as fear twisted through her. Her mother's warnings had become reality; the monsters had come.

The rock frame of the ledge crumbled under her grasp, and Isobel slid along the cobblestones, her body curling into itself as she dropped to the ground.

Visions raced through her mind like a movie reel rapidly ticking images across a screen; her mother, pale and lifeless on the floor, a strange man cradling her head. Thomas, crumpled in the corner, his neck bent at an unnatural angle. A strange man propped in the doorway, blood dripping from his long, razor sharp teeth.

The shouting came from the man kneeling on the floor. He was angry. Angry with—

"Dario!" he yelled again.

That must be the man with the fangs. And the one proudly responsible for draining the life from her mother and husband. Isobel covered her mouth, silencing the scream that filled her throat, and a darkness threatened to take her sight.

Her family was dead! Gone from her forever.

And gone from the stranger who sat on the floor equally distraught.

Dizziness consumed her. She clung to the ivy for support, closed her eyes, and swallowed down the bile that burned the back of her throat. She had to help her mother. Her eyelids flipped open; she couldn't be afraid.

On shaky legs, Isobel pulled herself to stand and moved to the window once again. The shouting had stopped, and now all that filled her ears were the deep sounds of sobbing. Of pleading. Of begging.

Buried in the nape of her mother's neck was the face of the man who had held her so gently minutes before. His fair hair intertwined with her mother's dark as his shoulders shook.

"How will I live without you?" His tone turned more angry than heartbroken as a rumble of laughter emerged from the vampire propped in the doorway.

Isobel's knees locked in place.

How would *he* live without *her*?

A cold sweat beaded across her skin. How dare this stranger make such a declaration. Isobel's love for her mother was fierce. Until she wed Thomas, it had been just the two of them, mother and daughter. What right did this man, this stranger, have to lay any claim over her mother?

Isobel drew in a slow and steady breath, but before she had a chance to blink, the man pulled away, blood stained tears trailing down his face, his eyes wide with their crimson irises spinning rapidly. He threw his head back, unhinged his jaw and exposed his razor sharp fangs, venom freely spilling from their tips. Isobel dropped below the pane of glass, her heart exploding in her chest as she collapsed against the cottage and gasped for air. She grasped the five pointed star that hung from her neck and brought it to her lips.

As she mouthed the broken words of a spell she had never mastered and pledged an irrational willingness to do anything if it would bring her mother back, she overheard his confession. The truth behind why the grieving vampire who knelt on warped floorboards and cradled her mother's lifeless body so lovingly cared. A sudden coldness hit at her core, and the charm fell from her lips.

"Mother!" Isobel screamed, and like the flip of a switch, the energy that surrounded her turned feral.

They had heard.

Chapter 2

A haunting stillness surrounded Isobel as she raced along the river's edge. No birds called nor animals scurried; even the water traveled silently as it poured downstream between the muddy banks near her feet. The only sounds were those of the dried leaves that crunched between her boots and the soft, damp earth.

"Fara, are you there?" Wide eyed, Isobel searched, pushing aside the low thorny branches that clawed at her arms and face like pointed, brittle fingers.

The magpie's harsh caw broke the silence as she spiraled from the sky. Her glossy black wings stayed tucked in tight until she reached Isobel's shoulders. Spreading them wide, she raced along beside her. Fara was Isobel's familiar.

Without warning, the energy that surrounded the two tensed, and Fara soared for the skies. Looking over, Isobel spotted the clearing and beyond it their refuge; the tangled brush and archaic white oaks and tall pines that outlined miles of dense forest along the northern border of Massachusetts.

"There!" she blurted. Pointing, she redirected Fara towards the trees on the horizon, and the two changed their course.

They had managed to escape before the vampires fled outdoors in search of the scream that still faintly echoed in the open air. Isobel wasn't sure how long she would remain hidden. Tears blurred her vision, and a sob choked in her throat; she had been too late to save her mother and husband. But she wasn't too late to protect herself. She pressed her lips together. She had to keep moving.

Fallen limbs and clusters of jagged rocks had formed a weak dam at a narrow point in the waterway. Splashing across the shallow water, Isobel flung herself onto the other side. Dry, decayed branches that lay beneath a carpet of fallen leaves snapped under her weight. Isobel rolled on her back and threw her arms across her stomach.

"I know; I should be more careful, quieter," Isobel said as Fara nudged at her hand. "But there isn't time."

Cloudy bursts of breath expelled from her lips as she spoke. The temperature was dropping.

"Fara, they are catching up to us. We have to keep moving." The bird flapped her wings and screeched.

Isobel brought her finger to her lips. "He will hear you." Fara's feet patted the dirt nervously; they had to go.

As her hand brushed against her face, Isobel caught sight of the limp roots and tiny blue flowers that dangled from her fist. She had grabbed a handful of the herb that grew hidden in their garden hoping it would grant her protection as she fled.

"You can't drop them, not one," she murmured. As if saying it aloud made it more real, more convincing that she would stay alive.

Jumping up, Isobel struck the ground harder, faster, her pace keeping time with the ever pounding of her heart. Overhead, Fara ascended high and out of reach again, but not out of sight. Just when Isobel believed herself to be lost, a feat that only her hurried desperation would allow to happen, for she knew the way through the dense overgrowth better than anyone, a clearing appeared. She would be visible as she made her way across the open field. If she could make it.

The sky above opened, and Isobel squinted from the sudden brightness of sunlight. She prayed the density of the woods ahead would grant her a few more seconds of freedom; that's all she needed.

Then, like a bullet, a burning sensation drilled into the back of her neck while a gust of icy air slammed into her and shoved her forward into the warmth of sunlight.

"Your God cannot help you now!" A voice shouted from behind as an intense pressure in her head caused her to stumble. She pressed her fists to her temples, clenched her teeth against the pain, and projected herself forward. She couldn't falter and she couldn't stop now.

In her Mind's Eye, long, stony fingers stretched out behind her. The hand belonged to Dario, the vampire who had slayed her family. Fara swooped and pecked at his taut, pale skin, and for a brief moment the pain in her head to subside. Dario reached for

Fara, but she dropped, ducking below his arm before spreading her ebony wings and climbing high once again.

The vampire's jet black hair blew away from his face as he returned his attention to Isobel. His skin tone, golden and brought to life by the magic of her mother's blood, glowed under the sunlight as he moved from underneath the canopy of branches and into the open field. His fitted white shirt and tan breeches made a striking contrast against the warmth of his flesh.

He stood well over six feet tall, his body fit and lean with muscle. The color of his brows and lashes mimicked his hair while his angular nose and chiseled jawline made him look as though he were carved from stone. Breath-taking and nearly God-like easily described his appearance. Had it been a different time under different circumstances, Isobel might have fallen for his glamour. But she knew that a demon, one she had witnessed only moments ago, resided below the surface of that impossible beauty.

Dario's full lips parted, the dried blood in the corners cracked and made him look even more sadistic. "I can hear your witch's blood racing through your veins. I will catch you, and when I do, I will drain you of life like your mother!" The roar of his promise shook the ground. His manner was neither charming nor manipulative. It was pure evil.

Her mother had warned her of dangerous creatures, ones that took joy in spilling blood and leaving hollowed bodies by the wayside. Isobel knew the aura he was experiencing from her mother's magic, but she also sensed a seething hatred Dario had for her. He pursued her for a reason. She wasn't prey, but rather a pawn. For what, she had no idea, but if he caught her, he would make good on his vow and kill her. Isobel, however, had no plans to give the blood-thirsty vampire that satisfaction.

Besides, he was wrong.

The blood that ran through her veins wasn't like her mother's. The years of failed attempts at reciting successful incantations had proven that a thousand times over. She resembled her mother in looks—tall, slender, wide-eyed with long, dark hair— but as for magical abilities, she had not been equally gifted.

Gritting her teeth, Isobel sealed her lips shut and swallowed the scream that again, rose from her lungs and begged to be released. She knew what she had to do. She looked at the heavens and gave a silent command. Fara dove in front of her.

"We have to go home. Your home. We will go see Mariam." The magpie screeched, the sound song-like as she circled overhead. Iridescent colors of blue and green shimmered off her long black feathers as she turned and twisted in flight beneath the open sky.

Isobel knew of a place where her existence would be less known and her past had yet to happen. Dropping her hands to her abdomen, she whispered, "I will keep you safe." The three of them would be welcomed but not completely free from danger. Other hunters would exist, but Mariam would protect them just as she had when Isobel and her mother had unexpectedly arrived at Elden Castle's door thirteen years ago. Isobel was only a child, but she remembered the comfortable warmth in Mariam's face as she opened the door that night.

Looking ahead, the shadowy edge of the more than three-hundred-year-old tree appeared. Their exposed knotty roots and woven slender limbs had formed a natural barrier against the outside world. But it was the darkness that lurked behind them that mesmerized Isobel as she said the words she had been born to speak, the only spell she could recite successfully. The sole form of magic Isobel possessed was the ability to travel through time.

Fire, water, wind, and earth, the time I'm in please reverse.

Take me to a past I've been before; I call ahead the open door.

Hazy particles of silky bands and shimmering silver threads emerged. Isobel coached the elements to weave together and take shape.

Ribbons of dark, and strings of light, bind together and hold on tight.

The circular motion became clearer, gaining speed as the black eye in the center pushed outwards; the portal was opening.

The space surrounding Isobel turned dreamlike, and as the energy from the gateway grew stronger, it guided her in. She no longer recognized the jarring of her body. Her lungs burned, and her heart beat remained fierce, but as always, Isobel never experienced the constricting pain, or shortness of breath. Easily, she stayed one step ahead of her hunter while her mind quickly searched for a time from the past.

Isobel envisioned the mountains, the heather-covered crags, and the glens and hidden lochs that she had explored as a child. She recalled the glistening falls and listened for their steady, splashing sounds as they moved and spilled into the glassy pools that formed below.

Gloomy skies came into view and the memorable dampness saturated Isobel's senses; thick and velvety air pressed against her face as its rich woody scent of heather filled her lungs.

The clouds parted and the familiar gray stone castle that stood majestically along the uneven cliff bordering the North Sea materialized. They would be far from home but amongst family. Isobel finished the spell.

In my mind, the place you see. Take me there and set me free.

Fara's screeching cries warned Isobel that Dario had caught up to her. She wrapped her arms around herself just as an unholy bellow of laughter exploded from behind.

Grabbing her hair, Dario jerked her head back.

"Noooo!"

The deafening command sounded in front of Isobel, and instantly her hair was released. Skidding to a stop, she searched for the voice that had ordered her freedom and found it standing at the edge of the open field, opposite of the portal. Unsure if the man in front of her, the one who had argued with Dario in her kitchen, and the reason she was running from her life, was real or a vision.

Drawn into the pools of his bright blue eyes, the richness of their color sharp and as deep as her own, Isobel found herself unable to look away. An unexpected rush of warmth filled her from head to toe, and unconsciously she took a step towards him. True to his command, anyone who looked this angelic couldn't have anything but her best interest at heart. She took another step. His brows narrowed, and he moved out of the shadows. He was real.

"Stay back!" Isobel threw her hands outwards and accidentally released the herbal protection she had carried this far. The tiny flowers and crumpled roots fell from her grasp and floated to the ground.

Pulling his lips back, the fair haired man freed an evil hiss and his eyes, now cold and black, looked fixedly past her. Isobel turned and discovered that his stare was for Dario, who stood motionless and silent behind her. For a moment she had forgotten him. He lifted his chin and sniffed into the air. Lowering his eyes, he met hers and his lips curled.

The rumble of a growl sounded, and slowly Isobel turned to the stranger. The expression on his face remained grim and forbidding, leaving Isobel unsure which one of them, she or Dario, the man directed such a chilling hostility towards. Her gut told her he was restraining himself from what he wanted to say, or worse, what he wanted to do. But to whom? she silently wondered.

Isobel planted her feet firmly on the ground. The frigid air that encircled her closed like a fist and made her light-headed, but she refused to cower in fear. As long as there was breath in her lungs, she would fight for her and her unborn daughter's life. She was not helpless; she was strong and fast. She had outrun Dario almost to the portal; if only the second vampire had stayed away she and Fara would already be safe with Mariam.

You knew he would appear, the logical part of her mind dared to say, *but he didn't return just for his own selfish reasons.*

"Stop!" Isobel yelled before remembering that she stood sandwiched dangerously in the middle of two blood thirsty hunters.

Lifting their brows, they tilted their heads as if they were waiting to hear more.

In the distance, the whirring sounds of the gateway became stronger. If only she could free herself and escape from the vampire's hypnotic stare that had returned. Instead, they remained frozen, each trapped in their own reverie. Which on some conscious level might unite—

No! Isobel silently screamed. She would not allow her thoughts to go there.

Despite the wide open space, a tightness pulled across her chest and her mouthed turned dry. Her hands, slick with sweat and numb from the cold, remained extended in front and behind her like a shield. The flowers she had clung to for protection now lay withered in the grass, useless, for they only worked if they were alive.

A pair of black-capped chickadees called in the distance. The lone sound, *Hey Sweetie*, carried above the open field from east to west and then back, over and over again. Isobel lifted her head to the tree line. Hidden safely among the interwoven branches, Fara waited, and she was not alone.

Her gaze returned to the vampire who stood in front of her and an unexpected heat tumbled in her core. His eyes, blue again, softened, and he spoke not from his mouth but from somewhere deep within her.

Isobel.

Her body faltered, and she stepped to the side to keep from falling.

His enchanting tone caressed her ears and filled her with uncontrolled emotions: love, admiration, sorrow, and pride. The feelings, however, were not her own. They belonged to the vampire who stood in front of her. He had a weakness, a vulnerability, and for a brief moment he allowed her access to it.

Fear paralyzed her. She fought to regain control of her mind, to break free from the trance he had pulled her into when a collection of images flashed through her head: her childhood in the garden, her adventures with Fara, her runs beside the ocean before daybreak, her wedding, the life that grew inside her. She gasped, and cold prickles of nausea flooded her gut.

How was this happening? How did he know?

The dry grass behind her rustled; Dario stirred. Isobel listened as he released an exaggerated sigh and cracked the bones in his fingers, a subtle reminder that he remained close.

A faint ringing sounded in her ears. The man's silent voice spoke again.

Breathe.

How could this be? she asked as she obeyed his command and carefully let the air out of her lungs. He's a monster. Cold. Hard and dead inside. His revelation this morning couldn't be true. Isobel's mind rebelled against the memory of his words; this man was not her father.

It's all true, daughter, but you have no reason to fear me. I have and always will protect you, he said, and then his words went silent. His brows pulled together and the dark look returned to his face. Another growl rumbled from his chest, and his eyes were once again black and focused on the vampire behind her.

The tension in Isobel's muscles lessened, and the warmth returned to her hands. His thoughts no longer filled her head; he had released her. Standing tall, Isobel squared her shoulders and pushed aside her fear, her sense of apprehension receding into the background.

Unsure if the vampire standing in front of her and claiming to be her father could read her mind or just project his own ideas, Isobel refused to think through her plan any further.

"Fara, now!" Isobel yelled, and they raced towards the portal.

Chapter 3

Feeling stronger than she ever believed herself to be, Isobel lifted her right foot, and as her body crashed through the outer edges of tangled brush and into the spinning black hole she had summoned, she jumped.

"Isobel, no! You are safe with me!" His shout entered the portal just before it closed.

Isobel tumbled end over end, her body weightless as it swirled through the rift towards another place in time. The vampire's words echoed off the invisible walls and filled Isobel's ears until they faded and a steady humming sound took their place. Her arms jerked out into the blackness, but other than the magical current that sent tingles throughout her body, the space she fell through was empty.

Warm, stale air smothered her face, and Isobel gasped for breath. She was terrified, but the cause had little to do with traveling through portal. The images the man had projected in her mind were memories. He had watched and made a mental note of her every move; the visions had unfolded the story of her life. His words that chased her into the past may have been silenced, but Isobel knew his claim to her would haunt her forever.

Flashbacks unraveled, stories of a man so gallant and selfless, brave and honorable who had died for his country shortly after Isobel had been born emerged and clashed with the visual images the vampire had shown her. Her mother had described her father as noble. Trustworthy. A loving and dedicated father and husband. She had made him sound real. Human.

But was he?

So many questions combined with the suffocating darkness blurred Isobel's mind, and a rush of heat soared through her veins. Painfully, her body bent and twisted as the suction of the portal turned abnormally strong and forced a wave of fatigue over her earlier than normal.

In the past, Isobel's time travel had been carefree, gentle and quick; this was taking too long. It was as if the veil between the two worlds was obstructed, impassable. Her body always required rest afterwards but never while she was in the portal. She could barely keep her eyes open. Something wasn't right. Maybe it was the pregnancy.

Isobel feared for her daughter's safety as the unborn child hardened within her body. Forcing her hands towards her abdomen, she fought against the current, desperate to offer the comforting touch of a mother, when suddenly, a whisper of voices bounced off the gateway wall and struck at her from every angle. Their words, as they intermingled with the dull hum of the portal's vacuum, were indecipherable, but the essence of their energy—every vibration, every wave, every particle—alerted Isobel that they came from the past: souls of the dead, mortal and immortal.

Ghostly visions of flames and dripping blood flashed behind her closed lids; death had not come easy to many of them. An unrest weighed heavy in the underworld of witches and vampires; an injustice that would be made right. The curse had long been spoken. A prophecy set in place. The sounds grew in volume. If only she could fully make out what they were saying.

In time. They were the only words spoken clearly just as her air became restricted.

Isobel clawed at her neck as terror squeezed at her closing throat. Her thin, delicate skin clumped under her nails as she tore at her flesh, drawing the wetness of blood and the stinging of pain while the indiscernible walls of the portal closed in. Then she landed.

A storm had blown through, but the soft earth and lush rain-soaked grasses did little to pad her fall. Lightning streaked across the sky, and crashes of thunder shook the wet ground. Rolling to her side, Isobel coughed and allowed the perfume of the damp air to fill her nostrils as she gasped for breath. Thankful for the open space, she waited for the spinning of her vision to stop.

"Fara?" Her voice cracked, its sound not more than a whisper as her eyes grew heavy and exhaustion set in.

Trembling, Isobel ignored the dry, burning sensation that lined her throat and gulped back the tears that tried to escape between her closed lids. She moved her hands to her stomach and waited. A flutter, then a kick bounced against her. Then Fara landed in the grass beside her.

"There you both are." They were Isobel's last words before helplessly falling into a deep sleep.

Isobel had not time walked since becoming pregnant for fear of harming her daughter. The physical toll it took on her body alone was one thing. Not to mention the threat that she could become trapped and not make it back. Growing up, her mother had warned her repeatedly that her time traveling ability would not last forever. Returning to the Highlands had been a dangerous risk, but at the time she hadn't seen another choice.

"We made it," she said in a voice that she finally recognized as her own. Sitting up, she wondered how long she had been asleep.

Thick thunder clouds tumbled between her and the black sky; it was night.

Isobel caressed her belly and the soft black feathers of her familiar. But as she sought to regain her composure, a wariness developed around her, and the hairs along the back of her neck stood on end. It was too dark to see clearly, but Isobel's surroundings were not like she remembered.

Getting to her feet, she quickly moved into the shadows. Her heart slammed into her chest and sweat beaded across her forehead as she probed her surroundings.

"There is more land, and the trees—" Isobel had difficulty finding the right words for what she was seeing. Or rather, what she wasn't.

"The wall around the castle has fallen, or could it be that it's being rebuilt? And the gatehouse—where is it? It isn't here."

Frowning, Isobel stepped slowly into the open field. Through the leaves and tall grasses, the air swirled and whispered of a haunted time; a history Isobel knew all too well. She covered her mouth and ran back to the darkness as the stench that encircled her head slid down the back of her throat and she gagged. Fara nervously patted the wet grass beside her before flying to a nearby branch; she sensed the danger, too.

"Fara, I know this smell." A vision of evil entered Isobel's head as she leaned into the tree for support.

It was exactly how they had described it: putrid, yet sweet. Isobel scanned the darkness again, slower this time, and as she recalled the gruesome tales that her mother had once shared, she wondered if it were daylight, would she see a sky filled with the tendrils of smoke from a persecution. A fire smoldered somewhere in the distance, but Isobel saw no flames, no stake mounted on a platform, and no rope, or worse, swinging from a tree.

"It's the smell of burning flesh, Fara." Isobel was horrified, and the magpie squawked.

Bile rose in Isobel's throat. Death by fire was not something that should be wished upon for anyone. She braced herself against the Scots pine's scaly trunk for support and heaved again. Her fingers dug into the rough bark and a crack sounded, the base of the tree shifting under Isobel's touch.

"Gentle, Isobel," her mother's reminder of caution spoke in her head. "You cannot draw attention to yourself. Your strength is far too great and will not go unnoticed." Releasing the trunk, Isobel sought self-control. If she were going to stay hidden, the trees were going to have to remain upright and in place.

Looking out, she focused all her attention on the castle she had called upon for safety.

The fortress sat on perfectly leveled ground that left one to believe it had been created specifically to hold such a magnificent structure. Isobel took in the smoothness of the stones and the coarseness of the dark mortar that bound it together. The sheer gargantuan size, tall towers and massive, oversized wooden doors held her just as captive as they had the first time she had seen it.

Isobel had lived within the comfortable walls of her mother's small home in Massachusetts since she had been born, December 21, 1862. Its simplicity in design was not remotely comparable to the castle before her. Elden Castle looked as magnificent as it had thirteen years ago, an emblem of majesty, dedication and protection, and Isobel felt a sense of relief that they had made it here.

"Mariam will help us," she said as she fought to ignore the thick taste of death that coated her tongue.

Her stomach churned, but as she stepped from under the shadow of pine branches once again and into the light of the moon, she realized she wasn't alone. Isobel froze, her eyes locked on the sudden movement of a small figure approach a side door at the base of the castle.

Shaking off her cloak, the girl unleashed the most beautiful amber colored curls laced with golden strands. The colors came alive as they shimmered down her back under the bright moonlight that glowed between the passing clouds. Isobel's mystical senses stirred and the hairs along her neck crawled. The girl was a witch.

With one hand on the lever, the girl turned and looked in Isobel's direction before she slipped inside the narrow opening and closed the door behind her.

In the distance, a clanging of church bells rang, and Isobel spun in their direction. The sound was faint but distinct as it echoed off the mountains. *Impossible!*

She and Fara looked at one another. The monastery was crumbled into rubble the last time they were here.

Fara paced along the branch as Isobel squinted into the blackness of night, searching for anything that was recognizable other than the stone stronghold that towered above her. A moist breeze blew past and carried the bells reverberating sound across the land.

Resting her palm against the rough bark of the tree, Isobel closed her eyes and searched for Mariam's earthy heather scent. But what filled her nostrils instead were scents of the Highlands; lightly flowery and sugar candy sweet, briny, and wet, then finally burned flesh.

She channeled deeper for the soft yellow illumination of energy that had radiated around her ancestor the night she and Isobel's mother worked together. Neither had shown any response to Isobel's spying; instead, they seemed only aware of one another, the small book that lay opened between them and the magical tinctures they whispered over. The chemistry between the two women had caused Isobel's own skin to tingle those nights. However, tonight she detected nothing.

Isobel studied the highest arched window of the north tower. A faint glow suddenly lit the opening, and a silhouetted image stood in the open space.

"It's not Mariam." Isobel sighed and her shoulders fell as she exhaled, unaware that she had been holding her breath. "The frame is too large."

Bolts of lightning again streaked across the sky and were followed by an explosive crack of thunder. In the brief seconds of light she had caught a glimpse of the stranger that stood in the tower window.

"It's a man."

Fara stilled.

A large, icy raindrop fell on Isobel's head. Then another and another. The heavy sky that hung repressively over the castle threatened to give way to the weight of the rain that filled it.

"Another storm is approaching, Fara. I need to get inside.

Will you be well?" The magpie bobbed her head.

"As soon as I can, I'll open a window so you can come in. Mariam will be happy to see you too, I am sure." Fara walked to the edge of the branch and cocked her head towards Isobel.

"I'll be fine, I promise," Isobel reassured her. Fara bobbed her head once more, then took flight towards the tallest turret.

Surefooted, Isobel followed the rock lined path toward Elden Castle. Despite the bumpy terrain and slippery cobblestones that felt cool and hard through her leather soles, she made it with ease along the narrow winding path straight to what she remembered was the entrance; the beautiful, handcrafted set of doors whose arched peak where they came together was greater than twice her height.

As Isobel reached the oversized, dark wooden doors, a sensation ran through her and an unsettling feeling formed in the pit of her stomach.

You shouldn't be here, it warned; *you won't be welcomed.*

Isobel threw her fists outwards, ignoring the forewarning, but before she made contact, the door opened and a pretty but timid looking woman peered around its edge.

"Hello?" she spoke, and her eyes grew big.

Isobel knew how disheveled she must look; water soaked and hair a tangled mess.

"Mariam," Isobel said. She lifted her chin and took a step closer. "I need to see Mariam."

This was not the same woman Isobel had seen slipping inside the castle moments ago. Rather, this woman had golden hair that hung straight below her shoulders, and she appeared taller, standing eye-to-eye with Isobel. The light that glowed behind her illuminated her silhouette, making it difficult for Isobel to see her clearly, but she sensed no connection or shared magical powers as the two stood face to face. This woman was undeniably human, but the only gift that ran through her veins and wafted from her body was kindness.

"Mariam?" the stranger repeated as she fumbled with the heavy wool shawl around her shoulders. Her eyes narrowed. "There's no Mariam."

Isobel swayed and grabbed the edge of the opened door.

No Mariam?

As she opened her mouth to ask the curious looking woman who she was, the skies opened and the rain came down in sheets. Tiny splatters of mud bounced off Isobel's boots, the downpour hammering the ground around her.

The woman pulled the door open a little wider, and a waft of heat warmed Isobel's face.

"Please come in."

Chapter 4

"Elspeth! Who's there?" shouted an irritable voice as the woman inside reached for Isobel.

A large hand caught the door, and a man stepped in front, forcing Isobel to take a step back and into a shallow puddle that was quickly forming. Towering over her by at least a foot was the man whose silhouette Isobel had seen in the tower window minutes earlier.

His blond hair hung in long, thick waves, and its ends pulled Isobel's eyes to the heaviness of his shoulders that filled the open space where she and the woman once stood. His size and obvious strength was intimidating, but it was the glare from his piercing blue eyes that made her so frightened she was unable to look away. This man was the exact definition of a battle thirsty warrior.

"Mariam; I'm looking for Mariam," Isobel repeated, forcing the words from her tight throat.

Her voice was firm, but its sound was lost to the heavy rains that fell behind her. The warrior narrowed his brow in reaction. She hoped this giant of a man would know Mariam, and that, despite his obvious annoyance, would whisk her inside and deposit her at her ancestor's feet before she said another word. Instead, the angry scowl spread across his face, and Isobel's knees buckled.

She threw her hands forward and grabbed ahold of the first thing within her reach: the strip of blue plaid that lay proudly across his battle scarred chest. He didn't falter as she clung to him, nor did he offer her any assistance. The heat from his body sent a shock to her fingers and another warning of danger shot through her.

You are not safe.

Her fists pressed against him, and Isobel regained her footing and stepped back. Lightning illuminated the sky and reflected off the metal bracket pinned at his left shoulder. The family crest was not one she recognized.

"Gavan, move! Let this lass come inside before she drowns!" The command came from Elspeth, and she pushed her way between the two. Taking Isobel by the hand, she pulled her indoors.

"Wait here."

Shivering, Isobel watched the woman scurry down the hallway and disappear through an arched opening. Her eyes scanned the foyer in search of the elegant paintings, woven rushes, and enormous firelit sconces she remembered admiring as a child. This entrance had once looked regal, but tonight the gray stone walls looked as cold and dank as Isobel.

She craned her neck, following the curvature of the grand staircase in front of her and each of the stone steps; wide at the bottom, then narrowing before leveling off at the second landing. Missing was the ornate floor covering that lay centered down the steps, giving it warmth and character, and the intricate carvings that dug deep along the posts and banister.

Was Mariam in the process of renovating? That would explain the missing features both inside and out of the castle.

Isobel returned her attention to the warrior, whose eyes seemed to be watching everything at once, the door behind him wide open. She brushed the wet hair from her eyes. Being inside filled her with a renewed sense of energy, and she met his haunted stare.

"Thank you," she said. "For allowing me to come in, that is. I apologize if I've intruded. I won't stay long. I need to speak with Mariam. My name is Isobel. I haven't been here since I was a child, but she will know me." She forced a thin, nervous smile around her chattering teeth as she spoke.

Gavan adjusted his arms across his chest, and in one step, moved within inches from where Isobel stood. The sound of the pounding rain filled Isobel's right ear while the crackling of firewood sounded in her left. Color flushed her cheeks as the brooding man—whose face tensed with anger— furrowed his brows even tighter and slowly studied her from head to toe.

Isobel shook the water from her skirt and adjusted the bodice of her dress where his eyes seemed to have fixated. However, her attempt at modesty did nothing to break his glare.

Returning with a blanket, Elspeth threw it over Isobel's shoulders, closed the heavy wooden door and led Isobel into another room.

"Come by the fire; we need to get you dry," Elspeth said as she rubbed Isobel's arms to generate some heat and calm her shivering.

The brute in a kilt followed them, the stomping of his heavy steps sounding right behind them. Isobel sensed that if she stopped, he would step on them both. Had she not been so uncertain of who these people were or caught from the corner of her eye the swinging motion of his sword, she would have done so just to irritate him.

"Elspeth!" he commanded.

Isobel jumped.

"What are you doing? We don't know who this woman is!"

"Come, sit," she told Isobel and lowered her in a chair by the fire, ignoring the man.

Isobel wondered if he were a guard who had been left in charge. Other than the stories her mother had told her, those of her ancestors, of witchcraft and strong matriarchs from centuries ago, Isobel didn't know much about daily life in Scotland. Mariam had had guards, even though she was completely able to protect herself. But this woman kneeled before her wasn't a witch, although tonight she did appear to be in charge.

The chair swallowed Isobel's slender frame, and both

looked miniature as they sat in front of the massive stone fireplace. Large pieces of wood stacked at least four feet tall filled the firebox, and for a moment Isobel sat hypnotized by the elongated flames that danced in the enclosed space.

Looking around the room, Isobel recognized the large lofty ceiling and windows on the south side. Missing, however, were the long, heavy plum colored drapes that had flanked them on either side. No, tonight the room was bare and unfamiliar, its furnishings unrecognizable compared to Isobel's memories.

"Lass, what happened to you? Were you attacked?" Elspeth pointed to her neck as she spoke. Her soft tone was filled with as much concern as her wide, clear blue eyes. Eyes, Isobel noticed, that were identical to the warrior's.

"Where am I?" Isobel whispered as she reached for her throat. The raw skin from where she had clawed at her neck in the portal stung under her touch.

Elspeth propped Isobel's feet and covered her with another fur. Isobel waited for the kind woman to answer. The heat from the blazing fire warmed her face, and she shrugged the blanket from her shoulders and allowed the rest of her body to absorb it.

"You're in the Highlands, of course," Elspeth answered, smiling now. "At Elden Castle in Dunkinshire."

"Elspeth!" Red faced, Gavan charged toward the two women, the vein along the middle of his brow throbbing. Isobel gripped the arms of the oak chair.

Dunkinshire. Elden Castle. She was in the right place, but who were these people?

Isobel considered summoning the portal when a stream of energy entered the room and pulled her from her thoughts. The scent of lavender surrounded her as invisible tendrils of magic so intimate and familial wove together with her own. For a brief moment, Isobel felt so overcome with homesickness and nearly cried out *Mother!* when a sudden sense of darkness gripped her—the smell of witching.

Swoosh, swoosh, a faint swinging motion reverberated in Isobel's ear. The sound grew louder, slowing her heart and rocking her bones with the continuum of motion. Isobel's hands held tighter to the arms of her chair, and she prayed that she could remain still. The wood beneath her fingers cracked under her grip. The splintering sound was distant against the pendulum but close enough to alert Isobel she had to let go before it disintegrated in her grasp.

In her Mind's Eye, Isobel saw the perpetrator: the girl with the shimmering curls. Her beauty was unmistakable yet deceiving. Isobel's mind became dizzy, and her eardrums seared with pain while the young witch probed through her subconscious and searched for clues as to who Isobel was.

Who are you? The words slithered from Isobel's mind, and she looked past Gavan and Elspeth, neither showing any reaction to the vibrating sound, and into the darkness of the corridor where the girl hid.

Rush! The swiping movement of a hand seized the swinging, and the hypnotic motion silenced; Isobel was released.

"Meg, come in here." It was the Highlander who spoke as he turned toward the arched doorway they had walked through minutes earlier. An amber lock bounced in the dim light at the wall's edge.

"Meg? Who's Meg?" Isobel asked, her voice hoarse and body rigid in the chair. Slowly, she worked to steady her breathing.

"Gavan, you called for me?" answered a sweet, song-like voice as a young woman stepped gracefully around the corner and stole all of their attention, her slim hand slipping inside the pouch at her waist as she did.

Her large round eyes were shaped identical to the Highlander's yet their color was the deepest blue Isobel had ever seen, like sapphires and diamonds. Isobel followed them as they roamed the room, looking everywhere except at her. Her knowledge regarding how the eyes mirror one's soul came to mind.

Those whose eyes are a rich shade of blue often lead multiple lives, so you must be cautious, Isobel, her mother had warned. *They don't believe many would understand their ways, so they keep to themselves and often don't speak the truth.*

Isobel's gaze remained on the girl as she proceeded across the room toward the warrior as he had commanded. The invisible stream of energy that flowed from her tightened the closer she got to the hearth.

A sweet smile, one that Isobel sensed was full of secrets, pulled at the corner of Meg's lips and her defiant eyes finally looked up and met Isobel's as she stopped in front of Gavan. Isobel's blood recoiled, sending a shock throughout her system. The fire in the hearth popped, and Elspeth jumped.

A dark blood brews beneath her fair skin, whispered a voice deep inside of Isobel.

"Meg, fetch her some ale," Elspeth said, and she took a step away from the fireplace.

Plaited spirals still sat atop Meg's head, and they created the illusion that she was wearing a halo. Random strands of golden hair had broken free and jutted out around her face. The disheveled look suggested that Meg had been moving carelessly and at a hurried pace.

Isobel pushed the heavy fur from her shoulders. The heat and sudden sweet scent of honeysuckle that filled the room had become too much. Her thoughts turned hazy, and she felt off balance.

"Meg is our sister," Elspeth explained, smiling. "The youngest, you know. Gavan is the oldest, and me in the middle."

Elspeth's words sounded distorted and distant, indistinguishable to Isobel's ears. She needed to speak, but the words she wanted to say fled from her mind. Her onlookers' brows drew together and their eyes squinted, the looks on their faces ones of confusion. Isobel stood, and Elspeth took hold of her hands.

"Lass?" Elspeth questioned.

"No ale, please," she whispered as a flash of honesty washed over her; there was no Mariam.

The buzz of nearing unconsciousness rang in her ears, and her vision clouded.

No! Isobel silently screamed. *Stay awake!*

Her grip on Elspeth's hands tightened, and the woman cried out in pain. Isobel knew she was crushing the woman's delicate fingers, but she couldn't let go. She couldn't close her eyes and lose sight of these strangers. It was too dangerous.

Gavan stepped forward and caught Isobel just before she hit the floor, the invisible current between her and Meg snapping against his intrusion just as total darkness threatened to take Isobel's sight. Instantly, her mind cleared, and she gasped, her lungs begging for more air, her eyes wide open.

"Please put me down," she stammered.

But Gavan didn't budge; his arms pinning her to his chest. Standing steady, he appeared unaffected by her added weight. His eyes met hers and then traveled downward until they reached her mid-section. His body stiffened.

Isobel wanted to disappear, to summon the portal and escape once again. But her body had not fully recovered, and she feared how its weakening would affect her unborn child. Besides, the chants only worked if spoken aloud. If she opened her mouth, death would come for certain. She had to get away from this castle and these people, whoever they were. Her mind struggled as to where she would go. Returning home wasn't an option. The vampires would be looking for her.

Gavan lowered her in the chair. And as she inhaled, Gavan's scent of strength and knowing filled her nostrils. The warning that spoke to her before she had knocked on the castle door echoed in her head again.

"Isobel?" It was Meg who spoke, her tone smug. She stared at Isobel thoughtfully, then turned to leave the room.

Isobel's glare bore through the long shimmering curls, and the girl stilled. Meg was unlike her brother and sister. Isobel looked back and forth at Meg's siblings. Elspeth showed no reaction to her younger sister's peculiarity, but Isobel detected a slight quickening of Gavan's heart, and his once dry brow was now glazed over with sweat.

Meg stopped in the doorway and looked back, a repressed smile on her lips.

"What is the time? The year?" Isobel whispered.
"It's the year of our Lord, 1597," the Scottish Highlander answered, his tone thundering in the near silence that surrounded them.

Panic rose in Isobel's chest, and she clutched her belly; she had landed one hundred years too early! The eyes of the three strangers standing before her fell to the wet clothing that clung to her like a second layer of skin.

"Oh my!" Elspeth threw her hands to her face. "How did I not notice?"

Damn the rain.

"My daughter"—Isobel found the words as she slid her arms protectively around her waist— "will be here in eight weeks."

"A girl?" Gavan moved his hand to his hilt. "And how do you know it's a girl?"

Deep creases returned to his brow. Isobel couldn't tell them how she knew she was carrying a daughter. That she had sensed her pregnancy from the day she conceived and had witnessed it from the inside as her daughter's tiny body grew. Or how she knew the baby had green eyes and the shadow of dark hair like her mother, and her father's mouth and long fingers. And that since the moment they learned of her creation, they had called her Charlotte. No, Isobel couldn't tell them any of that.

Looking first at Gavan and then Elspeth, Isobel locked eyes with Meg and chose a more suitable answer.

"The sickness I've had points to the child being a girl."

Nodding her head, Elspeth understood, and she put her arm around Isobel's shoulders. "This is your first?"

"Yes," Isobel answered, and her eyes returned to Gavan.

"Well, it could be a wee bit longer. Sometimes the first one likes to take their own sweet time."

True, thought Isobel, but the child had a greater chance of arriving early, according to the birth of female children in her family.

Elspeth patted Isobel's hand, but Isobel's full attention remained on Gavan. His features had turned stoic and unreadable. His eyes were serious, and his lips now sat closed in a hard, flat line. Isobel liked it better when she could see his anger.

Gavan held onto the hilt of his sword, and his eyes veered from Isobel to Meg and then back again.

Isobel stood silent, unsure what to do next, when the explanation for Gavan's behavior became apparent; he wasn't as oblivious to his sister's abilities as Isobel had first thought. But why glare at her? What did his sister have to do with her?

The answer, Isobel sensed, was what sounded the warning through her veins.

Chapter 5

Meg's breath sounded loud in her ears, the thundering of her heart even louder. She left the hall before the others; she had to pull herself together. Slumping into the wall, she sucked in a breath and focused on the rise of her chest as her lungs filled with the damp air from the storm and the heavy scent of lavender that wafted from Isobel's skin. Sliding her hand into the pouch at her waist, Meg grasped her mother's ring and the delicate chain that it dangled from. Her little finger tingled as she pushed it through the circular opening until it sat secure at the first knuckle. She exhaled.

Meg had sensed Isobel's energy when she approached the castle minutes before, but she hadn't known where it was coming from. She had been standing with one hand on the lever of the door when a swarm of Highland midges encircled her head and sounded an alarm. Meg recalled the reverberating noise of their wings as they beat frantically in an attempt to stay aloft. The sound translated into the words Meg first refused to believe she had heard but now knew were true: *She is here.* Meg had shooed the annoying insects away, but as she swatted the air around her face, she discovered it was empty. Although her skin felt alive with their touch, there were no flies.

Afraid that one of the villagers had seen her viewing the execution and followed her home, Meg slipped quickly inside and locked the door behind her. It wasn't until she stood in the shadows at the top of the staircase and watched the trio move from the foyer to the hall that Meg got her explanation.

With her mother's charm in hand, Meg had moved down the steps once the three were no longer in sight. A glimpse: that's all she wanted of the stranger who had her own skin tingling and her siblings' emotions at war with one another. None of them would ever know she was there. But as Meg peeked around the corner, she gasped. Isobel was already staring in her direction.

The striking dark-haired witch with electric green eyes who sat warming herself next to the stone hearth was the vision from her dream two nights ago. Meg remembered the images that had woken her with a fright.

Refusing to be charmed by the light that illuminated around Isobel, Meg stepped back into the corridor and leaned into the wall. Squeezing her eyes shut, she attempted to block out the numbered vision and bring forth another, one that would be more useful and that Meg would understand.

Move! Meg thrust her hand forward, and the ring that hung from the chain swayed.

Faster! she commanded as she stood still and concentrated, her eyes wide open and her focus solely on the woman who sat on the other side of the wall. The charm swung steadily as commanded. The answers she sought stirred inside, but what came forth Meg couldn't comprehend.

An unsettling feeling formed in the pit of her stomach as an image from the stranger's mind appeared. Meg's palms grew slick with sweat as a cold and evil presence bore a wicked smile. Venom oozed from the tips of sharp white teeth over smooth red lips and down the chiseled jawline below it. Meg watched the poisoned string of saliva hang suspended in the air and then release, dropping to the floor.

Snatching the pendulum, she forced the swaying motion to stop but remained hypnotized from the vision that had yet to fade from her sight. Magic surrounded Meg, yet her heart raced and her knees trembled.

The blood that flowed beneath Isobel's skin was as mysterious as her own; chilled, and haunted, and fed a strange craving within. Much like herself, a world of dark secrets lay hidden inside Isobel. One, in particular, was powerful. And dangerous. And strangely familiar.

~~~~~~~~~~~~~~~~~

"Well, we can't put her out in the rain, Gavan; be sensible," Elspeth pleaded, placing her hands on her hips.

"I don't like it. I get a bad feeling," he responded, bracing his feet apart. The frown returned to his face as his fists rested on his hips.

"Oh, you frighten too easily, brother, listen to too much

talk. She is a fraction of your size and with child. What do you think she's going to do?"

If they were attempting to speak in private, they were not successful. They turned and looked at Isobel as if they expected her to answer. She returned the blank look then shifted her attention to her surroundings.

The circular room was cold and hard with its bare stone walls, and until a fire was built was rather uninviting. Upon the mantle sat several heavy candleholders, and Isobel watched as Elspeth captured a small flame from the firebox and lit the candles for a bit more light. She freed the woven tapestry from its peg; ceasing the cold, damp wind that blew between the slats of the wooden shutters that covered the room's only window.

"We can sort the details tomorrow. I'll go and fetch the midwife to look at her head and those scratches and make sure the bairn is fine, and then we can help her on her way," Elspeth said as she shook the blankets and laid them across the bed.

"And thank you for building the fire," she continued, nodding in Gavan's direction.

"A good night's rest is what we need." Meg forced a yawn. "Rest will make everything much clearer."

Gavan ran his hands through his hair and clasped his fingers behind his head.

"Get some sleep, lass; don't you worry," Elspeth reassured Isobel with a gentle smile. "You can wear this for the night." She placed a folded white smock on the end of the bed.

But Isobel did worry. Despite the fire Gavan had roaring in the hearth, the room was frigid. And strange, and these were strangers and she was in their home. Isobel knew she should be afraid, but something unexplainable kept her at ease.

"You two go to bed. I'll be in the great hall if you need me for anything," Gavan said. The footfalls of his boots sounded heavy against the floor as he followed his sisters without giving Isobel a second look.

The lock in the door clicked into place.

Meg bid her siblings goodnight at the end of the corridor and quickly moved toward her room. Time was running out, and she couldn't be late. Her life, and that of Gavan and Elspeth, unbeknownst to them, depended on it.

She closed her door and rushed to the window. Pulling open the tapestry, Meg took the pendulum from her pocket and wrapped it carefully in a pair of stockings that she had left folded on the ledge. She had been five years old the night Elspeth lowered the charm into her hand, but she remembered it like it was yesterday.

"I have so many questions, so much to learn," Meg whispered as her fingers doubled the soft fabric again and again. Her charm safely hidden inside. "But I will learn, Ma, I promise." She tucked the sacred piece away where it wouldn't be found and gathered her things.

Rolling up a few blankets, Meg stuffed them along with a couple of pillows under the coverings on her bed in case Gavan looked in on her. She pulled on her darkest woolen cloak and slipped off her shoes, shoving them under her arm as she made her way to the hidden stairwell.

Placing her hand on the stone wall, Meg crept counter-clockwise down the winding staircase. The complete darkness had once spooked her, but that was years ago. As a child, Meg had spent weeks counting steps, sixty-one to be exact, along with memorizing the pattern of their varied sizes: narrow, narrow, wide, narrow. The pattern repeated itself in reverse until she reached the bottom.

"Sixty-one." Meg stepped softly onto the landing below the last step.

Taking a few more seconds before she slipped out, Meg made sure Gavan had settled himself as promised.

A dim light from the hearth filled the hall. The flames that had soared when they were together had disappeared. Now the only glow came from the mounds of deep orange colored embers amongst the ash. Gavan shifted in the chair next to them, his back to Meg.

Standing, he scooted the chair away and paced. Meg pushed herself flat against the wall. Blanketed in the dark, Meg knew Gavan couldn't see her, but his sudden movement had caused her heart to accelerate.

Gavan was a worrier. Ever since their father had died, he had put his obligation of protecting Elspeth and her above his other duties. Meg knew that having a stranger whom he didn't trust bedding in his home, even a mere girl with child, would make him anxious and life miserable for them all. Gavan agreed to one night and would expect Isobel to be gone tomorrow, but Elspeth was equally stubborn. When her siblings got something stuck in their heads, it was nearly impossible for them to concede.

Shaking her head, Meg pushed aside her prediction of Gavan and Elspeth's wants. She had more pressing matters to attend to before she focused on tomorrow.

Creeping towards the exit, she lifted the lever and opened the door wide enough to squeeze through before gently pulling it closed. Reaching under her arm, she grabbed her shoes and slipped them on.

Meg slinked along the walls of the castle until she was certain she couldn't be seen. Pulling her hood over her head, she took off downhill, winding around the slickened cobblestones as her feet slapped through the rain filled puddles. The skipping of her heart increased, and mud splattered the edge of her smock and filled her shoes, but Meg was oblivious.

She looked ahead, thinking she had to be close, but from the moonlight that glowed between the broken clouds, the tree line appeared to retreat as she moved forward.

Thunder rumbled in the distance, and Meg pushed herself

faster; she had to get to the edge of the cliff before Cristian came looking for her. For them all.

"I. Am. Coming." Meg prayed the vampire was close enough to hear the sputtered words between her ragged breaths.

Chapter 6

Cristian ducked under the arched opening and headed north.

"Cristian!" The shouts came from behind. They would have to wait.

Stepping onto the road, he veered away from the crowds in an attempt to distance himself from their all too familiar and tedious conversations.

"What would be their focus tonight?" he muttered under his breath.

The weather? Politics? Or would it be their ridiculous ideologies regarding religion and witchcraft, their visions of the world warped until they were convinced they met God's plan. Whatever the topic would be, Cristian was in no mood to listen to their rationalizations once again.

"I wonder what they would say if they knew about my kind." He winked at the women who passed by and chuckled to himself.

Whispers concerning Violet McDonald, the eighteen-year-old girl who had been sent to the gallows last night, interrupted his good mood. Witchcraft had more than challenged their social order.

"Sensationalists." He shook his head and turned away.

Their conversations were mind numbing; if only he could block them, and their self-fulfilling prophecies, out. Unfortunately, Cristian would be far from town before their voices would silence in his ears.

Sharp intakes of breath brushed against his ear drums as his scent saturated their senses. Cristian's mere being had cleared a wide path around him as their stares drank him in from the top of his flaxen head to the bottom of his laced-up leather boots. Superficially, Cristian fit in among the elite in his fine linen shirt with deep cuffs and pleated velvet breeches that tapered off below his knees. Fashion these days. Such pretenses annoyed Cristian, but he chose to comply most of the time. His dress epitomized the look of a gentleman, but gentleness was a trait Cristian hadn't possessed in years.

Delicate whispers sounded behind him. "He is so handsome." They giggled to one another behind opened gloved hands.

A tightness formed between his legs. Women—he could make them swoon by just looking at them if he chose. Looking ahead, he allowed them to freely gawk and made his way out of town. Tomorrow night, however, he sensed things would go quite differently.

Thunder rumbled. The threatening sound of the storm approaching was too distant for the human ear to hear, but it easily interrupted Cristian's sadistic thoughts about tomorrow. His eyes narrowed and cut through the thick veil of heavy mist that blanketed the air outside of town. As he scanned the glen, white feathers illuminated along the belly of a magpie, catching his attention. He stopped and met the tiny pair of glowing eyes. Perched high in a tree, jutting its beak, the tightly tucked-in bird leaned forward and narrowed its gaze, and for the second time tonight Cristian knew he was being scrutinized. This time an uneasy feeling washed over him; one he didn't like. The condemning stare bore through him as if it were searching for his soul.

"Good luck, bird." Parting his lips, Cristian flashed a glimpse of wickedness that lived inside him. He could break the magpie's neck without even trying, crush it into mere dust. That was if he could escape from its stare and move.

The bird spread its wings and took flight above the treetops, the rich blackness of its feathers blending in with the midnight sky the higher it climbed. It glanced over an open wing and cawed, releasing Cristian from his stupor. He suspected he had been warned, and even though he hadn't felt cold in decades, an impossible shiver ran down his spine.

Ridiculous.

He feared nothing.

Well, that wasn't completely true; there was one thing that terrified him. Agitated, Cristian pushed aside his unsettling feelings before they spiraled beyond his control and focused on tonight.

Tiny drops of water beaded across the shoulders of his cape and dampened his hair. Cristian tightened his fists underneath the fine velvet fabric that was more for show than comfort and stepped forward, shivering again.

November made him restless, anxious. Every year, as the onset of winter forced shorter days and longer nights, an invisible clock inside him counted down the time, reminding him of the night his life was taken.

"Or stolen," he mumbled.

Leaving deep footprints in the moist ground, Cristian moved with unrelenting stealth, uprooting and hurling through the air anything that grew in his way. Each step that carried him further from town brought him that much closer to Meg, and that was all that was important. The revelation should have been calming and reassuring, but instead, a tightness pulled across his chest.

Where discipline and patience were once easy, Cristian was now demanding, impulsive, and plagued with the guilty pleasure of satisfying himself much sooner than necessary. This change in his character came one hundred eighty years ago—the day he was made a vampire.

The attack had happened without warning as he slept alone under the light of the moon outside of Loch Lomond. He had been returning to the Highlands, his homeland, when he stepped off the footpath to rest for a few hours. Leaning against an old white pine, he sat hypnotized by the blazing sun as it bathed the calm waters in golden splashes of light before it slipped effortlessly behind the mountain and his heavy lids closed. It was the last thing Cristian saw through human eyes.

He awakened, startled, pinned against the pine by an unbearable weight that dug into his side. Thousands of burning needles stabbed at his arm and forced streaks of heat upwards from his wrist. Cristian fought hard to free himself of the painful heat that ignited throughout his body, but in the end, his tortured humanity was no match against his assailant's unnatural strength; no, the element of surprise lay solely in his attacker's hands.

As suddenly as it had appeared, the weight vanished, and Cristian was alone. As he twitched uncontrollably on the ground, he tried to process what had just happened, but a darkness pulled him under. To an outsider, Cristian appeared dead; his breathing was nonexistent, nor was there a ticking of his heart, but he was very much alive.

Without warning, the crisp scent of apples filled his nostrils and triggered a violent hollow throughout his core, a hunger like never before. His lids flipped open at the unexpected smell. Apples were known symbols of both love and death. Sin and mortality. Cristian, who had never been a follower of such superstition, was now most assured that an omen had encircled him. He lay motionless under the heavy weight of darkness, fearful of another sign to come.

It wasn't until a small magpie flew directly towards him, beating her wings harshly until she was a feather's length from his face and then soared upwards through the canopy of woven tree limbs that Cristian understood the nature of his hunger. He lunged for the bird, but she released a screech so shrill that he fell to the ground and covered his ears until his thirst won out.

He used to count the time—the hours, the weeks, the years—after he changed. He didn't remember when he stopped keeping track or the moment when his past life faded to the present. Or when living became irrelevant because time had become irrelevant. Or when he stopped caring. Time ticked by, serving no real purpose except to brutally record the length of his immortality and distance him from the life he once knew. His body became frozen in time at the age of twenty-nine.

From the outside, not much had changed. Except his eyes. Their shade, when not a fiery, crimson red, were a cold and calculating deep blue that missed nothing and now mirrored a faint hue across his ghostly white complexion.

Not many reacted to the color of his skin; rather, it was the temperature that wafted off him that was most alarming. Cristian saw it in their eyes and heard it in their whispers as they walked past.

Standing six foot three inches tall, Cristian had remained broad-shouldered and thick with muscle; a physique he had earned working on his family's sheep farm. The word he used to define his physical self now was *indestructible*; his strength was unyielding and his body rarely tired.

He had used this physical gift to frighten and to kill, sometimes mercilessly and sometimes with a vengeance. And sometimes just for sport. Cruelty and violence filled the world these days, and at times, he believed that this new version of him fit in rather nicely. He hadn't asked to be a monster; in truth, he hadn't even known such a being existed; he was a demon without a soul.

Cristian met others like himself, but he only felt a deep-rooted hatred towards them. It wasn't long before he ventured into the world on his own and his desire for vengeance lessened. His nomadic lifestyle suited him well. Being alone had proven to be better. Easier. Simpler. The dead made him uneasy and quite anxious when they were near. No, it was around the living where Cristian oddly found comfort.

Perhaps over time he would change, he once told himself.

But then again, maybe not. After all, it was a vampire who had attacked him. Everything he had treasured had been violently ripped away, the breath from his lungs, the blood from his heart, and the very love of his life. But over the last one hundred eighty years, Cristian had never let go of what he held closest to his heart—the love for his mortal family and Catarine. And although his promise was uttered through silent cries, he vowed to never make room for anyone else.

That was, until he met a girl whose honeysuckle scent drew him out of the woods and onto the trodden path where she walked. Alone. A girl with hair that matched her mother's and eyes so hauntingly familiar that they sent an unraveling in his chest. It was then that Cristian understood why he hadn't attached to the undead. His humanity had not abandoned him after all.

The muscles in Cristian's jaw ticked. He blinked and snapped back to the present; he was at the backside of the woods.

As always, he had arrived early. He liked to study her—her quick breaths, the rapid blinking of her eyes, her jumpiness—as she waited for him to appear. He never left her alone too long. His need for the world that her blood opened up to him wouldn't allow it.

Meg's existence was precious to him. A gift he first believed he had inadvertently stumbled upon, and for a brief moment, the memory of their first encounter replayed in his head.

A second chance, he had mumbled under his breath that night, captivated by what he believed was a ghost from his human life. But as her magic lured him in and fed him life, Cristian realized that without a doubt, Meg was his perfect mate. After nearly two hundred years, it was time; it was lonely being dead.

The light from the full moon cast his shadow, oversized and disfigured, across the ground. With his hands clasped behind his back, Cristian kicked the loose stones in his way and sent them plummeting over the cliff. He stopped for a moment, cupped a hand to his ear for dramatic effect, and waited to hear the scratching of claws as the woodland rodents scurried for safety. His only voyeur, however, was silently perched high above.

Refusing to acknowledge the tiny pair of glowing eyes that stalked him from the treetops, Cristian finished his one-sided conversation as he waited for Meg's arrival.

"She needs me." And again, the will to suppress his thoughts failed and the memory of that night flooded his mind.

"You need protection," he had told her. "After all, Meg, how long do you think you can hide? This is a dangerous time in Scotland. All anyone needs is a suspicion to take the law in their own hands, thanks to your king." Cristian's tone had been harsh. He had then gathered her in his arms that trembled with both anger and fear.

"I will not let anyone bring harm to you, Meg," he vowed softly. His words had been more for himself, but Meg had been quite in tune with his motive and stiffened in his icy embrace.

"And who will protect me from you?" she spat as a frightening discomfort collected in the air.

"Everything comes at a price, my darling. Allow me to protect you or burn at the stake. You make the choice." He lifted a dismissive shoulder and released her.

His tone had been calm, as if he didn't care what she did, but in truth, Cristian's last sentence was meaningless. Meg had no choice to make; she belonged to him.

Cristian brought his forefingers around to his lips, smiled, and dismissed the past.

The rain had not yet reached the tree line, but a damp breeze off the water carried the promise that it wouldn't be long. Thunder rumbled again in the distance, and the leaves on the ancient oaks swayed. Cristian ran his tongue across his lips. Soon Meg's sweetness would replace the saltiness left by the sea. He closed his eyes and envisioned his fingers tangled in her hair, the warmth of her flesh pressed against him, and her magical blood that would soon fill him.

He smiled, and a drop of venom fell soundlessly to the ground.

Chapter 7

Raindrops tapped in rapid succession against the shutters.

Isobel rolled to her side, her legs tangling in the long smock Elspeth had loaned her to sleep in. Her mind raced as the drumming sound of rain grew louder.

One hundred years. How had she traveled so off course?

She kicked at the folds of linen fabric until she was free, pushed up and stared at the closed wooden door.

Isobel frowned as she imagined the Highlander propped on the other side like a barrier, his sword in hand and ready to strike if she so much as stepped one foot outside.

While his sisters had busied themselves making sure she was comfortable for the night, the man did little more than lean against the small fireplace mantle and scowl. Resisting the urge to fidget under his scrutiny, Isobel had crossed her arms and met his stare, mocking his pose until her curiosity finally won out.

Slowly, her eyes had wandered from his translucent blue ones to his square jaw line and cleft chin beneath the shadow of sandy blond stubble. Not shaving had served him well as it intensified his already barbaric presence. His brows remained pulled together, and his lips, once again, sat in that hard, flat line. He was looking at her but not at her face.

Her gaze continued to his bare shoulders and followed the

scars that cut across his upper body and arms before finally resting on his large, calloused hands. The tension between them grew, as did her inability to stay still until Elspeth finally spoke, a welcome distraction.

Throwing aside the layers of furs and blankets, Isobel slid off the bed. She stretched, and her body shivered from the chill in the room. Her daughter stirred in reaction to the sudden jerky movements and sent a fist, or a foot, into Isobel's ribs.

"I'm sorry if I woke you," Isobel said. "It's so drafty in here."

The fire Gavan had lit continued to blaze, but a chill remained heavy in the air of her small circular space.

Turning back to the warmth of her bed, Isobel draped one of the furs around her shoulders. Moving towards the door, she thought to peek out and see if her premonition of Gavan standing guard was correct, but as she gripped the lever, it refused to turn. Her heart raced, and her palm immediately became slick with sweat. She had heard right last night; they had locked her in.

With trembling hands, she reached for the woven rush along the side of the bed and dragged it to the only other opening that led outside of the room. She pulled back the plaid tapestry, and the wind whistled through the wooden slats of the shutters. Releasing the iron bar from its fastener, Isobel flung the shutters open, and cool, damp air rushed in. Leaning forward, she closed her eyes and drew in a breath. As her heart slowed its erratic beats, the fear of being trapped inside lessened. Her daughter shifted again.

"You're restless too, I see." Isobel pulled the blanket tightly around herself again and swayed as she opened her eyes and waited for them to adjust to the darkness.

"I can't shake the notion that we are meant to be here," she said to Fara, who had joined her at the window's ledge.

Adjusting the fur around her shoulders tighter, Isobel froze when a faint scent of lavender blew in with the breeze. Like a punch to the gut, she doubled over and braced herself against the cold, hard stone.

"Mother?" she whispered, and her surroundings began to turn. Quick breaths burst from her lips, and her hands, slick with an icy cold sweat, tingled until they stung with a heavy numbness. Tears poured from her eyes, and for a moment, Isobel forgot where she was.

An uncontrolled trembling shot through her body, and she squeezed her eyes shut. Her mother. Thomas. She would never see them again. Her daughter would never know her father or her grandmother. They had planned to stay together, always, yet here Isobel was without either of them. The realization left a large, gaping hole in her core, and she began to sob. The gruesome images of their lifeless bodies filled her head, and a series of dry heaves rhythmically rattled her insides. Isobel let her grief consume her body until it could no longer react.

Laying her cheek on the cool stone, she waited a few more minutes, then pushed herself to stand on shaky legs and sucked in a deep breath. The damp air no longer smelled of lavender. With the back of one hand, she wiped at her cheeks while Fara brushed her head against her other hand.

"Everything happened so quickly, Fara. If only—" Isobel started when a figure running away from the castle caught her attention, and the dizziness dissipated. The individual made its way, without haste, across the water-soaked grasses and in the direction of the woods that stretched from the edge of the glen to the open sea.

"Fara, look! Do you see that?" Her voice quaked as she pointed into the darkness. Fara patted her feet against the cold, damp stone.

Looking over the treetops, Isobel searched for land on the other side. But all she saw were the rapidly moving waves that the wind from the storm blew in.

Isobel clasped her hands to her chest. "Fara, the cliff," she whispered. "Whoever that is must be heading to its edge." Fear gripped her; she could not witness death again today. She swallowed hard against the bile that lurched into her throat.

Leaning forward through the window as comfortably as she could, Isobel squinted and caught sight of the white trim from an undergarment trailing below the hem of the cloak. She had assumed that the small stature was that of a woman, and now

Isobel was certain she knew who it belonged to.

The moon, showing itself between broken storm clouds, cast a bright glow just as the hood of the cape slipped off and unleashed the reddish golden curls Isobel expected to see. They shimmered and bounced with each fervent step that moved the girl further from home and closer to the woods.

Meg.

The young witch stepped with such grace that it reminded Isobel of the smooth movements of a pendulum. She would be asking Meg her reasoning for probing into her head as soon as she got her alone, but at this moment, Isobel's first concern was where the girl was going at this hour unchaperoned.

Without warning, a recognizable scent of danger blew through the window, filling Isobel's nostrils and catching her off guard. She stiffened and swallowed the heartbeat that climbed up her throat as the hair on back of her neck and arms raised.

Pushing herself inside, Isobel leaned into the stone wall for support and sank to the floor. Curling into a ball, she rocked back and forth, burying herself beneath the fur that had slipped from her shoulders. Her heart thundered, and her breaths came in such loud, desperate gulps that she feared they would awaken everyone in the castle. Bright pin pricks of light filled the edges of her vision as a cold sweat glued the linen sleeping gown to her body.

Isobel prayed that Gavan had placed himself outside her room, for at this moment he seemed to be the lesser of two evils.

True, he may kill her, but he may be merciful; end her life quickly and painlessly before she had time to give it a second thought. What lurked outside in the darkness had already promised Isobel no mercy. She stared at the door, but it remained closed. The castle was silent. The air that encircled her was tumultuous and feral.

Her face tingled as did the skin where the pentacle lay; danger was near. Her daughter fought inside for more room, but Isobel drew her knees in and pulled herself tighter. She grasped the charm that hung from her neck and—

Her necklace! That's what Gavan had been staring at. Isobel had wondered how he could show such resentment when he didn't even know her. His continual grip on the hilt of his sword and glaring look of distrust made sense now. It wasn't who Isobel was, but rather what. Gavan hadn't been angry; he had been afraid. The gift she had worn around her neck since she was seven years old would get them all killed if she were discovered.

A gust of wind blew through the window, causing the flames in the firebox to dance and the shutters to slam against the walls. The banging pierced Isobel's eardrums, but she was so frightened she couldn't move.

"Gavan knows what I am, Fara. And there's a vampire outside the castle walls." She lowered the fur from her face, and the air that filled the room smelled untamed and daring. Reaching over, Isobel lifted the magpie with a shaky hand and held her close to her chest.

"We have to leave before it's too late. The portal," she said. "I don't know where we will go, but there is too much danger here. I need to get the three of us to a safe place."

Fara flew to the window ledge, and Isobel stood. Closing her eyes, she tried to envision the smoky ribbons and silvery threads, but her own fears combined with Fara's sudden pecking at her hands left her unable to concentrate.

"Fara, stop. We need to get to Mariam. We don't have much time."

Gripping the charm that hung from her neck, her thumb and forefinger grasped the tip of the star that pointed upwards; the one that represented *spirit*. She could do this.

"Look into my mind and you will see what haunts me most and why we must flee.

From here to there I call you to find a place of safety not in this time."

Isobel stood spellbound and waited for the portal to appear. Instead, an inexplicable heaviness filled her body and anchored her in place.

She squeezed her eyes shut and spoke the words again, this time with more conviction, but again the circular motion of the gateway failed to materialize.

Her daughter's forceful movements had ceased with the gift of more room, but Fara continued to pace and flutter and now pecked at Isobel's feet.

"If they followed me here, they could follow me anywhere. We need—" Isobel looked at Fara, the pain from her sharp beak distracting her thoughts.

"Fara, stop. What is wrong?" Isobel shifted her weight as she rubbed her foot against the other in an attempt to soothe the lingering sting.

The magpie flew to the window ledge, and her beady black eyes guided Isobel toward the woods.

A vision of the young witch who ran wildly towards the trees and right into the hands of danger emerged. Isobel recalled Meg's nervousness this evening and the desperation in her hurried steps as she fled from the castle. Maybe the girl knew what hid beyond the trees. If she was going willingly, maybe she wasn't entirely afraid. Or maybe she wasn't given a choice.

"Fara, perhaps it isn't what I think." Fara became at ease, and the mysterious weight lifted from Isobel's bones.

"It doesn't feel like they are after me; at least not yet. I don't think it's *them*, but maybe others like them." Isobel hadn't forgotten the stories her mother had told. Myths that warned of creatures, witches and vampires alike who roamed the lands from one end of the earth to the other as far back as the stories went.

"Fara, the men who hunted us are still in Massachusetts. Neither could have entered the gateway unless I brought them with us, and that I did not do. Whoever is waiting in the woods is a stranger and nothing more." Isobel exhaled. She couldn't let her guard down, but right now it was Meg's safety she needed to be concerned about.

Fara's gaze remained locked on Isobel, and a silent voice warned her that her time at Elden Castle might not be easy, but she was meant to stay.

Turning to the window, Isobel, with Fara perched beside her, searched for the girl, hoping she hadn't already disappeared.

"There!"

Isobel's eyes sparkled as she pointed to the edge of the woods, but Fara was already staring in that direction.

The self-assured, controlling witch who had pranced in front of Isobel, pried into her subconscious and eyed her sinfully hours ago was gone. Rather, the girl with overly bright eyes staring up at her now rocked back and forth on the balls of her feet at the shadows' edge of the trees.

Meg's head tilted upwards toward the castle, stopping at the last arched window of the north tower, the one Isobel and Fara looked out from. The one their silhouettes stood motionless in, just as Gavan's had hours ago.

The wind gusted and jerked the woven tapestry from Isobel's hands, forcing her to grab at the stone ledge for support. It was cold and slippery from the steady fall of rain, but Isobel held on, her cheek pressed against the edge of the arch, not taking her eyes off of Meg. Fara, too, stood entranced; her feathered body was rigid and her head cocked as if she were listening to something. Or someone.

Isobel wanted to call to Meg but feared it could send an alarm to Gavan or the vampire that remained hidden in the darkness. Fara patted her feet along the stone and cawed, the sound lost to the rumble of thunder that rolled across the sky.

Isobel couldn't read the minds of others, but she could feel their emotions. However, Meg had the ability to get in Isobel's head. If the girl could hear Isobel's thoughts—

Fara bobbed her head up and down.

Ignoring the sounds of the falling rain and the thunder that grew louder, Isobel focused on the silent message she wanted Meg to hear.

I can help you! You can trust me! Please return to the castle!

Meg stood unmoving and showed no response to Isobel's silent pleas. Maybe she could only hear with the use of her pendulum. Isobel tried again.

Lightening cracked across the sky and briefly bathed the space around Meg in a brilliant white. In those few moments of light, Isobel caught a glimpse of Meg's fair skin and wide, frightened eyes before she all too quickly returned to a silhouetted form and blended back into the blackness of night.

The wind blew steadily, and large drops of rain slapped against the stone ledge. The window tapestry, now free from its restraint, whipped against Isobel's back. She clung to the slippery stone, wide-eyed and motionless, unaware that her face and sleeping gown dripped with water. The witch's silent response as she disappeared behind the front row of trees was all that filled her ears.

It is hopeless.

Chapter 8

Meg stepped to the edge of the cliff, pulled the opening of her coat tightly closed and fought back the tears that filled her eyes. She wanted to defy him, to run back to the safety of her home and into the arms of her family. But Cristian had made it clear early on that if she ever attempted to escape from him, it would be a death sentence for her entire family. Besides, only half of her wanted to flee. The other half—her body trembled in anticipation at the thought, and her shoulders slumped.

Memories of the first night she secretly met Cristian replayed in her head—the field of wildflowers she trampled as she hurried on her way, the abandoned stable whose shadows she hid amongst, and the eerie silence that weighed far too heavy on her shoulders. Too quiet, Meg regrettably realized after she took a deep breath and stepped into the light to return home.

Cristian had appeared out of thin air, his face so colorless that he resembled a ghost against the darkness. It was as though he had waited in the alcove of the barn shadows for the precise moment to show himself. To pounce.

A horrified scream had collected in her chest, but as Meg opened her mouth, all that escaped was a gasp of fear, the moisture of her breath freezing into tiny ice crystals as she found her words.

"Wh-where did you come from?" Her blood soared through

her veins. She didn't remember him looking so pale this afternoon.

A wicked smile spread across Cristian's face. Digging his fingers into her upper arms, he lifted her until they were nose to nose and the toes of her shoes dangled above the icy grasses between them. Holding her breath, she stilled in his grip, unable to look away from his eyes as they transformed from their mesmerizing blue, a shade identical to her own, to a rich and glossy black. But none of these visceral reactions were necessary; the energy in the air alone dripped with Cristian's anger.

Wind gusts scattered a cluster of fallen leaves across the dirt path behind her, their dried dead stems scratching against the hard ground before taking flight and swirling overhead. The sounds were lost to the raging pulse that pounded in Meg's ears, but they were excruciatingly irritating to Cristian's.

"I'll allow this once," he said as he pulled his lips back and drew her attention to the points of his incisors; they weren't normal. "You run from me again, and the next time I won't be so gracious." His eyes glowed an unnatural red just seconds before returning to black, and he lowered her to the ground. His body trembled, but Meg wasn't sure if it came from anger or fear. During the moments he had held her captivated, she saw a weakness hiding deep behind those ever changing eyes

The memory haunted her mind, causing her many nightmares since. When it came to Cristian, Meg had quickly learned that there was only one option: obey. However, he wasn't the only one who benefited from the command—an unexpected shock to them both and the reason behind why the other half of her desired to meet him.

Closing her eyes, Meg focused on the waves as they crashed into the rocks below. The sound was explosive, and she silently begged for the noise to drown out her memories of him as the toes of her shoes clung to the ledge. One wind gust too strong and this could all be over. Cristian's mandates of where she was to meet him had become one of the many games he played with her life. She could fight against his demands, but his strength and vows to harm her family gave him the upper hand. Besides, he seemed to enjoy it when she challenged him. Smiling, he would recite the same line of reasoning no matter what she questioned.

"Ah, my darling, it's what keeps it exciting," he would claim. "For both of us."

"Not for me; it's terrifying." Meg attempted to sound bold and in control when she stood up to him, but Cristian always laughed at her admission.

"Terrifying, exciting; isn't it one and the same?"

And then he would take her.

Meg rubbed her thumb across the raised scars on her wrist, the immortal wounds of a vampire, and images of that first night and the many thereafter flipped vividly through her mind. Cristian had woven himself into her life, but Meg wasn't so sure she hated herself for it any more. He was terrifying, and what happened between them went beyond reason. She couldn't live with him, but Meg wasn't so sure she was ready to give up whatever it was that his venom awakened as it paired with her magic. Her silent words that she had whispered just minutes ago to the strange woman locked in Elden Castle had never been more true. There was no escaping this.

Meg's chest constricted so tightly she couldn't breathe, and she braced herself.

"You called for me?" His words blew past her cheek, and her eyes flew open.

The temperature of his body as he stood mere inches behind her own caused her body to tremble. It hadn't taken Meg long to learn that the throbbing of her heart was what called Cristian to her side.

"You please me, Meg," he said as he wound his fingers through her hair and pulled her head to the side, exposing her neck. "The way your heart hammers out the syllables of my name, calling me to you. It's both soothing and exhilarating." He buried his face into the nape of her neck and drew in a breath.

"Your scent alone is nearly enough, my darling. I can almost see their faces, hear their voices." He inhaled again. "Maybe soon, just breathing you in will be sufficient." There was a moment of silence and then he laughed. "Whatever am I thinking?" And he grazed his teeth against her flesh. "I will never deny myself your magic. It is the only thing that completes my existence."

He stepped forward, barely leaving a feather's width between them. His closeness stirred a familiar warmth, and Meg fought to suppress it as she tried to focus only on the temperature of the air and the coldness that enveloped her. But the magic that raced through her veins refused to comply to her silent demand and quickly awakened in her body.

Meg craved Cristian's strength but not him. Not the painstakingly dark and harrowing place he took her to before his venom mixed with her magic and she was able to find the light again and take the upper hand. Meg stood fixed in place, her speech paralyzed as her body surrendered to the attention Cristian gave it. He made her weak and confused, and she shifted her weight. Couldn't he just hurry up and get it over with?

No sooner had she silently wished for it, Cristian released her hair and slid his hand over her shoulder until his palm found what it always longed for: the throbbing of her heart.

Stranded on the edge of the cliff, Meg remained motionless. Time rooted in place as did their bodies until a darkness encircled them and her footing slipped. The crashing sounds of the ocean below faded to the ringing in her ears; she had forgotten to breathe. No longer able to stay rigid, she went limp in his arms. The time had come.

Tiny dark spots filled her vision as Cristian carried her, the hardness of his bone pressing painfully into her flesh as he crushed her to his chest. Her head hung from the crook of his elbow, her hair swirling in the wind and the mist stinging her cheeks. She should feel chilled to the bone, but instead, Meg was on fire, and she turned in to his embrace.

Laying her down, Cristian lifted her arm and ripped away the sleeve of her gown; the tearing sound of fabric sent a shudder through her. A hiccup of laughter escaped between her lips—Elspeth would be mad.

Another sleeve to be mended. How do you manage this? her sister would ask.

Dreamlike images of the witch as she stood looking down from the castle tower emerged. Isobel. It was too bad Isobel couldn't be right, that she wasn't able to help like she believed.

Meg closed her eyes to the fogginess that blurred her vision. But before the darkness completed its task of rendering her unconscious, the pain as Cristian pierced the thin layer of her skin consumed her. Her back arched, her eyes flew open, and a heat exploded within: he had joined them as one. Meg's magic travelled from her core in long, smooth bursts as Cristian suckled at her wrist. Gritting her teeth, she fought unconsciousness until she recognized the onset of her pain disappearing into near oblivion when her blood began mixing with his venom.

Her eyes rolled back, but before her heavy lids closed, she caught a glimpse of Cristian's feral state that loomed over as he surrendered to instinct—his wide eyes glazed over, his teeth buried below her flesh, and the blood that stained the corners of his lips. Her blood.

Her body softened against the boulder, and a final thought before her surroundings went black passed through her.

In just a few moments, they would be trading places.

Chapter 9

Cristian's mind went into a frenzy as he drank. Meg's magic filled and warmed his hard, hollowed veins and well-preserved organs, and the reaction was painful, like being pricked by thousands of blades from the inside. His corpse-like body that immortality had gifted him with so many years ago slowly came to life, and his heart and body jerked in response.

With each feed, Cristian's senses magnified to a level he hadn't known existed. Unable to resist, he kept Meg's wrist pressed against his lips, opened his eyes and waited for the magical effects to begin. With a shaky hand, he scrambled to unfasten the black velvet cape that now hung too tightly from his neck. After the third try, it fell to the ground.

Except for the occasional gleam of moonlight when the heavy clouds thinned and drifted apart, the nighttime sky blanketed the woods with darkness. But the world through Cristian's eyes, although distorted as he struggled to focus, illuminated brilliantly; trees and leaves, shrubbery and tiny flowers, both dead and alive, were drenched in countless shades of brown and green in a variety of textures; smooth, glossy, rough, prickly, even decayed and broken. Overwhelmed but not yet satiated, he buried his fangs deeper. He needed more in order to see them. Hear their voices. Feel their touch. Bring them to life.

Meg's flesh was velvet against his firm, icy lips. Her warmth melted his coldness, quickly muddling the distinction of where her body started and his ended. Cristian drew long and hard against her vein and swallowed. Her blood coated his throat, sending impulses into his arms and legs then out to his fingers and toes. His heart caught, stumbled, and restarted again. Words tangled on his tongue. Words he so badly wanted to say: *Thank you for giving them back to me.*

Lifting her arm, Cristian's eyes shifted to Meg's face.

The challenge of denying himself had become more painful as each day passed. He struggled daily over just the thought of her, not to mention what she gave back to him. Meg weakened his self-control more than anyone in his immortal life, but Cristian knew he had to be cautious. He understood what could happen once her body had absorbed his venom, but if he wanted to be reunited with mortality, even for the briefest amount of time, he had to concede. Truth be told, he hadn't found the thought of dying that hard to accept, especially if it happened in the arms of those he loved the most. Ideally, wasn't that how everyone wished to go?

Releasing his hold, Cristian pulled away from Meg's scarred, bloody wrist and moved his hands across the dip of her stomach to the ridges of her rib cage. His palm paused under her breast for a moment to absorb the desperate thuds of her heart, then slinked upwards to her shoulders. He pressed his fingertips lightly at the base of her throat where her skin was thin and delicate, and a burning sensation soared through his hands as though he had submerged them in a bed of hot coals. The beating of her pulse accelerated. Cristian had learned that it would be only minutes before he was the one to slip into unconsciousness and Meg would be—well, he didn't know exactly what she would be other than strong enough to kill him if she so desired.

He leaned forward, only a feather's width from her face, and inhaled the sweet breath that faintly escaped from her lips. Her looks, her scent, and the magic in her blood was nearly identical to his one and only love. A storm filled his eyes and his mind tumbled as memories of Catarine held him in ecstasy. A craving deep inside emerged, and the last thread of his self-control snapped.

"Meg, I have to have you," Cristian growled. He pulled himself on top of her lifeless body, and his weight forced the air from her lungs.

"Cristian." Meg breathed.

No sooner had he found comfort in his position than a switch flipped, and Cristian spun onto his back in one fluid motion, his movement so quick that he startled himself. It was Catarine's voice that had sounded in his ears, not Meg's. Giddy with excitement, he forgot how soon his fate would be in Meg's hands and anxiously scanned his surroundings.

"Catarine?" He gurgled as Meg's blood bubbled in his throat. But the voice didn't respond. A wave of heat rushed to his head, and white flashes clouded his sight. The tree limbs above swirled, and now it was Cristian who found his body faltering. As he slid off the rock and landed on the ground, his back pressed against the boulder for support, and he saw the familiar dark cloud form in front of him.

The magic that swam in the blood he had ingested pulled from Cristian's memory and summoned his most cherished recollections. One by one, the members of his mortal family materialized from tiny specks of floating dust to distinguishable figures: his mother, father, and brother. Cristian's mouth moved to greet them, but no sound came out. They smiled, and his mother waved as though she were welcoming him home after a long journey. Then suddenly, he was gathered in their arms, his father and brother locking him and his mother tightly in the middle. Diluted rust colored streaks stained Cristian's cheeks as tears poured from his eyes; his mind completely fooled that his loved ones stood before him speaking. Touching. He inhaled their familial scent so deeply he choked; his longing for his human life satiated for the moment.

"Cristian." But this time it was Meg that spoke.

His name was the last word Cristian heard before the voices in his head took over and talked to him all at once. *We've missed you so much. How long has it been, son? I got married and have a family; come meet them.* And so on. Cristian drowned in euphoria while his lungs sputtered for air until the three of them faded from his sight and behind them, in the distance, Catarine appeared.

First, her hair—fiery and coiled. Then her legs—long and slender and shapely under his touch; he could still remember. And lastly, as all her features came into a clean, crisp view, her eyes—a crystal clear blue, not the unique, telling sort like his own, but still ones that held him mesmerized every time he looked into them. Something warm and tender brushed against his cheek, and he shot out a hand to grab it, but nothing was there. A rush of honeysuckle swirled around him and filled his nostrils as an invisible weight pressed into his side. It slowly encircled his shoulders and held him in a tight embrace.

A scattering of memories raced through his mind, ending with the last time he saw Catarine through human eyes—leaving town and unbeknownst to them both, never to return. At least, not as the man he had been.

Catarine! he silently cried as he reached out and swiped at her image. Her body sliced in half, exploding into thousands of swirling, pixilated specks before regrouping and making her whole again. Cristian froze, terrified that if he moved towards her again, she would disappear for good.

The sensation of weight returned to his side. Except this time, she wrapped her arms around his, lay her head on his shoulder, and whispered in his ear. Feelings worked their way into Cristian's bones like water that spilled across a surface, filling the cracks until they overflowed. He feared he would shatter from the sense of fullness as he sat captivated, lost in a moment he never wanted to end.

Catarine's nearness was all he wanted. Well, that wasn't entirely true. For them both to be alive, and human, and her image not to be some hallucinatory ghost that left him in an agitated state when the stupor dissipated was truly all he would ever want. Love was wicked.

Cristian's heart ached, the muscles stretched so tightly now that he worried the newly awakened organ might leap from his chest or worse, burst and never give him the chance at life again. Then a calmness settled over him. The wind howled through the trees and rushed away the intoxicating scent that proved it could hold him captive even after more than a century. Catarine's ghostly presence disappeared, and Cristian found himself in the woods. Alone. And undead, just as before. Meg hadn't killed him. At least not this time.

How long he had been out? *Seconds, minutes, hours?* The sky was still dark, but the moon had begun its descent towards the horizon. His normally hardened skin had returned, and deep creases formed along his forehead as his brows narrowed. He sniffed into the air to see which way Meg had fled. He wouldn't go after her, but as always he was aware of where she was. Both of their lives depended on it.

"You may be a witch, my dear, but you are also human. Weak and emotional. The race of your adrenaline and your scent in the air tells me everything I need to know." They were like that. Humans, that is. Too easy to read, too easy to manipulate, and far too easy to frighten. His venom had gifted Meg with a momentary burst of strength and speed, and it terrified her. If he listened close enough he could hear her heart and feet pounding as one as she had fled through the glen earlier, far from Elden Castle, and now circling back to return.

"Please protect her, Cristian. Just as any father would." It was Catarine's last whispered request before her body disseminated into the darkness.

Convinced that she was safe, Cristian closed his eyes and tuned in to the organ that Meg had fed life to—his heart. It was weak and strained to pump what little blood remained. Cristian sensed its desperation as it worked selfishly to hang on to every drop. He waited until the last thump sounded in his chest and his body went silent before he stood.

Cristian regretted not being able to save her mother, a mistake he wouldn't make twice. He could no longer live without Meg, and she simply wouldn't stay alive without him. For 1597 was a dangerous time to be a witch.

"And your brother, my darling, leads one of the more prominent witch hunts in the Highlands. If he only knew." An evil smile parted his lips as he reattached his cape around his neck. "Ironic how things work sometimes."

Stepping back, Cristian took in his surroundings once again. With each feed, he believed himself to be invincible well beyond what immortality had granted him so many years ago. Sounds from each direction resonated in his ears. As his mind filtered through them, he focused on the ones of fear that came from those both near and far. Oddly, they were calming to his now restless mood.

Men abruptly awoke in alarm as a warning in their gut flooded the darkness with distress. Their bodies were wet with sweat and shook as terror filled their minds; something was coming for them. Those who were married clung to their spouses. Those who lay alone held on tightly to the bed sheets. All begged for daylight as they gasped for breath and prayed it was simply a nightmare. But they knew better.

Animals who found themselves too close scurried for protection, their nails scratching anxiously into the ground as their hackles stood on end. And the magpie, with her critical eyes and condescending stare, also kept her space as she looked down on him from high above.

"No need to worry," he said to the animals, his tone heavily contradicting the gentle nature of his words.

Gusts of winds returned through the trees, and the tall grasses bowed in response. Leaves snapped from their branches and floated to the ground, a single black feather landing near the toe of his boot. Discarding the wrongness of what he was about to do, Cristian planted his feet firmly in the dirt, looked up and spoke, hoping that his voice would carry across the glen for Meg to hear.

"Until the next time we meet, my love."

And then he was gone.

Chapter 10

Isobel collapsed onto the mattress, her head hitting the pillow as her eyes closed. But sleep didn't come that easy. Tossing and turning, she struggled to get comfortable and put her mind to rest.

"Just one night, a few hours of sleep," she begged of herself.

For as long as Isobel could remember, she hadn't required much sleep. As a child she often found herself listening to her mother's deep breathing while she lay there thinking, drifting in and out of consciousness for no more than a couple of hours.

Tonight Isobel sensed she would need sleep, unsure as to what may come tomorrow. The vampire in the woods, the Highland warrior down the hallway, or the witch burnings in the village; no matter which way Isobel turned, danger surrounded her.

Her body soon grew heavy and found comfort in the center of the bed. Her racing thoughts silenced, and Isobel drifted off. Deep sleep had come, and it was there that the demons she had kept locked away for the past twenty-four hours came alive.

Deliberately, they chased and taunted her, their silent footfalls shaking the ground beneath her. Isobel's witch's blood burned through her veins, and her heart pumped faster as she fled.

She jerked and twisted, and the bed coverings slid to the

floor as she fought to escape. Then, as quickly as they had appeared, the spirits vanished, and a cold, eerie silence filled the space as the terrifying maze of zigzags she ran through came to a dead end.

The darkness lifted, and Isobel found herself standing in front of a full length mirror, her eyes meeting those of a child who stared at her, their rich emerald green color identical. The girl's long, dark hair was disheveled, and Isobel recognized the favorite pale pink night gown she wore. The reflection was of herself as a child of only four years.

The child stood alone, her face relaxed and her arms limp as they hung motionless by her side. Behind her, familiar furnishings slowly came into focus the longer Isobel gazed into the mirror; the house was her mother's.

Isobel reached towards the glass when the vision turned and ran, her bare feet padding across the painted wooden floor as she bolted in the direction of a dead end hallway.

Isobel gripped the frame that encased the mirror and peered in more closely so as not to lose sight of her childlike self.

"Mama! Mama!" the little girl cried as she stopped at the end of the corridor. But there was no answer.

Where was her mother?

The child stood on her tip toes and reached for the round glass knob on the last white panel door to the left.

"Mama!" she cried again and flung the door open, stopping

as she stepped inside.

Dozens of bodies filled the room. Crouching, they snapped their jaws as they moved towards a bed. Black capes hung from their necks, the edges sweeping gracefully along the floor behind them. Their eyes were bright red and their teeth a shade of white more brilliant than their skin. Single-handedly, they ripped one another off the body that lay across the bed, tossing them to the back of the room. Blood spilled from the corners of their mouths as they stumbled forward, their eyes dazed and their thirst desperate for another drink.

Isobel's eyes sat fixed on the bed where a pair of arms and legs could be seen. They were bruised and punctured with dozens of small holes, a few crusted over with dried blood. Bodies shifted in place, and a pair of eyes slowly turned towards her as the head on the pillow moved.

She studied the dark brows and long lashes that framed the same blood red eyes as the others. She followed the long, dark hair that was splayed across the pillow and along the bare shoulders.

Mother? Isobel mouthed.

The room fell silent, and one by one, the demons surrounding the bed turned their attention to the child standing in the open doorway. Drawing in a deep breath, their crimson irises rolled in their sockets before turning glossy and wild with excitement. A unified growl rumbled through the room as they crouched and moved towards the entryway; their hunt had begun.

Isobel stood frozen, her mind paralyzed and her knees locked in place. Pressing her hands on the glass, she suddenly landed on the hardwood floor where her childlike self had stood.

"H—how did I do that?" Isobel whispered. A cold sweat covered her body, and she trembled. She had fallen through the mirror.

Isobel's child-like self turned and stared. Isobel had to warn her; she had to get her away from that room. She opened her mouth, but the words wouldn't come. Isobel sensed that the girl had somehow silenced her.

Slowly, the young face transformed. Parting her lips, small white teeth, sharp as razors, emerged, the tips dripping with what Isobel sensed was venom. Tiny flecks of red swirled within her emerald irises as her lids peeled open and her eyes glazed over. The specks spun faster and faster, multiplying until they filled the circular space with the same brilliant shade of red as those that moved behind her.

She opened her mouth, her throaty tone feral and bloodthirsty as she spoke to Isobel. "The vampires have come for us."

Dropping the small pink blanket clutched in her hand, she too hunched her shoulders and stepped in unison with their march. A man with long blond hair, the one who had called himself Isobel's father before she escaped through the portal, stepped away from the crowd and opened his arms.

Bolting upright, Isobel's heart thrashed against her chest and eardrums.

"It was only a dream; it was only a dream." Isobel gasped for breath. She threw her legs over the side of the bed and fought to remember where she was. The hearth across from her bed cast a soft glow. The flame from the fire had died out long ago, but its smoldering coals lay along the base, giving her just enough light. Isobel looked around the circular room; she was in the tower at Elden Castle. She had time walked, she had escaped them; it was all coming to her. The child and falling through the mirror was not real. But the vampires?

Isobel pushed aside the tapestry that covered the window and peeked through the wooden slats of the shutters. It was dark outside. Cool, damp air whistled through the cracks, and her body shivered in reaction as it blew against her damp skin. Uncontrollable sobs rose from her chest, but Isobel forced them to stay quiet as images of Meg disappearing into the woods resurfaced. *Had she returned to the castle yet?*

Fara climbed onto the back of her hand and rubbed her small head against Isobel's skin.

"Oh Fara, I think you are right. We are meant to stay here for now."

Resting her forehead against the boards, Isobel closed her eyes. She lifted the pentacle to her lips and prayed. Not just for the strange young witch she realized she had to help, but also for the courage when she went to see Mariam. She needed answers.

~~~~~~~~~~~~~~~~~~~~

A slight rap on the door startled Isobel, and her eyes flew open. Under the blankets, she grabbed the heavy, bronze candle holder she had taken from the mantel before returning to bed after her terrifying dream.

"Isobel? Are you awake? May I come in?" It was Elspeth. Isobel let go of the heavy ornamental piece and sighed.

Rubbing her eyes, she sat up. The stone walls around her swirled and forced her to collapse into the warm depression left by her body. Her head throbbed as it hit the pillow.

"Yes," she answered, and the lever on the door clicked.

"It's freezing in here. Let me relight the fire before you get out of bed," Elspeth said as she dropped a stack of clothing near Isobel's feet, causing her legs to bounce. The sounds of wood being added to the fireplace and furniture being scooted across the floor filled the silence before Elspeth spoke again.

"Lass, are you feeling ill?"

Yes, she was ill. The dizziness had made Isobel queasy, and the lack of sleep kept her from thinking clearly. She didn't want to talk, or move, or anything.

Please leave.

Guilt washed over Isobel. Elspeth had been more than kind

to her. If it weren't for her, who knew what would have happened last night? Or where she would be right now.

"I just need a little more sleep, that's all." Isobel looked at Elspeth, but her eyes closed against the dizziness that consumed her again.

Elspeth rested her hands on Isobel's shoulders. "Sleep. It's early; no need to get up yet. I brought you some clean water to freshen yourself and clothes to dress in before you come downstairs. I will leave them by the fire. If you need any assistance, please don't hesitate to come find me. I am happy to help. Oh, and the chamber pot, if you haven't already discovered, is under your bed."

A cool, wet cloth was pressed against Isobel's forehead, and she sighed at the relief it brought. Elspeth pulled the blankets and furs to Isobel's chin and tucked her in like a child. Isobel never heard the door close. Fara, who had been listening, came out from under the bed and perched herself on the window ledge. Nuzzling her beak under her wing, she, too, found some much needed rest.

This time, Isobel had no dreams, and when she awoke, she found the bed coverings in the same place Elspeth had left them. Feeling rested, she decided to take her chances and venture out. Stretching, she stood and made her way to the shutters. Slivers of sunlight shone between the boards, and Isobel was thankful the storms had passed.

"I will meet you outside as soon as I can," she reassured

Fara, who paced along the window ledge, hesitant to leave. "I promise, I'll be fine." Looking into the sky, Isobel squinted. She welcomed the warmth and the light to be able to see what the darkness had hidden from her last night.

After staring at Isobel one last time, Fara stretched her wings and quickly disappeared into the blinding light. Isobel's stomach rumbled, and a sudden feeling of nausea nearly made her gag. She latched the window coverings and moved towards the foot of the bed, trying to remember when she last ate. *Yesterday?*

Yesterday!

Her body faltered, and Isobel grabbed the arm of the chair beside her. It was as if the space that encircled her unexpectedly gave its permission and Isobel's feelings of fear and grief that she thought were concealed suddenly exploded, huge and recklessly.

Squeezing her eyes shut, Isobel tried to force the images of the last twenty-four hours back into hiding as she did last night. The ones she had buried deep within her subconscious; the murders, the chase, the vampire's confession, and the witch who had taunted her.

Isobel shook uncontrollably. *Get out!*

Her lungs fought for air between the wretched sobs that filled her ears. Her grief and fear grew big, bigger than herself every time she cried out. "I can't do this now." *Maybe not ever.*

Isobel sucked in a breath and another scream made its way out. Each one asking—*how had this happened?* Each one understanding that what had happened was real.

Sinking to the floor, she threw her hands over her ears and tried to silence the horrifying sound. The gut-wrenching pain. Fara pecked wildly at the closed shutters, but Isobel couldn't move. Her mother and husband were dead. And vampires were near. Terror took over Isobel. Charlotte stirred within her mother's womb, the swaying movement was gentle and repetitive, as though she were rocking her mother. Comforting her. Unafraid. Isobel's hands slid down to her abdomen and encircled her waist. Her throat felt scorched and her eyes dry, but the screams, her screams, had finally ceased.

Again, she inhaled, her body shuddering as she breathed out. In and out, Isobel repeated the process until her body stilled and the voices in her head slowly faded to the crackling sounds of the firewood in the hearth. She didn't want to think of the vampire, or her dream, or Meg. She needed some air.

Fara's wild and endless pecking on the outer side of the shutters had silenced, but Isobel knew the magpie would be frantic until she saw her. Pushing herself up, Isobel stepped to the window, but before she had the shutters completely opened, Fara dove in and landed on her shoulder. Cocking her head left then right, the magpie surveyed Isobel until she was convinced that she wasn't harmed. Isobel turned and made her way in small, shaky steps to the basin that Elspeth had brought, forgetting to close the partially opened shutters. Fara hopped down and perched herself on the back of the chair.

"You need your strength; pull yourself together," Isobel coached, splashing the cool water on her face, and rinsing her mouth. She wet the edge of the linen cloth that sat folded over the basin's lip and held it against her eyes. Clumsily, she backed away and moved towards the fire in hopes that the warmth would ease her muscles and calm her mind. A long time passed before Isobel was ready to move.

Thankful to have watched her ancestors dress once before, Isobel gathered the pieces of clothing Elspeth had left on the bed and hanging neatly over the back of the chair. She layered them as best as she could remember, and except for being a bit snug around her waist, the gown was a near perfect fit.

Isobel had been confined to her room last night, the lock clicking into place as Gavan shut the door behind him and his sisters. But as Isobel turned the lever today, the door freely swung open. Looking back, she gave Fara a weak smile and watched as the magpie flew out of the opened window.

She moved down the stairs towards the main hall and further back towards the kitchen. Thirteen years had passed since she walked these corridors, but she remembered the route as if she had travelled it yesterday. The soft shoes Elspeth had shared left Isobel's footsteps silent, and she made her way through the winding passages, her gaze roving over every dismal gray stone from ceiling to floor like she was assessing it for the first time.

Cautiously, Isobel moved towards the voices and thick aroma of freshly baked bread. Without warning, her stomach reminded her of its emptiness and she heaved. Isobel stopped and braced a hand against the wall and inhaled deeply. She had to regain her composure. She could do this.

Pushing away from the wall, her palm left a slight indentation in the stone. Her mother's words, *Easy, Isobel*, came to mind. She had to be careful.

Surely, it won't be noticed, Isobel hoped. She closed her eyes and silently reminded herself to move naturally and not forget the power of her strength.

The thrust of Gavan's words came at her as she rounded the corner. Unable to sense any magic nearby, Isobel assumed he was speaking with Elspeth. The closer she got, the clearer his voice became, and Isobel soon learned the reason for their argument. Her.

Taking a deep breath, she strode towards the doorway and acted as if she had heard none of Gavan's insistence on sending her on her way even if it meant dragging her from the bed himself.

Stepping under the arched opening, Isobel sucked in another breath. Like the rest of the castle, this room was different, and for a moment, it held Isobel captive. Gone were the maids who had fed and looked after her when she was a child. There was no tall stool for her to sit on and watch the chopping and slicing of meals as they were being prepared. Also missing was the gigantic brown dog, Mac, who, despite being shooed out of the kitchen repeatedly, always returned, begging for more scraps.

Along the length of the back wall stood a wooden table dusted in its middle with flour. On either side sat bowls of varying sizes, each covered with a linen cloth, and a large wooden rolling pin, also covered in flour, lay nearby. Underneath the table, a tall wire basket of fruits and vegetables sat on the floor.

Isobel's eyes darted towards an open flame where a large, upturned bowl with a thick liquid bubbled and sent a delicious steam upwards into the air.

As usual, Elspeth was busy with purpose, and Isobel remained silent for a moment and watched as she brushed a glaze over the pie crusts laid out in front of her.

"Good morning," Isobel said, a little too emphatic as she looked at Elspeth. "I'm sorry I slept so late." Isobel hoped Gavan hadn't heard the slight quiver in her voice. Standing tall, she looked him in the eye and forced a smile.

"You look much rested," Elspeth said. She wiped her hands on her apron and ignored the glare her brother cast in their direction.

"Are you hungry?" Grabbing her skirts, Elspeth moved around Gavan and placed a platter stacked with breads and cheese on the table.

"Sit; I will make you something to eat."

"Oh no, please don't go to any trouble. This will be fine."

Isobel grabbed two large hunks of bread. Their outer crusts were warm and smooth against her fingers. The rich doughy scent filled her nostrils, and as her stomach gave a noisy growl, the acidic taste of bile rose in her throat.

Oh no, not here. Not in front of Gavan, whose scowl from last night remained etched in his face. Isobel forced herself to take a bite and fight her nausea; she shouldn't have waited so long to eat. She begged herself not to get sick. Not to show him any sort of weakness that he could choose to misinterpret or manipulate.

Don't give him any excuse to have your head. Isobel glanced at Gavan's weapon that hung from his waist.

"I'd like to go outside and get a little fresh air if that's alright," Isobel finally said after forcing down one of the pieces of bread while looking between the siblings. She wasn't asking for permission, but if it sounded like she was, it might go over a little better with Gavan.

Gavan's surly demeanor, however, stood unchanged. Their mannerisms were so different that it made Isobel wonder if he and Elspeth were really brother and sister. Elspeth's warm smile and gentle eyes offered a genuine kindness, and she refilled the plate with more for Isobel to eat.

"May I plait your hair before you step outside? It is not appropriate to wear it unbound as it is now. For your husband's sake, lass?"

But before any of them had a chance to respond, the door

swung open and crashed into the wall behind it. A brightness of sunlight, along with a rush of outside air, burst in and diluted the rich baked aroma that had once smothered them. With his hand on the hilt of his sword, Gavan raised his arm and spun around as Meg skidded to a stop inches in front of the tip of his blade.

Chapter 11

A loud clatter broke the silence, pulling everyone's attention to the floor as Meg's shoes fell from beneath her cloak and landed in a heap next to her dirty, bare feet.

Her deep blue eyes were unnaturally wide, and her mouth hung open as if she wanted to speak but couldn't. The paleness of her skin alerted Isobel's senses. Meg's powers were weak, and Isobel had trouble holding a connection between the two. The girl's blood raced, and an unmistakable heat radiated from her; oddly, it was a heat similar to what wafted from Isobel on her morning runs. Isobel studied Meg from head to toe, looking for any signs of an attack but found no visible wounds. Isobel's own blood tingled, and she shivered as dread stirred in her gut. The vampire had gotten to Meg, she was most certain, but there was something else. Something different with her. Gavan lowered his sword and replaced it in its sheath at his side. His hands were visibly shaking.

"Oh," Meg finally said to the three of them still rooted in place. Her hands pulled at the torn jagged edge of her sleeve, stretching it into her palm before she turned and pushed the door closed with more force than necessary.

She closed her eyes and grimaced as it slammed shut, sealing the kitchen from the cool morning air once again. From the corner of her eye, Meg had seen the three of them jump in reaction to the banging sound. Letting out one last anxious heavy breath, she opened her eyes, and returned to face Gavan, Elspeth, and Isobel.

Isobel's insides buzzed as Meg's heart rate accelerated.

"I didn't know anyone was in here. Excuse me; I'll be out of your way." Meg's cheeks flushed, and her eyes shifted to the ground. Again, her hands fidgeted with the sleeve of her gown, pulling the loose frayed fabric to her fingertips.

"I could have killed you!" Gavan bellowed. "What were you thinking, busting in here like that—never mind." Gavan shook his head slowly and exhaled, the muscles in his jaw tensing as his brows pulled together. "Where have you been?" He asked the question through clenched teeth, but Elspeth spoke before Meg could respond .

"Your smock is covered in mud, and your hair—"

The three of them stared at the matted mess atop of Meg's head. Folding his arms, Gavan braced his legs apart and blocked the space in front of his youngest sister. Grabbing her skirts, Elspeth scurried around Gavan, but he didn't budge when she bumped into his upper body, the collision causing her to lose her balance.

"You could move!" she spat as she picked up Meg's shoes and held them out to her.

"Meg—" Gavan said, but Isobel didn't stick around to hear

any of the lashing that the scowl on his face and the clipped tone of his voice implied he was about to give.

With Meg's unexpected entrance, Isobel's presence seemed to be momentarily forgotten. Carefully, she grabbed a large wedge of cheese and another handful of bread and backed towards the arched opening that led away from the kitchen. Grateful for the soft leather soled shoes Elspeth had left for her to wear, Isobel quickly but quietly made her way to the main door. Piling her breakfast into one hand, she used the other to pull the lever and let herself out. Leaning into the closed door, her pent-up breath rushed from her lungs; she was relieved that at least for now she was no longer the center of attention.

~~~~~~~~

Winding along the cobblestone pathway that had led her to the entrance last night, Isobel descended away from Elden Castle. The ground, a semi-circle made of tall grasses and patches of dirt along the base of the fortress, was soft from the heavy rains and the moisture that remained scattered shimmered in the sunlight. Shielding her eyes from the brightness, Isobel stopped and looked ahead. The dense outer row of trees where Isobel had witnessed Meg disappear into last night still felt dangerous. Turning, she made her way to the other side of the castle in the direction of a small garden bordered with large boulders and wildly growing heather.

The storms from overnight had left a cloudless blue sky, and the leaves along the tree tops swayed in unison with the breeze. Birds called to one another joyously as they repaired their damaged nests, and rodents scurried, recovering their buried treasures of nuts and seeds from underground. Tiny goosebumps rose along Isobel's flesh beneath her heavy skirts and long sleeves, but she was refreshed, not cold. The chill in the air was due strictly to the weather.

Making her way toward the patch of heather that bordered one side of the garden's edge, Isobel thought about Mariam. Her ancestor would know how to help with the vampires that had killed her mother and husband and chased her into the past, but would she know the answers to Isobel's parentage? Was it possible that her mother had confided in Mariam while they worked so quietly behind closed doors thirteen years ago? And if so, would she expose her mother?

Isobel stooped to pick a cluster of the tiny purple flowers that sprouted at her feet when a recognizable but unwanted sting prickled through her. She reached out to the nearest boulder for support.

Meg.

The young witch was probing in Isobel's head again, no doubt looking for answers to her past and present. Pushing off the rock, Isobel stood and held her ground, desperate to keep her mind to herself. Meg's focus was still a bit clumsy, but her will to know was intense. Isobel, however, was stronger this morning. If she wasn't ready to face her own fears, she certainly wasn't about to let anyone else see them.

Shielding her eyes from the sun once again, Isobel tilted her head back and looked at Meg, who stood staring in her direction. Meg's hair was unbound, the curls twisting and shining magically under the bright light that glinted off her bright blue eyes, their color mimicking the clear open sky. From the outside, Meg was a beautiful sight and painted a magical scene with the enormous stone castle looming behind her. But there was more to Meg than beauty. The lore behind the intense color of her eyes reminded Isobel to be careful while she fought hard to keep her own secrets hidden.

Swooping from the trees, Fara landed on the rock beside Isobel, her tail feathers turned toward the castle and Meg. Her tiny feet patted against the stone, and the spell that had held Isobel entranced was lifted. The tightness across her chest loosened, and Isobel exhaled. Reaching across, she handed Fara a small piece of bread.

"Thank you," she whispered. Isobel wanted to stroke her small, sleek head but resisted. Sitting beside her familiar, Isobel, too, turned her back on the castle and Meg, who still stood staring down.

"Fara, I have been thinking this morning. We need to go

see Mariam now more than ever." The magpie stopped pecking at the bread crumb and cocked her head toward Isobel.

"We have been here less than a day, and I have more questions than before we entered the portal. I need to know about my mother and father, but also, who Meg, Gavan, and Elspeth are and what they are doing in Mariam's home. She has to have some answers; at the least, she will advise what to do about the vampires when we return home."

Fara's tail feathers fanned, and Isobel stilled.

"I haven't seen a bird come so close." It was Meg's young voice that spoke from behind and interrupted Isobel's conversation. Isobel looked over her shoulder; she hadn't heard the girl approach.

"How is it not afraid?" Meg asked, pointing at the magpie.

Caught off guard, Isobel forced a smile and gave a quick but logical answer. "I think she's hungry and wants some of my bread."

A cold sweat glossed over Isobel's palms. Pulling a small piece of bread loose, she handed it to Meg and nodded for her to offer it to Fara. Meg hesitated and held out her free hand, the other remaining buried deep in her pocket. Fara fluttered and flew toward the trees. Perched a few feet away, her beady black eyes stared at Meg, but she refused to come any closer.

"You called her *she;* how do you know it's a girl?" Meg asked.

"My mother." Isobel choked on the word *mother* and drew in a breath before she continued. "When we came to the Highlands many years ago, I asked her the same thing, and she said a mother just knows these things."

Isobel was anxious to get to know Meg. She didn't know how much longer the girl would stay, or how much of her own pain she could keep hidden if she continued to speak of her own family. An awkward silence suddenly filled the air as the two women looked at one another, each waiting for the other to speak.

Meg wore a simple, ankle-length cream colored gown with long sleeves and brown shoes. Isobel wondered what Gavan had said to her after her outburst in the kitchen. She didn't look as if she had been crying, and he hadn't locked her away, so it must not have been too bad. Odd, considering how angry he had appeared.

It was Isobel who finally spoke, unsure how much she should share with Meg. "Fara is not just a bird; she is part of my family." Anything she said Meg could tell her brother, and Isobel knew she didn't need to give Gavan any reasons to further dislike her no matter how short of a time she was planning on staying.

"Your family? Like a pet?" Meg asked, frowning as she looked at the magpie, who hadn't taken her own eyes off of Meg.

"Yes. She is my familiar."

Meg scrunched her nose. "A familiar? What does that mean?"

"There are many different ideas defining a familiar. Some

even speak of them as grotesque and frightening and evil, but Meg, that is not at all true. A familiar is someone who is the truest of friends and serves as a guide or protector. They can see and understand everything about and around you, and often know us better than we know ourselves."

She should know this, Isobel thought. *She is a witch.*

"But it's just a little bird; how can it protect you?" Meg sat next to Isobel, and the tension between the two lifted slightly. For a moment, Meg sounded so young, like a curious child. But her balled up fist bulging at the bottom of her pocket alerted Isobel to keep her guard up.

"Fara and I have a special connection, Meg. I'm not sure how to describe it other than I am able to read her feelings, or sense her energy if danger is nearby or she wants me to see something in another way. We have learned how to communicate with one another. Surely you know what I mean when I say that some people are able to do special things that others can't."

Meg ignored Isobel's statement and studied the magpie that had returned to Isobel's side. Fara's shiny black feathers gleamed as they caught and absorbed the rays of sunlight from overhead. Meg was intrigued, but the look on her face remained indifferent.

"Fara means 'traveler'," Isobel continued, trying to keep Meg engaged in conversation. "Since the first day we met when I was seven years old, she hasn't left my side."

"You mean she goes everywhere you go? She doesn't stay

outside in the trees with other birds."

"Well, Fara does like it better outdoors, but she doesn't leave me for long."

"How did you find her?" Meg asked.

"I didn't. She found me."

Wondering as though she had already said too much, Isobel was ready to change the subject. She wanted to know more about Meg and the pendulum. She handed Fara another piece of bread, and the magpie hopped to the ground with it.

"Meg—" Isobel said when a movement behind the girl caught the corner of Isobel's eye. Elspeth smiled and waved her hands as she made her way down the incline toward them.

Meg turned to see what Isobel was looking at and sighed. "They are not going to give me a moment's peace," she said, her eyes squinting towards the castle. Pulling her balled up fist from her pocket, she laced and unlaced her fingers together, fidgeting empty handed while she waited.

As Elspeth came closer, Gavan emerged from the shadows and took his place outside the castle. The expression on his face looked more inquisitive than angry, Isobel thought, and she wondered why. In the short time she had been in Dunkinshire, Isobel had become accustomed to his frown and menacing glare. She could read him better that way. This new look threw her off, and like his appearance last night, Isobel wasn't so sure she liked it.

"I'm sorry to interrupt you two," Elspeth said, "but I need Meg's help inside."

"It's a beautiful day," Meg stated in hopes of persuading her older sister to leave her be. "Can we not take a break from work today and enjoy it?"

"I'll be fetching the midwife tomorrow, Meg, and I'll be gone a day or two. Please don't give Gavan another reason—"

"Aye!" Meg said, and she threw up her hands.

Eyeing the ground, Meg looked for Fara as if she planned on telling the magpie goodbye, but Fara wouldn't be showing herself in front of Elspeth; she knew when to be discreet.

Meg stood and sighed. Slumping her shoulders, she gathered her skirt and followed Elspeth uphill towards the castle, never giving Isobel a second glance.

"Is there anything I can help with?" Isobel called out after the sisters.

"Of course not; you are our guest. Please rest and enjoy yourself. When you get hungry, I will be in the kitchen." Elspeth turned and trailed behind Meg.

Isobel kept her eyes on the two until they disappeared behind the stone wall. Moving between and around the boulders, she resumed gathering the musky smelling flowers she loved. It was winter here, so the garden was mostly bare other than some grasses that grew in patches. Isobel wondered what was grown here and if the garden belonged to Meg. Did she have a knowledge of herbs? Or maybe the garden belonged to Elspeth? Isobel made a mental note to ask the sisters next time she spoke with them.

Fara stayed close by, pecking at bugs and seeds that she found on the ground between the large boulders. The air surrounding the two was peaceful, but as Isobel turned her back away from the blinding glare of the sun, she sensed she was being watched. Isobel willed her ivory colored dress to make her difficult to see, but as time passed, her voyeur held his position until Isobel couldn't take the scrutiny any longer.

Rubbing her brow with one hand, she squeezed the stems together in her other and made her way toward the castle.

Not too quickly, she reminded herself as the sudden need to march uphill tried to take over. *Move naturally*.

Her eyes narrowed as she slowed her gait and stared in Gavan's direction. He had made it obvious that Isobel would get no privacy while she was beyond the castle walls, so she would go inside and leave him to his precious outdoors.

"And that's exactly what I'm going to tell him," Isobel snapped under her breath as she grabbed her skirt and headed straight in his direction.

Chapter 12

By the time Isobel reached the top of the hill, she had regained her composure and didn't tell Gavan exactly what she thought of him watching her. Instead, she dismissed him altogether. She sensed his eyes following her movements and was cautious not to step with too much force as she often did when she was angry.

Don't give him any reasons to have your head, she reminded herself and stared straight ahead, refusing to give him the satisfaction of even one last look before she entered the castle's main entrance. As she closed the heavy cathedral doors, the caws of her familiar, who was flying overhead, cried out.

Expecting Gavan to charge through the door after her, Isobel stepped forward and stood in the entry for a few minutes and waited. Nothing. No one. Except for the sounds of Isobel's rapid shallow breaths, the foyer was silent.

"Good! I guess he got the hint." She wandered around the lower level and took in how different, from floor to ceiling, the inside of the castle looked compared to when she was last here.

Who are Gavan, Elspeth, and Meg? she questioned as her fingertips trailed along the dismal gray stone of the corridor before finally arriving at the Great Hall.

Stopping in the entryway, she squinted at the display of

ornamental weaponry and unfamiliar coat of arms that were mounted above the mantle. There was an inscription, but Isobel was too far away to make it out. Moving into the room, she stopped in front of the fire and looked up. *Le claidheamh cuir sgiath.* By sword and shield. The arms must belong to the Highlander.

Reaching out to warm her hands, black script and a lion insignia encircled with the words IN MY DEFENCE GOD ME DEFEND caught the corner of Isobel's eye.

Daemonologie.

Her fingers traced the title; she couldn't believe she was looking at an original copy. Isobel yearned to read through the book written by Scotland's King James VI. Her mother had recited stories of their ancestors who had lived during this tumultuous time and the remembrance of their told persecutions sent Isobel's heart clattering. She glanced behind her before returning her gaze to the pamphlet. She was still alone. She would take a quick look and return it. No one would ever know. Isobel's heart maintained its racing pace as she reached down and lifted the pamphlet from the stack; this indeed was a different time. One of fear and violence, and one she too should be frightened of. King James VI's writing sought to educate the misinformed people regarding prophecy and black magic and why those who practiced such sorcery should be brought to justice under church law. Isobel knew it was beliefs like the king's that led to the witch hunts and burnings, and in times like these, anyone could have been a suspect. She also knew that anyone who was accused rarely went free.

You shouldn't be here. The reminder sounded deep within her bones, but she ignored it and trailed her fingers across the simple stitch binding and thin parchment covering. Had Gavan bound it himself or had it been done and given to him as a gift?

It was a popular read, so Isobel didn't question why he had it, but if he had any idea of his youngest sister's abilities, which Isobel had sensed last night that he might, she wondered why he left it out on display. Perhaps it was just for show. Something to keep the villagers at bay and trusting that he too believed in the evilness. Of course, he might believe. Isobel didn't know him well enough to know the answer.

Turning the thin skin cover, the pamphlet close to her nose, Isobel pored over its contents. Page after page, she became so engrossed reading about demons and witches and vampires and necromancy that she forgot where she was. At this moment in time, the history of witchcraft came to life. Everything her mother had told her about the past seemed true.

The crinkling sound as she turned the thin pages was the only noise that filled Isobel's ears until suddenly the back of her neck tingled and she froze; someone was watching her.

Please let it be Elspeth.

"What are you doing?" Gavan's voice boomed, piercing Isobel's eardrums as it bounced off the bare walls of the hall. "Are you reading?"

Isobel whipped around, crumpling the edges of the paper in her haste.

The harshness of his tone was startling, and the two watched the pamphlet fall from her hands and to the floor. Isobel stooped to retrieve it. With shaky hands, she grabbed at the edges multiple times when the toe of Gavan's polished boot appeared and stepped on one corner.

"I'm sorry," Isobel stammered, staring at his bare knees braced in front of her.

Her heart beat like a caged animal desperate to escape, and the walls of the Hall swirled. How could she have been so careless? At the least, she should have sensed when Gavan had entered the castle.

"You didn't answer my question. Were you reading?"

Isobel knew the best way to answer that question was with a no. But the same part of her that refused to cower to the vampires chose not to recoil from him. She stood and straightened her skirt, then she shifted her gaze to him. Gavan's eyes were wide, and his jaw hung open as he waited for her to speak. The pamphlet remained on the floor, trapped under his boot.

"I apologize for not asking first. I have heard of the pamphlet but never seen an original copy before." She doubted he would believe her. The publication was well known and had been circulated throughout the villages. If you lived in this time period, that is.

"And yes, I was reading. I am quite curious about the king's ideas." Her voice was strong and confident. Her fingers held tight to her skirts, but their trembling had stopped. "You know, Gavan, some women are interested in politics and do read. Those who have been properly educated. Surely, Meg and Elspeth have been suitably educated?"

The muscles in Gavan's jaw ticked. Isobel knew that Scottish Highlanders had tempers and wouldn't hesitate to strike a woman if they believed she deserved it. She should have left his sisters out of it, but Isobel was desperate for a distraction. She raised an eyebrow as his knitted closer together, and the vein across his forehead became more defined. Isobel opened her mouth to continue, but he spoke first.

"My sisters are none of your business." Gavan's voice was low and controlled, and his balled fists moved to his hips.

"Well, if you kindly remove your foot, I will pick up your leaflet and place it where I found it. I would like to return to my room. I didn't sleep well last night and want to lie down." To her own ears, she heard the weakness of her words and wished she could take them back.

Gavan stepped forward, closing the distance between the two to inches. Isobel stared into the dark blue plaid that lay seamlessly across his bare chest and exposed muscles that bespoke long hours of physical endurance. His loose hair was damp and fell across his shoulders in waves, and the rich, crisp scent of soap filled the sliver of space between them. Straining her neck, Isobel looked up.

"You may have fooled my sisters but not me. No more reading as you have no reason to make yourself comfortable. You will not be here for long," he said in a clipped tone.

Gavan's icy blue eyes sent a chill throughout her, and Isobel feared that his deadly stare saw right through everything she tried to hide. He was a protector and would stop at nothing to keep his sisters safe. She matched his glare and slid her arms possessively around her stomach. Charlotte pushed against her mother's touch. Isobel's movement pulled Gavan's eyes downward, and the lines at the corners of his lashes deepened.

The undergarments Elspeth had left for her this morning made Isobel look larger than she was. Gavan's eyes remained locked on her swollen belly, and the space of time before he spoke again confused Isobel.

"Where is your husband?" he suddenly demanded, and Isobel's head snapped upright.

"Considering your condition, how is it that he allowed you to travel, especially without an escort?"

Isobel opened her mouth, but before she had a chance to answer, Gavan asked, "It is his child?" he whispered, and his eyes were contemptuous as he searched her face.

Appalled, Isobel spat, "Of course, this is my husband's

child! How dare you insinuate otherwise. I came here looking for my relatives, as I told you last night. And the reason why I travel alone is because my family—my husband and my mother—were murdered." Tears filled Isobel's eyes, and the trembling returned to her fingers. She wasn't sure how much longer she would be able to stand up to him. "It is only my daughter and I left." It was the truth, sort of—enough of the truth that Isobel chose to believe anyway.

"And the bird?" he questioned. "I saw you talking to a bird." He moved his arms across his chest.

Caught off guard, Isobel's body faltered, and she took a step back to steady herself. She hadn't seen Gavan outside until Elspeth approached them, yet he had been watching her. For how long? And where had he been?

She was close to breaking. "You're going to ask me about a bird? If you must know, I was talking to myself, and the bird flew beside me. I shooed it away, but it saw the bread I had. I tore off a piece and didn't give it another thought."

The Highlander didn't believe her; Isobel sensed it as she studied his face. She had to get away before Gavan asked her anything else, demanded answers that she couldn't, absolutely wouldn't, give. She wanted to go to her room, but she was worried he would follow her. Isobel couldn't risk being alone with him any longer. She needed to find Elspeth.

"If you will excuse me, Elspeth told me to find her in the

kitchen when I came inside," Isobel said as one arm cradled her unborn daughter and the other hand grabbed her skirts.

"Elspeth!" Isobel called out. Her voice quaked and sounded much softer than she would have liked considering the boldness of walking away from him.

Isobel stepped around Gavan, but not before he caught her upper arm and pulled her body into his. His grip was tight but not painful. The look on his face was unreadable as he bent his head and stared into her eyes so deeply it was as if he were looking right through her again.

"You have secrets, Isobel," he finally said through gritted teeth. His warm breath blew against her cheek and his voice rumbled in her ears. "And until I find what they are, I will be watching you."

And he let her go.

Chapter 13

Isobel and Elspeth ate supper in the Great Hall alone that evening.

"I'm not hungry," Meg had announced as she passed by the kitchen earlier, and Gavan had not yet returned from tending to business.

"So, have you chosen a name?" Elspeth asked as she blew on her spoon. The mutton stew that sat before them both had simmered the majority of the day, its rich, meaty scent filling the castle's lower level and whetting everyone's appetite.

"What?" Isobel had heard Elspeth speak, but she hadn't really been listening; her thoughts were lost on Gavan and Meg. What if Gavan were in town asking about her? Telling everyone how this strange woman who wore the symbol of witchcraft around her neck had shown up at their door last night. What if he was planning her persecution and gathering a group to assist? At any moment, he could come busting through the doors ready to end her life. And Meg. She has disappeared for a bit late this afternoon. Where had she gone? Had she met with the vampire again? Isobel dragged her spoon through the meat and vegetables that once made her stomach growl with hunger and no longer felt safe.

"A name for the baby. Do you have one?" Elspeth repeated.

"Yes. Charlotte," Isobel answered, her voice shaky. She

laid her spoon down and looked up at Elspeth. "And if it's a boy?"

It's not a boy.

"There is a chance it could be a boy. Some children are boys, you know," Elspeth said with a smile. "You should be prepared."

"Yes, I suppose I should," Isobel half-heartedly agreed, and she looked down into her bowl. "If the child were a boy, he would be named after his father, Thomas." Even to her own ears, her voice sounded distant, as though she were speaking from the end of a long dark hallway on the other side of Elden Castle.

A gut-wrenching sob filled her body as she thought of her husband. The fear he must have had when he saw her mother lifeless in the arms of the vampire, not to mention when Dario attacked him. Isobel hoped he went quickly so that he hadn't even known what had happened and didn't suffer any pain. All afternoon, she had forced herself to dwell on their times of happiness. It was all she had; that and her nightmares. Charlotte pressed against Isobel's stomach.

You're right, I have you, she silently agreed.

"Lass, your hands are trembling." Elspeth placed her spoon on the table and drew her brows together as she studied Isobel. "All the color has left your face. Are you in pain?"

Yes! Isobel thought sadly and stood, forcing herself to be strong.

"Can I carry these to the kitchen for you?" Isobel's legs were so weak she wasn't sure they could carry her, but she needed to move around and get out from under Elspeth's scrutiny.

"No, please leave them here. It's not much, and I can see you're tired. You didn't eat, lass. Are you sure you are not feeling unwell?"

"Thank you, Elspeth. You have been so kind to me, and I do appreciate it. I know that it can be hard having a stranger in the house, especially one who has caused so much turmoil in such a short time like I have. I am sorry for that. But I am still tired and mourning my family."

"I understand your loss," Elspeth said with a gentle smile, and her brows relaxed. She leaned back into her chair. "The three of us were young when our parents were killed. Our mother first, then our father. It was hardest on Gavan and me. Meg was just a wee one, too young to understand. She kept Gavan and me busy and often distracted. We knew how to run a household by helping at a young age and watching our elders, but we had never been left in charge. Along with our grieving and trying to keep Meg safe, we often felt lost and angry. So much responsibility was placed on us overnight after our father died, but we had one another, and I believe that is what got us through. I am so sorry you are having to go through this alone. Are you certain you have no other family? Even a distant relative who could help at least until the baby has come?"

Isobel shook her head no. "We lived very isolated, my family and me. If there was anyone else, my mother never spoke of them. My husband's parents had already passed. He was an only child."

Elspeth gave a sad smile and nodded. Her eyes dropped to Isobel's abdomen, then to her face. "So you can understand why Gavan is so overprotective? He was forced to become the man of the house, even though he was barely a man himself. It's not been easy for him."

"Well, I suppose that's how a brother should be." Isobel didn't have siblings, so she was unsure how a brother should be, but if it was anything like a husband or a father, then being overprotective was right.

My daughter will never have a brother or a father, Isobel thought, and the image of Thomas's pale, crumpled body that terrorized her in her sleep flashed in her mind. Charlotte shifted herself again, and Isobel leaned against the wooden table for support.

"Good night, Elspeth. And again, I do apologize for any trouble I have stirred. Perhaps I should try to return home tomorrow," Isobel said.

Elspeth pushed her chair back and stood. "I will not hear of it. You cannot travel in your condition. You are too weak; you can't even finish your meal. It will only take me a few days to retrieve the midwife and return. By that time you should be rested.

Once she can confirm you are well enough, Gavan will escort you or have Kenneth ride with you to your home."

An escort won't be necessary, Elspeth. You will never see me leave. Tears filled Isobel's eyes. She nodded and quickly left the Great Hall before another word was said.

Grabbing the wooden handrail for support, Isobel's fingers trailed the innately carved grooves as she climbed the stairs to her room. She was thankful not to have anyone glaring at her or hounding her with questions, but the quietness she moved into as she stepped into the room had demons of its own.

Closing her door, Isobel let the tears pour down her cheeks. The sobs that begged to escape released again, and Isobel doubled over in agony. She kept one hand over her mouth and swallowed each one until she regained her composure and her ragged breaths no longer came in uncontrollable gulps.

The fire in her hearth had been lit, and soon Isobel was mesmerized by the dancing flames, her mind numb and silent. Moving to a chair, she sat and welcomed the warmth as her body relaxed and her trembling stopped. Looking at the glowing coals, Isobel wondered when Elspeth had lit it. The woman didn't stand still for long, that's for sure. Many times throughout the afternoon, it was as if she had vanished and Isobel had to search for her. She had been careful making her way around the lower level of the castle, glancing here and there as she wound her way through the little connecting rooms, most of which were sparse of furniture and other items. She didn't touch anything that could cause questioning, or worse, Gavan's promise of uncovering any of her secrets.

Isobel hadn't seen Gavan again after their confrontation in the hall, but she did notice that another man had been in and out of the castle, looking around until he lay eyes on her.

"Who is that?" she had asked after he left the kitchen the first time earlier this afternoon.

"That is Kenneth. He is the stable master," Elspeth replied, a bright red flush coloring her cheeks. Isobel wanted to ask more about Kenneth, but Elspeth's sudden fumbling of kitchen tools and the near drop a freshly baked pie told plenty.

"Gavan must have ordered Kenneth to keep an eye on me," Isobel said. The corners of Elspeth's lips pulled up, but she didn't respond.

Isobel fought the urge to tell Kenneth precisely what she thought of his spying after the third time she felt him staring. Instead, she ignored him and refused to acknowledge his presence just as she had Gavan earlier.

A slight tap at the shutters tore Isobel's attention away from the flames. She stood and made her way to the window, pulled back the fabric and wooden coverings, and let Fara in. Leaning against the ledge, she stroked the magpies head before closing and securing the latch, shutting out the cold.

"How does it feel to be home?" Isobel asked.

Fara patted her feet and bobbed her head, making Isobel smile. Untying the layers of skirts and undergarments, Isobel washed her face and hands in the basin of water before sliding the white linen smock over her head. A quiet knock at the door sounded, and a recognizable tingle alerted Isobel's senses. *Meg.*

"Yes?" Isobel was surprised. She hadn't expected to see Meg, or anyone for that matter, until tomorrow morning. She pulled her nightdress down until the hem hit the floor.

"It's Meg; may I come in?"

"Of course," Isobel answered, and the click of the door knob sounded.

"I just wanted to say good night. And…" Meg trailed off as her eyes darted around room. She shifted from one foot to the other.

"Yes?" Isobel questioned, raising an eyebrow.

"Well, I wanted to ask how you are feeling and apologize for my brother's behavior today. Well, really, since you got here." Meg looked at the floor and not at Isobel. "I'm sorry; if you are ready for bed, we can visit in the morning." Meg's voice cracked and she toyed with the sleeves of her gown. They had not been torn, but they had been stretched to the center of her palms.

"Thank you, Meg, but truly there is nothing to apologize for," Isobel responded cautiously. "Elspeth explained Gavan to me at dinner. Your brother has the right to feel uneasy. After all, I am a stranger in his house."

Meg stood uneasy. She was different tonight compared to last night and when they were together in the garden this afternoon. Her nervous energy formed an invisible barrier between the two, and it left their magic disconnected and Isobel unsettled. Her stomach tumbled, and for a moment Isobel feared she would be ill. She sensed Fara's uneasiness too as she patted her feet on the stone floor under the bed before exposing herself and flying beside Isobel.

"Fara!" Meg gasped, and her hand flew to her chest. Instantly, the invisible barrier between the two women vanished, as though Fara's appearance had broken the spell. Meg reacted as if she had forgotten about the magpie that had held her so captivated this afternoon. "You let her inside the castle?"

"I told you, Fara rarely leaves me." Isobel studied Meg before she continued. "She and I are a lot alike. Like you and I, Meg." A spark flickered inside Isobel and feeling bold, she pounced on the sudden opportunity to question Meg. "Your brother and sister may be fooled, Meg, but I can see you for who you are. Why did you taunt me like that last night?"

"I have no idea what you're asking me." Meg shoved her hand in her pocket and looked away.

Fara fluttered between the two, and Isobel sensed her familiar's desire to interrupt the conversation. Isobel rushed a finger to her lips to motion her to stay quiet. The magpie lowered her wings and settled on the back of the chair between Meg and

Isobel. Stepping away from the edge of the bed, Isobel made her way towards the center of the room. The smugness Meg had displayed last night was non-existent, yet she wasn't vulnerable and frightened like this morning in the kitchen. Isobel sensed the young witch's confidence slip and her anger rise the closer she got.

"You will not threaten me in my own home!" Meg spat and took a step backwards. "I have done no such thing to you."

She lies.

"Meg, you have no reason to fear me." Isobel thought of the inexplicable familial pull she had towards Meg the first time she stepped into the Great Hall and then again this morning in the kitchen. "More so than even I understand," Isobel whispered as she covered Meg's hand with her own. "And I know you have to feel it too."

Where their skin touched, a tingle traveled across Isobel's hand and up her arm. The sensation was warming and caused a ripple of goosebumps to rise over her body. Meg jerked her hand back as though it had been burned, and her lips pulled in a thin line. She lifted her head high. Despite her air of confidence on display, Isobel sensed the girl was disentangling on the inside, the magic between the two bouncing invisibly around the room like strikes of lightning.

"We are not alike!" Meg spat. "I don't even know you!" She shook her head and continued stepping backwards until her heels bumped into the door and her hand clumsily searched for the knob. Her blue eyes had clouded, and like last night, they darted around the room and made contact with everything except for Isobel.

"The pendulum in your pocket," Isobel said. Her Mind's Eye saw the pendulum lying at the bottom of Meg's deepest pocket.

Isobel wondered if she carried the sacred charm everywhere she went. Who had given it to her? But more importantly, who had taught her to use it?

Isobel grasped the silver pentacle that lay against the base of her neck, the five-pointed star warming her thumb and forefinger. She had spent her childhood practicing magic, but to no avail. She wasn't able to alter or change things or find the answers to unanswered questions or heal the sick. Yet, it had taken Meg only minutes, and she was in Isobel's head, digging around for information that even Isobel didn't understand. That fact alone spoke to the power within her.

"I told you, Meg, you cannot hide yourself from me," Isobel said as she exhaled. She had to keep her composure if she was going to get anywhere with Meg, but a rush of anxiety filled her veins and she had to grip the chair beside her in order not to fall. She looked at Fara, whose dark eyes bore into her. Isobel opened her mouth ready to question the magpie, but then turned to Meg and spoke, ignoring her familiar's warning to stop.

"I, too, am a witch. And your choice of witchcraft,

especially towards one of your own kind, is a dangerous one." Isobel thrust the charm she wore around her neck forward for Meg to see.

Meg's glassy blue eyes went wide, and she backed over the threshold and into the corridor, the lever of the door grasped tightly in her hand.

"Surely you know that!" Isobel called after her, but Meg was gone, the door between them slammed shut.

~~~~~~~

Meg sat on the bottom step of the winding staircase that led to the east tower. Her heart raced, and the rough edge of the stair cut into her thighs and her lower back, the coolness of the stone soothing the fire that raged inside of her.

"How can this be happening? How dare Isobel talk to me like that! Make such accusations!" she spat into the tight, empty stairwell.

How dare she know.

Meg had hoped the invisible current that awakened her blood and drew her to the dark haired witch from her dream had been a mistake. But as she pulled out her mother's ring and was silently rewarded with some answers, she discovered there was no mistake.

Elspeth had given her their mother's ring when Meg was

just seven years old.

"She wanted you to have this," Elspeth had explained. "Meg, this is very special, and you mustn't lose it. I have put it on a chain for you," she continued as she lowered the keepsake over Meg's head. "Don't ever take it off."

Meg had nodded, but as soon she stepped outdoors and away from her older sister's watch, she slipped it off. Moving towards the stables to see what Kenneth, the stable master was doing, she began to swing the chain back and forth. As she stood mesmerized by the flickers of sunlight that glinted off the ring, she heard Kenneth's voice. Meg stopped, stilled the chain, and looked around. The stable master was nowhere in sight. She swung the chain again, and again she heard him speaking. His words, ones that promised to follow Gavan's request and stop his pursuit of Elspeth, came not from his mouth but from his mind. Meg was unsure how she knew this, but she felt it deep within her bones.

As she grew older, Meg learned that if she closed her eyes and envisioned a person as she commanded her pendulum to swing, she could hear their secrets—their wants and desires, who they loved and who angered them, but mostly their fears. Sometimes the voices were muddled and made little to no sense while other times they spoke to her clearly. Additionally, it didn't work with everyone, like her brother and sister.

At first, Meg had thought it odd since they were related, but over time she began to wonder if maybe her mother also had the gift of hearing others' thoughts and had placed a spell on the ring. However, despite her limited magic ability to pry into the heads of her siblings, Meg had learned to read Gavan and Elspeth perfectly; they were like open books. Elspeth's soft smile but distant eyes and the tick in Gavan's jaw gave them both away. Of course, often their distress came from Meg, but even if it didn't, Meg was easily in tune with their emotions.

A new fear surfaced within her, and she frowned. Reaching into her pocket, she pulled out the pendulum and stared at it as it warmed her thumb and forefinger. The dark, dank air in the tower weighed on her heavily, and she held her breath. They could not keep another witch in the castle. If Isobel said anything in front of Elspeth or Gavan, gave anything away—

She shoved the ring back into her pocket and stood. Her bare footsteps slapped against the cold, hard steps heavier than usual as she climbed the stairs to her room, unconsciously mouthing the pattern that led her in an upwards spiral, *narrow, narrow, wide, narrow, repeat*. Gathering her skirt in her left hand, the fingertips on her right brushed against the smooth wall for support, and Meg made up her mind.

Gavan was right. Isobel needed to leave.

Chapter 14

"Ready for another?" the barmaid asked.

Cristian glanced her way then returned his attention to the group of Highlanders gathered across the room. Their voices were hushed, but their thick, knitted brows and doubled up fists sent a nervous energy into the air, one that reeked of an oncoming battle.

"My name is Fiona if you need anything," she said, dragging out the enunciation of *anything*, as she slid her finger along his shoulder. Cristian sat motionless; his ale untouched.

The corners of his lips turned up slightly as he continued to eavesdrop from the back of the overcrowded tavern. He was partially responsible for the warriors' excitement, but the killings last night were hardly worth summoning a meeting of vigilantes. The victims were known criminals—swindlers, pillagers, even a rapist— Cristian had done the town a favor. But the restlessness that brewed near the front door wasn't about them being murdered; it was more a matter of how. Perhaps he had been a little eccentric, leaving their bodies bloody and somewhat dismembered in the street for all to see, but again, it was all in the town's best interest, right?

Cristian sat with his back to the corner, rigid and unnoticed by everyone except the barmaid, who had walked away sulking when he ignored her invitation. Glancing over, he watched as the girl toyed with her bottom lip she had now jutted in a pout.

"You have no idea who you are playing with, my darling," he muttered under his breath.

While the feed last night had satiated his craving for blood, Cristian found another desire stirring as she licked her lips in an effort to keep his attention. He should teach the little whore a lesson, one regarding how dangerous it can be to play out of your league.

But that could be risky. There was a chance that one of the patrons would see them walk out together. Cristian didn't want to draw any attention to himself when she didn't come home tonight. It wasn't that he couldn't protect himself, but he didn't want to have to kill everyone in town; he liked it here. And he would never leave Meg. He couldn't.

Cristian returned his attention to Gavan. A smokey haze now hovered over the men's heads as they puffed intensely on their pipes. The anxiety of what loomed outside in the darkness as their discussion deepened formed creases across their foreheads.

"It's the witches, I tell you; we must burn them all." Fists pounded on the table and rattled their cups, sloshing the ale.

"We will go house to house—" The men all talked at once.

The tension that rose within Gavan went unnoticed by everyone except Cristian, who idly leaned into his seat and watched the tic in the Highlander's jaw become more prominent as his adrenaline surged and his heart pounded. The sound was soothing to Cristian's ears. If he had been hungry, it would have driven him to advance as soon as the warrior stepped outside and into the shadows.

Calm yourself, my friend; this is business as usual. Don't let your sister be a distraction; you know what you must do. The words came without a sound from Cristian's lips to the warrior's ears, and Gavan stilled upon hearing them.

Turning, he looked over his shoulder, but of course there wasn't anyone there, only the inner wall of the tavern. Gavan's pulse slowed to a near normal pace, and Cristian sat pleased as he waited for the commander at the table to speak.

Raising a hand, Gavan stopped the men's passionate speeches that ordered a mandatory witch hunt and shook his head in disagreement. As he processed his thoughts, he conveyed them both rationally and fearfully to the clan that sat amongst him. It was a method Gavan was well accustomed to using in order to keep his family safe, but his final words took Cristian by surprise.

"This is not a sacrifice from witches, but an attack from something more like an animal."

"They were drained of their blood—"

"Their bodies broken and ripped apart—"

"They had been fornicating with a witch—"

"Aye!" They raised their cups and continued, interrupting one another with their theories explaining the victims deaths.

"Silence!" Gavan ordered. The men stared at their leader in

disbelief.

Gavan usually jumped at the chance of a persecution if believed necessary to keep the clans safe. Cristian knew this because over the last six months he had followed Meg's brother and listened to the superstitious conversations that gathered around him. Overall, Cristian didn't care whether the life of an alleged witch was taken or not, unless of course it was Meg's. He was always ready to protect her in case her brother or anyone else in the Highlands questioned her reclusiveness.

Cristian gave Gavan's reaction some consideration. If the Highlander didn't believe that witches were responsible for the mutilations, what did he believe? Cristian was unsure why this assumption, although it was correct, bothered him, but it did, and he shifted in his seat. He wondered what kind of animal Gavan thought had attacked. What kind drank the blood of its victims and left them ripped apart in the streets? Perhaps the warrior was more open-minded than he let on. If that was the case then it was possible he was aware of Meg's abilities.

Narrowing his eyes, Cristian studied how Gavan took control of the conversation. He no longer had any interest in what the Highlander was saying. Rather, he was more intrigued with the man himself. Gavan's voice remained low and controlled, and his posture stiffened; his fists clenched, his exposed muscles flexed, and his spine was so rigid it looked as if it would snap.

Cristian deduced that they were of the same height.

Gavan's physique outsized his immensely, but Cristian knew his immortal strength couldn't be overpowered by a human, not even one as skilled as Gavan.

Light reflected off the hilt of the Highlander's sword and pulled Cristian's eyes to his scabbard. Gavan was a trained warrior, and the crest he wore pinned to his shoulder left no questions as to his allegiance.

Gavan grew up on the battlefield, and Cristian knew his reputation for being relentless was rightfully earned. Fighting had made the man's instincts sharp and his reflexes quick. If he ever sensed Meg was in danger, Cristian knew her brother wouldn't hesitate to use his resources to protect her. As would Cristian.

He drummed his fingers on the table. Their shared love and desire to keep Meg alive bothered him. Even though protecting Meg had been expected after their father had been killed, Cristian didn't want another man responsible for keeping her safe, not even her brother. That was his job.

Feeling agitated, Cristian shifted his eyes away from Gavan's table and searched for Fiona. He didn't need another drink, but rather a distraction. Her back was to him, and he listened as she talked nonstop to the man behind the counter. The barkeeper was thin and lanky, and stood no taller than Fiona. The man's eyes lowered from the barmaid's face, and Cristian remembered how her dress showed off her ample bosom.

"Why don't you go upstairs and wait for me, love," the

man smacked, spittle flying from his lips. Fiona tilted her head and squinted at him as though she was considering the offer.

Cristian's hungry stare bore into the barmaid until she visibly shivered and turned to look. Between his long, dark lashes, his eyes softened and returned to the same pools of blue that had first caught her attention. Her heart escalated, and she smiled in return. The barkeeper gazed past Fiona to see what had pulled her interest away when the tavern door crashed open.

"I'll be right back, lass; don't you go nowhere," he told Fiona, winking and giving her a toothless grin as he licked his lips.

Cristian, too, zeroed in on the man who had stumbled indoors. He managed to stay on his feet long enough to grab an empty chair at the warriors' table. Between shaggy golden eyebrows and stubbled cheeks lay a pair of bloodshot eyes; this man had already consumed more than his fair share of the drink. He opened his mouth to speak, but all that emerged was a sickening belch, and then his head collapsed on the table.

Riotous laughter and cheering emerged as an oversized Highlander tightly gripped the flagon of ale in front of him and threw it back in one long gulp before slamming it on the table, sending the drunk and dozens of empty tankards tumbling. For a moment, the seriousness that had hung heavily over the table was forgotten. Humans were miserable, ridiculous creatures. Yet Cristian preferred their company over the dead. *What does that say about me?* he wondered and then returned his stare to the barmaid.

Folding her arms along the ledge, Fiona rested her breasts on the bar top and gave Cristian a better view of the deep cleavage her shallow, scooped neckline made visible. His eyes held hers captive, and he narrowed his brows, hoping to make her nervous, even scared. If she had any sense, she would be terrified. Pulling his lips back, he displayed the sharp incisors at the corners of his mouth, giving her a brief glimpse of the evil that lurked inside him. It was her last chance to escape. But rather than shy away, Fiona smiled again and shifted her weight, leaning further across the wooden counter. Was she inviting him to take her right there?

Cristian held her stare for a few seconds longer before standing. Stepping into the dim light cast from the lantern on his table, he played her game and drew her eyes to his arousal that now pushed against his fitted stockings. Her heart skipped.

Without another glance, Cristian turned and exited through the rear of the building, immersing himself in her shallow breaths and the rapid clicking sounds of her heels that followed behind. He was completely tuned in to her every move.

Despite the heat that rose inside her, the cool wind whipped and sent a shiver along Fiona's spine as she slipped through the open back door. With one hand trailing along the wall, she searched for Cristian in the darkness; the escalating beat of her heart thumping deliciously in his ears the closer she got.

As she stepped from behind the tavern, Cristian grabbed and pinned her to the stone wall, hiding them within the shadows.

His mouth covered hers, silencing her scream, and she squirmed under his touch. He felt her fear, and his excitement escalated. He had warned her, had he not?

Fiona's soft warm skin sent him into a frenzy, and he grabbed the top of her dress, ripping it down the middle. She wore nothing underneath. Her breasts more than filled his hands, but it was the frantic drumming of her heart against the heel of his palm that sent him into ecstasy beyond his control. Cristian pressed his throbbing groin against her warmth, and it cradled him as a woman's body should. The only barrier that lay between their flesh connecting was his stockings.

"Not here," he growled against her lips.

By the time Fiona screamed again, they were out of the town's shadows and halfway up the mountainside. Cristian held her tightly as she collapsed against him, fear pulling her into unconsciousness. He wanted to shake her awake. He required her full participation. After all, wasn't that what she had offered him minutes ago?

Weaving through the overgrowth at speeds too great for the human eye to see, Cristian fantasized of how Fiona's heat would soon envelope him. How her softness would cushion his firmness, and how her quiet moans would transform into guttural cries, pushing him over the edge to finish.

Fiona wasn't Meg. He didn't have to be careful. He didn't have to fear losing himself to her, and most of all, he didn't have to worry if he killed her. With Fiona, Cristian could be himself, the monster he had been bred to be.

Propelling his body faster, his mind warned him to take it slow. Impatience, his biggest flaw, would keep him from satisfying the physical desires his body hungered for if he didn't.

He lunged into the air, and a faint scent of honeysuckle blew past. *Cristian.* His mind snapped at the scent and the sound of his name. Catarine!

Tremors shot through his body at her memory just as the soft sounds of Fiona crying filled his right ear. Cristian ignored the warning that pounded in his head and begged him to slow down. To pace himself.

He leaned his head back and forced himself to tune into the quiet, feminine sobs that jerked against his spine; the barmaid was awake. Catarine's voice had been nothing more than a memory that escaped during a moment of weakening. After all, it had been years since he heard her voice without the aid of Meg's blood. He forced her image from his head.

"We're almost there; a few more seconds." Cristian's words were strained as he spoke. His need for Fiona's flesh wrapped around his own skyrocketed, and he felt alive. Together, they would bring his fantasies to life. And together, they would put them to death.

But as he approached the sacred place he longed to share with the barmaid, Cristian recognized the shift of his instinct taking over, igniting the internal war of man against animal. Suddenly, he wanted nothing more than to sink his teeth into her delicate, tender flesh and bleed her dry.

Agony ripped through him; he hated his inability to separate and control his wants from his needs. It was as if his body understood a reality that his mind continued to deny, his immortality challenging his longing to be human again. He would be satisfied either way but was desperate to stay in control of his actions. He didn't need her blood. Not yet.

Fighting against the intense craving was arduous. Every step a test to his self-control. The urge to ravage her soft, warm body that clung to him drove him mad. When he thought the mania would leave him no other choice than to surrender to his own neurosis, they reached the familiar clearing.

In an effort to stay in control, Cristian focused on the open, secluded space around him and the near naked body that lay molded against his back. Fiona's warm, shallow breaths against his neck and her fierce heartbeat along his spine quickly lured his physical needs back to the surface.

There wasn't anyone for miles. Fiona's cries that would soon come would fall silent to everyone except Cristian. His eyes became wild and mindless as he imagined the sound, and the heaviness between his legs returned. The air around them was tranquil, and the brightness of the moon illuminated the open field. They would be able to watch one another perfectly as the mood switched seamlessly from blissful satisfaction to utter terror.

Releasing her arms, Fiona slid down his back and collapsed on the tall, soft grass that grew at Cristian's feet. He turned, and she looked up into his soulless black eyes. Her tear-stained cheeks drained of color, and their creamy white shade now matched the nakedness that her open dress left exposed for his viewing. Cristian stared. Her wide hazel eyes were frozen open in horror, and Cristian thought she never looked more beautiful. He knew that if she could speak, she would plead for him to set her free. A smile tugged at the corners of his mouth. Never. He unclipped his cape, and it fell to the ground in a heap.

As he dropped beside her on his knees and freed himself from his fabric restraint, Cristian had only one hope: that he hadn't waited too long. Then the demon within him took control.

~~~~~~~~

The air hung heavy with Cristian's misdeeds. He stared at Fiona's bloodless, mutilated body at his feet and waited for regret to consume him. It never came. His eyes remained pooled into two circles of black ink, even though the longing that once throbbed between his legs had been satiated and his bloodlust content.

The barmaid would be missed, but only briefly. It was why Cristian had given in to his desires. She was a wanderer, no family, no one expecting her to return home after her shift at the tavern.

Cristian had learned this when the bar keep asked if she had a husband to go home to tonight. Fiona's solitary life was much like Cristian's—desolate, lonely, and self-contained.

He hadn't been entirely selfish tonight, but the cruelty he inflicted upon the girl as her cries of pleasure turned to screams of terror was wrong. He had tasted every inch of her flesh and dared himself to count the bite marks he had savagely left: seventy-three. Again, he waited for guilt to overcome him. He had no right to take her life, even though becoming a vampire had granted him that exact ability.

"I can give life, take it away, or savor in it," he stated into the darkness, his tone straightforward and devoid of emotion. "It is who I am."

He reattached his cape at his throat just as the winds from the north gusted and a brush of feathers sounded in his ears. Turning on his heel, a sliver of brightness against the midnight sky caught his attention. Cristian zeroed in on the pair of glossy black eyes and breast of white feathers that glowed under the moonlight. There, perched on a branch in the tallest tree, sat the magpie who had suddenly made a habit of watching him.

The bird pulled him into its stare and held him there as if it could communicate by clairvoyance. Oddly, he felt as though it was disappointed in him and perhaps sad. The bird had witnessed the malice his touch had inflicted on Fiona and was warning him that he would be punished. Cristian understood its presence;

magpies were associated with divination. However, he left the believing of such superstitious nonsense to the humans. He had, though, had enough of the bird.

A harsh, rising call emitted from the magpie, and it took flight just as Cristian thought he heard Catarine call cut his name again. His eyelids fluttered and he looked around, but all that sounded in the open air was the swift beating of the magpie's wings.

Cristian sprang into the darkness, mercilessness weighing heavy at his fingertips. He lunged towards the sky, but as he reached the treetops, Fara was nowhere in sight.

Chapter 15

Caught between wakefulness and sleep, a scream in the distance pulled Isobel from her slumber. Her body jerked, and she thrust her arms forward to catch herself, only to discover she was lying flat on the bed. Sitting up, she pushed aside the furs and stared wide-eyed into the glowing coals cast by the fire, her pulse raging in her ears. She was in Elden Castle, in the circular room at the top of the north tower. Placing her hands on her abdomen, she waited until a gentle nudge pushed against her palm. Her breaths slowed, and the beating of her heart soon followed suit. She turned towards the window. *Meg.*

Untangling the smock from her legs, Isobel climbed out of bed and made her way to the window. Peeling away the woven tapestry, whose navy colors mirrored the plaid Gavan wore proudly around his body, Isobel slid the metal latch from the shutters and looked out. The crescent shaped moon shined high in the clear, dark sky, and its light drew Isobel to the endless stars that flickered in the background. Shivering, she wished she had grabbed a fur to cover herself before leaving the bed. Afraid to walk away from the window, in fear that she might miss something, she stilled and tried to ignore the cold air that settled around her.

Beside her sat Fara. The magpie's tiny, glossy eyes stared

towards the mountains and not at the heavens above, like Isobel's. She was not entranced by the stars, but instead by something Isobel could only sense, and she felt the weight of her familiar's worry as though it were her own. Fara sat motionless for minutes, and then, without warning, she was gone.

Above the treetops, the magpie soared. Under the bright moonlight, the iridescent colors of blue and green reflected off her ebony wings until she was finally swallowed into the blackness of the sky. Isobel wanted to call to her, but she was afraid to disrupt the dangerously quiet space between them.

Isobel shivered again and hoped that Meg wasn't out there. Her eyes lowered to the open fields of heather and tall grasses, and she searched through the white oaks and Scots pines that filled the space from the glen to the water's edge. She detected nothing—no magic, no coldness, no danger nearby. Meg could have wandered farther from home this time. For her own sake, Isobel hoped not.

Closing the shutters, she returned the tapestry over the opening and moved toward the fire to warm herself. After placing some new logs on top of the glowing coals, Isobel crawled back into bed and settled herself under the layer of furs. Her feet were ice cold after walking across the bare stone floor, and as she rubbed them together to generate some warmth, another chill shivered through her. The wood sizzled and popped as it ignited, comforting sounds Isobel had become accustomed to. Heat quickly spread from the firebox, and along with the flickers of orange and red flames that danced against the black backdrop of her closed lids, Isobel was soon lulled to sleep.

She would see Fara in the morning.

~~~~~~~

After tying her boots, Meg left through a side door, one far from where Elspeth was rushing around, and went in search of Gavan. Her sister had already gone over the list of chores twice, and Meg didn't want to hear it again, or worse, be told that more tasks had been added. No, her mind was focused on a more important responsibility this morning. Last night, she had tossed and turned as thoughts of Isobel sleeping in the tower next to her flooded her mind. Isobel could ruin her life. She could get them all killed.

She bent down, gathered a small cluster of heather in her fist and inhaled the rich, musky scent. Closing her eyes, she slowly released a long breath and made her way toward the stables, her mind concerned with what Gavan would say when she agreed that Isobel needed to be gone. It wasn't often that she sided with him, with either of them really, so she expected an interrogation. But she knew exactly what to say to Gavan. She had practiced all night while she lay there awake.

There is something suspicious about Isobel, brother. And I'm feeling too uncomfortable with her in our home. I think you were right last night; she can't stay here.

Entering the barn, Meg heard Kenneth sneeze in rapid succession and wondered if he was taking ill. Looking ahead, she saw that Gavan's stallion, Ahearn, wasn't in his stall; the gate to it was wide open.

"Good morning, lass," Kenneth said without looking in Meg's direction. The man had been with her family since before the three of them were born. His senses were keen and without ever looking up, he was aware of his entire surroundings. As a child, Meg had learned that fact the hard way more than once when he would mysteriously appear just before she fell head first into mischief.

"Is my brother here?" she asked as she stared at her family plaid that pulled across his back.

"No, I'm afraid not." Kenneth turned to Meg, and his emerging frown formed deep creases across his forehead. It was a look Meg had become used to.

"I am fine, Kenneth," she said with a sigh. "I needed to speak with him. It is urgent; do you know when he will return? Soon, I hope?"

"Not before dark, lass. A woman's body was found, one who worked regularly at the alehouse. A bloody mess it was." He shook his head, and now it was his turn to let out a sigh. "Your brother went to see."

"Another sacrifice from the witches?" Meg asked, keeping

a stoic look on her face.

He shook his head again.

She didn't think so. Taking a step back, she looked at the barn ceiling and focused on a mountain spider who was weaving its silk between the rafters. Its long but thin brown legs worked feverishly as it reached the roof's edge and bound the loose strings that flowed from its abdomen. Immediately, the threads swayed, and the spider ran across its web towards the midge that frantically worked to disentangle itself.

"An animal, from the looks of it," Kenneth said. "Bite marks covered her body, and her clothes had been ripped away, shredded by some very thick claws."

Or teeth, Meg added silently. She pulled at the sleeves of her gown, stretching the soft light blue fabric until it lay across the palms of her hands, hiding the wounds at her wrist that suddenly itched. Looking away from the spider, who was mending the damaged web, its prey now still and wrapped in silk, she returned her attention to Kenneth.

"At least her arms and legs were still attached, not like the men found the other night. But like the men, she was stark white, and not a drop of blood anywhere." His brows pulled together again. "Don't go wandering too far today; your brother's orders." He stood, crossed his arms and looked Meg in the eye.

Kenneth was a kind man and a loyal one too. Stocky and barrel chested, he wasn't as tall nor as large as Gavan, but he could be as intimidating with his dark eyes and equally long, dark hair that over the years had become threaded with strands of silver. He was not a native of Scotland but as a young man had made the Highlands his home. Kenneth embraced the fiery and bold patriotism and willingness to personally defend the country until he took his very last breath. A vow he had honored since he spoken it.

Over the years, as Elspeth became a better cook, Kenneth's middle had softened, but his time on the battlefields had not diminished. Like her brother, Kenneth remained a dangerous warrior.

Before her pendulum allowed her to pry into his private thoughts, Meg believed that Kenneth would marry Elspeth when she became old enough, and by the amount of attention he gave Elspeth as she grew into womanhood, her sister may have thought so too. But after the death of their father, the dynamics of their household changed. All of the kitchen maids and stablemen left, and the visitors who used to drop in regularly stopped coming. Slowly, their small family became isolated from the rest of the village.

There was still time, Meg thought. *We aren't children anymore.* Once she removed Isobel, she would focus on getting Elspeth and Kenneth together.

"You won't be taking the horse neither, and if I can't see you, I'll come lookin'. And lass, please don't make me come lookin'. You know your brother; he won't like it if I have to tell him." Kenneth shook his head again, and Meg, who was smiling at the thought of Kenneth and Elspeth wed, turned and disappeared from of the barn without another word.

The thought of missing an entire day before she could put her plan in place did not sit well with Meg. She would have to handle Isobel on her own. Perhaps she could trick her, lead her away from the castle on a mission that would land her right into Cristian's hands. Once he caught Isobel's scent, detected the power of her magic, which Meg did not understand but sensed was far greater than her own, she knew he would become frantic. If he found another to feed from, he would forget about her. There was one thing that made her hesitant. If Cristian were gone, she would no longer be able to relish in the burst of energy and strength his venom gave her. It was something neither of them understood, but the freedom it gave her to explore well beyond the castle walls and her brother's watchful eye was exhilarating, no matter how short lived it was. Then another thought crossed Meg's mind, and her shoulders slumped.

"How could I even think about sending a pregnant woman straight into his bloodthirsty hands?" she asked herself, although she already knew the answer.

She was desperate, that's how. She had no choice but to put a stop to Isobel's potential treachery before it could ever start. If her secret, their secret, was exposed, they would be taken to the gallows, their lives gone before they knew it. And not just their lives, but those of Elspeth, Gavan and likely Kenneth too. Meg didn't know if she could trust Cristian's words, his promise to keep her safe. He was only one man, and there must have been at least one hundred just in town. Meg didn't know who she could trust, and Isobel was just too different.

And too much like you, a voice whispered in her head.

The words reminded Meg why she had put the plan together in the first place—she would make the sacrifice. She would just have to find another way to sneak around and enjoy time to herself. She had done it plenty as a child; surely she was wiser now and could do it again. She didn't need Cristian's venom, and it wasn't worth the loss of her family's life. The loss of her life.

Cupping her hand above her brows, she shielded her eyes from the sun and looked across the glen. Near her parents' grave markers stood Isobel dressed in another one of their mother's gowns. Stopping, she picked at the tall, rich purple-colored flowers that grew in abundance. The same flowers that now lay wilted in Meg's own clenched and determined fist.

Gavan would be gone for two days, one to escort Elspeth to the midwife and one to return. Meg stepped forward. That didn't give her much time to waste.

Chapter 16

Isobel felt the recognizable tingle and looked over her shoulder. She watched as Meg stared at her for a long minute before stepping away from the stable doors and heading in her direction. She sensed that Meg wanted to speak, but her hesitation as she bit down on her lower lip and her pulse that elevated the closer she got warned Isobel that she wasn't going to like what the girl had to say. Turning back, Isobel studied the wildly growing heather and let Meg move toward her at her own pace. Her accusatory tone when she came to her last night wouldn't get her anywhere with the young girl. The minute Meg had slipped her hand back into her pocket and refused to continue looking Isobel in the eye, she realized she had acted with haste, been too forward. That kind of approach certainly wouldn't build Meg's trust, and that was exactly what Isobel needed. For many reasons, but primarily so she could stay alive.

"When I came to the Highlands the first time, when Fara found me," Isobel said when the dried grass behind her crunched and she knew Meg was close enough to hear, "I was seven years old."

She didn't expect a response, but Meg replied, "I would have been a wee one, and you would have met me, Elspeth, and Gavan if it were this castle you visited. You are only a few years older than me. Five years older, to be exact."

Meg had paid attention and already given thought to Isobel's story claiming that her own distant relatives had lived at Elden Castle and that was why she had returned. Of course, Meg would be correct if they were discussing the same century, but they weren't. And Isobel doubted that this was the right time to announce that she could travel through time but had somehow made a serious time jump mistake. She had to be careful.

"Yes, you are right. I was just a child. I think I imagined that the castle I visited before was Elden Castle," Isobel lied. Meg nodded, and a bit of the tension that tethered between the two loosened.

"So, do the three of you live here alone?" Isobel asked, turning to face Meg.

"Well, not completely alone," Meg answered. "Kenneth, the stable master, also lives here." Meg pointed toward a cottage not far from the barn. It was small and circular, topped with a thatched roof, and built from the same gray stone that was embedded in Elden Castle. Two small windows sat parallel on either side of a wooden arched door that Isobel felt certain Kenneth had to stoop to walk through.

"That is his home. A few others come on occasion to work with Gavan when he requests it, but as far as family, yes, it is just the three of us." Isobel still eyed Kenneth's home. The one room living quarters was probably sufficient for a single occupant. But why not allow him to stay in the castle where so many of the rooms went unused? Perhaps he had been invited into Elden Castle but preferred his privacy. Isobel nodded to herself.

"What happened to your mother and father?" she asked.

"They are both dead." Meg's eyes shifted downward to Isobel's side and said, "The crosses belong to them, although only my father's body is buried there.

Isobel frowned and followed Meg's eyes to the grave markers. She had been so wrapped up in her own grieving at dinner last night that she hadn't thought to ask Elspeth anything more after she said their parents were dead.

"I overheard Gavan and Elspeth talking about it once when I was a child. I tried to ask where our mother was buried if she wasn't with Father, but Elspeth barely let me finish asking before she said that I mustn't ever bring it up. Then she sent me out of the kitchen. Elspeth doesn't get angry often, but she had spoken so harshly that she made me afraid, and I never asked again. I've always thought maybe my mother was buried with her own family, although I don't know how they would have gotten her body there; she wasn't from the Highlands."

"I'm sorry to hear that, Meg." Isobel looked at the two unmarked wooden crosses staked in the ground. Odd that they had no inscription—no name, no dates. She wanted to touch Meg on the shoulder, offer a gesture of sympathy for her loss, but she resisted. Touching Meg's hand last night had been a mistake, one

Isobel chose not to make again so soon.

"Thank you. They've been gone for a long time," Meg continued. "We used to have a bustling household. Until my mother died, that is. And then after my father was killed, the few remaining servants that had stayed on left. Elspeth claims that they left because we couldn't afford them any longer, but I have never believed her."

"Why is that?" Isobel asked, raising an eyebrow.

"Something in the way her eyes darted around when she said it made me believe she wasn't being honest. I can read my brother and sister well, and I know when they are avoiding telling me something or when they don't speak the truth. They still treat me as though I'm a child. Honestly, I think Gavan likes having a small household. Too many people in and out of the castle makes him irritable."

Isobel nodded. She couldn't believe how much the girl was telling her without a single prompt. The invisible magical current between the two flowed steadily, so Isobel remained quiet and let Meg speak.

"My mother died after my birth," Meg continued. "But there are times when I can remember her. See her face so clearly. Elspeth used to tell me stories, her memories of our mother, and she always stated that they were what made my mother appear real to me, but I'm not sure. Sometimes, specifically when I'm alone in the garden or right before I fall asleep, I can hear my mother's voice faintly singing or speaking to me, or feel her touch, the gentleness of her hand holding mine. Those are not things my sister could capture through stories." Meg's eyes were distant and haunting as though she was lost alone in a painful memory. Quickly, her gaze returned to Isobel and she continued; a faint pinkness coloring her cheeks.

"My father died when I was seven years old. I definitely remember him; his smile, the way he smelled and carried me on his shoulders. The tone of his voice when I got into mischief." A smile tugged at the corner of her lips. Her head lowered slightly, and as she talked, a sadness filled her round blue eyes.

"I never much liked staying indoors and helping Elspeth; I preferred to be outside chasing my father, or brother, or even Kenneth around. Well, it was more like they chased after me."

Stories that served as memories of Isobel's own father filled her mind as she listened to Meg. She wanted to ask how her father had died but was fearful Meg would ask the same question in return. She didn't want to talk about the loss of her own family or the father she never knew. Or even worse, the one who had recently claimed her.

"Both Gavan and Elspeth say I'm like my mother—the way she carried herself, how she dressed, her daily habits, but mostly the way she looked. Other than the color of our eyes, we could have been twins, I have been told. Of course, I couldn't have copied the things she did because I didn't grow up with her; they just came to me naturally. Maybe it's because I am named after her and we share the same birthday. Like a destiny?" Meg looked over at Isobel with one eyebrow raised, her blue eyes telling more than her story.

Isobel also thought about her own daughter and how they, too, would share a birthday, the same as Isobel's mother. She opened her mouth to ask about the date, but Meg spoke first.

"The dress you are wearing—it belonged to her. She wore yellow on Sunday, blue or sometimes lavender on Monday, crimson on Tuesday along with—" Meg stopped in mid-sentence and suddenly stiffened.

Isobel recognized the wide-eyed look of fear on Meg's face. It was the same one she wore as she had backed out of her room last night. She prayed she wouldn't lose the girl now, not when she was opening up. Worried that she may turn and run back to the castle, Isobel quickly thought of something to say.

"Well, she must have been a very beautiful woman. And no, I did not know the dress belonged to her. If you are uncomfortable with me wearing what your sister brings to me, I understand. I can wear my own clothes," Isobel said as she looked down at the light pink gown Elspeth had laid over the chair for her this morning. Meg was wearing aqua, and Isobel, who hadn't given the days a single thought since she arrived, made a mental note that today was Friday.

"No, it's fine," Meg reassured her. "When I was much

younger, Elspeth caught me in my mother's wardrobe playing in her dresses. She shooed me away and told me not to go in there again. The sad look that filled her eyes when she saw me twirling around in my mother's gowns that were much too big scared me. I hadn't seen Elspeth cry before. I know it's been hard for her and Gavan more than myself."

Isobel smiled. "What was your mother's name?"

"Catarine Margherita Delgado was my mother's given name. After marrying my father, she took his last name, Mannering."

"My parents are both gone as well. I guess that's one of the things we have in common." Isobel kept a watchful eye on Meg as she spoke, but Meg turned away and continued her story as though Isobel hadn't spoken.

"When Elspeth and I were alone, working in the kitchen or washing or mending our clothing, or when Gavan was away, she would tell me stories about our mother and father. They were always times that were happy, with both of us laughing at the end. Elspeth said it pained Gavan too much to hear, so we were never to speak of them in front of him. So we don't."

Then, as though she had remembered something, Meg faced Isobel.

"I'm sorry to hear that your parents are gone, too. Did they leave behind anything special for you to remember them by?"

"Yes." Isobel touched the pentacle that hung from her neck.

"My mother gave this to me as a gift on my seventh year. I never take it off."

Meg stared at the symbol that shimmered under the bright light of the sun. It was what Isobel had tried to show her last night. Meg knew the five pointed star represented the elements of earth and wondered, but didn't dare ask, how Isobel used it. She wasn't supposed to be enjoying their conversation, but she was, and she became immediately frustrated with herself.

"You?" Isobel asked as her fingers toyed with the charm, hoping Meg would tell her how she got the pendulum and who had taught her to use it. But Meg remained quiet and the energy between the two heated up.

"Meg, tell me about the Highlands," Isobel said, changing the subject.

"What do you mean? You have been here before."

"Yes," Isobel agreed. She started walking across the open land and hoped that Meg would follow. Looking over her shoulder, she said, "But it's been a long time, and I'm sure things have changed over the last thirteen years."

~~~~~~~~

Isobel opened the shutters for Fara to come in. The clouds had returned this evening, along with a cold wind, and Isobel shivered. The milder temperatures over the last two days had been a welcome surprise, but this was more how November should feel.

Looking down, Isobel saw Meg's silhouetted shadow run for the woods. Her cloak hid her from the top of her head to the top of her boots, but the loose hairs that had managed to unplait and escape from under her hood as she moved gave her away. The wind gusted and snapped the window tapestry around just as the girl disappeared into the trees. Closing the shutters, Isobel rested her forehead against the wooden slats and spoke to her unborn daughter.

"I made progress with Meg today, Charlotte. We even laughed a few times as she told me stories of her family and the Highlands." Charlotte shifted inside Isobel as though she were acknowledging her mother's words.

"But the moment was brief, as Elspeth once again interrupted us, stating that she needed Meg's help indoors before supper."

Isobel rested her hands on her stomach and sighed.

Elspeth was supposed to go fetch the mid-wife this afternoon, but Gavan's leaving and not returning until well after dark had kept her at the castle. They would go tomorrow, when Gavan could escort her himself. Another day without the brooding Highlander was a welcome day for Isobel. And without Elspeth, she and Meg shouldn't have any interruptions.

"When it's just the two of us tomorrow, I can help Meg with her duties, and that will give us more time together. She opened up today, but I sense that she is fearful of me, Fara."

Fara rubbed her head against the back of Isobel's hand and then hopped to the chair back to watch.

Isobel placed the purple flowers she had picked into a wooden bowl and was reminded of Meg's mention of her mother's daily habits. Isobel was aware of such beliefs, specific colors worn on certain days to bring forth good fortune and positivity, and so on.

Her mother had also followed such rituals, going so far as to plant and tend the garden, or read, bake or cast spells on certain days, even teaching herself how to do something new.

"It's all about balance, Isobel. If one area of your life becomes too heavy, you will have instability. Your days must be equal, with your interests and duties divided so that you can give them the proper time and attention and allow you to free your mind." The remembrance of her mother's explanation was so clear it was as if she were standing beside her telling it again.

Isobel had memorized her mother's routine for each day of the week, even though she hadn't adapted to it herself.

"I never felt the need or desire to fill each day with specific elements to create a balance," she suddenly spoke out loud as she separated the flower stems to dry. Rather, what Isobel craved the most, even to this day, was her time outdoors where she and Fara were alone and free to be themselves. With Fara in the air and Isobel on the ground, they traveled at their own speeds and explored without being judged by fearful eyes. Their cravings for such freedom soon became their rituals, and for the two, a supernatural aura only they could understand emerged.

"Perhaps that is why I haven't been good at magic," she told her familiar with a smile. "I was not properly disciplined, Fara." The magpie cocked her head to the side, then moved to be closer to Isobel.

Removing the soft pink gown, Isobel pulled her nightdress over her head, the linen fabric sliding over her protruding belly and then falling to the floor. As she crawled into bed, Isobel wondered if the smock had also belonged to Catarine. As she lay on the soft mattress and under the layers of warm fur, images of her own mother played in her mind. Caressing her stomach, Isobel waited for Charlotte to respond to her touch.

"I wonder if my mother felt as alone as I sense Meg feels."

And as alone as I am now, she silently added, saddened that she too seldom had anyone to speak to. Charlotte stirred.

"Yes, you are right, my daughter." Isobel smiled at the thought of her daughter's birth that was quickly approaching. "Once you are here, I will not be alone." Closing her eyes, Isobel rested her hands across her stomach.

Tomorrow was Saturday. Meg would be wearing black, and the day would be filled with opportunities to work hard and clean. How fitting, considering that Elspeth would be gone. A smile pulled across her face as she thought of the list of chores that the older sister had recited to Meg.

"Time to clean away the negative and make room for the positive," Isobel's mother would say as she devoted her time to tidying the house and whispering spells to remove obstacles that came in their way.

Rolling to her side, Isobel's eyes quickly grew heavy; she was more tired than she had realized. Closing her lids, she wondered if there could there be a connection between her mother and Catarine? Their habits, three hundred years apart, were nearly identical, but they were customary. Also, what was it that drew the thirst of a vampire to her mother and Meg, yet not to Isobel? And what about Catarine? Had a vampire drank her blood? A form of magic ran through their veins, but what made Isobel's so different, so undesirable to the vampires? In order to discover the answers to her questions, she would need rest, and a lot of it, for she had one more place to go before returning to her time.

"A trip to the seventeenth century," she mumbled before drifting off to sleep.

That night, Isobel slept soundly and dreamed of new ways to connect with Meg. She had to gain the girl's trust before it was too late. Especially, if she was taking her to meet Mariam.

Chapter 17

"Kenneth said you were looking for me yesterday?" Gavan asked, raising an eyebrow. His voice was low and sounded a bit suspicious to Meg's ears.

"Yes, I had a question, but Elspeth helped me to resolve it," she lied.

"Are you sure? You've been quiet this morning, and our sister said you were quite helpful yesterday, which isn't exactly like you." A smile tugged at the corners of his mouth, even though his tone maintained its skepticism.

Gavan's hair was damp from his bath, and his clothing did not smell of horses, tobacco, or ale, at least not yet. He looked rested, and for the first time in days, the lines that trailed across his forehead and around his eyes had relaxed. There had been a lot to distract him lately; Isobel, the witch hunts, the two animal attacks, not to mention the clan disagreements that constantly erupted around them. Gavan took his responsibilities seriously, which, in Meg's eyes, left him little time for himself. She studied the reddish-blond stubble that shadowed his chin and upper lip before speaking; he looked at least thirty-five.

Tilting his head, Gavan sighed. "What now?" he asked with hesitation, dropping his shoulders as she smiled at him.

"You know, you are quite handsome when you aren't

glaring." It was a fact that Meg had reminded him of more than once.

"Smiling does not win on the battlefield," he responded. He leaned against the counter and folded his arms, the movement pulling the tartan sash tightly across his chest.

"There is more to life than battle, brother." Meg shook her head, knowing that was what he would say. "What about a wife? You will never catch one if you look angry all the time. And children? Well, you will frighten them so badly they won't come near you."

Gavan laughed. "Did I frighten you as a child?" he asked, knowing full well the answer was no. To their family's dismay, not much ever frightened Meg.

However, this morning an uncertainty gripped her as she sat across the table debating on whether she should speak to her brother about Isobel or remain silent. Gavan could be so reactive at times, and she didn't want to stir trouble so early in the day. Besides, if he sensed Meg had any qualms with Isobel, he would give her no choice but to accompany him and Elspeth, and Meg had no intention of wasting the next two days on her horse. She rarely objected to time spent with her aunt, especially since her own children were married off and she and Meg's uncle were often home by themselves, but today she had too much on her mind. Besides, the winds had turned last night, and riding against them as they blew from the northwest would be exhausting and frigid.

"I'm fine, I promise," she lied again. "And I thought you would be pleased that I didn't give Elspeth a hard time yesterday." Still smiling, she mocked his one raised eyebrow, but his face remained stoic.

Meg had chosen a simple black woolen dress this morning. It had a high neckline, long sleeves and an attached skirt that fell to her feet. She had draped their plaid across her shoulders, the family crest pinning it in place at her breasts. She was warm for sure, but Meg also knew Gavan would approve of her modesty; she wished for no delays on his and Elspeth's departure, not this morning. After dressing, she had pinched her cheeks fiercely, hoping to bring about a rosiness that her lack of blood from Cristian's feed last night couldn't provide on its own. She only felt slightly weak, but the last thing she needed was Gavan or Elspeth following her around as though she were ill.

"More like skeptical, Meg." He eyed her up and down before finally settling his gaze on her face. "If you are sure you are well, I am going to escort Elspeth to retrieve the mid-wife today. I expect to be gone for a day due to the weather that moved in overnight, but Kenneth is here should you need anything. I'll be back tomorrow afternoon."

"With the amount of work Elspeth has left for me to do, I shouldn't have a spare minute to need anything. I swear, I think our sister makes things up to punish me for my behavior when I was a child." Meg sighed and rolled her eyes.

"Meg—" he warned, and the once relaxed creases along his forehead deepened.

"Gavan, please go. I will behave. It is much too cold outdoors for me to do otherwise." And she shooed him towards the door before he could change his mind and demand that Kenneth prepare her horse, and her to ride with them.

With his hand on the hilt of his sword, her brother turned and walked out of the kitchen.

Meg was relieved that he didn't want to fight today either. She watched until he stepped over the threshold, closed the door behind him, and began to make his way toward the stables. It was the same door she had stumbled through a few mornings ago, startling herself, her siblings, and Isobel. Meg remembered the look on Isobel's face as she examined Meg from head to toe, as though she was searching for something. For a few moments, the scrutiny had left Meg afraid, worried that Isobel somehow knew about everything and would speak. But instead, she had stayed silent and slipped away unnoticed, leaving Meg to fend for herself.

Meg went to the window and waited while Gavan and Elspeth mounted their horses and steered them north. Gavan would escort their sister there, and one of their uncle's men would return with Elspeth and the mid-wife. Her sister had planned to be gone for three days, two of which would be travel days. This would give her time to visit with relatives and purchase supplies that weren't readily available in Dunkinshire. That was as long as the weather didn't worsen; hence, the long list of tasks Elspeth had recounted in anticipation of an extended absence.

As soon as her siblings disappeared and Kenneth slipped behind the stable doors, Meg left the kitchen window in search of Isobel. She was used to taking care of herself, so why not seek her own way of ridding the woman from their home before involving their brother? After all, she had spent most of last night devising a plan; she had to try it. If she weren't successful, she would speak to Gavan when he returned.

~~~~~~~~

Meg found Isobel sitting in the Great Hall near the fire Gavan had rekindled before anyone else was out of bed. The stack of wood stood at least three feet high and filled the bottom of the cast iron fire box. The logs crackled and popped, and long, reddish-golden flames shot up through the flue. The room was filled with warmth, the heat too much for Meg as it smothered her face as soon as she walked under the archway. Isobel, however, looked cozy and unaffected.

"The weather is so blustery, I worried they wouldn't go," Isobel said, not looking away from the needlework Elspeth had given her yesterday when she had begged to help.

"Me too."

Meg attempted to ignore the stifling heat that continued

suffocating her and watched Isobel stab a threaded needle through the linen she held tightly in her hands. One of her brother's books that usually sat stacked near the fireplace lay open beside her.

Odd, Meg thought. Gavan wouldn't have left it out like that.

Her fingers toyed with her plaid shawl, and she shifted her body, feeling awkward and unsure how to proceed. It had all seemed so simple last night as she paced in her room and practiced what she would say. But now with Isobel just across the room from her, Meg wasn't so sure.

"Why don't you sit, Meg? Elspeth gave me plenty to share." Isobel looked over her mending, pulled the open book she had been reading earlier closer to her, and made room for Meg. But when she looked up, she found Meg's pale face frowning at her. "Are you feeling alright?"

"Of course." Meg forced a smile and hoped that Isobel hadn't heard the jitteriness in her voice. "I was thinking of your suggestion that I help you. I am not good with a needle; it is the one chore that Elspeth never leaves me to do." A quiet laugh escaped from both of the women's lips. "Besides, it is quite warm in here, don't you think?" Waving a hand in front of her face, Meg fanned herself before reaching for the pin and removing the plaid from around her shoulders.

"Well, I am happy to do all the needlework then. I overheard Elspeth's list of household duties that needed to be done, so if there is anything I can help you with, please let me know. It looks like we will both be stuck inside as I have no desire to be out in the cold today."

Isobel's comment regarding the cold made Meg realize there was much she didn't know about Isobel. Was she not used to the cold winters? Did she live somewhere warmer? Or maybe she just didn't like the cold. And what about the book that now sat against her leg. Could Isobel read? They were all such simple questions, but the answers were important. Yesterday, the two had spent a brief time discussing Meg's family and life in the Highlands, but Meg didn't ask of Isobel's life. Truth be told, she hadn't planned to converse with Isobel at all; it just happened.

"Yesterday, I didn't ask about your family, Isobel, and where you live. I apologize for being so rude." Meg remained standing while she spoke, her fingers now fidgeting with the sleeves of her gown. If she didn't relax, she would soon have the hems unraveled and stretched to her palms.

"My brother's book." She pointed beside Isobel. "That's not like him to leave his belongings scattered. I can put it away if you like."

Isobel lowered her sewing to her lap, and Meg felt a surge of anxiety race through Isobel's veins.

"Oh, it is quite all right. I was the one looking through it; I hope you don't mind. I will be certain to put it away just as I found it," Isobel said.

"What do you mean? Can you read?" Meg's question was a whisper.

"Of course. Can you?" Isobel knew the answer but wanted to act as though she didn't. Last night as she lay in bed thinking of Meg in the next tower over, she thought of ways to connect with Meg. If the girl truly could not read, which Isobel didn't think she could, then perhaps she would teach her.

"Well, not really. I recognize a few words here and there, but that is about all." A rosiness colored her cheeks, and Isobel immediately felt guilty for embarrassing her.

Standing, Isobel smiled and locked an arm through one of Meg's. It was a bold move, but Isobel took a chance. Meg stiffened against her touch, a movement that didn't go unnoticed. The connection between the two was unnerving as it wavered back and forth, each trying to suppress any reaction brought on by what the other said or felt.

"The book is titled *Ninety-five Theses,* and it speaks of Reformation, primarily the start of Protestantism. Let's go to the kitchen. I know you have much to prepare before Gavan returns. We can talk while we work."

Isobel's touch and the sudden knowledge that she could read interrupted Meg's thoughts, making her feel weak and not at all in control like she planned. Their eyes locked, but she remained silent and unmoving. Yes, she wanted Isobel to speak freely and openly, it was the only way her plan would work. But what she wanted to hear about was the darkness that haunted her. She wanted Isobel vulnerable, desperate, and afraid, and to beg her for help. Instead, Isobel had taken charge, become the stronger of the two, and by the crook of her arm, tried to lead Meg around.

"Similar to you not knowing your mother, Meg, I never got the chance to know my father. My mother told me stories of him and how he served his country, but I never met him, not even as a babe. He died in battle after I was born. I grew up alone with my mother, and it was she who taught me how to read amongst so many other things." Isobel opted to refrain from mentioning that she attended school as that concept had not hit this century. "I can teach you if you would like."

Meg's skin prickled where their arms remained locked. She was afraid to move, captivated by the idea that Isobel was about to tell her story. The coolness of her touch chilled Meg's insides, and her mood, despite how hard she tried to hide it, was anything but calm.

"My mother was a healer," Isobel continued as the two stood in the center of the Great Hall. "Her talents included a combination of great knowledge and the herbs she grew. And despite the harsh temperatures we endured every winter, her garden would come back the following spring twice as fruitful as the last. She could cure most ailments by making tinctures and blessing them with specific chants she had learned throughout her life. She was a remarkable woman—gentle, kind, and patient—

and even though our lives end at some time, she did not deserve to die in the manner that she did."

"What did she look like?" Meg blurted out. She was mesmerized by Isobel's words. "I mean, you are most beautiful, Isobel. If she looked anything like you—"

Isobel smiled, and a vision of her mother formed in her mind. "I do look much like her," she answered. "We are the same height, and her eyes were more hazel than green. And like my own, her hair was long and dark and fell in unruly waves down her back."

"She sounds beautiful."

"She is." *Was.*

"My mother had a natural beauty about her, but it wasn't something you would notice if you passed her on the street. Her real gift was her ability to help others. She had a genuine kindness that never seemed to waver, no matter the situation. She was gentle and caring and took to anyone who sought out her care."

"Are you a healer too?"

Isobel shook her head. "I am quite in tune to others' feelings, but no, I am not a healer; my abilities are limited. It's not because my mother didn't try though. For years, she worked with me, but I never spoke the words correctly. For when I tried, nothing would happen. I didn't inherit her gift. She told me we would work together until I learned the spells, that magic was our destiny together as mother and daughter."

Isobel looked at Meg. "This gave me hope, but if I were to be honest, I would tell you that I knew the life my mother taught me was not mine to live. Inside, I possessed an otherworldly power, but it wasn't the same magic that stirred within my mother. I was aware of it; I just didn't understand it. It's still not completely clear, I am afraid."

Meg was entranced.

"Of course, I had no ill feelings towards her constant teachings. Rather, I prayed, even begged, night after night that when I woke the next morning, I would be able to do as my mother instructed. I would tell myself to just repeat the words and think them to be true and they would be. But it never happened. Despite my pathetic requests, I would fail. I may not have known who I was, but I knew who I wasn't."

Isobel hoped that would be enough to satisfy Meg's curiosity for the moment. She would need to trust Meg before she gave the full explanation of all her gifts; her unrelenting mental and physical strength and, of course, her ability to travel through time, the single magical gift she had been granted. Unfortunately, Isobel didn't have that much time, so she would need to build their relationship quickly.

"Do you ever wish you could be someone else?" Meg suddenly asked as her eyes shifted away from Isobel's.

A thick silence weighed on both women's shoulders as they waited for Isobel's response. Her answer wasn't an easy one to admit, but it was an honest one. Isobel only knew about half of herself. Half her past and her own story. The magic half that stemmed from her mother. Her entire life, she had denied asking more questions about her father, afraid that perhaps she favored him rather than her mother, and maybe that was the reason she couldn't do magic.

"I do." Isobel released Meg's arm and walked out of the Great Hall.

"Now let's move to the kitchen and get the breads going," Isobel suggested without turning back or waiting for Meg to follow. She needed a minute. The charm around her neck burned her skin, and Isobel was uncertain as to why. A few deep breaths and a little space between the two women who knew more than they trusted to tell one another should help.

Busying themselves in preparation for the meals of the day, Isobel told Meg stories of her childhood and how it had been when she and her mother lived in a place not as far north as Scotland, but sometimes as cold and blustery as the Highlands.

"It sounds like you and your mother shared a close relationship," Meg said, and she was anxious to hear more.

"Yes, we did. And I don't believe it was because it was just the two of us until I met my husband. The same bond has already been forged between my daughter and me. I can feel it."

Fara, who had flown inside one of the many times Meg opened the door for a cool breeze to cool her face from the heat of the ovens and open flame. She perched with her claws wrapped around the top spindle of a chair and eyed the women's movements back and forth across the kitchen. Isobel sensed a calmness from the magpie, and the feeling helped her to calm her own nerves.

A comfortable cadence filled the room, and as each woman became lost in her own thoughts, their actions became methodical; chop, knead, mix, wash. They cooked and cleaned as Elspeth had instructed and made more progress than if Meg had done it on her own. They were dusted in flour and the fine hairs that framed their faces sprang from their braids and coiled in damp ringlets from the heat. Isobel was surprised at how well Meg knew her way around the kitchen, considering all the complaining she had voiced during her stay so far.

Puffing her feathers, Fara tucked her smooth black beak beneath her wing, and under the thick aromas of yeast and meats, she drifted off to sleep. It was then that Isobel decided to give Meg more of the information she had been probing for. Perhaps if she answered a few more of the girl's questions, she may get a few more of her own answered.

"The Highlands was the first place I had thought to hide," Isobel said as she laid the blade on the wooden countertop and looked at Meg. "But wait; let me start from the beginning."

Chapter 18

Wide-eyed and her jaw hanging open, Meg leaned forward and listened to Isobel recite the story that had forced her to run for her life—the murders of her mother and husband as she stood outside their kitchen window.

"They both lay so impossibly still that I knew they were gone." A twinge of guilt struck Isobel as she recalled the scene that morning, almost one week ago. In that moment, as she peered through the narrow, clear pane of glass, she had been relieved that the wall stood between herself and her family's blood thirsty killers, but now pangs of guilt stabbed at her without mercy. She hadn't even tried to help them. Instead, she left her family in the hands of their killers. Isobel lowered herself onto a stool, closed her eyes, and took in a deep breath. Her fingers and lips tingled as a whiteness clouded her vision. She was going to lose consciousness.

Breathe.

Isobel's eyes flew open at the sound of his voice, and she gripped the edge of the table so tightly that the thick wooden slab she clung to cracked. She jumped up, and her stool toppled over, making a loud clattering sound behind her. She scanned the room as quickly as her heart pounded in her chest, but he wasn't there. It was only her, Fara, and Meg. The command that had replayed in her head was just a memory.

"Isobel, are you alright?" A genuine concern sounded in Meg's voice, and her eyes softened.

Isobel nodded. She was safe. She took in a couple of deep breaths and slowly let them out before continuing.

"Fara and I left the house early that morning." Isobel's voice quivered at first, but as she replayed the events of her last morning at home, she sounded stronger, more certain. The stinging sensation had left her hands, and her legs felt solid. "It is our routine to go on a run. Well, I run, she flies," Isobel corrected. "The open space away from family and the village gives me a chance to clear my head, and Fara the opportunity to stretch her wings. We were barely gone an hour when I heard my mother scream." Meg's eyes never veered from Isobel's as she listened to the deadly incident that drove Isobel to the Highlands.

"They were both so pale and lifeless. One of the men knelt next to my mother, while the other leaned into the doorway, a huge, awful looking smile spreading across his face It was a brutal attack. One that my mother could have prevented, I believe, if she had used the knowledge my ancestor Mariam had taught her. They were both aware of her vulnerability."

Vampires, Meg thought as the words *pale* and *lifeless,* and *vulnerable* turned in her mind. Vampires had been after Isobel's mother and had killed her but left Isobel alive. This wasn't the darkness Meg had seen through the pendulum, but perhaps it was a start. Her brows pulled together. "Is that why you came here looking for Mariam?"

Isobel nodded again. "I thought it would help me to understand, but I also needed a place of refuge. If I had stayed much longer, I too would have been killed. I couldn't risk that for my daughter."

You are safe with me, Isobel. The vampire's words sounded in her head, again.

Closing her eyes, Isobel gritted her teeth. She hadn't invited him inside to haunt her, so with all her mental strength, she forced his words away from her mind. Dropping her hands to her swollen belly, she sought comfort from her daughter. Charlotte moved against her mother's touch immediately, and Isobel's rigid posture lessened.

"Do you think the man meant to kill your family?" Meg asked.

"Yes. As a matter of fact, he bragged about it as he chased me, promising to do the same to me once he caught me."

"Your mother sounds so kind; why would anyone want to harm her?"

He wasn't just anyone, Isobel thought.

"There are many different people in the world, Meg, some not as you would believe them to be. Not humans, or witches, but others who are far more dangerous. In plain sight, they can fool you. Yes, sometimes they may seem out of place, but in truth, their existence is more powerful than all of the rest of us together and deadly to all who cross their paths."

Isobel watched for a reaction. She knew she wasn't wrong about what she had detected in the woods her first night at Elden Castle. She had smelled his coldness, seen Meg run into the woods where Isobel sensed he hid. She hadn't made any of that up. Meg knew of the danger she was talking about, but the blank look that splayed across her face as her chin now rested in the palm of her hand gave nothing away. Getting the young witch to admit what she was involved in might be more difficult than Isobel imagined.

"I believe the magic that lived in my mother's veins was transferable. Meaning that if an individual drank her blood, some of her power would be temporarily granted to them."

"Why would you think this?" Meg asked slowly as her pulse elevated in her ears.

"In addition to my mother warning me that it could happen, there were several things I sensed that weren't normal about the man who killed my mother—his warm flushed skin, wild black eyes, and the rush of power and strength that I witnessed him executing as he came after me. My mother told me stories and said that people could appear to have my best interest at heart, but it could be trickery. When I was a child, I didn't fully understand, but the eerie look in her eyes, the way she clung to my hands and held me close, told me that I needed to listen to her. And to believe. As I got older, I became afraid, and then my fear turned to curiosity. I had never met such a person who wanted to harm me, but again, I knew my mother wouldn't tell me something that was untrue." Meg nodded her head.

"We live in a world of mysteries. Women like us—you and me—we trust our intuitions even if we don't fully understand; it is 'our way'. However, most men and villagers, like Gavan and those who lead the witch hunts, need to have a clear explanation as to why things happen." Meg shifted her weight and, without taking her eyes off Isobel, up-righted the stool that lay behind her and sat.

"But there was one mystery my mother hid from; one I think she hoped would change." Isobel's mind awkwardly worked to put the pieces of her life together. So much was still missing. "I am different, Meg. My abilities are not completely normal for a witch, nor for a human."

"I bet you were terrified they would kill you," Meg said, now pulling at the hem of her sleeves. *What is it that kept you alive?* Meg wanted to ask out loud, sensing that the answer just might be the one to explain everything.

"Yes, at first. But then something happened, and for a moment I forgot about dying." Isobel walked around the counter, stopping beside Meg.

Bewildered, Meg asked, "What could be more terrifying than a couple of vampires hunting you down and threatening to kill you like they did your mother?"

Isobel froze. She hadn't called the men vampires. "One of

them claimed to be my father," she said calmly, and wondered if Meg realized what she had said.

Meg's body wavered, and she gripped the table's edge to keep herself from falling just as Isobel had. "How is that possible?" There was something cold and dark that lingered beneath Isobel's skin, and Meg had yet to put her finger on exactly what it was, but Isobel wasn't a vampire.

Isobel finished her story. "I believe Dario initially attacked for a different reason. But once my mother's blood awoke his senses, he couldn't have stopped himself. Her body wasn't mutilated like my husband's. Thomas must have put up a fight or done something to anger Dario for it to turn so violent. For whatever the reason, I'm certain death for both was eminent once they were discovered. Maybe even before that. Something tells me that there is more to their intrusion and to the warnings my mother issued throughout my life. Having abilities that are beyond what is considered normal doesn't always give you the upper hand, Meg. Rather, it can leave you exposed. You mustn't ever forget that."

~~~~~~~~~

Meg lay on her bed that night and waited for darkness to fall. The day had not gone at all as she had planned, and she blamed herself. She had been so afraid of Isobel, of what she could do to the family, but the more she spoke, the more Meg found herself drawn toward her. Isobel had been right. The two had a connection.

She replayed Isobel's story in her head. A sadness she had never experienced consumed her, and suddenly she found herself mourning the loss of the mother she wasn't given the opportunity to know. Her loud sobs came in gulps and shook her body over and over again. Rolling to her side, she pulled a heavy fur over her head and let herself go. She had never felt more alone.

Meg had been told that she was three days old when her mother died of complications from childbirth: a common event. But as she had explained to Isobel, and to Elspeth countless numbers of times, she remembered what it felt like to be cradled in her mother's arms. She could also recall the sound of her mother's voice and the gentleness of her touch.

"I know it is hard to grow up without a mother; we all miss her," Elspeth said. "But you mustn't tell such stories, Meg, especially around Gavan. It upsets him greatly. Now we've discussed this enough. No more." And then Elspeth had dismissed her to run along.

On her seventh birthday, Elspeth pulled Meg aside and handed her a small bundle wrapped in a soft cloth and tied with a ribbon.

"Mother wanted you to have this. She made me swear I would keep it safe until today."

Carefully, Meg untied the ribbon and opened the cloth.

What lay in the very center was a ring. The ring that Meg now carried almost everywhere with her.

"What is it?" she asked her older sister as she held the silver circle up and turned it in the light.

"It's a keepsake, Meg," Elspeth explained. "She said that it was given to her, and she wanted you to have it."

Elspeth then pulled the chain forward from her neck. On it hung their mother's wedding ring. Until the moment her sister lifted the chain over her head, Meg had thought her mother had overlooked her. Especially since she had been a wee infant when she died. But as the ring lay warm against her chest, Meg realized she had never been forgotten.

Had her mother known what the ring could do? Is that why she left it to Meg? And if so, what was it that had alerted her to Meg's specialness? Meg had prodded at Elspeth for years for more information, but her older sister claimed she had no knowledge of anything beyond their mother's request.

Lifting the ring to her lips, Meg pushed into hiding the memories of a mother they both said she couldn't possibly remember. Rolling to her side, the corner of the book she and Isobel had looked at after they cooked and cleaned poked at her side.

Isobel had been calm and patient as she worked with and taught her how to sound out the letters that formed words. All afternoon until dinner, Meg had practiced reading. Isobel never gave up on her, even when she made mistakes, and it was because of her small successes that Meg realized she couldn't bring Isobel any harm. They had a connection, deeper than what Meg wanted to acknowledge and was still yet to understand. She was still afraid they could be exposed, but she would not be the cause for a child, if it were to survive the brutal attack of a vampire, to live without a mother. That was something she would never wish on anyone. She would find another way to escape the hold Cristian had on her, even if it meant killing him.

Meg unfastened the plaits Elspeth had wrapped around her head that morning and shook out the curls. It was Cristian's preference for her hair to be loose. The thought of his cold, stony fingers raking through her hair sent a shiver down her spine. Just this morning, she had planned to send Isobel running straight into the woods, yet here she was going again instead.

Tucking the heirloom charm away, she grabbed her shoes from the floor and left her room. Time had gotten away from her, and she realized she would be late. However, with both her siblings gone and Isobel tucked away in the north tower, it would be easy to slip away without fear of being missed.

Pulling the outer door of the east tower closed, Meg slipped on her shoes and cloak, grabbed at her skirt with both fists, and raced through the heather-filled glen. The stems whipped at her ankles as the northwesterly wind blew, and she winced against the stinging pain as they slapped at her bare skin. Tomorrow her legs would be streaked with thin red lashings. She would need to wear her boots and keep herself covered from Gavan's sight.

Dropping her skirt, she slowed her pace and climbed the last grassy knoll. Her eyes followed the length of the bell tower that remained upright amidst the crumbled, scattered ruins until she found his silhouette perched in the opening—arms folded and watching for her arrival. A rush of cold air blew through her hair and encircled her so tightly that it nearly squeezed the breath from her lungs before exploding and releasing her.

Meg waited in the shadows for a moment before advancing; she needed to catch her breath. However, in a few minutes, the demand for air would cease to exist. She would then run as fast as she could, push boulders off cliffs, and pull up trees with her bare hands. She could drive herself well beyond all physical human limitations because, however short-lived it would be, her humanity would lie hidden. The strength Cristian's venom gave Meg still scared her, but tonight she welcomed it. She had realized today that there was no use fighting against it; she belonged to him. For now.

Meg sighed and took a step into the moonlight. And then, as if a pack of wild dogs had attacked, Cristian's body enveloped her, and they fell to the ground.

Chapter 19

Diarmad Abbey was a sacred place for Meg. She had stumbled upon the run-down monastery when she was ten years old after slipping away from the castle unnoticed late one morning. If Gavan had ever found out about the countless days she had spent climbing through the rubble, chasing butterflies, and picking wildflowers, all in her best gowns that Elspeth had made for her, he would have locked her in the dungeon forever. Over time, however, as she aged from a child to a young woman, the abbey had become more of a refuge—her private space. She embraced the ability to do absolutely nothing but daydream if she so desired, which she often did. But there were other times she had to be alone, such as dark nights like tonight.

Cristian's venom that raced in her bloodstream made it difficult for her to stay still. With quick, light steps, she paced around the outer edges of the building that had once been hallowed ground and thought about his listless body she had stepped over before leaving him to relish in his magical stupor. He had been mumbling, his words slurred and impossible to make out. As she had walked past him, the hem of her gown had brushed against his leg, and he reached out, one large hand swiping into the cold dark air. She had looked down and wondered what he was grabbing at, and then decided not to care. She turned and was gone, making good on her promise to destroy whatever grew in her way. When she was finished, she found herself outside of Diarmad Abbey, her heart racing and all her frustration gone.

As she moved past one of the barred windows, a flickering of light from inside caught her attention. She stopped and watched as the glow brightened and filled in the surrounding cracks. *Odd,* Meg thought. The abbey had been deserted for years. It was why she liked it. No one to tell her what to do or choose to answer her questions with lies. It was quiet and desolate and perfect.

Placing her hands on the large, jagged rock that made up one of the outer walls, she peered through one of the holes and gasped. Pushing away, the stone under the weight of her hands shifted, and a stream of pebbles tumbled to the ground, stirring a cloud of dust over the tops of her shoes. The twinkling of light on the other side of the wall came from dozens of lit candles around the perimeter of the tiny abandoned sanctuary and atop a makeshift altar. Meg's heart thundered in her chest, and she feared the sound would give her away. Leaning forward, again, she stared at the small circle of women on the other side of the wall, their thin white smocks spinning around their bare ankles as they danced.

Proper young women would not be staring into such danger. Her thoughts were wrong earlier; if Gavan or Elspeth found her here, she would be banished to Elden Castle's underground rooms and never seen again. Her anxiety rose as she stood, unable to look away. The five women moved and twirled with steps so graceful that they appeared to be hovering just above the floor. They were humming, and Meg strained to hear as their voices were nearly inaudible. Without Cristian's venom, she imagined she wouldn't have heard the unfamiliar tune at all. The glow of the candlelight, the women's constant spinning, and the low drum of their unified voice held her entranced and lured her into another space. Fear spiked around her throat as an unseen force spread through her limbs like a flame and held her motionless. Could they see her through the cracks? Heard the movement when the wall shifted? Or maybe her beating heart had given her away.

Meg opened her mouth to cry out in protest and break the spell she had been pulled under when an enchanted wind gently blew past, filling her nostrils with a recognizable spice. A cool breath brushed against her neck and sent her blood soaring.

"You should not be out here alone in the dead of night." Cristian's voice rumbled like that of a storm building in the distance.

His feral scent of heavy cinnamon and ice left her weak. His venom suddenly no longer existed in her bloodstream. Meg turned into his warning but found she was alone. Righting herself, she propelled her body away from Diarmad Abbey, the unholy ritual taking place inside, and Cristian's warning, and ran all the way home, her human legs carrying her faster than she ever knew they could.

How long had he been there watching her? Waiting to make his move when he thought she would least expect it. She never expected it. Cristian never came for her twice in one night. How had he recovered so quickly? Could the magic in her blood be weakening? And how had he found her? Diarmad Abbey was miles away from where she had left him.

Frantic, Meg reached into her pocket, grasped the ring that lay at the bottom, and willed herself to move even faster. With every step toward Elden Castle, she braced herself for Cristian's attack, but it never came. She listened for any sound that would acknowledge he was with her, chasing behind her and ready to pounce, but all that sounded in her ears were the beating wings and cries of the magpie overhead that was suddenly leading her home.

~~~~~~~~~

Cristian stared at Meg's silhouette until she was out of sight, and then he snapped and became guided by instinct, rage coloring his sight red. The ungodly being the women summoned was alive; however, it now took shape inside Cristian's body instead of hovering above the altar. A deific impulse surged through him and a growl, savage and predatory, rumbled across the room. The light from the candles was snuffed out, and the magic of the night was over in a single breath. Screams echoed off the stone walls as sounds of tearing flesh and cracking bones filled the sanctuary; true darkness had been invoked. Cristian's destruction of the women's evocation lasted only seconds before all fell silent and the heavy scent of iron rich blood, sweat, and fear permeated the air.

He looked around; he was shameless. His job was to protect Meg, to keep her safe, and that was exactly what he had done. His temper hadn't gotten away from him; no, it was his possessiveness.

Meg belonged to him.

He moved up the crumbled stairwell of the bell tower. With his bloodlust more than satiated, he was sluggish and thought to stay at the abbey for a while. Meg would be home now, safe within the confines of Elden Castle, but from the tower he could see a great distance and keep an eye on the neighboring villages, just in case. A witch burning was taking place tomorrow. Cristian had heard the magistrate bellowing this morning that the girl had cursed his wife, who had now turned against him, refusing to so much as speak or sleep under the same roof. However, Cristian knew the truth. The magistrate had advanced on the girl, but she had denied him. He beat her into submission but not into silence. His wife had believed the girl. Humans could often be just as dangerous as the monsters that they feared lived in the dark. This was why he had to be certain Meg stayed far away.

The early morning rays of sun finally lit the edge of the horizon, and as Cristian moved into the darkness of the shadows for safety, he inhaled the scent: honeysuckle. A single thud clamored in his chest.

What was she doing back here! Hadn't he frightened her enough last night? Cristian wanted to jump down, grab her by the arms and ask those exact questions, but instead, he froze.

Breaking the silence, a gasp sounded in his ears. Cristian lowered his head just as Meg appeared at the entrance of the abbey. Stepping backwards, she moved slowly until her feet hit the solid, hard earth. She grabbed fists full of her skirt, the one she had been wearing last night, turned, and ran toward the bottom of the grassy knoll. As she reached the edge of the open field, she skidded to a stop and looked over her shoulder. Her blood pulsated through her veins frantically, and Cristian smelled the cold sweat that slickened her palms and trailed down the center of her back. His desire resurfaced.

Lifting his head, he inhaled deeply, and pain stabbed through him, taking his breath and hunger for her away. The force was so excruciating that his body begged to double over and give in. Thankfully, the slab of stone behind him held him upright. Meg's stare had followed the bell tower until it reached the shadows of the highest peak.

Their gazes—hers wet and bright, his dark and haunted—locked, and an awakening tingled in Cristian's fingertips, climbing upwards and numbing his arms, before finally crushing his chest. His vision clouded with tiny flickers of white that for a moment extinguished his sight. He leaned heavily against the stone tower that encircled the bell, unable to pull himself away and go after her. Feelings of humanity, ones he thought had died years ago, thwarted in his chest.

Meg had returned. Had she thought to betray him? The idea that she could so easily share herself with anyone else crushed his heart and left a hole in his empty, lifeless soul. And then he remembered.

The corner of his lips twitched as they pulled sideways and formed a disfigured and evil smile. His fangs lengthened and dropped over his bottom lip, a single drop of venom falling to the stone at his feet. Oh, how disappointed she must have been to see what he had done!

Chapter 20

From the shadows of the bell tower, Cristian's eyes narrowed through the clusters of tall Scots pines and on the deadly platform that had been erected at the base of the mountains. The air entombed within the circular barrier of towering trees hung thick and with oppression. Brisk northern winds howled against the outer, rough protective bark, but the sound and the chill in the air were lost to the focus of the task at hand. It didn't take the vampire long to locate the oversized Highlander and worm his way into the man's thoughts. Cristian loathed listening to humans but would always make the sacrifice when it came to Meg.

Gavan stood amidst the crowd, oblivious to the whispers that circled around him, his thoughts lost to Elden Castle and the dangerous guest who had appeared on their doorstep less than a week ago. He had sensed a warning the moment he saw her outside his front door, the pentacle around her neck shimmering with defiance as she stood drenched from the rain. But it was the spark that stung through his calloused fingers as he wrapped them around her upper arm after catching her snooping that had confirmed it. She was one of them. A witch.

He had allowed her inside, even agreed that she could stay; what had he been thinking? He had been frightened the entire time he had been away, worried that when he returned it would be

Meg's persecution he would be viewing. Exposing Isobel would be a death sentence for them all, but he could escort her from their home and make sure she was never seen again. His sisters would never forgive him if they found out he had harmed her in any way, so feeling trapped, Gavan decided to remain silent.

"For now," Cristian heard the warrior mutter as he listened to the afflicted man's rants from the abbey.

Agitation spread through the vampire, and he paced in circles around the tower. Had Gavan housed one of his whores in the castle? One he feared could draw attention to Meg and possibly bring death to them all?

"What was he thinking!" Cristian shouted. This was exactly why he kept Meg close. "He better make good on his plan of disposing this woman on his own, and quickly!"

Animal instinct raged inside and cut off his thoughts. It took everything Cristian had to still himself and return his attention to the warrior.

Letting go of his blade, the Highlander widened his stance and ran his hands through his hair, his mind unable to rest. Hurried movements surrounded the platform, and Gavan forced himself to focus on the preparations before him. In the northernmost Highlands, he had sought the company of females akin to the girl who remained in her underground cell, awaiting her death. All were flesh and blood women, looking for comfort and who, like so many others, felt the strain of living in such a cruel and unbending world.

The most daring took a stand; they had a passion, a claim to a higher power, and a desire to be heard. Gavan wasn't so sure he believed in any of their declarations, but he wasn't so sure he didn't. He had been young at the untimely death of his mother, but he had been aware of her oddity as far back as his memories took him: the regimented patterns of her daily life, the continual growth of her garden even during the harshest of winters, and her ability to bring unexplained aid when she saw fit.

"The devil's work," the disbelievers had preached. The phrase was often alive in Gavan's mind as he sensed a similar strangeness in Meg.

Meg. The hanging this afternoon had delayed his return home, something he hadn't expected. He hoped his sister had behaved herself as she had been told.

"What an annoying, complicated man," Cristian mumbled, already bored with Gavan's internal monologue regarding women. "But not to worry; your sister is safe. I have made most certain of that."

A group of magpies swooped down through the clouds, and a single caw pulled Cristian's attention from the viewing. Cocking its head to the side, one of the birds tried to lock its black beady eyes with the vampire's. Cristian's gaze shifted to the ground to avoid being trapped in its trance, and from the corner of his eye, he watched as the bird ascended between the mountain ridges toward a thick canopy of leaves above the hanging.

Gavan's eyes sat fixated on the victim. *Guilty or innocent*, he wondered; who really knew?

"Or cares," Cristian interjected again as he shook off the annoyance the bird had jilted him with and surveyed the glen below.

Curled near a guard's feet lay a girl. Her eyes were closed, and her right cheek lay pressed into the hard, cracked earth where she had been dropped after being brought up from her cell. Her body gave the illusion that she was dead, but her faint heartbeat and earthy human scent told Cristian otherwise. He tuned in to her labored breaths—they paused, then resumed, only to pause again. He folded his arms, leaned into the stone wall, and stared as the spectacle unfolded with feigned interest.

The victim's frailty was an effect of purposeful malnourishment and beatings believed to release her from the demons. She had confessed, lied rather, under the torturous pain, but her admission of cursing the magistrate's wife against her husband had left her in a no-win situation.

Her torn smock was caked with dirt and clung to patches of dried blood along her back, and the loose sleeves exposed her bruised, bony wrists bound behind her. Lacerations lined her calves, and the torn red flesh both crusted over and oozed with septicity. One of the witnesses shook his head in disgust and kicked her. From their individual vantage points, Gavan and

Cristian stood unmoving and watched.

Beatrix McDonald had been kept in a hole dug deep into the earth while the court listened to her petitioner. The unanimous guilty verdict had filtered throughout the town at record speed. Cristian had lost count of the days they had waited, but Gavan bet the girl hadn't. He felt sorry for her, but she wasn't a girl he needed to protect; she wasn't his sister.

Dropping his arms to his side, Cristian wondered if he should have put the girl out of her misery days ago, honored her with a quick death. But he had learned that sometimes you have to let things run their course, and this was one of those times. Protecting Meg came before all else, and while everyone's attention was on the accused before them, Meg was safe.

The crowd of purists had gathered closer, filling the open space between Gavan and the platform. Towering over the women, children, and many of the men who had come to witness, his view was unblemished. A fevered chant buzzed from their lips as their gloved hands grasped the edges of their cloaks and held them closed beneath their raised chins. "Burn the witch, burn the witch!"

Gavan's unwavering focus remained on the girl. Cristian's remained on Gavan.

A large hand from one of the guards reached down and jerked the girl upright. Her hair, the color of black ink, hung knotted around her face and down the length of her torso. Murmurs from the villagers filtered around the Highlander. "Never trust someone with hair the color of midnight—a sure sign of a witch."

The corners of her mouth were turned down, as were her eyes. The heavy lids that were barely open showed lines of sadness. The rope that bound her wrists was tightened, but she showed no resistance as her captors dragged her between the parted crowd and towards the scaffolding. Gavan wondered if she had made peace with dying. Again, Cristian didn't care.

The onlookers' chant grew louder as her waif-like body was lifted onto the wooden stool. *Humans were so predictable; meek, mere followers of the assertive.* Cristian braced himself as
their internal monologues flooded his ears all at once, their voices dizzying his thoughts.

Skepticism ran through the nay-sayers' minds; there was no way any of the accusations were true. But just as passionate were the rationalists who believed the young girl was delusional and ill. The romantics alleged the witchery to be quite real but a bit distorted, and at last, there was the opinion of those who blamed the stress of modern society for the weak girl's actions.

The villagers were simple people, unable to stand alone for what they believed in for fear of persecution. They looked at one another for assurance, obediently nodding their heads in unison, justifying what needed to be done. And for that, they knew their life would be spared another day.

"Did they not understand that one had to believe in

witchcraft for there to be a witch hunt?" Cristian mumbled, shaking his head. He loathed their conflicted views and wanted to release them all from their miserable human lives. How was it that he preferred their company over those like himself? It made no sense. Restless, he paced along the narrow ledge around the bell, talking himself out of annihilating the entire village.

The actions that followed in the distance had been done so many times that the hangmen's movements were swift and mechanical. It was rumored that a few of the officials had one arm a bit longer and more muscular than the other. It came from flogging the innocent into confession. With the men's cloaks covering them, you couldn't tell, but the villagers all believed it to be true.

Gavan had stood witness a few times to the brutal torture of the accused; lashing of a whip over and over again, flaying the suspect into submission or the loss of consciousness—whichever came first. He had been in many battles and brutally taken the lives of many men but watching such cruelty against a woman always made his stomach turn.

Looking through lowered lashes, Beatrix suddenly lifted her chin, pulled her shoulders straight and stood tall. She stared ahead with a dead calm, and the gathering before her drew in a breath and waited.

Moving in front was a man of average height with a high forehead, heavy jowls, and a wobbly chin. His hands, which were exposed in the bitter cold, were delicate in nature; small, with narrow fingers and cropped nails at the tips. One of his gentle hands gripped the top of a wooden stick, and his body shifted forward. His fair skin was smooth and undamaged, giving the impression that he hadn't labored outdoors a day in his life. He branded the look of a gentleman and not the type who could orchestrate such an event, but it was clear to anyone who looked on that he was the one in control.

"Beatrix Dunbar," the magistrate began, "you have been tried by the esteemed court of Dunkinshire and, on this 23rd day of November 1597, been found guilty of witchcraft, a crime punishable by death." A collective nodding of heads rippled across the crowd followed by shouting.

Beatrix's dark eyes, now high and proud, met the magistrate's grayish blue ones. His gaze drifted downwards and stopped at her mouth. Her lips moved endlessly, and anger reddened his face.

"Do you have something you wish to say? Another confession?" he asked, a smile teetering on his lips as the crack of a whip exploded beside her. A hearty blend of fear and dismay thrummed through the crowd as they leaned forward and strained to hear.

Then a whisper of words rang out. Beatrix's voice was hushed but firm with conviction. However, what the villagers heard was far from another confession.

"Our Father who art in heaven—" It was the Lord's prayer that emitted from the young girl's lips, not a curse. A gasp swept across the crowd.

Releasing the cane, the magistrate waved a shaky hand for the hangmen to hurry, and a white cotton sack was placed over her head.

They could do this in their sleep. Gavan and Cristian's thoughts became one.

"Thy kingdom come, thy will be done, as earth as it is in heaven." Her voiced remained strong, although muffled through the sack.

Bright, empty eyes darted from one end of the crowd to the other as an unanticipated flutter of doubt passed through them all. Their silent thoughts rang loud in Cristian's head; witches couldn't recite *The Lord's Prayer*. Beatrix Dunbar was innocent.

A smile now tugged at the corner of Cristian's mouth. "It's a little too late, you fools," he said under his breath.

His eyes shifted back to the girl, and he watched the rise of her chest as she filled her lungs with what she believed to be her last breath. Cristian leaned his head back and drew in a breath with her. Her heart stalled just as Cristian's gave a single, loud thump.

The hangman's noose, its one end anchored to the stake, was lowered and pulled tight beneath Beatrix's jaw. Her raven head cocked to the right, her body now waiting in the balance between life and death. The crowd drew in another unitary gasp and fell silent.

This could be Meg.

Through pursed lips, the magistrate's visible breath came out in rapid puffs, and he gave the nod to proceed. In one smooth motion, the stool her toes had rested upon was kicked out from under her. Its legs skidded across the platform and broke the frightened silence as her neck snapped.

This will never be Meg.

Her body hung motionless as her head sagged at an impossible angle inside the bag; she was dead. Cheering erupted.

He would make certain.

A fire was set beneath her lifeless body, and the onlookers went silent. They gripped the fur lining around the edges of their hoods and covered their mouth and nose against the stench of burning flesh. Then, moving as one, their free hands made the Sign of the Cross, and they mumbled from beneath their cloaks, "The fires of damnation." They dropped their heads and prayed.

From the bell tower, Cristian followed the acrid smoke as it swirled upwards along the length of the trees and disappeared into the dimly lit sky. Whenever there was a hanging that was too close for his liking, he commanded Meg to meet him. But after last night, Cristian chose to leave Meg at Elden Castle, thinking that might be safer this time.

He thought of the woman her brother was harboring in the castle. If the villagers discovered their family secret, the three would be subjected to grueling and unrelentless torture. Meg and her sister would be raped and beaten repeatedly, impaled, and even disfigured, especially given Gavan's position. The warrior would be viewed as a traitor and quite possibly the leader of the threesome. The pain that would be inflicted would be slow and unmerciful before the final word to light the pyre and put them all to death would be given.

Of course, Cristian would never allow any of that to happen. He had no real concerns for the Highlander, but he wouldn't allow another man to come near Meg, cause her pain or distress, or even worse, to violate her. The mere thought stirred a recognizable force within him and ignited a seething desire to kill, again. The corners of his lips twitched, and as an agitated growl thundered within his chest, his fangs emerged.

"I would slaughter the entire village for her protection," Cristian vowed through clenched teeth.

He would do that for Meg.

He loved her.

Chapter 21

"I'm going to take you to market today," Meg announced, closing the book she had been reading through while waiting for Isobel to wake and come downstairs. "Elspeth needs me to purchase some items, and it's no fun going with Kenneth." Meg's voice and the sparkle that filled her eyes made her look like a child.

Isobel raised an eyebrow and glanced at the copy of *The Faerie Queene* that lay on the table.

"Oh, don't worry," Meg said. "Gavan isn't here. He left early this morning and likely won't be back until supper."

"That's a rather large book for someone who is just beginning to read," Isobel said, clasping her hands together, her index fingers pointing at the bound manuscript.

"Oh, I know, but it gives me plenty of words to practice." The child-like smile returned to Meg's face. "You will come with me today, yes?" she begged, changing the subject as she grasped Isobel's hands. The air between the two sizzled with mystic energy, and their finger tingled in response.

"Please don't make me go alone. Farmers and craftsmen from the nearby villages come and sell their wares. They bring wool and pottery items, animal hides and jewelry and a variety of foods. There are musicians and dancers that often perform in the street and animals that do tricks. You will enjoy it. Besides, it is Thursday," Meg explained as she pulled her hands from Isobel's.

"Thursday?" Isobel asked in an uncertain tone.

"Thursday is the day that one's spiritual pursuits and good fortune are attributed. I thought you were familiar with this," Meg said, biting her lower lip.

"I did not pay attention to all that my mother did. Sometimes I was away tending to my own spiritual pursuits." Isobel smiled. "I would love to go though; I just need to retrieve my cloak."

"Oh thank you! This is the last one before the harsh winter weather settles in. But wait, I have something for you!" Meg called from behind. Isobel turned and tilted her head to the side.

"It's a gown, a purple one. 'Tis the color for our adventure." Meg beamed as she held it out, twirled once, and waited for Isobel to answer. Its violet shade was much darker than Meg's, and the fabric looked new. It had a high neckline, long sleeves, and looked as though it would keep her warm. Isobel wondered if it had belonged to Meg's mother.

"If it pleases you, I will change. I am surprised"—Isobel placed one hand on the banister and looked over her shoulder at Meg—"that Gavan is letting us go after the persecution last night. I would think he would be most afraid to let you leave the castle." The smile disappeared from Meg's face as her mouth fell open.

"How did you know?" she whispered. Meg had learned of

the event after eavesdropping on Kenneth in the stables. But Isobel hadn't stepped outside the castle the last two days.

"The scent filled the air, Meg." It was all Isobel said before turning and heading up the stairs to change her gown.

~~~~~~~~

Riding side by side, with Kenneth a few feet behind them, Meg and Isobel led the way to market. The gaits of their mares were in sync—even and focused—and Meg and Isobel's bodies rose and dipped in unison.

"I am so happy to have you here, Isobel. Over the last two days, you feel more like a sister to me than a stranger. And I believe Gavan has relaxed about you staying here. I mean, I don't think he would leave the castle otherwise. I can read my brother well, and I think his worries are more focused on what is going on in the villages instead of you," Meg said.

"Oh, I'm not so sure of that." Isobel gave Meg a sideways glance.

True, Gavan hadn't been there much the last couple of days, but before he'd left, he had scrutinized her every move. She had told him lies, kept secrets from him. Of course, it was for his own good, but Isobel knew that was partially why he didn't trust her, and she couldn't argue that it wasn't for good reason.

Meg tugged the reigns of her horse toward Isobel, leaned over and whispered, "Isobel, there is something I want to tell you."

"Is it about the romantic material you have been reading?" Isobel teased, wondering when she was going to bring it up.

"The book, it is romantic?" Meg questioned as she blushed. "Perhaps, I need to practice sounding out all the words and not skipping through them."

Isobel laughed.

"No, it is not about my reading," Meg whispered again, her head tipping toward Isobel. The rhythm of the two women's hearts skipped the same hurried and frightened beat. Isobel swallowed and forced herself to remain at ease.

"Of course, you can tell me anything," Isobel replied with a strained smile. Her hands clenched her horse's reins so tightly that her fingers cramped within her gloves.

"Isobel, I think I am a lot like your mother. I can't heal, at least I don't think I can, but I am good at growing herbs in our garden when Gavan and Elspeth let me. And you know that I can often hear other people's thoughts. But there are other things."

Isobel wobbled, and she jerked the leather straps to keep from falling.

"Lass, are you alright!" Kenneth called out to her.

Isobel looked over her shoulder at Kenneth. "Yes, I'm sorry. It's been a while since I have ridden." She had never ridden, but that wasn't the cause of her near fall. She longed to hear Meg's story, but before she could open her mouth and ask anything, Meg continued.

"I have managed to keep myself hidden from Elspeth and Gavan. It is why I hated you at first. I was terrified you would give my secret away. If that were to happen, Isobel, you know what they would do to us."

"Meg, you needn't worry of that. I would never say anything to anyone. I have my own secrets to protect."

"Yes, I know. The first night you were at Elden Castle, when I used my mother's ring to learn who you were, I saw a secret hidden deep inside of you that I shouldn't have. I don't understand it. There is magic inside of you—I can feel it—but nonetheless, I saw something different. Then, after you told me that a vampire confessed to being your father, it really made me question what I saw. I do apologize for prying, sister." Meg reached over and gently patted Isobel's hands. "I promise not to do it again."

All the color had drained from Isobel's cheeks, and for a moment Meg thought she might fall from her horse.

"Isobel, are you ill? Do we need to stop for a minute?" Meg glanced over her shoulder at Kenneth. He remained about ten feet behind them. She pulled her lips in a thin, tight smile and turned her attention back to Isobel.

"No, I am fine," Isobel mumbled. "Please go on." *What was it that Meg saw?* She couldn't imagine that it was too alarming, unless she learned that Isobel could time travel. But it sounded like her vision had nothing to do with magic. Isobel opened her mouth to ask, but Meg cut her off again.

"Wait, me first."

Entering the edge of town, the loud, harmonious sounds of bagpipes filled their ears, and Kenneth wedged his steed between them. Isobel hadn't heard him approach.

"This way," he said and guided his horse to the right. "I will water the horses and catch up to you two. Meg, do not wander far."

"Of course not, Kenneth," she answered. "I will be getting the usual supplies."

Kenneth nodded.

Offering them a hand, Meg and Isobel dismounted and handed their reins over to Kenneth. Meg locked her arm through Isobel's and led her toward the crowds of people littered along the cobblestone path ahead.

The anticipation of what Meg wanted to share made Isobel anxious. She pulled at the sleeves of her cloak, her palms dampening the fur trim. Meg still had her arm looped through hers, and she leaned into the girl. The street was crammed with carts and carriages, and Isobel made herself dizzy looking left and right and then left again. She and Meg worked their way into the middle of the celebration when Isobel suddenly blurted out, "Meg, you have to be careful."

She pulled Meg closer. "Whatever it is that you are doing that you have to whisper is likely dangerous. Like your use of the pendulum. You are putting yourself and your family in danger.

You must be discreet and refrain from using it no matter what. These times of witch hunting will pass, but it will be after your own time." Isobel paused and wondered if Meg would question what she meant. But she stared straight ahead, looking lost in thought.

"If anyone were to learn what you can do, you would be hanged and burned to death. Like the girl last night and the one the night I arrived. You know this—it is exactly why you wanted me away from Elden Castle." Isobel's voice was low, but her tone was firm.

"Isobel, like I said, you don't have to worry. I understand the danger, but I can protect myself. I am safe. Let us sit and rest for a minute," Meg said, worried about the paleness that had suddenly colored Isobel's face. She led them to a set of steps nearby, and both the women sat.

Meg closed her eyes, and a sense of uneasiness webbed itself between them. Isobel folded her hands in her lap and sat impossibly still and waited for Meg to speak.

"Last night, I had a recurring dream. However, lately, since you have been at Elden Castle, it has visited me almost nightly." Meg looked at Isobel. Her rich blue eyes had dulled, and by her lack of expression, Isobel knew Meg's mind was somewhere else.

"I am listening," Isobel said.

"It is of my mother. We are in the garden, and she is kneeling, holding my small face in her hands." Meg closed her eyes as she spoke. "I can feel her, Isobel, smell her lavender scent in front of me. She whispers that I am not a fair maiden like Elspeth; rather, I am a warrior. I am confused by her comment, for only men go to battle, so I ask her, 'Like Gavan?'

"She smiles down on me with so much love and faith and says, 'No, darling, Your strength is within, created specifically to protect you.' I ask her, 'You will show me how to use this strength?' Her eyes then brim with a sadness that I am unable to forget, and she tells me, 'My darling, I fear I may not be here to show you. This is why I am telling you now that it exists. But this is a secret, one just between you and me. Do you understand?' I am afraid, but I nod that I do."

Meg opened her eyes; their brightness had returned, and she turned toward Isobel.

"What a beautiful dream," Isobel said, her eyes filled with tears.

"I believe it to be more than a dream. I believe it to be a memory, Isobel. I have no way of proving this, but it is what I believe is true. My mother was aware of my abilities from the beginning, I don't know how, but I am determined to find out." Meg stood. Pleased to see that the coloring had returned to Isobel's cheeks, she offered her a hand and pulled her to her feet.

"Meg, you are not safe!" Isobel exclaimed. "Whether it be a memory or a dream, your mother isn't here and has no idea what you are involved in. Your brother is a mighty warrior who I know would defend you until his own life was taken, but he is not enough to protect you from an entire village of witch-hunters, I am sorry to say. If you are discovered, they will take Gavan and Elspeth down with you."

"I'm not talking of Gavan. There is another who has vowed to protect me, to keep me safe and from harm. He has to, Isobel; his life depends on it."

Isobel stopped, a cart full of bright red apples was parked on her right. A small child, a boy with round, dimpled cheeks and reddish-blond curls, raced around the two and held one out to Isobel. He smiled, and she noticed that his top front teeth were missing.

At any other time, the polished skin and fresh, crisp aroma would be so tantalizing that she wouldn't be able to resist indulging, but at this moment, the sweet fragrance made her stomach tumble and her thoughts race; death, immortality, sin. Her magic recoiled at the words that echoed in her head, and a chill settled in her bones.

Meg purchased a dozen apples from the boy and patted him on the head. The tone of her voice was soothing and oddly distant, even though Isobel was standing beside her.

"Ready to move on?" Meg asked, turning to face her. "Isobel, you have turned as white as a sheet. Is it the baby? Do I need to have Kenneth escort us back?"

Isobel shook her head and quickly but quietly found her voice. "Who has vowed to protect you, Meg? And why does their life depend on it?"

"Oh that; yes, do not fret," Meg whispered as she linked

her arm with Isobel's once again and the two women stepped forward. "I am safe from persecution; Cristian has promised me that," she added. "He can't let me die."

Isobel stumbled. Cristian must be Meg's vampire. His vow, Isobel assumed, was probably much like the one told to her mother. She felt the color leave her face and fill her heart.

"I never heard his approach that first day." Meg's words came out fast at first, her voice quivering as if maybe she were afraid to share this secret. "I was returning to Elden Castle, and I thought I was alone, but suddenly, he was beside me. His eyes were as black as the night sky and wild. He dropped his chin as if to speak, but instead, he just stood staring. It frightened me for a moment and I tried to look away, but I couldn't. It was like he wouldn't let me, and then something about him changed, as if he were remembering something. Or someone. I remember a feeling of warmth and security filling my insides."

Isobel thought of the moments before she had entered the portal. The feelings that had overwhelmed her were much like what Meg was describing. The vampire who had clearly cared for her mother had felt much the same about her. A flood of fear over the similarity ran through Isobel, and she shuddered in reaction.

Meg took a deep breath, oblivious to the tightening hold Isobel had on her arm and continued. "It was then that he called me by my mother's name, his words choking in his throat as he spoke. Of course, I told him that Catarine was my mother and that people often commented that I look like her. I explained that she had died many years ago and asked how he had known her."

Meg looked down and sighed. "He never answered; he just stared and refused to let me look anywhere else but at him. I thought him to be odd, but I wasn't afraid. There was something quite charming about him, and he did behave like a perfect gentleman as he walked with me through the field. But as soon as we approached Elden Castle, he vanished. I never even saw him leave. I received a note from a messenger the following day, asking me to meet him. I knew that I shouldn't go without a chaperone, but I was most excited. Besides, if I had asked Gavan to escort me to meet a strange man in the woods, he would not only say no. He would have locked me in my room or sent me to live with our father's relatives in England like he has threatened so many times before." The look of mischief that briefly filled her eyes as she spoke of Gavan's punishments quickly faded.

"It wasn't until that night, as I stepped into the shadows, Cristian suddenly by my side, that I learned I should be very afraid. He held me so tightly and made a promise that harm from the villagers would never come to me as long as I was with him. He would protect me and keep my secret safe."

"You are not being protected, Meg; you are being hunted. You will not be free of danger as long as you allow this to happen," Isobel said, and the image of the raised red scars that marked her mother's arm came to her.

Fearing that she was right, Isobel grabbed Meg's wrist. She pushed back the fur trim that lined the sleeve of her cloak and exposed the two circular wounds she had sensed were there.

"Isobel, not here, please," Meg said as she scrambled to pull the sleeve down and hide the marks. Isobel's grip was too strong though, and for a moment, Meg was frightened.

"You claimed you were safe, Meg. Isn't that what you told me?" Isobel held Meg's wrist up for her to see, her voice no longer controlled.

"You're hurting me, Isobel; please let go before you snap my arm in two. And you're drawing attention to us; walk with me and lower your voice."

"He is using you. It will only be a matter of time before he drains you of your blood and leaves you lifeless in the woods. You need to stay away. Stop going to him before he kills you. How long has this been—" Isobel let the remaining words drift away into the music and conversations that had suddenly moved closer to them. She let go of Meg's forearm.

"A few months," Meg mouthed.

"Meg, my mother bore the same two marks on her wrist. It was a vampire who drank her blood and a vampire who killed her. He bragged of draining her of life. Do you not remember me telling you this?" Isobel's words were whispered, but her tone was harsh.

"I remember, but that was your mother, not me. And besides, you weren't harmed?" Meg asked, wrapping her arms around herself and out of Isobel's reach. "Do you not wonder why that was? How is it that the daughter of a witch does not possess the same magical blood? And does not draw to her the same deadly thirst of the vampires that killed her mother?"

Every day since her mother's death, Isobel had wondered that exact thing. Bagpipes played loudly in their ears as they passed a group of musicians and performers, dressed in traditional garb, weaved in and out of the crowd while they performed a Scottish dance. To be polite, Meg and Isobel stopped and let the women cavort around them, and they applauded briefly, along with the crowd, when the performance ended.

The distraction helped Isobel regain her composure, and she and Meg moved forward and away from the crowd before speaking again. *Magic is in her veins; it's just different.* But this was not what Isobel wanted to discuss.

"Meg, the morning I witnessed the violence through my mother's window, I was afraid for my life. If the vampire who fed from my mother had vowed to keep her safe, he failed. He didn't appear to be the one who had harmed her, but he wasn't the only one capable. Meg, in the end, he wasn't able to protect her from someone like himself."

Meg stopped and looked ahead. "Isobel, there is more, but I am going to need to tell you quickly as I see that Kenneth is motioning for us to return."

Following Meg's stare, Isobel watched as the stable master waved his hand. Meg nodded and the two women stepped forward, Meg hoping that would keep Kenneth in place for just a few more minutes.

"Something strange happens when Cristian"—she hesitated—"well, when he bites me. When his venom mixes with my blood."

"What do you mean?" Isobel's eyes widened in horror. Was this something her mother had experienced too? She had never seemed different, but then again her mother had kept many secrets from her.

"He becomes weak, collapses on the ground, and starts talking. He told me that the magic in my blood allows him to see his human family, and that is why he won't ever let me die. He remembers and misses them, Isobel. But that's not all."

They had nearly reached Kenneth, despite their slow steps.

Meg talked fast. "Isobel, my magic makes him weak and vulnerable and like a human, while his venom turns me more like—" Meg couldn't say the words aloud. Instead, she quickly explained how Cristian's venom temporarily gave her the similar physical strength and endurance of a vampire.

The same strength and endurance that flowed naturally within Isobel's veins.

Chapter 22

"I enjoyed our visit into town yesterday," Isobel said as she and Meg walked along the flattened grass beyond the stables and towards the other side of Elden Castle. She wanted to finish their conversation where it had left off yesterday before Kenneth motioned for them to return. He had eyed them suspiciously after mounting their horses and wedged himself between her and Meg the entire way home. Except for the clopping of the horses' hooves along the beaten path, the trio had traveled in silence. Gavan had greeted them as soon as they arrived and kept his place beside Meg until the two women excused themselves to their room, leaving Isobel no opportunity to speak with Meg alone.

"I'm glad you liked it. The market is a festive time. Unless, of course, one of the farmers catches a thief." The exaggerated look on Meg's face made both the women laugh, even though stealing was no laughing matter.

Meg appeared relaxed this morning, and the light blue gown against her fair skin and dark sapphire colored eyes was most flattering. She wore her hair loose down her back, and it fell in perfect curls over her shoulders, much like it did the first night Isobel saw her sneaking back into Elden Castle. There was a gentleness in her smile, and her eyes sparkled as though she had not a care in the world. Had she really already forgotten Isobel's warning?

A loud whistle commanded their attention, and both women turned to look. It was Kenneth, standing in the stable doorway with the reins to his horse in hand. Meg waved to him and smiled before pointing in the direction of the garden ahead. Kenneth frowned, but Meg grabbed Isobel's hand and led her towards the boulders near the cliff anyway.

"I swear, that man frets like a lady. He and my brother both. He can see us just perfectly," Meg mumbled under her breath.

Whether Gavan was aware of Meg's magic or not, Isobel understood why he kept her so close to home. Her looks and the way she carried herself could be enchanting when she wanted them to be. Isobel had only known Meg for two weeks now, but it seemed as if she had blossomed more into womanhood with each passing day. Men would not restrain themselves if given the opportunity to get her alone, and then swear to their wives, as they begged for forgiveness, that Meg had put a curse on them and should be sent to the gallows. Isobel closed her eyes at the image of how Gavan would react if anyone harmed his youngest sister.

"Meg, thank you for entrusting me with your secret about Cristian. I fear for your safety regarding so many things. Life in Scotland is not safe for many people right now, and it seems that you have placed yourself right in the middle of two dangerous entities; a vampire and the witch hunters. I hope you know I only want to help you."

Isobel looked toward the stables again.

"What is it, Isobel? Kenneth has gone back into the barn. He will leave us as long as we can be seen."

Isobel smiled. "It's not that."

"Well, out with it. I can tell you have more to say."

"Yes, I do."

Isobel had already made up her mind to go see Mariam, but after Meg's confession yesterday, she wanted her to go with her in hopes that Mariam could help the girl understand the danger she was in. Meg was young and foolish, Isobel reminded herself as she remembered her boast about being protected from persecution. And from a vampire of all things. What was it she believed he was doing to her? Also, the fact that Meg was able to channel a pendulum and seek desired information spoke of the power within her. Power that Isobel didn't know how to help her with. Meg needed someone with magical abilities more like herself.

Isobel sucked in a breath of air. She would need to choose her words carefully. In order to get Meg to agree, she would have to tell her she was from the future, and until this moment, Isobel had been most certain that would remain a secret she would never have to expose.

"Meg, I need to tell you something very special about me, really about what I can do. I know it may be hard for you to understand, but I will explain the best that I can. All I ask is that you listen to me with an open mind."

"Yes," Meg said, and she sat on the boulder next to Isobel.

Clasping her hands together, Isobel spoke. "There is a reason I am different from you and your family and those in the village, but it isn't because I traveled from another place in our world. Rather, it is because I came from another time."

Isobel paused. Meg sat quietly as promised, her mouth was closed, but slowly, as she took in Isobel's words, her eyebrows pulled together.

"My mother was gifted with the power to heal through potions and herbs and magic spells, all gifts that I did not receive. She worked with me for so many years, but I was never successful. I was a clumsy child; too fast, too strong. None of the other children wanted to play with me because I would beat them at their games or I broke their things. Of course, I never did any of this intentionally, but magic, I believe, runs different in my veins."

Isobel hesitated, and her heart thumped so loudly in her chest that she was certain Meg could hear it. "The only magical gift I inherited from my mother, Meg, is the ability to travel through time."

"I don't know if I understand," Meg responded, her brows still furrowed together.

"Meg, I came to you from the future, a time that doesn't exist yet. I was born December 21, 1862, almost three hundred years from now, and granted with the power to summon an invisible gateway that can move me through time—the past or future—to any place that I desire." Isobel spoke her words carefully.

"Two weeks ago, when I called the portal, I was desperate to return to 1697 and reunite with my ancestor Mariam. I hadn't seen her since my seventh birthday, the last time, truly the only time, I ever visited the Highlands. But instead, the portal dropped me on your doorstep one hundred years too early."

Isobel stopped and let her words sink in. Sharing her secret allowed a huge weight to be lifted from her shoulders, but it also unleashed a great fear. What if Meg didn't believe her? Or worse, what if she ran straight to Gavan and he dragged her to the gallows? Isobel would not allow herself to be burned at the stake and have her daughter's life end in such a torturous, barbaric way before it ever began. Her hands fidgeted in her lap as did Charlotte's beneath her mother's skin.

You have the portal, Isobel reminded herself. Her breathing eased, and she looked at Meg. *If Meg seems at all suspicious, you can call it and return home immediately. You do not have to stay.*

"December 21 is my birthdate, Isobel. And my mother's."

My mother's too. And it will be my daughter's.

Before Isobel could acknowledge the frightening coincidence that they were all born on the same date in December, Meg spoke again.

"Can all witches travel through time?" she asked, thinking

of the irrational theory that witches flew through the air. She had a hard time grasping what Isobel had told her but sensed that she was speaking the truth. After all, Meg knew that things not easily understood existed.

"No, it is not a common ability. I asked my mother that same question."

"Could your mother travel through time?"

"She could go with me, but no, she didn't have the power to call the portal."

"How did you know you could travel through time? Is it possible that I can too?" A giddiness welled up inside of Meg. Maybe she could take herself to a place or time where she would be safe. Somewhere she didn't have to hide or be in fear of who she was or the vampire who stalked her. She could walk the streets freely and live the life she had been born to live without judgment or persecution. Now it was Meg's blood that sent an alert to both women as it thumped excitedly in her chest.

"Meg, you would know if you could. When I was very young, I used to disappear from my mother's sight and return at random. When I returned, she would demand that I tell her where I had been and if I had been alone. She was so frightened. I was too young to explain but shook my head against the idea that I had disappeared with someone. Finally, when I was four years old, she took me by the hand and asked me to take her with me. I will never forget the look of relief on her face, nor the serious conversation we had once I brought us back home safely." Isobel smiled at the memory.

"Meg, I am being honest with you because I need to go see Mariam. I need to know why the spell she taught my mother to protect herself against vampires didn't work. I don't have much time as I have to return home before Charlotte is born. I want to be able to protect us and not fear that every time I step outside he may be there waiting, ready to end our lives too."

"I don't know that I fully understand, but if you can travel through time as you say, why haven't you returned home already? Or gone to see your ancestor Mariam once you realized she wasn't here? Why have you stayed in Dunkinshire so long and kept yourself in danger?"

"I have considered it several times. I did attempt to return home the first night the vampire's cold scent blew through my window and I saw you running into the woods toward him. But Fara stopped me. She helped me realize that he was after you and not me, and that we needed to help you."

Meg's eyes widened.

"Fara is sensitive to my safety, Meg. If she senses that I am in danger, her guard goes up. Not being honest with me at first, along with the vampire scent on your skin, has raised her alertness, I am sure."

"Isobel, a few nights ago after I met with Cristian, I fled to a sacred place that I have been visiting alone for years." Meg wanted to tell Isobel the whole story—what she had witnessed through the broken window, how Cristian had frightened her, and what he had done to the women inside the sanctuary—but she decided to remain quiet about all the details for now. "Anyways, on my way home, a bird, I couldn't really see what kind because it was so dark, but it flew overhead with me until we reached Elden Castle. Do you think it was Fara?"

"It is possible. She may have been worried that someone would harm you or follow you home."

The bird had every right to be worried, terrified even, Meg thought as she remembered the coldness in Cristian's words and the terror he had deliberately caused.

"I have so many questions concerning myself and my mother, and I feel that Mariam has the answers I am looking for," Isobel continued. "She and my mother spoke for hours, their voices so hushed that even when I stood with my ear to the keyhole, their conversation was only the faint sound of a whisper."

Isobel grabbed Meg's wrist and turned it over, exposing the bite marks. Thin skin had sealed over the wounds, but the raised red nodules looked tender. "And I know she can help you too."

"But how do we go to the future?" Meg removed her arm from Isobel's grasp and pulled at the sleeve of her dress until the hem reached her palm.

"When will Gavan be leaving again?"

"In the morning," Meg answered. "He is riding to a

neighboring village to purchase a couple of new horses. He said he should be home by sunset."

"I can see the stables from my window. We will meet as soon as he leaves. In the woods at the edge of the tree line where Kenneth can't spot us."

"Can we do this in a day? If Gavan finds us gone, it won't be good. For either of us, Isobel."

Meg looked at Isobel as a sister in some ways more than Elspeth. In such a short time, the two women had grown close, and Isobel's safety was important to her. Two weeks ago, Meg hadn't cared what happened to the strange witch who had found herself banging on their front door, begging to see someone who didn't exist. But now as she stared at the kind soul who glowed from the nearness of motherhood and looked so lovely in her own mother's turquoise colored gown, Meg knew she would risk her own life to save Isobel's if needed. The two had a bond that was indescribable but evident to them both. And it ran deeper than the magic in their blood and a shared birthday.

"Yes, we can; we have to. I'll tell Mariam we don't have much time."

"Isobel?" Meg's voice quivered, and she pulled at her sleeve again.

"You have to trust me, Meg. We need to do this." Isobel squeezed Meg's hands in her own.

"But what if we don't make it to Mariam. What if we go

somewhere else, like you did?"

"We won't. I was scared and in a hurry last time; I must have made a mistake. I will keep us safe, and we will return."

For the remainder of their outing, the two sat in silence, shoulder to shoulder, each lost in their own thoughts. The sounds of nature around them soothed Isobel's nervousness despite her climbing curiosity of what tomorrow held. They both had so many questions and wondered if they would ever find the answers.

The days had grown shorter over the last two weeks, and dusk fell upon them quickly. As the two made their way to the castle, a brisk wind picked up and blew off the water, forcing the temperature of the air to drop just as the light from the sun disappeared below the horizon. Thankful for the few days of mild weather, both women knew that another storm was approaching just as it should in late November.

Isobel spied Fara perched on the window ledge outside of her room and Kenneth watching them from the door to his cottage. Gavan would return any time, but at least the two were standing at the castle doors.

"Good night, Isobel. I will be there in the morning. If you are strong enough to do this, so am I." Meg smiled, gave Isobel a quick hug, and then made her way to the opposite end of the castle.

No messages had been delivered from Cristian today, so she would be staying indoors for the night and she was grateful. She had a lot to think about and didn't want to be weak or tired tomorrow.

Winding through the hallways, she turned through the last arched opening on the right and sat on the bottom step. To see the world in a new time, one that didn't exist, intrigued her.

"If Mariam lives in Elden Castle one hundred years from now, and Isobel has been there and has no knowledge of me or my family, we must all be dead," Meg spoke aloud as she wound the silver chain of her pendulum around her finger.

Or could it be that she was still alive one hundred years from now but had married and moved with her husband. Would Mariam be able to tell Meg of her future? The idea suddenly danced in Meg's head, and she became more excited and less afraid.

Her mind wandered, and the ideas of what the future held for her soared. Smiling, she stood, placed her hand on the wall, and made her way up the dark, spiral staircase. *Narrow, wide, narrow, narrow, wide, repeat…*

Chapter 23

Meg met Isobel at the edge of the woods early the next morning. The idea of learning her own fate had overcome any anxiety of what it meant to travel through time. Fearful she would give away her excitement, she had waited in her room until Gavan slammed the front door behind him, mounted Ahearn, and headed west.

"Hold on and don't let go. It will be dark, but quick," Isobel said as she grabbed Meg's hand. Fara sat on her shoulder and as she closed her eyes, she pinched the pentacle between her fingers and called forth the portal.

I close my eyes and I see
One hundred years in the future in front of me.
From here to there I call you to find
The Elden Castle in this time.

The air in front of them slowly churned clockwise. As the magical particles clung together, the spinning motion gained speed and brought forth the portal. Its suction pulled at the two, and before Meg had a chance to change her mind, Isobel pressed Fara to her chest and jerked Meg through the opening. No sooner had they disappeared, the two found themselves dropped on the ground in the same woods they had just left.

"Meg, are you well?" Isobel rolled to her side, placed her

hands on her stomach, and waited for Charlotte's movements. The brush of Fara's wings sounded in her ears, and her sleek head nudged against her cheek. Isobel's surroundings swirled, the weight of her body feeling as if it was filled with lead. Her eyes closed against her will; she would need time to recover, but time was something they didn't have much of.

Meg lay beside Isobel, her fingers clenching the tall grasses beneath her as if she were trying to anchor herself in place. Her eyelids were pulled back and her eyes were wide and bright like those of a frightened child.

"What just happened?" she mumbled. "Isobel?"

Isobel remained asleep. Meg watched the rapid rise and fall of her chest until her breaths became more even and the rosy color returned to her cheeks. On their way back to the castle last night, Isobel had explained that her body required sleep after moving through the gateway. Meg wondered how long it would be before she awakened. She wasn't afraid, at least not yet.

She opened her mouth, but whatever she had thought to say stayed silent as Isobel's eyelids fluttered, and she clumsily reached out to push herself up. Looking ahead, Meg stared at the castle that towered above them as if she were seeing it for the first time.

"Are you well?" she asked.

Isobel nodded. "Can you help me stand? How long was I asleep?"

Jumping up, Meg reached for Isobel's hands and pulled her

gently to her feet. "Not long."

Isobel shook out her skirt. "Come on; we don't have much time."

Fara flew ahead and waited for them along the top of the wall across from the castle entrance, her feet pattering nervously across the uneven cobblestones.

"This looks much the same," Meg whispered as the two made their way to the front door. Her steps were not as swift and graceful as Isobel's and the grass tangled around her ankles, causing her to stumble. "How can you be sure we are in a different time, Isobel?"

One hundred years had passed from the moment they had stepped in the portal, but the castle that stood proud on the landing above them looked just as glorious and complete as Isobel had expected the first time.

"Yes, I am certain this time. See how the trees have grown, and the wall where Fara is sitting has been built from the top of the pathway all the way around the castle. I can also feel Mariam's energy." They reached the oversized arched doors, and Isobel raised her fist and knocked. After the third time, it opened.

"Isobel? Fara?"

There in the entryway stood Mariam just as Isobel remembered. Her musky, heathery scent filled Isobel's nostrils with a comfortable familiarity, and tears pooled in her eyes. Their mystical energy intertwined, and as it strengthened, a soft amber glow illuminated off Mariam's fair skin. Nothing about her had changed; not her long, pale hair, nor her high cheek bones that lifted her narrow face, nor her mesmerizing bluish-green eyes. Mariam looked like Isobel had expected. Radiant and beautiful.

With her hand still grasping the door handle, her other balled on her hip, and Fara now perched on her shoulder, Mariam watched the tears stream down Isobel's cheeks and waited for her guests to speak.

But before Isobel could nod and acknowledge that it was indeed herself and her familiar, she fell into Mariam's arms, relief sweeping over her.

~~~~~~~~

"Are you sure, my dear?" Mariam asked as she led Isobel and Meg into the Great Hall to sit. Meg lagged behind, and her eyes darted from one wall to the other, taking in the strange ornamental objects that now embellished her home.

"Yes. I need to know who I am. The truth. My mother kept many secrets, and with her gone now, I fear that there is no one else who may know."

Seating herself across from Meg and Isobel, Mariam folded her hands in her lap. Meg's eyes roamed the room, looking everywhere except at her.

"I can't believe you are here, my dear. Please forgive me for staring, but I'm a bit in shock. I always wondered if you and your mother had made it back safely and if you would ever return."

Isobel sat quietly, unsure how to begin. She felt it odd that Mariam hadn't asked who Meg was, but truly, all she could think about was wanting the answers to her questions. She needed to give Mariam time to get acclimated to seeing her though; that was only fair.

"You have grown into such a lovely young woman." Pride showed in Mariam's gentle smile, and the invisible thread of magic that wove between them warmed and pulled Isobel closer.

"Thank you, Mariam. And you look the same. Just as beautiful," Isobel said as she tried her best to be patient. "My mother is gone. The vampires—well, I believe it was only one—but they killed her. And my husband, too. You were the only one I knew to turn to. Please, Mariam, I need your help."

Her ancestor cleared her throat and stared into Isobel's pleading eyes. She had kept Isobel's mother's secret safe for the last thirteen years as promised. She never thought she would be the one to expose it, but Isobel had a right to know who, or rather what, she was. Mariam had told Bonni, Isobel's mother, that long ago, but the woman wouldn't hear of it.

"After he's gone. When I know for certain he is dead, I will tell her," Bonni had whispered behind closed doors as they blessed the sacred herb to perform a quick death. It was too bad that time never came.

Mariam drew in a deep breath and began. "Many different creatures roam the lands and other than humans, during most of our existence, we have lived in peace, side by side, as our presence as witches has never been a direct threat. But there have been times when an outsider has stumbled upon a rarity that has been born among us. It has been during times like those that we become endangered."

Isobel had difficulty following where Mariam's story was going and how any of it applied to the many questions that rattled inside her. She glanced around the room at the memorable handmade furniture pieces and woven tapestries she had expected to see when she stepped through the Elden Castle doorway two weeks ago. The material items brought a comfort to Isobel, but more than anything she wanted answers.

As much as Isobel felt safe here, safer than anywhere she had been since her family's murders, she and Meg couldn't be gone for too long. Gavan would return by sundown. Glancing through the window, the sun sat bright and high in the sky. They had a few hours but mustn't lose track of time. Finally, Mariam got to the point.

"Isobel, your mother was special. She had been returning home one evening when a vampire lurking in the shadows detected her scent and attacked. He would have likely left her for dead, but as soon as he tasted her magic and experienced its effects—his body awakening in ways it hadn't done in years—he knew he had to keep her alive. For months, he visited your mother, nearly draining her of life before leaving again on his own. Your mother kept her secret, afraid that most wouldn't believe her or, worse, think that she was cursed and kill her. Feeling desperate and alone, she finally devised a plan in hopes to make him weak and vulnerable; she seduced the vampire." Isobel's jaw dropped, and she felt an immediate embarrassment for her mother.

Mariam continued. "But the plan didn't work. She said he drank the tainted blood and his strength diminished, but not for long like Bonni had hoped. His behavior became erratic, first fearful and then enraged. He screamed, asking what she had done to him. She tried to fight him off, finally confessing that she had meant to lure him into a moment of weakness and kill him. For the longest of moments, she said she feared for her life. But instead, he took what she had initially offered. Your mother immediately became pregnant with you. She even claimed she could sense you growing inside of her within just a few days. She believed you to be a miracle, Isobel, but she was also terrified at what she had done."

The color had drained from Isobel's face, and she trembled. Meg reached over and placed a hand on top, offering Isobel comfort. The lavender-colored sleeve of her gown had been pulled to the middle of her palm, hiding the vampire's bite marks, but Isobel felt the wounds pulse as Mariam continued her story.

"You must understand, your mother was alone and at his

mercy. She knew the shame she had brought upon herself carrying a child without being married, so she allowed him to take her into seclusion. He claimed he hadn't known he could father a child and vowed to protect your mother, promising that no harm would ever come to either of you."

You are safe with me. His words resonated in Isobel's ears.

"He limited his feedings while your mother was pregnant and never touched her intimately again. But as soon as you were born, his desire to feed nearly non-stop returned. The first couple of years, she was so weak from feeding both you and him, she wasn't sure she would survive. But he kept his word and neither you nor your mother were ever harmed, so she decided to bide her time and in the meantime took care of herself the best she could. As you grew, it became obvious that your abilities mirrored him more than your mother and he became fascinated, watching you day and night."

Isobel thought to when she was a child but couldn't recall anyone ever seeing anyone she didn't recognize from the village watching her.

"When you were seven years old, Bonni decided she couldn't endure it any longer. They had made a deal, but she was afraid that as you got older you would discover the truth or, worse, he would start feeding off of you. Your blood is different and wouldn't satisfy him like hers did, but Bonni knew she couldn't prevent him from trying. That is when the two of you came to see me."

Isobel jumped from her seat. "But why didn't she just kill him? You taught her; I remember your conversations. I didn't understand them at the time, but I knew that what you were teaching her was—" Isobel stopped mid-sentence.

Her father was a vampire.

"Maybe he can't die," Meg suggested softly. "I've heard the tales about immortals."

"An immortal can live forever, but that does not necessarily mean that they do, my dear," Mariam explained.

"Mariam, what was my father's name?" Isobel asked.

"I don't know; Bonni would never tell me."

"Do you know what he looked like? Where he came from? Where my mother was when he first found her?"

Mariam shook her head. "Bonni stayed silent to protect you. I gave her the tools, but I also know she was afraid that if her plan failed, like it had the first time, he would harm or take you away. When it came down to it, she must have decided she couldn't take the chance and didn't try again."

Isobel sat quietly and looked at her hands folded in her lap. She had rebelled against following witch protocol this morning and had dressed in red. However, she discovered that the color was not very forgiving and emphasized the roundness of her belly as she sat. Her pregnancy hadn't been cumbersome—even to this day she could move as she wished—so at times she failed to notice how much her body had changed.

"You're with child?" Mariam asked, her question sounding more like a statement. The look on her face was inquisitive, but Isobel wasn't sure why. Mariam would have sensed the pregnancy as soon as she opened the front door.

"Yes," Isobel answered, resting her hands on her daughter. Charlotte pushed against the weight and rolled a foot or an elbow across her stomach.

"My husband was human, but my daughter? I'm wondering, Mariam, what will she be?"

"We will have to wait and see. But I believe she will be more like her father or your mother's side rather than your father. After all, in order to be a vampire, even half, you must be created by one, one way or another."

A momentary sense of relief swept over Isobel. She didn't want her daughter to be anything like her alleged grandfather.

"But, Isobel, you can't let your guard down."

"Mariam, my mother once warned me that my powers wouldn't last forever. Do you know what she meant by that?" Isobel asked, changing the subject.

"You are half witch, half vampire, Isobel. There are others out there like you, but your existence is rare. You have been gifted with a multitude of abilities, but your one weakness, and we all have one, is that your magic isn't everlasting."

"What does that mean?" Isobel was panicked. What if she couldn't make it home? What if she was stuck here or, worse, got trapped in the portal?

"Your magic feeds your vampiric needs: your speed, your strength, and your resiliency. Although it is different with each individual, this half is the more dominant side of you, Isobel, and the most demanding. Over time, your magic will be drained as it feeds your physical self. The more you use it, the quicker that time will pass."

"Mariam," Isobel said as she wondered how she could fight against such odds. "How do I stop it? How do I keep the magic in my blood?"

How do I stay alive?

Chapter 24

Mariam cast her eyes downward and shook her head, confirming what Isobel had already concluded without saying a word. She had been given a life sentence. Simply put, she was killing herself day by day, spell by spell, movement by movement.

"Did my mother know this?"

Fara hopped onto the seat between Meg and Isobel. The magpie had been motionless from the back of a chair while Mariam had spoken.

"Yes." Mariam's tone was solemn, and her lips pursed. She tilted her head, and her eyes went from Fara's to Isobel's. "She only suspected it at first so she began a journal noting your sleep patterns, your moments of high and low energy, your physical strength, and the levels of the small amount of magic she could sense in your blood during these times. She shared her theory with me when you two came to visit, and after a brief consultation with someone of extensive knowledge it was confirmed."

Isobel's understanding of her father's identity was destroyed. The stories her mother shared of him being a soldier, the vivid details as she explained how dashing he looked, the way he carried himself when he moved; confident, strong, and protective.

"He was so handsome, daughter," Isobel remembered her

mother saying as she sat with her chin in the cup of her palm, her eyes cloudy and distant. Her stories, Isobel now realized, had not been about her father; rather, they were about the man her mother had dreamed of and wished for him to be.

Isobel's heart hammered in her chest, and she grabbed the small decorative vase off the table next to her. Without any effort, she closed her fingers around it and the *pop!* of shattering glass filled the room. Opening her hand, shimmering particles that resembled salt crystals spilled to the floor, her hand unblemished.

"Over the years I have learned to be careful with most things I touch, but I can crush anything, dissolve it to dust with ease." Isobel's voice was cold and detached as the pieces of her life wove themselves together in her mind. "My mother would tell me, 'Careful, Isobel. Be gentle.' But as she said the words, there was always a pooling of sadness in her eyes. Like a guilt or a knowing that she was afraid to speak about."

Isobel looked at Mariam. "For my seventh birthday, just before we came to see you, my mother clasped this around my neck." Isobel held the pentacle out for Mariam to see.

"She said, 'Daughter, you must never show anyone what is inside of you.' I thought she was referring to my magic, my ability to call forth a portal that could move me through time. But now—"

"Your strength will go too," Mariam interrupted, and her eyes shifted to the floor. "Once your magic dies, your body will no longer be able to replenish itself like it requires, and your strength and all your physical abilities will fade away."

"Mariam." Isobel hesitated for a moment. She looked down and Fara, and then to Meg before returning her gaze on her ancestor. "When this happens, will I die too?"

Mariam met Isobel's wide-eyed stare and nodded as her own filled with tears.

"So, I am half vampire, but I am not immortal?" Isobel's question hung heavy in the air as she waited for Mariam to answer.

"No, you are not immortal; you will never drink the blood of others, and yes, you will die. If you lose too much blood, use too much of your energy, particularly at the same time, your life will be in grave danger."

Isobel's thoughts turned to death. No doubt it came to her as it did for everyone, but she imagined that hers would not be gentle. She would not close her eyes in sleep, never to wake up. Rather, if she understood correctly, her body would starve itself, weakening as her blood ceased to flow and nourish herself, forcing her muscles to atrophy before finally turning into stone. The vision before her was frightening. Isobel would know when death was coming, and she wouldn't be able to stop it. Her mother had known this too.

Isobel thought of Charlotte. She wanted to see her daughter live a full and beautiful life, wanted to be surrounded by grandchildren until finally, naturally, well into old age, her time to die would come. Isobel wanted to be human.

The three women and magpie looked at her swollen abdomen in silence before Mariam turned her attention to Meg and studied the young unruly witch who now fidgeted nervously under her scrutiny. Should she let Meg know? Address her in the familial way that a niece speaks to her aunt? Would Meg be able to grasp the concept that she and Mariam were blood related?

Meg resembled her brother, all except for the striking shade of her blue eyes. Her hair was more red than golden, but the shape of her eyes and face and the fiery spirit that brewed inside of her was nearly identical to Gavan's, Mariam's father. Throughout Mariam's childhood, he had told many stories of his family as she sat on his knee after supper, her mother, Gavan's wife, Amity, beside them listening as well.

Without Isobel, Mariam may not get another chance to see Meg. As soon as she stepped through the threshold, her honeysuckle scent filling the air, Mariam's heart thudded and a sadness for the loss of her father hit her all over again. But now staring into her aunt's face, Mariam could see her father alive and well, youthful and just beginning his life.

Closing her eyes, Mariam hoped this wouldn't be more than her guests, her family, could handle.

"Meg?"

"Yes," she answered softly as she looked at Mariam.

"How is your brother?"

Meg's once sparkling, bright blue eyes suddenly clouded,

and her brows drew together. "My brother? How do you know I have a brother?"

Mariam sucked in a deep breath before a smile tugged at her lips. "Gavan—" Mariam began.

"You know his name? How is this possible?" Meg turned towards Isobel, who looked just as surprised.

"I have always lived at Elden Castle; it is where I was born," Mariam said. "Gavan was my father, which makes you my aunt."

The rosiness that once colored Meg's cheeks vanished, leaving her face ghostly white. "Aunt," she whispered. "How—"

Mariam watched Meg's mind count the years that lay between her own time and the time she sat in now. "How can this be true?"

"Like yourself, Meg, I inherited Catarine's magic. I can grow the most lavish gardens even in the dead of winter, conjure a remedy to heal most ailments, and I age, but it doesn't show. And also like you and your mother, I was born on the shortest day of the year, December 21, the winter solstice."

Meg's jaw dropped. "But my brother—"

Is only human, Meg started to say, but the words silenced on her tongue.

Then, as if Mariam heard Meg's unspoken words, she answered, "Yes, I know. So was my mother, Amity, who your brother wed."

Her brother had married. And had a child. Suddenly, fear struck at Meg, and she looked frantically around the room. "Is he here?"

"No." A sadness filled Mariam's eyes, ones that Meg suddenly recognized were identical in color to Gavan's.

"He died many years ago, Meg. He had been injured; his wounds, no matter how hard I tried, wouldn't heal. He went peacefully in his sleep though. My mother was heartbroken; she missed him so much. She took to her room in seclusion and within a few months, she passed in her sleep, too."

"Do you live here alone?" Meg asked, looking around for any evidence that someone else was here.

"Yes. I was married and gave birth to twins shortly after my wedding day. My daughter and husband have passed, but my son, who I mentioned earlier is much like myself, lives elsewhere. It has been years since I have seen him. For the most part, he has abandoned his gift of magic and chooses to live a bit more recklessly, I am afraid."

An eerie silence weighed heavily in the room as the three women absorbed all that had been told. They looked from one to the other, wondering who would speak next. It was then that Mariam stood.

"I have something for you," she said to Meg and exited the Hall, leaving her and Isobel alone.

"Isobel, did you know?" Meg whispered.

"No."

"I wonder if your mother knew?"

"It is possible, but she never shared it with me if she did." Meg's hands fidgeted in her lap, tugging at the hem of her sleeves while Isobel remained impossibly still. Fara hopped onto Meg's leg and rubbed her head on Meg's hand.

Mariam returned quickly with a small leather-bound book in her hand. "This is yours," she said and held it out to Meg.

Meg reached for the book. She grasped it tightly and a stinging sensation prickled her fingertips. There was magic in this book!

"What is this?" Meg asked as Mariam returned to her seat.

"I found it when I was a child, in a secret room in the north tower." Mariam's eyes shifted upwards as though she was drawing Isobel and Meg's attention to the place.

"My brothers never survived their childhood, both of them passing in infancy, leaving me to be my own playmate. I was rarely afraid of anything and would often slip away unnoticed for hours. This, of course, drove your brother mad with fear and more than once, he would shout, *'Meg!'* upon my return before addressing me by my real name." Smiles pulled at the corners of Mariam and Meg's lips.

"Yes," Meg admitted. "I did the same for most of my childhood. I do it still, I am afraid to admit. At least, he didn't move you away."

"Oh, he threatened many times to send me to England to live with relatives, but I knew deep in my heart that my father would never allow me to leave. I was his only surviving child."

Meg looked down at the book in her hands, still wondering what it was.

"That is your mother's diary."

Meg's eyes, round and wide, slowly lifted and met Mariam's and then Isobel's. Fara, who had been still in Meg's lap suddenly patted her feet nervously and rustled her feathers. "What is wrong with her?" Meg asked Isobel.

"Fara, stop," Isobel said, but the magpie continued to show her agitation.

Lifting the book over Fara, Meg carefully opened the cover and studied the inscription on the first page. She didn't recognize the words, so instead of trying to sound out the words, she traced over the numbers at the top of the page; 1415.

"I could talk for days, perhaps even weeks, about our family if given the time. I remember my father's temper and agree with Isobel's impatience that I am sensing; it is time for you two to go back." A sudden anxiousness sounded in Mariam's voice, one that hadn't been there before, and instantly Isobel knew Mariam wished they could stay. The sun had moved low in the sky. It wouldn't be much longer before its outer rays would touch the horizon.

"Much of what you are searching for is written on those

pages. Catarine also speaks of a spell she cast and a prediction of the future. There were generations of women before her and many after, each has or will give birth to a surviving child primarily a daughter, although there are a few sons, who is a version of their mother; not identical, but not completely different. The bloodline changes, altering itself as commanded by fate, or by the prophecy, if you wish to believe. The one thing they all have in common is the date of their birth, December twenty-first, the date of the winter solstice."

Meg stilled. *She was part of a prophecy?* Her eyes darted to Isobel, who shared a similar look of shock.

"That is the date of my birth," they both murmured. Mariam nodded as though she was already aware.

"And my mother," Isobel continued softly. "And it will be my daughter's."

"As Catarine's, and myself, and my son, not to mention their children and so on," Mariam said with a smile.

"But not Elspeth," Meg answered, shaking her head.

"No, Elspeth was not a part of the prophecy. Not every child born will be called upon."

"You said, 'was'. Elspeth—"

"I'm sorry, Meg. She too is gone. She married a man named Kenneth, and they had three sons, none of them gifted. They have all passed. Elspeth and Kenneth are buried here, below the castle.

Isobel dropped a hand on her abdomen, and Charlotte pushed against it in return. Her daughter wasn't expected to be born until January. Was it possible that Isobel was wrong and that Charlotte would make it to her expected date and skip the prophecy? Tears came to her eyes. She wanted her daughter to be safe, needed for her to be safe. Both her and Meg's mother had been killed, yet Mariam stayed alive and untouched, as had Isobel and Meg. Being born on the winter solstice didn't necessarily mean death. Isobel needed more answers.

"What about me?" Meg asked softly. "You didn't seem shocked to see me, like you would if you were seeing a ghost. But I also don't reside at Elden Castle any longer. Do you know what happened to me?" Meg wanted to know but was very afraid of what Mariam may tell her.

"I'm sorry, Meg, I don't know much. No one did. One day, you just disappeared. And until the day they died, both my father and Elspeth looked for you. They loved you very much and would want you to know that."

Taking her by the hand, Mariam uncovered the puncture wounds etched in Meg's wrist. Wounds that resembled snake bites but would require more than a scab in order to heal.

Mariam's voice was strong but quiet. "You have to put a stop to this. If you don't, you will not survive."

At Mariam's words, Fara suddenly took flight, whipping her wings and cawing as she flew around the room.

"Fara!" Isobel called and put out her arm for her to land. The magpie, however, landed in Meg's lap and pecked at Mariam's hand until she let go of Meg's arm.

Isobel had been preoccupied with thoughts of Catarine, Meg, and Mariam. They had a connection, a blood connection. But what about her? What about her mother? Were they also descendants of Catarine Delgado? Meg had made the comment more than once that Isobel felt like a sister, and Isobel remembered the pull she had to the girl the moment she first saw her. It wasn't possible for them to be sisters, as nearly three hundred years separated their birth, but perhaps they were family. It was the only possible explanation. If this were to be true, then her mother would have known and it would have been the reason why she had chosen Mariam to visit all those years ago.

There were still so many unanswered questions, and they left Isobel torn between leaving and staying. But Mariam was right; they had to go. Looking out the window, only a faint glow of sunlight remained above the horizon. Gavan would certainly have returned by now. Perhaps once she returned Meg back home safely, she could return to Mariam.

"Meg?" Tilting her head, Isobel gestured toward the door and stood.

On shaky legs, Meg stood, clutching the book to her chest with one hand and Fara with the other.

"Can you teach me what you taught Isobel's mother before

it's too late? I won't be afraid to use whatever you give me."

"You don't need me, Meg. Isobel knows the tincture to make." Mariam smiled. Reaching forward, she extended a finger and tapped it against the back cover of Catarine's book. "Everything else you need to know is told in here."

Chapter 25

"Meg!" Gavan shouted as he threw open the front door at Elden Castle and stepped inside. All he was greeted with was silence.

The stomping of his boots echoed in the empty, open space as he made his way across the foyer and toward his sister's room. Stopping mid-way, he reached for the banister of the main staircase, his long fingers wrapping around the hand-carved wooden railing.

Isobel.

Gavan took the steps two at a time. Landing on the platform, he drew his sword, and headed to the north tower. His legs bulged and flexed in reaction to his long, powerful stride as he ascended the winding staircase. Reaching the top, he lunged around the corner towards the single, circular room where Isobel had been staying only to find the door wide open and the room empty.

"Dammit!" He kicked the door and sent it crashing into the wall, the solid piece of oak cracking on impact.

"I shouldn't have left Meg here alone. I should have forced her to go with Elspeth and me." Shaking with fear and anger, Gavan replaced his sword into its scabbard and ran his hands through his hair.

"And that witch, that goddamn witch! As soon as I get ahold of Isobel, I will kill her with my bare hands!" His face flushed, and the vein that trailed along his forehead throbbed.

He searched the room—one hand returning to the hilt of his sword—but didn't find anything out of the ordinary. He made his way back down to the main floor and in the direction of the Great Hall.

The firebox was empty; not even embers glowed from its base. No one had been in this room for hours, perhaps not at all. Feeling confined and unable to sit, Gavan stepped outside and resumed his pacing. The sun, which was set high in the sky when he'd returned to Dunkinshire, had begun its descent behind the trees and toward the horizon, and the loss of daylight came much too quickly for Gavan's liking. He should not have spent so much time in the village when he first arrived, but he had done so to learn if anything had gone amiss while he'd been away. And he hadn't anticipated Meg to leave their home. She was out there somewhere, and more than likely with Isobel. He had no idea where to look and couldn't settle himself long enough to think.

He ran his hands through his hair and moved away from the castle, searching the stables, Kenneth's cottage, and the garden. All were empty, so he circled the castle once more before making his way up the path, his mind lost in thought. He was a skilled warrior. One who was more than keen against his enemies on the battlefield. But Meg wasn't his enemy, and where he stood now was at the entrance of their home, not on a battleground. More than anything, Gavan knew his youngest sister needed protection from herself, something she never seemed to understand.

The phrase *the devil's work* sounded in his head.

Gavan braced his legs and watched the sun slip from sight, leaving brilliant shades of orange, red, and purple streaking upwards in the sky. He couldn't wait any longer. Returning to the stables, he mounted Ahearn and raced out of the barn. It was then that two figures emerged from the woods, his sister's loose hair shimmering under the moonlight. He pulled back on the stallion's reins, and in a matter of seconds, he was at his sister's side, his heart slamming against his rib cage.

"Where have ya been!" he shouted, shaking Meg by the arms before embracing her.

The minutes before Isobel and Meg had stepped from the woods, Gavan had envisioned his youngest sister bound and beaten, with a noose around her neck, and a ring of fire spreading her way. It was a constant fear he experienced nearly every time she stepped outside the castle doors and wasn't where he or Kenneth could see her.

"Gavan, you're squeezing me too tight. Isobel and I went for a walk, and we lost track of time," Meg said as she fought to free herself from his grasp.

"Kenneth, is he with you?" Gavan shouted again.

Meg shook her head.

"I told you not to leave the castle when I am gone. And you—" Gavan released his sister and stepped towards Isobel, the toe of his boot touching the toe of her shoe, the brawn of his chest in her face.

"Was this your idea? To lure my sister away from her home? To keep her out past daylight?" Gavan looked down at the top of Isobel's head and spoke between clenched teeth, his anger seething and out of control. Without giving Isobel a chance to respond, he said, "I will make sure this never happens again. You're coming with me."

Wrapping his fingers around her upper arm, Gavan guided Isobel toward the castle and through its main door, Meg racing behind to catch up.

"Gavan, stop! You're out of your mind with anger. Let Isobel go; you're going to hurt her. I can explain," Meg pleaded with her brother, but he refused to break stride and continued forward, ignoring her cries that chased after him.

Winding their way around the main floor, past the kitchen and toward the back of the castle, Gavan swung open a single wooden door and, with Isobel's arm still in his grasp, led her into the darkness. After taking a few steps downward, they stopped. The space around Isobel was as black as night, so she listened as a door beside them slammed shut and the click of a lock sounded. Squeezing her arm, Gavan pushed her forward, and they resumed their descent. The dampness and musty odor that filled her nostrils and layered thickly across her tongue told her that they were moving underground.

Meg's pounding and her shouts for the locked door to be opened immediately could be heard clearly from the other side of the door, but as Gavan moved them further into the darkness, his sister's protests faded, and finally silenced altogether.

Reaching the bottom, a flame mounted to the wall lit the small, circular area, and as Isobel's eyes adjusted to the sudden gift of light she noticed a single, metal door standing open. The air was considerably colder, and Isobel shivered as she quickly glanced around—the door had a small window carved out near the top, but there were no other doors nor windows to be seen. Fara would be panicked that she couldn't get to Isobel tonight, and Isobel worried what the magpie might do.

"This will be your room for the remainder of your stay, which I promise isn't going to be long. You brought this on yourself, Isobel. I did warn you." Those were Gavan's final words before leading her into the small, dark room, slamming its door and locking her inside.

The faint light from the flame at the base of the stairwell leaked in through a small opening, and Isobel was just tall enough to look out. There was no fireplace and no other source of light visible either in or out of the room. After some time, her eyes adjusted to the darkness, and she made out her surroundings.

A few furs were strewn across a straw mattress on the

floor; they were the only comforts she would be having right now. It was a far cry from the room she had spent the last couple of weeks in, but at this moment she was grateful to still be alive. Taking Meg had been a mistake and one Isobel knew she couldn't undo. Gavan's statement was true; she had left him no choice.

Outside the door, Isobel heard the Highlander's shouts, forbidding Meg from entering not just Isobel's cell, but the crypt altogether.

"She is a witch and can't be trusted. If she is discovered here, the three of us will be persecuted, Meg. We will burn. What is it that you don't understand about that!" And then the door at the top of the stairs slammed shut.

~~~~~~~~~~

Isobel sat and wrapped the heaviest fur around her shoulders. Deep in her bones, she sensed that Gavan would have no regrets killing her. The way he dug his fingers into her arm as he dragged her into Elden Castle, pulled her down the dark stairwell, and shoved her into her cell had made it clear how angry he was.

She needed to leave, but she didn't have the strength to call the portal again. She placed her hands on her stomach while she listened for the tiny heartbeat to pulsate against her insides; Charlotte hadn't moved since they'd returned, but she was alive.

Isobel didn't know if either one could survive another trip through the portal so soon. She would take the risk for herself, but not her unborn daughter.

"I need a little rest, and then I can try," she whispered, her heavy eyelids drooping as she covered herself with the remaining furs and settled into the bed.

She had slept in the woods when she and Meg returned but only briefly as she had asked Meg to wake her after a short period of time. The sky had been almost dark when the portal deposited them in 1597, well past when they should have been back. Despite Isobel's extreme exhaustion, Mariam's explanation of her existence replayed itself in her head as did the echo of words: *You are safe with me,* and *it is all true, daughter.*

Her thoughts chased themselves round and round until Isobel thought her head would explode. Elspeth would return tomorrow. If Gavan still had her down here, surely his eldest sister would let her free. That was, if Meg doesn't beat her sister to it.

"Just a little more time. And perhaps a few more answers," Isobel whispered as her eyes finally closed and she fell in a deep slumber.

No sooner than she had drifted off, Isobel bolted upright. Gasping for breath, she looked around at the bare stone walls of her cell. She was still at Elden Castle, locked away in the dungeon. And alone. Isobel grabbed the leather waterskin that lay next to her, leaned back against the wall, and drank. The answer had come to her in a dream.

Isobel had been safe from harm the moment she had been conceived, the moment her father smelled his scent in her tiny, growing body. The moment he recognized that her blood was different. If he had fed from her even once while she was a child, he would have started the process of her body dying. If he had fed more than once, he likely would have killed her. Isobel was more like him—like her father—than her mother. Her magic existed for the pure sake of feeding her vampiric needs just as Mariam had said, and just as he had known.

Isobel assumed he kept that little secret to himself and had never told her mother. Instead, he allowed Bonni to remain afraid and vulnerable so that he could keep himself alive, keep himself strong, and keep himself near his daughter; a child he had biologically fathered, and one as close to a replica of himself as she could be.

A click sounded, and Isobel looked at the bright light that now filtered through the door as the mechanism in the lock disengaged. She had been so lost in her own thoughts that she hadn't heard anyone come down the stairs or approach her cell. She took a slow deep breath in and searched for Meg's magic, or Elspeth's kindness, hoping that either of the two were here to save her. Unfortunately, Isobel detected neither.

The door swung open, and its hinges creaked loudly against the hollow, tense silence around her. Flamed torches now framed the base of the stairwell and poured light around the bulky body that stood in the doorway. Isobel shielded her eyes from the sudden brightness.

"Get up!" Oversized shadows crept along the cell's walls as Gavan advanced, reached down, and pulled her upright. He squeezed her arm and pulled her into him, his grip much tighter and much angrier than before.

"Go!" he commanded.

His face remained hidden in the shadows, but the gruff tone of his voice let Isobel know that she had been anything but saved.

Chapter 26

Gavan and Isobel climbed the staircase with quick, hurried steps, his hard muscled, chest against her back, pressing her forward until they reached the main floor. Gavan gripped Isobel's elbow and steered her down the dark and silent corridors toward a side entrance that led them outdoors. Isobel recognized where they were at once. It was the same doorway she had seen Meg slip through the night she arrived. Isobel wondered about Meg's whereabouts tonight; was she asleep or had she fled for the woods, assuming that her brother would be guarding, non-stop, the door that led to the underground cell.

Gavan's hold tightened as they wove around the cobblestones and down the grassy hill. Isobel considered pulling away and fleeing. She had managed to stay one step ahead of a vampire, so she was certain she could escape the Highland warrior, but she remained weak from time hopping and lack of sleep, and she feared what might happen if she couldn't outrun him.

Disappearing into the dense forest, their dirt path was familiar until Gavan turned them towards the sound of the water; he was taking her to the cliff. Isobel opened her mouth, but Gavan spoke first.

"I knew you were a danger the moment I saw you." His voice was soft but filled with a loathing hatred, and had he not leaned forward and spat the words in her ear, Isobel would not have heard him. "I should have gone with my gut and thrown you over the cliff that first night."

Isobel slowed her steps. He would have to drag her to the edge if that was where he wanted her; she would not go willingly and allow him to harm her daughter. "I haven't hurt you or your family. I wanted to help Meg. If you could understand that and understand your sister, you might see things differently."

Gavan spun Isobel around so quickly that she lost her footing. He jerked her upright and brought them nose to nose, the silver chain from her neck wrapped tightly around his fingers. "I understand plenty."

Isobel didn't move for fear he would destroy the only tangible item she had left from her mother. Her body trembled, making her angry. This was not the time to appear weak and helpless. She drew in a breath, and a wave of magic warmed her insides, giving her the strength she needed to stand on her own.

"You think you are the first woman I have come across who practices witchcraft?"

"Your assumption just shows how little you know. I have never proclaimed to practice such of a thing!" Isobel boldly spat.

Gavan ignored her outburst and continued. "Or the first one I have seen put to death? From my doorway that night when you begged to come inside, I studied you, Isobel. Your clothes, the way you spoke, even your mannerisms as a female, were not right.

They are still not right." Gavan lifted the pentacle to where Isobel could see it.

"My sisters may have glossed over these differences, but I did not."

His sisters had saved her life. Isobel held her head high, ready to respond, but he twisted the chain and cut her words off. Her mind raced with what to do next as she listened to him speak. In the distance, she heard the frantic whipping of a magpie's wings.

Hurry, Fara.

"I have been in the company of many like you. Traveling through the Highlands, they live hidden deep in the mountains and throughout the deserted lochs. Most are desperate for safety, so they choose to live in solitude. They are flesh and blood women, and personally, I don't care what they claim to possess. But at home, I have my sisters to protect. An honor bestowed upon me by my father as he lay dying, his enemy's sword planted in his gut on the battlefield."

His warm breaths came out in rapid burst fanned across Isobel's face as he spoke. Layered in his plaid and cloak, he appeared much bigger than normal but, again, now was not the time to show any fear.

"I am sorry, Gavan. I didn't know." She looked into his eyes as she spoke.

Gavan released the delicate silver chain, and the pentacle

fell to her chest. Isobel exhaled, thankful he hadn't yanked it from her neck and tossed it in the woods.

He took a step back. "I was seventeen years old when I avenged my father's murder. Coming from behind, I swung my sword with every ounce of strength I had and took off the bastard's head. I sent it flying across the field and watched as his body collapsed, blood pouring from the gaping hole my sword left. Unfortunately, I was a little too late. He had already planted his sword through my father's gut, pinning him to the ground. After freeing my father of his enemy's weapon, I lay beside him and feigned my own death as warriors searched for survivors of their own and slay enemies who showed even the slightest sign of life. The thought to give my father a quick death and not risk being discovered alive came to me, but I just couldn't bring myself to do it. So, we lay like that, my hand over his until he took his last raspy breath and the gurgling sound of blood that choked in his throat was silenced."

Gavan's voice strained as he shared the grim details of his father's last moments of life. He took a step forward, the toe of his boots stepping on Isobel. She stepped back. Looking up, she saw the pain that stormed behind his cloudy blue eyes. Tears brimmed at the edges of her own, and she recalled the violent deaths of her mother and husband. She had not actually witnessed the acts as Gavan had, but she could imagine. She and Gavan shared an unrelenting amount of pain and anguish over the loss of family, but

Isobel doubted that he would see their situations as being alike.

"It was two days before I sensed it was safe to leave. I carried my father home, and my sisters and I buried him beside our mother under the Scots pines outside the castle wall."

Isobel thought of the pair of wooden crosses that protruded from the ground and then back to her family. She wondered if they were still lying on the kitchen floor as Isobel had last seen them. In her haste for safety, she hadn't thought of what would happen to their bodies if she wasn't there. It had been more than two weeks, and Isobel knew that death had more than already set in. Guilt washed over her, and she felt the immediate need to return to her own time and bury them properly. How could she have been so inattentive?

Gavan finished his story. "That was eight years ago. Meg was seven, and Elspeth was twelve."

Lost in thoughts of her family, Isobel hadn't noticed how Gavan had inched them out of the woods; her heels now stood only a few feet from the edge of the cliff.

For a moment, neither spoke. A look of vulnerability filled Gavan's eyes, his mind still lost to the past. Isobel touched his hand, a simple gesture of sympathy she thought to offer, but he jumped as though her fingers had burned him.

"Elspeth and Meg are all that is left of my family, and they will not be taken from me. Not by you nor anyone in the village." Gavan resumed his steps, leaving Isobel no other option than to move backwards.

They stopped at the ledge, and Isobel heard clearly the caws of her familiar.

"I would give you the opportunity to jump, but I fear you won't take it."

"Gavan, please. You don't have to do this. I can return home now and promise that you will never see me again. If you will just step aside and let me go." She hadn't regained enough strength to time travel, but she could run. All she needed was a place to hide and a little sleep. As she formed a plan, one she prayed Gavan would agree to, her blood began to tingle with awareness; Meg was here, in the woods, and Fara was with her.

Feeling bold, she tried to step aside, but Gavan reached for her wrists, braced his feet apart and lifted her arms. Isobel closed her eyes so they would not give his sister's arrival away and cause Gavan to react hastily. Sweat slickened her palms, and her magic soared, invisibly connecting her and Meg. The ghostly thread wrapped around her body and anchored her to Meg with such a force that Isobel feared it would split her in two.

"Gavan?" Meg's voice was gentle as she called out from behind him. "Please, bring Isobel off the cliff."

Meg strove not to startle her brother and cause him to complete his intended action of dropping Isobel into the turbulent seas below her. Their magic had them bound to one another, but Meg wasn't sure if it was enough to keep them both on land.

With Isobel still in his grasp, her brother whipped his head around at the sound of his sister's voice. "Meg! What are you doing here?"

A few feet behind him, barefoot and dressed only in her sleeping gown, Meg stood motionless. Fara gripped the branch above her, tilted her head and bore her black glossy eyes directly into Gavan.

"Brother, I need to explain what happened and clear this misunderstanding with Isobel. I should have told you a long time ago, but I didn't know how, and I was afraid. Isobel has been helping me, not putting me in danger. That I can assure you." Meg slowly put out a hand toward her brother.

"Why are you wearing only a smock? Where is your cloak? And your shoes? You are not decent, dressed like that."

"When I discovered you both were gone, I knew I didn't have time to dress."

"You are supposed to be in your room, not wandering around the castle!" Gavan's shouting had returned.

"I know." They were Meg's only words as she stared at her brother and stood her ground.

Gavan looked between the two women before lowering Isobel's arms and pulling her away from the edge of the mountain. Isobel's breath caught in her throat. Meg grabbed Isobel's hand, led her to a nearby tree stump and sat her down.

She stood in front of Isobel as if to shield her from Gavan

and her brother lifted a brow; her protective gesture did not go unnoticed. He opened his mouth to speak, but Meg beat him to it.

"You should sit too," she told him.

Chapter 27

Ignoring his sister's request to sit, Gavan stood, his stance defensive and alert like the warrior he was.

"This may not make sense to you right away, but please hear me out. Isobel has become more like a sister to me than a stranger," Meg said. "In the two days you were gone escorting Elspeth to our aunt's house, Isobel and I discovered we have so much—"

"Meg," he interrupted. "I know. I have always known, and so has Elspeth." Gavan remained in position, but the lines around his eyes and across his forehead softened.

Meg frowned.

"I know why you and—" he gave Isobel a sideways, dismissive glance, then looked back at Meg. "You are like our mother, and I don't mean just how she looked, but how she was. The things she was able to do without a logical explanation."

He knows? Meg wasn't sure what to say.

"It is why I don't like you out of my sight when you are outdoors and also why I have been at the forefront of the persecutions, Meg."

"What! Did you plan on killing me too?" Meg's tone teetered on the edge of hysteria and she stepped back, bumping into Isobel.

"For God's sake, Meg, no! I have been there to protect you. To lead suspicion away from you, and away from Elden Castle. If the villagers see me as a leader among the witch hunts, they will have no reason to suspect my family again." Or at least, that is what he had hoped.

Running his hands through his hair, Gavan sighed and told the true story of their mother, the one he had planned to keep secret from his youngest sister forever.

A ringing sounded in Meg's ears, and her surroundings swirled the longer he spoke; her mother hadn't died at childbirth; rather, she was ripped away from them when Meg was three years old. Meg felt Isobel's arms around her waist, guiding her down to the tree stump to sit beside her and Fara.

Her memories of their mother hadn't come from Elspeth's stories. They were her own.

"How could you—" Meg barely computed her brother's words, and she strained to keep up. Isobel squeezed her hand, but Meg was lost in the memory of her mother's touch and the connection she remembered the two had shared. Her brother and sister had dismissed her recollections, yet it had all been real.

Gavan's lips moved rapidly as he rushed to finish his story. "Elspeth and I never spoke of what happened because we wanted to protect you. We hoped you would never have to know the truth, but Meg, our mother was persecuted."

"What? Why?" Her words were no louder than a whisper.

"She was accused of placing a spell on another man's wife. But Elspeth, Father and I never believed it to be true. Father fought to have her released, but the villagers threatened to turn on you and Elspeth. Mother begged him to stop, to keep you both safe. She promised that everything was going to be fine. He refused to give up, though. When he went back into the village the next morning, he found her standing on the platform and a pyre built up around her. An official claimed that she had confessed during the night and asked to be put to death immediately."

Meg leaned into Isobel, and her stomach turned. "No!" Meg cried. "The pain and suffering she must have felt. Oh, Gavan—"

Her brother glanced toward the treetops, and his weight shifted. "Father was there, in the back of the crowd. He said once the wood was lit, it was difficult for him to watch, but he did so for our mother's sake. Mother never screamed or cried out, so it was believed that she died from the smoke before the flames got to her. But once the smoke was so thick that she couldn't be seen, he said the oddest thing happened."

Tears rolled down Meg's ghostly cheeks, but she had silenced her cries.

"A small black bird projected itself from the center of the flames, its wings beating frantically as it moved away from the village and into the hazy sky above. It must have been nesting somewhere in the sticks and was lucky to get out alive."

Isobel's heart pounded as she thought of the small black bird Gavan had described. She looked down at Fara, who now stood protectively between her and Meg. Inside the dark beady eyes that stared back at her, Isobel was pulled into the tiny blue flecks spinning in the magpie's iris' once again. She gasped and threw a hand over her mouth. Fara leaned forward and brushed her head against Meg, and at that very moment, everything about her familiar—why she had chosen Isobel all those years ago, why the portal redirected to 1597, and why she wouldn't let Isobel call on the portal to take them home that first night—made sense. Using her magic, Catarine had somehow changed herself into the magpie. Isobel trembled.

"Gavan, I want to know more about our mother before she was—" Meg said.

"Elspeth and I will tell you more when she returns home." The lines around his eyes suddenly deepened, and the energy between the three tensed.

Isobel turned away from her familiar, speechless and questioning what, if anything, she should do with her new-found insight. Of course, she would be talking to Fara as soon as they were alone, but Meg—what would she ever tell her? *Meg, it's possible, highly probable that your mother is still alive but shifted into the form of a bird.*

Meg squeezed Isobel's hand, and Isobel looked away from the magpie. She wondered if Meg was sure she was ready to divulge her secrets, and if Gavan was equally sure he wanted to hear them.

"There is another reason I was out in the woods tonight. It is true that I searched the castle to see where you were before I—well, I was supposed to meet someone here," Meg said softly as she looked up at her brother.

"Who?" he demanded. "Meg?" Gavan's brows hadn't lifted, nor had his head cocked with curiosity, but rather a scowl, one that Isobel imagined he wore during war, spread across his face.

"Gavan, he gives me no choice. I have to go to him. If I don't, I will die. We will all die, and it will be far worse than burning at the stake!"

"Him? A man? Who is this, Meg?" His voice thundered and sent an echo throughout the woods. "Did he harm you? I will kill him!" Outraged, Gavan reached for his sword. The idea that someone had defiled his sister turned his stomach and made his blood boil.

"It's not what you think." Meg stumbled over her words, unsure how to explain Cristian to her brother. Tears pooled in her eyes, again, and then suddenly she was in his arms.

Gavan removed his plaid, wrapped it around his sister, then tucked her back under his arm and stared at Isobel as if she were the one to blame. Of course, none of this was her fault, but she could give Gavan the explanation he was asking for. Feeling as though she had nothing to lose, Isobel stood and spoke for Meg.

"Gavan, if your mind is open enough to believe that forms of witchcraft exist, I believe you will understand the story I am going to tell you. There is an evil that is neither man nor witch that roams in the darkness while the world sleeps. Its mere existence is ancient and beautiful and designed to overpower and kill. They drain both humans and animals of their life and toss their bodies to the side, sometimes dismembering them in the process. I know you have seen what I speak of, so you will know that it is true. In human form, they roam the world in search of blood in order to keep themselves strong, but they are not human; they are vampires. I know you must have heard the legends, as they have been told for hundreds, if not thousands, of years. And Gavan, they are true."

Isobel stopped for a minute and studied the Highlander. He hadn't moved from his place, but Meg, who remained tucked under his arm, had turned to listen. Gavan's silence encouraged her to go on despite the pecking that Fara began to do along the back of her legs. Isobel swished her hand behind her, but the magpie refused to stop and started jabbing at her fingers.

"On rare occasions, a vampire comes across a person who has a special kind of blood, one that is only detected after it has been tasted. This blood feeds the vampire's mind and body like no other has done before, and for a period of time they feel as though they are alive again. But it is a false feeling, a delusion, you could call it. Desperate to continue the high, this blood magic fills them with they keep their victim alive, rather than kill them, and continue to feed. My mother had this kind of blood. And until the moment she died by the hands of a blood thirsty killer, she had fed another for years, giving him unrelenting physical strength and power. She became an obsession for him just as Meg has for the one that found her." Isobel stopped and let her words resonate with Gavan.

"Meg, what is she saying?" he asked as he rubbed the back of his neck.

Lifting her arm, Meg pulled back the plaid and linen sleeve of her gown and showed Gavan the circular marks etched in her wrist.

"Meg has a magical blood similar to my mother and perhaps her own mother. If she didn't, she would have been dead the first time he met her. Gavan, Meg is in grave danger; he will never leave her. She can't fight him off or hide from him. He has attached her scent to himself and can find her anywhere she goes."

"Over my dead body!" Gavan interrupted, and both women jumped.

"Yes, even over your dead body. Again, this is not a man. He is a monster, and one that cannot be fought and won against. He has to be killed. And I know how to do it." Isobel was going to say that was why she had taken Meg to see Mariam today but knew that if she admitted luring his sister anywhere away from Elden Castle, Gavan would finish what he had come here to do without a single hesitation.

"My mother had a tincture, a recipe, if you please, that will poison a vampire and render him dead within minutes. I believe that she failed to use it for reasons I'll never know because she is gone, but I can help Meg by making it and telling her how to administer it to him."

"Enough!" The single word sliced right through Isobel's explanation. "I knew you were behind this!" he shouted. He released Meg, shoving her behind him.

Leaning into the tree stump, Isobel braced herself. Behind her, Fara took flight, her wings grazing the side of Gavan's head before disappearing into the shadows next to Meg. With Gavan's back to her, Meg bent down and scooped up the magpie and held her to her chest.

Standing toe to toe with Isobel, Gavan bent over and said, "My sister is none of your concern. I will bludgeon this bloody bastard, tear him to pieces if I have to, but you, Isobel, will not interfere. Your intrusion and introduction to this man has caused my sister and my family enough pain." Then he turned on his heel. "Meg, we're going home. You and I will talk more of this in private. I want this man's name and where you are to meet him. He will have quite the surprise the next time he expects you to bend to his demands. As I will take off his head."

"Gavan, you are a fine warrior, but I must warn you. You cannot fight him off. He is too fast and strong and will detect you coming before you are ever in his sight. Believing in monsters is not the same as meeting them in the flesh. Please let me help. I can do this."

"Do you not ever know when to keep silent?" Grabbing Isobel's upper arm, Gavan pushed her towards the edge of the cliff.

Fara sprang from Meg's hands and screeched as she flew feverishly between the two. Letting go of one of Isobel's arms, Gavan swatted at the magpie, but she had already landed out of reach, though ready to interfere again if needed.

"I promise you, if I fail, you can throw me over the ledge to my death," Isobel said.

"No. " Meg moved between Isobel and the rocky edge, her wide blue eyes demanding Gavan to stop. "If she goes, I go too, brother, "

For a moment, the three stood in a standoff with the fate of Isobel's life once again sandwiched in the middle of her hunter and her protector.

Moments passed as brother and sister stared one another down. They were equally stubborn, but since the loss of their parents, Gavan had more of a soft heart toward his sisters than he ever thought was possible. They were his responsibility, and he was their only protector, but more often than he liked, he found himself compromising against his better judgment.

Running his hands through his hair, Gavan pulled his eyes away from Meg and toward Isobel. "I will say this one last time.

My family is not your concern. You will not help with anything, and you will not speak unless I allow it. That is the only way you will walk away from this cliff tonight, Isobel. Is that understood?"

Isobel nodded.

"Let's go." And he motioned to the other side of the woods from where they stood.

The two women flanked Gavan on either side and made their way back to the castle. They traveled in silence; not even their breaths made a sound as they wound their way around to the large cathedral doors at the entrance, Fara flying overhead, lost in the darkness of the nighttime sky. Dismissing Meg to the Great Hall to wait for his return, Gavan escorted Isobel in the direction of the basement again.

"Brother, please. Let Isobel sleep in the tower. She is with child and exhausted. She needs a fire to keep her warm and a soft bed to sleep on. She will need her strength if she is to ride away from here tomorrow. You can lock her in there; I'm sure she would understand it was as much for her safety as mine; right, Isobel?"

Isobel wanted to be strong and defiant and hold her own against Gavan, but she knew this was one fight she would not win. If he locked her in the basement, she would be separated from Fara and unable to prepare the herbs needed to kill Meg's vampire. She had to agree, to be obedient, one last time, if for no other reason than to save Gavan's sister. After that, she would leave Elden Castle without another incident and return to her own time.

Remembering his command of her silence, Isobel again nodded.

"Oh, and brother, if you take her back to her room, I won't go near her door. I give you my word."

Looking at the lass he had held in his fist, Gavan saw the dark circles that had formed under her eyes. Her belly looked larger, yet she had no trouble moving or keeping at his pace. And her flesh that he held in his grip was lean and hard with muscle, not soft like most women. Isobel's peculiarity bothered him more than he wanted to admit. She would remain locked up until Elspeth's return, and then, regardless of anyone's pleas or excuses or threats, he would see to it that she was gone, one way or another.

Gavan circled Isobel around and followed her to the main staircase. He had forgotten about the splintered door, but as he moved it on its hinges, he determined that it would be secure for one more night. A pile of logs sat on the hearth, and he presumed she knew how to light them.

Isobel sat on the edge of the bed, her body heavy with exhaustion, but her eyes opened and locked on him. She would not speak as he requested, but she would not cower in fear.

Gavan moved toward the door but turned once he got to the threshold.

"Again, I am most certain you put these wild ideas in my sister's head. Or if they do exist, you introduced them to her.

Elspeth will return with the mid-wife tomorrow, and after she has examined you, I will ask her to take you away. Far from Elden Castle and Dunkinshire, and Isobel, you are never to return. If you do—" Gavan's chest rose as he filled his lungs with air.

Releasing the lever on the door, he removed his sword and walked toward her.

"If you do, I will have your head. Do you understand?" he asked, standing in front of her.

And again, honoring his request to remain silent, Isobel nodded.

Chapter 28

Thankful not to be secluded underground and in the cold dark cell tonight, Isobel moved to the window and opened the shutters so Fara could come inside.

"I was so worried I wouldn't be able to see you tonight," Isobel said.

The magpie flew past and landed on the back of the chair beside the hearth on the other side of the room. Her claws wrapped around the top wooden spindle, and she tilted her head. It wasn't like Fara to keep her distance.

A second wind of energy filled Isobel unlike ever before. "Thank you for trying to dissuade Gavan from throwing me to my death," Isobel said. "I know all of this must be very hard, considering—" Isobel's words faded as she moved toward her familiar, finally taking a seat in the chair Fara clung to.

Again, Isobel replayed Gavan's story regarding his mother's execution and the frightened bird that had shot out of the flames just before the pyre was completely engulfed. Squinting, she searched for the blue flecks in her familiar's black glossy eyes that she remembered seeing in the portal, but she found none. Fara hopped into her lap and brushed her head against one of Isobel's open palms, and the energy that had mysteriously filled her minutes ago vanished.

Mariam's warning about overextending herself rang loudly in Isobel's ears as she began to relax, but there was one more thing she had to do before she could let her body collapse.

She scooped Fara up from her lap and returned her to the back of the chair. "I have a mission for you tonight."

Isobel retrieved the small wooden bowl Elspeth had given her from the kitchen a few days before and showed the magpie the purple flower that was dried inside.

"I doubt I will be free of this room until Elspeth and the mid-wife return, so I need you to bring me some more of these. Stay close to the castle so that I can instruct Meg that she won't have to go far to find more. I am going to light the fire so the room will be warm, but I will leave the shutters cracked for you to return and come inside." Fara stilled and studied Isobel.

"I will be fine, I promise," she said, assuming that Fara's concern was about leaving her alone. "I am going straight to bed. We will need our rest for tomorrow. We need to help Meg, I am convinced now more than ever that this is why the portal brought me here. If Elspeth returns as expected, we will be leaving Elden Castle sometime tomorrow. Now hurry."

Taking flight, Isobel watched as her familiar disappeared through the open window. Pushing the shutters together, she left an opening wide enough for the magpie to hop through when she returned.

But Fara had no intentions of returning with the deadly

herb Isobel had requested. She had great disdain for Cristian's behavior toward Meg, but a greater threat had just returned to the Highlands, and she needed to know why Dario was back.

Isobel's eyes, heavy with the need for sleep, looked into the day old basin of water on the table. Immersing her hands, she splashed the cold water on her face. She peeled the red woolen gown from her body and let it drop to the floor.

"I'll pick it up in the morning," she mumbled and left the dress in a pile where it fell as she slipped the clean linen smock Elspeth had left folded for her over her head.

Moving to the firebox, she stacked several logs inside, and with one of the candles Gavan had lit before he left, she started a small fire. She hoped it would be enough to warm the room.

Burying herself beneath the layer of furs, Isobel stretched the tightness in her legs and back that she hadn't realized were there. Charlotte shifted in unison, and soon they both settled, sleep pulling them under.

A slight breeze blew through the room and slipped underneath Isobel's door. The whistling sound as the air raced through the splintered wood caused by Gavan's ill temper yesterday alerted him that the window inside was open. He leaned back and debated whether he should go inside or let the witch freeze to death. It was unlikely that she had escaped through the window, seeing that the room was at the top of the tower, but if she had somehow found a way and he no longer needed to plant himself outside her door, that wouldn't be so bad. Returning to his room and stretching out in his oversized bed certainly sounded more comfortable than the cold, hard slab he was currently sitting on.

However, Isobel's explanation in the woods tonight still lingered in his mind. A tale she had spun he wanted to believe without a doubt, but there was a small part of him that couldn't completely dismiss the idea of such a violent being out there on the loose. After all, he had seen the aftermath of two separate attacks—human bodies destroyed like he had never witnessed before. A true vampire, he doubted, but perhaps a madman.

Another whistle of wind blew past his ear, and the sudden awareness that someone or something could be on the other side startled him, and he stood. Slipping the key inside the small hole, he turned it and pushed open the door. The room was dark, and it took his eyes a minute to adjust. Then, as he suspected, the plaid tapestry in front of the window swayed back and forth as cold air filtered in, chilling the room. Staring at the bed, he saw a lump underneath the covers, and the long dark hair that spilled out from underneath the edge.

Isobel hadn't escaped.

He searched the tiny room but found nothing out of place. After latching the shutters, he hung the plaid tapestry in place and moved to the hearth to refill the firebox with logs. Quickly, the flames blazed with heat and cast a faint glow around the room.

Turning away from the hearth, he noticed the single stem of blue flowers on the small table beside him. Picking up the wooden bowl, he tossed the contents into the fire and watched until the blossoms turned to ash. He knew all about magical potions and spells that claimed to alter the moods or thoughts of an individual, and he was damned if it was going to happen under his roof. Looking back, he stared at the bed once more. Isobel hadn't moved. Satisfied that no one had breached the castle, yet also disappointed that he wouldn't be returning to his room for the night, Gavan stepped back into the hall and quietly closed the door behind him, the mechanism clicking as the key turned again, this time locking the door in place.

~~~~~~~~~~

Cast by the flame mounted in the hall outside of Isobel's room, Meg studied Gavan's shadow. It sat distorted and unmoving against the corridor wall; her brother was alert and on guard for the night.

In stocking feet, she quickly descended the stairs to the main hall and toward one of the castle's side doors. She would be gone long enough to gather a handful of the flowers that grew near her parents' graves, and then she would return; Gavan would never know she had been gone.

Stepping outside, a feeling of awareness formed in Meg's

gut, and a chill trickled down her spine. She shivered at the physical reminder that she hadn't met Cristian earlier tonight as expected.

She slipped on the shoes she had tucked safely under her arm and muttered, "Surely, this one time he will forgive me." Technically, it would be the second time she would need Cristian's pardon. "He says he can't live without me, so he can't really kill me."

From the shadows of the castle, Meg stared into the darkness and wondered if he was out there. Waiting for her. Watching, ready to appear like he always did. Her heart thundered at the idea, and she braced herself. But no vampire. The air surrounding her remained quiet, so she stepped away from the castle, slowly at first, then more quickly as the light from the moon and stars above guided her downhill.

Sprinting toward the small, flowery field, Meg caught sight of Fara's tail feathers as she came out of the window at the top of the north tower. The magpie soared high and circled the castle once before turning and heading east. Meg watched the white breasted magpie until she disappeared from sight. As much as she had gotten used to Fara being around, she was thankful the magpie hadn't noticed her. She needed to be quick and didn't want any distractions.

Slipping off her gloves, she stowed them in the pouch underneath her cape. It was too cold outdoors for bare hands, but she wanted to be gentle with the stems as she plucked the flowers from the ground.

A handful or two should be plenty, Mariam had told them before they left as she reminded Isobel of the tincture. Meg wasn't sure they would need the herb right away, but she wanted to be prepared. And with Gavan occupied outside Isobel's door, she had to be the one to collect them. A gusty breeze blew past, and the light of the moon dimmed slightly before returning to its glow. Meg looked up. The thin layer of clouds seemed to appear from nowhere, and a warning settled in Meg's gut; she needed to hurry.

Bending forward, her fingers brushed across the tops of the tall grasses for the tiny purple flowers. As she plucked their stems from the ground, a jolt of something silent and unseen slammed her to the ground, knocking the air from her lungs and leaving the flowers beneath her crushed. The weight that held her in place was hard, heavy, and icy cold, but it was the voice that emerged out of the darkness, against the tender flesh of her ear lobe, that kept her frozen in place.

"Meg?"

Chapter 29

Meg tensed at the sting of Cristian's hiss against her ear drum as his body pressed her deeper into the ground, forcing out what little air was left in her lungs.

"You should ask the barmaid what happens when I lose my control." Although his tone was harsh, he smiled, his brilliant white razor sharp canines bared like weapons behind her back. "Oh wait, you can't!" He threw his head back and laughed.

Meg had assumed he was responsible for the young girl's death—*bite marks, dozens of them, and not one trace of blood to be found*, she had overheard Gavan tell Kenneth. Her brother had spoken of other crimes the girl's attacker had taken liberty with, but Meg forced herself not to think of them, even though her blood was all he had ever taken from her.

"Of course, the girl was no match, but oh, how I enjoyed playing the game all the way to the blissful end." Cristian sighed and flipped Meg over to face him.

Above, a beam of moonlight escaped between the drifting clouds and illuminated the ground where they lay. Meg gasped. Cristian was strikingly handsome but not in the way of the gentlemen who paraded in court with their possessions and influence. No, Cristian's beauty of paleness and sharp defined angles was unmistakably dangerous. Evil. A beautiful nightmare that would forever linger in Meg's mind.

Carefully, he wrapped a hand around her neck and pulled her to him, wisps of his hair brushing against her lips as he bent forward. Her pulse tapped against his fingers, and for a moment he got lost to the tempo before finally resting his lips below her chin.

Meg stared overhead, and watched as the clouds thickened, enveloping the moon until the last splinters of light were snuffed out and darkness blanketed the ground. Bright flecks danced in her vision, and she blinked, hurrying her eyes to overcome their sudden blindness. The sharp angle of his chin pressed into the base of her throat, nearly cutting off her air supply; she turned her head to the side.

"Are you angry with me? Is that why you didn't come tonight? I know you wouldn't purposefully defy me. Again," he said, slowly enunciating the word *again*.

With her cheek now pressed to the ground, Meg drew in a breath, her lungs aching for more as Cristian's body got heavier. The crushed bed of heather that cradled her head filled her nostrils, and with each shallow breath, their leaves brushed back and forth against her lips and nose.

"Meg, you are much too quiet this evening," he said as he shifted his weight. "Have you no explanation as to why you kept me waiting? And why I had to come looking for you at Elden Castle?"

His voice sounded kinder now, but Meg knew better than to

assume that he had forgiven her, and she sensed that he was smiling although she couldn't see his face.

"I—I was with my family. I wasn't able to come." Breathing felt impossible. If only she had gathered the flowers before he had attacked. She could have quickly ingested them and ended Cristian's life at this very moment.

Without any warning, Cristian grabbed the front of her cloak and in a single movement was on his feet and taking her with him. The whites of his eyes glowed, but what stood more alarming were the red iris' that had transformed within them. Cristian held them nose to nose, Meg's feet dangling above the ground; she was unsure what had startled him.

Letting go of her cape that was bunched within his fists, Cristian thrust Meg back onto the flowers they had just lain upon. He stood over her, wild eyed and glaring, his lips parted and his smile turning savage. Perhaps this time he would kill her as he had threatened before.

A sob welled inside Meg so large that she feared her lungs would burst. She swallowed to keep it from releasing. She couldn't make a sound; she was too close to the castle—Gavan would hear and know that the cry belonged to her, and that would mean death for them all. Gavan believed he could protect his family against Cristian, but he had no understanding of the monster that loomed over her, nor his capabilities.

"Cristian?" She hiccupped before he pounced, pinning her

to the ground once again.

"Where is she!" he said between clenched teeth.

"Who?" Meg asked softly, as if she had no understanding of what Cristian had detected: Isobel's scent.

And as Meg first predicted, when she sought to remove Isobel from Elden Castle and lure her into the vampire's hands, her scent was driving him into a frenzy. She was a fool for not bathing before she had left her room tonight; the thought never crossed her mind.

"I-I'm sorry; I don't know what you're talking about," she lied.

Cristian straddled her middle and pinned her arms above her head. Again, they faced one another so close that the tips of their noses touched.

"Do you think I'm daft? I can smell her powers. And my darling, they are even more alluring than yours." Leaning forward, Cristian inhaled long and deep against the nape of Meg's neck. It was where Isobel fingers had combed through the bound plaits, loosening the curls before they emerged from the woods after visiting Mariam.

"You smell like honeysuckle, my love," he said as he nuzzled her neck. "But today I smell—" Cristian hesitated for a moment.

"Lavender." He exhaled against her flesh. "And an

otherworldly scent that is dark and different yet familiar."

Cristian buried his face into her hair and drew in long, deep gulps of air. Meg wondered if he was hoping to quench his dying thirst with Isobel's sweet, sharp smell.

He won't be satisfied until—Meg silenced her own thoughts.

Her dream the night before Isobel stood on their doorstep, banging to be let in, had warned her that this would happen. Isobel and Cristian's paths would cross. Meg had been startled awake that night, her dream left interrupted; she hadn't seen how it would end.

She knew that filling his lungs with Isobel's scent wouldn't be enough to satisfy the vampire's dark and empty soul. He would need to taste her blood, absorb the powers that flowed through her veins and gave her exceptional life. Meg braced herself against his steady, fluid movements of inhaling and exhaling, and waited for his own self-awareness to evolve.

Silently, he moved away from the flesh of her neck and pulled her arm to his mouth. Sinking his teeth below the translucent skin of her wrist, Cristian locked his eyes with Meg and nursed against her vein. The pain which Meg had come to endure came in long, determined surges, and she wondered if he was searching for Isobel's taste, as if he could draw it from Meg somehow.

"Please stop. You are right," she said before losing consciousness. She didn't have the time or need for this tonight.

Cristian ripped her arm from his mouth and let it drop to the ground.

"You will bring her to me!" he demanded.

Interlocking his fingers through her hair, Cristian lifted Meg's head off the ground and gave her no choice but to meet his hungry stare. Blood stained his lips, and his iron scented breath blew against her face as he spoke, his words slow and deliberate.

"Tomorrow night, you will meet me at the abbey. If you don't come, if you don't bring her with you, I will find you both. And my darling, I will find you."

Cristian pressed his cold, hard lips to her ear and then vanished, letting her head fall back into the pillow of crushed flowers and grasses beneath her. The clouds thinned, and under the broken moonlight, Meg lay wide-eyed and trembling. No sound surrounded her; only the whisper of his final words echoed in her ears.

I won't be denied!

Chapter 30

Cristian raced across the darkness, hurdling fallen trees and the overgrown shrubbery that grew thick along the mountainside and blocked his way. He held his breath in an effort to keep the lavender scent alive that filled his nostrils.

He wanted to go back, break into the castle and find this mysterious witch for himself. He could capture her and eliminate the Highlander, who he expected guarded her door, within seconds. No one could stop him, and even better, no one would ever know. And then Meg and her guest would be alone and unprotected.

"I will hide them deep into the upper most part of Scotland or perhaps even further north in the Shetlands," Cristian said aloud, giddy over this new idea that formed as he fled. "They will be mine and safe from danger and the watchful eyes of the villagers." His heart, warmed by Meg's blood and magic, thumped with excitement.

No! an inner voice called out, and the abrupt jolt in his chest forced him to stop.

The scent he so desperately clung to was mesmerizing and more powerful than Meg's, but this stranger wasn't for him to devour, he suddenly realized as an odd sense of realization washed over him. He was drawn to her by instinct but not in the way of feeding. Rather, an inexplicable pull to protect, to cherish and keep her safe filled him—human feelings. The unspoken message that silently spoke from deep inside was clear and explicit; Cristian was to never lay his hands on this witch. Had he paused for just a moment instead of attacking Meg and then fleeing, this revelation might have hit him sooner.

Under the now cloudless sky and silver wedge of moonlight, Cristian moved out into the open basin between the mountains on either side of him. He inhaled deeply, and thoughts of his family emerged. He had not absorbed enough of Meg's blood to see them clearly or hear them speak, but faint, ghost-like images of his parents and brother stood whipping in the wind in the distance.

Cristian's heart thumped a large and painful beat again, and he fell to his knees. His emotions soared high in reaction and then plummeted in a downward spiral, sending blood stained tears streaking down his cheeks. He threw his head back and gasped unnecessarily for air as the pressure of what felt like strong arms, even stronger than his own, gathered around and held him protective as they lifted him to his feet. They were the arms of his father.

"Catarine!" Cristian bellowed.

The grip around him dissolved and his one true love's image formed in his mind and then exploded into thousands of tiny pieces. His cry that followed was angry, and it deafened him as it echoed through the valley. A breeze of honeysuckle blew past him and infused with the lavender scent he clung to, the smell bewitching him. His eyes rolled into the back and a slow smile spread across his face. He rocked back and forth on his heels, and he sank to the ground once again. If he had a pulse, it would have hammered through his veins, but instead a single thud struck against his ribs.

It had been sixteen years since he had last seen Catarine in the flesh. That day, against his better judgement, Cristian found himself drifting through Dunkinshire. It had been decades since he'd last visited the small town, and he came to a halt when he heard Catarine's name mentioned amongst a group of women. One of them turned his way, and he gave her a dazzling smile that made her swoon, then turned in the direction of Elden Castle, where they whispered she now lived.

She had been standing beside the stable, her hair down and blowing in the breeze and hands full of freshly picked herbs when she finally saw him at the edge of the trees. It had only taken them seconds to rekindle the passion that Cristian had feared was impossible after he became an immortal. That afternoon in the stable, it was as if more than one hundred fifty years and a change in his humanity hadn't passed between them. Their reunion was more than he could have ever asked for—until she confessed her marriage to another.

Betrayal had torn through him. Fearful of what he might do, he'd looked at her one last time, savoring every inch, and then fled without speaking another word. Five years later, when he learned of her fate at the stake, the news crushed the last bit of faith he had of them ever being together again.

    A tendril of smoke from far in the distance threatened to snuff out the lavender and honeysuckle scents that he was lost in, and Cristian snapped back to the present. Except for her mystical image when he filled himself with Meg's blood, Catarine was gone, and there was nothing he could do about it now. He reached into the pouch at his waist and pulled out a chain. Grasping the band that dangled from the bottom, Cristian lifted it to his face. A single blood-stained tear escaped over his cheek. More than a century ago, he had given the ring to Catarine and asked her to marry him. Tonight, when Meg fell to the ground and the ring landed in the grass beside her, he couldn't believe his eyes. He'd snatched it up and clasped in his hand, bewildered that it still existed. Catarine had kept it. Anger and loneliness overcame him, and his surroundings began to spin. He took a step forward and then another and another until he was racing at a speed far too fast for the naked eye to see toward his past; his human life.

    Throughout the first few years of becoming a vampire, Cristian had watched his family from afar. He feared getting too close; he didn't trust himself. They, too, would have been afraid, aware that he was different; he had changed just enough. He could explain his disappearance, and they would be grateful for his return. But he wouldn't have been able to give them any reasonable explanation as to the cause of his skin being so pale and so cold, and why his words and personality were now often clipped and reserved. It was better that they believed he was gone, even dead, despite the distant and saddened look that was permanently set behind his mother's eyes the remainder of her life. After all, it was a version of the truth; gone was the son and brother they once knew and loved.

Throughout their lives, Cristian had watched over them and made sure they remained safe, and on the night his mother's heart stopped beating, he wept silently as he leaned against their family house. It was as close to his family as he dared to be. His brother, Drew, had sat at her bedside, holding her frail hand until she took her last breath and her eyes closed, never to open them again.

Drew buried her next to their father and staked two rudimentary grave markers in the ground, marking their location. Cristian was thankful they weren't crosses as he would have hated to desecrate the ground where his parents lay in peace, but what other choice would he have had? Long gone were the markers and the single room stone cottage with slit windows and earthen floors in Burna where they had lived as a family, but Cristian never forgot. Moving in the direction of the small town north of Loch Lomond where he grew up, Cristian sucked in another breath, hoping to catch another glimpse of their images, but the flowery, lavender scent and Meg's blood was dissipating and barely detectable. Panicked, he inhaled again and again as his desire to be near his family intensified just as the first light of the morning sun rose along the horizon and unveiled the darkness of the overnight sky.

However, Cristian didn't need the illumination to see the movement that paralleled his own at the other end of the glen; he smelled them. Their horses galloped freely, following the winding trail well north of where Cristian dug his heels into the ground and came to a stop. Dirt and grasses uprooted with his sudden cease of movement, and he stood behind the earthen mound, transfixed. Two lone riders; he recognized the female and her mare. Their quickened pace seemed purposeful, but not due to a warning. At least not yet.

Forgetting about Burna, Cristian shoved the ring back into his pouch; he moved out of the emerging daylight and into the shadows of the trees, in the pair's direction. Miles separated them from one another. *But only for now*, he thought. He propelled himself faster, weaving in and out of the Scot Pines as a new plan unfolded in his mind and his animal instincts took control. Throwing his head back, he laughed, the sinister sound carrying past him by the north winds that raged against his face.

Cristian would return to Dunkinshire and collect what he rightfully believed belonged to him—Meg and the witch hiding in Elden Castle—and now he knew just how to do it without fear of being disobeyed again.

Chapter 31

From the window of her room, Meg watched Huxley, Elspeth's horse, gallop wildly across their land; her sister was not on his back. It took both Gavan and Kenneth to calm the gelding, grab hold of his reins, and lead the frightened animal into the stables. Rooted in place, Meg looked past Gavan, who now sprinted toward the castle, and combed the land as far as she could see; where was Elspeth? And her escort and the mid-wife? Surely, her sister hadn't ridden home without them. It wasn't safe for a woman to travel alone; Meg understood this more than anyone. Goosebumps rose along her arms, and she shivered at the thought of Elspeth out there unaccompanied. Then something far more terrifying flashed through her mind.

Cristian.

Panicking, Meg thought of their conversation last night as he pinned her to the ground and warned her that he wouldn't be denied. Had he somehow gotten to Elspeth?

Calm down, she told herself. It was Isobel who Cristian wanted, not Elspeth. But if that were true, why hadn't her sister returned? She stepped away from the window and began pacing from one end of the room to the other and back.

So much had happened since they were last together. Meg was desperate to see Isobel, to tell her all that had happened last night when she went to collect the flowers, but Gavan hadn't given her much opportunity as he rarely left her door, and when he did it wasn't for long. Her brother may be frustrated, even angry, over the chaos Isobel's arrival has caused, but Meg didn't worry about her brother harming Isobel. Instead, it was Isobel's safety from Cristian that concerned her. She had to find Kenneth or Gavan and find out what was going on.

Leaping down the stairwell, Meg took the stairs two at a time as she rushed to find her brother first. *Please let my sister be safe!* she prayed repeatedly all along her unladylike descent to the main floor.

Reaching the bottom, she turned the corner and ran into Gavan. His hard, muscled body didn't react to the collision of her slender frame, but to Meg it was as though she had hit a stone wall.

She gasped for breath as she fell backwards, but Gavan caught and pulled her to him.

"Meg!" he shouted.

She would have apologized, but there wasn't time.

"Where's Elspeth!" she cried as she held on tightly to his plaid. "I was watching through the window. I saw Huxley, but he was alone. And the mid-wife and their escort; did their horses return as well? I didn't see them. Gavan?"

"I don't know, but I'm leaving to find them now. Maybe they were watering the horses and Huxley got away and left them on foot."

Meg wanted to believe that was what happened. She searched her brother's face and sensed that he prayed for the same. Tears filled her eyes, and she released his plaid, but before she pulled completely away, Gavan grabbed her hands.

"Kenneth is preparing the horses and is going to ride with me. Meg, it is not safe to take you with us, but you are not to leave this castle while I am gone. Do you understand? Not one foot outside the door, any door, until I return."

Meg nodded.

She followed Gavan through the corridor and past the Great Hall, both of them stopping when they reached the main door. Turning around, Gavan took a step towards her, his brows pulled together and his lips set in a hard, flat line.

"Meg, you are not to go to Isobel. Do not go to her room; you are to avoid the north tower altogether. There is no one else who I can leave to guard her door, as I need Kenneth to travel with me. I don't have time to send for anyone else, but I won't be gone long. We are going to do a search along the border of our land. If nothing turns up, I will send Kenneth back, and I will gather some others from town to help with the search."

Meg nodded again. She wanted to keep her promise that she would obey, but she knew herself better. And by the look in her brother's eye as he braced his legs and crossed his arms, so did he.

"If you do not follow my orders, Meg, you will leave me no

choice other than to return you to England to live with our relatives as I did when you were a child."

Meg's jaw dropped as she gasped. She was shocked by Gavan's words but had no reason to doubt them. Only once had he made that threat, and he had made good on it then. She didn't want to be separated from her siblings again nor did she want to cause worry for her brother. This moment was about Elspeth and her safety, and the longer the two stood in the foyer and debated over her behavior, the greater the danger for Elspeth.

"Gavan, go and find our sister. And please hurry. I will be here when you return." She nodded and hugged him, then pushed him out the main door, locking it as he left.

~~~~~~~~~

Meg stood in the Great Hall, staring out the windows for some time after Gavan and Kenneth had disappeared from her sight. She knew that soon they would lose themselves in their thoughts as they raced across the moor and searched for the same woman that they so dearly, yet for completely different reasons, loved.

The sun rose from behind the mountain, and Meg wondered how long they would be gone. If they searched the entire perimeter of their land, it would be at least a few hours and then a little more time to return to the castle.

Moving into the kitchen, Meg grabbed a piece of bread and an apple from the large basket of fruit she had purchased when she and Isobel went to market. Pouring herself a small goblet of ale, she walked to the Great Hall and stood in front of the fire, wondering if Isobel was awake yet.

As she took a bite from the crisp red apple, the juice dripping down to her chin, she stilled. Had Gavan taken Isobel any food this morning? The sun had barely risen when Huxley broke through the trees and alerted them that Elspeth was missing. Gavan may not like or trust Isobel, but surely he wouldn't starve her. Setting her half eaten apple on the table, Meg returned to the kitchen.

"I'll just take her the tray and leave," she told herself after loading it up with bread, cheese, fruit, and a pitcher of cold water; it was the excuse she had been looking for. She had to tell Isobel all that had happened since last night. How the small patch of flowers she had gathered for them lay broken and lifeless in the field. How Cristian had appeared from nowhere and made the threat if she didn't bring Isobel to him. And the worst part of it all, how Elspeth hadn't returned home.

"He's watching me; I know it. But I can't do this alone," she mumbled, thinking of Cristian as she carried the tray stacked with food out of the kitchen. Her hands shook, and she whispered into the corridor, "Please, Elspeth, wherever you are, please be safe."

Turning toward the stairwell, she had just lifted her foot on the bottom step when a knock crashed against the main castle door. She jumped at the booming sound and bobbled the tray, nearly dropping it.

Who could that be?

Another knock hammered, rattling the iron latch that kept the door locked, but Meg stood frozen.

"Messenger!" a man called after a third, louder and more forceful, pounding flailed against the door.

Stepping down, Meg set the tray on the step, turned and faced the door. She didn't recognize the voice, but what if the man had news regarding Elspeth? Gavan had told her to stay inside, but this could be important. What if this messenger were holding Elspeth in his arms and waiting for someone to open the door so he could bring her inside?

Meg ran to the door and flung it open just as a large man, one she didn't recognize from the village, raised his fist to beat on it once again. He was dressed in plain, dirty clothing and wore no plaid or family crest that would distinguish who he belonged to.

"I have a message!" he yelled, spittle flying from his mouth. "Sorry, lass, I didn't mean to yell in ye face, but I have a message for a Meg." He wiped his mouth with the back of one hand, and then thrust a small folded piece of paper toward her. The paper she identified instantly.

Her heart slammed in her chest. "Th-th-thank you," she

stammered, and snatched the note from his hand. Closing the door, Meg slid the iron bar back in place and leaned into it heavily as if her weight was an added barrier of protection from the outside world.

She drew in a long breath and waited to see if the man would strike again. Her hands shook, and the perspiration from her palms dampened the paper she fearfully clung to. After a few minutes, when all remained silent, she slowly peeled open the edges of the paper and read the frightening words aloud.

Chapter 32

My Darling Meg,

If you want to see your sister alive again, you will meet me at Diarmad Abbey immediately. I will be in the sanctuary below the bell tower; I am sure you remember the place. And bring the witch.

Cristian

~~~~~~~~~

Tripping over the tray she had left on the bottom step, Meg raced toward the north tower.

"Isobel! I need your help!" Meg cried as she struggled to get Isobel's door unlocked.

"Meg, what is it? What has happened?" Isobel listened to the lever rattle under Meg's rough touch.

"I can't get the key to turn. It's stuck."

"Meg, calm down."

The spring unlocked, and the door swung open. Meg fell into the room, her hand clinging to the handle. Isobel jumped aside to avoid being hit as the door crashed into the wall behind it. *Crack!* The already splintered wood split again on impact and now hung lopsided off its hinge.

"There was a messenger. He came right after Gavan left. Isobel, you have to help me; we need to hurry." Meg grabbed at Isobel's hands and pulled her over the threshold and into the hall.

"Meg, what is going on? Where do we need to go? And where is Gavan?"

"It's Elspeth. He has her. And if I don't come right away, he will kill her."

"Who is going to kill Elspeth? Who told you this?" Isobel asked, pulling from Meg's grasp. Retreating to the side of her bed, she slipped on the shoes that Elspeth had loaned her almost three weeks ago. Meg grabbed Isobel's cloak that hung over the chair.

"It was a messenger. I haven't seen him before; I don't think he is from here. He kept banging on the door and I thought he might have Elspeth with him, so I answered it and he handed me this paper." Meg held the crumpled message for Isobel to read. "Cristian has her; that is why she didn't return this morning."

Isobel quickly scanned the crumpled paper. "Bring the witch?" she questioned, lifting her brow.

"I couldn't tell you because Gavan sat at your door, but last night I snuck out to gather some of the flowers near my parents' graves; the tiny purple ones that Mariam spoke about. Cristian was waiting for me, and he smelled your scent on my skin from when you unplaited my hair. Oh Isobel, I am so sorry, but we have to save Elspeth. She is innocent in this, and I'll never forgive myself if he harms her."

Isobel trembled. *She* was the witch the vampire had requested. Mariam had warned her of this if she stayed too close to danger. A queasiness churned in her gut, but as she watched Meg unraveling with panic, she knew she had to stay strong.

"Isobel, I've lost my mother's ring. I had it in my pouch last night, but after Cristian left, I reached inside and it was gone. It must have fallen out when he pushed me to the ground. I searched through the grasses, but it was so dark."

Isobel saw the sorrow behind Meg's eyes that now brimmed with tears. "Oh Meg, I am so sorry," she said, grabbing the girl's hands. "When we return, I will help you search. It couldn't have gone far, and with both of us looking, I am certain we will find it." Isobel wiped away Meg's tears with the back of her hand.

"Aye, thank you," she said, nodding. "There is something else I want to tell you, Isobel." Her shoulders dropped as she spoke. "The night before you arrived at Elden Castle, I dreamt of you. Of both you and Cristian. I know that sounds impossible, given you and I had never met, but the two of you were running at one another, and I was in the middle. I sensed that you would collide, but what struck me odd was that you were both more alike than different; the way you moved and how you smelled. I didn't understand how that could be. In my dream, I saw that three hundred years separated your lives. I thought I knew why Cristian was coming for me, why he always comes for me, but I had no idea who you were or how you fit in. Now more than ever I wish I hadn't awakened early; I didn't get to see how the dream ended. There is more to our story, Isobel. I can feel it. Somehow the three of us tie in together, I just haven't figured out how."

Isobel stood silent. Her mind raced with the knowledge of Meg's dream combined with her own previous thoughts of her connection to Meg. She had never linked Cristian to them. She didn't have magical blood for him to feed from; she wasn't like her mother, or Meg, or even Catarine. Her tie with a vampire was different; she had been fathered by one, but that was it. If what Meg was saying was true, and they killed Cristian, they may never know if they are somehow linked to one another. But then again, Meg's belief that they were connected was based on a dream. Nothing concrete, no facts; after all, how could there be? Until now, they had lived their lives three hundred years apart. The more Isobel thought about it, the more the idea sounded implausible.

"Isobel, the flowers! I gathered them, but they got crushed, and I wasn't able to bring any back. But I know where some others grow close by. If we hurry, we can pick them on our way."

Isobel had been so engrossed in her thoughts that it took her a moment to bring herself back to the present.

"Yes, we will go collect the flowers, but first I need your help," she finally answered. It was then that Isobel noticed the shutters had been closed and the brace across them latched. Someone had entered her room last night while she was sleeping.

Gavan.

"Fara!" Isobel cried out, looking frantically around the room, but the magpie was nowhere in sight. She must have gotten locked out.

The women retreated down the staircase, their energy infused with a feeling of renewed purpose. Following Isobel into the kitchen, Meg watched as she grabbed a goblet and knife from the mantle.

"He wants my blood. I need to fill this cup, and we need to carry it with us. Hopefully, it will be enough and he will return Elspeth and leave us all alone. We can finish the rest of the concoction after we gather the herbs. You do know where were the abbey is?"

Mesmerized by the sound of Isobel sharpening the knife against the smooth stone that Elspeth kept on the shelf, Meg nodded. "That's a large goblet, Isobel; what are we filling it with?" she asked, knowing full well that the answer was blood, but hoping that she was wrong.

"My blood, Meg. If we don't have enough for him to drink, it won't work, and he will come looking for me. If that happens, Meg, I fear the worst for all of us."

Wasting no more time, Isobel slid the tip of the blade across the tenderness inside her elbow. Blood poured from the wound and into the pewter cup below it. Meg turned away so as not to get sick.

"Meg, help me wrap my arm."

Isobel held pressure to the cut while Meg wound a white cotton bandage around it. Keeping her eyes on Isobel's and not the red stain that soaked through the bandage, Meg layered the strip of muslin around and around.

"Tighter, please," Isobel instructed. "We need enough pressure to force the bleeding to stop."

Meg wrapped a couple more layers until the gash no longer bled through.

"Yes, that is good. Now tie it in place and let's go."

They covered the goblet and stepped outside the kitchen door. Looking around, Isobel called out to her familiar again, and again no response.

"This isn't like her," Isobel said, pulling her brows together.

"Isobel, please. We have to get to Elspeth before Cristian does something terrible. I am sure Fara will catch up to us. Come on. I know where another patch of the flowers grows, just off the edge of the road ahead." Meg grabbed Isobel's hand and led her in that direction.

The two gathered a cluster of the flowers that grew just where Meg had said and crumbled them into the cup of Isobel's blood before continuing to the abbey. For fear of spilling its contents, they had to walk a bit slower than Meg would have liked.

"I am assuming that the abbey is abandoned?" Isobel asked,

still searching the skies for the magpie.

"Yes."

"An abbey is a strange place for a vampire to seek refuge, don't you think?"

"Yes." Meg sighed. "It is one of the many odd things Cristian relishes in."

She thought to share the night he had found her there with the others, but then decided against it. It was a memory that went to great lengths to haunt her without even speaking of it. Instead, she looked up and changed the subject.

"I wished I had a familiar," she said, combing the skies with Isobel. "Maybe I wouldn't feel so alone if I did."

Isobel remembered when she had first brought Fara home. Having a bird as a pet was certainly an oddity where she lived, and the townspeople hadn't been the least bit silent in letting that fact be known.

Meg pointed to the right. "This way." The two women veered north and walked against the wind. Isobel steadied the goblet in her hand and decided to share her story of Fara in hopes that it would help to calm their nerves and pass the time as they walked.

"It is true. Since I have had Fara, I haven't been alone. But many people were afraid of her and often avoided or criticized me for having a bird for a pet, they said it wasn't natural and many assumptions were made."

"What kind of assumptions?"

"Well, some are like they are now, even though the idea, or fear of witches no longer exists in my time. However, having a bird, or say a black cat, as a pet can cause alarm. Old superstitions and words like *familiar* were whispered. A familiar is believed to be the devil in disguise and the surest sign of a witch. No one called Fara a familiar, but she did cause some to suspect."

Curiosity sparked within Meg, but she stayed silent and allowed Isobel to tell her story.

"'Magpies don't come around here,' the elders of the small community would often say and then raise an eyebrow and glare at her. Of course, she followed me everywhere I went, refusing to be left behind. When I was much younger, I was often caught speaking to her. Because I was a child, it didn't come across as overly bizarre, but it was the cause of many stares as well as some question as to whether Fara understood what I said. As I became older, I learned to be more discreet, but discretion was not a strong suit for Fara." Isobel smiled.

"Oh," Meg said, surprised. "It is a good thing I didn't have a familiar as a child. She would have left me for all the trouble I got in."

"She does take great offense to insults and find ways to retaliate, like swooping, or fluttering her feathers and scaring people, or pecking at their garden when I'm not looking."

Stories of Fara eased some of the tension from the task

Meg and Isobel were on their way to perform. However, they both thought of little else. They climbed the last hill, and the ruins of the little abandoned abbey finally came into view. Centuries past its condemnation date, it looked both inviting and dreadful at the same time.

"There it is," Meg said. "Diarmad Abbey; it's where the messenger said Elspeth would be. Hand me the goblet, Isobel." Lunging toward Isobel, Meg took the filled cup from her hands. Thankfully, not a drop was spilled.

The closer they got, the faster Meg's pace became. *Diarmid Abbey;* the name was recognizable, and Isobel wondered where she had heard it. Her steps slowed, causing a great distance to grow between her and Meg as she sifted through her memory.

"Wait!" she called out as the story came to mind. But Meg walked faster as if the abbey were pulling her toward it.

Diarmid Abbey was once a sacred place. It was told that in the 1400s, a coven of witches who were said to practice black magic put a curse on the monks who lived there. Within hours, the monks fell dead, their corpses sacrificed and crudely buried in a semi-circle around the perimeter outside of the abbey. It was believed that Satan was the usurper who had commanded the attack; leading the witches there and forcing them to eliminate the heavenly body and replace it with hell. No wonder the vampire felt comfort there.

"Wait! Stop!" Isobel said, as she caught up to Meg.

Grabbing her by the arm, Isobel spun her around. Meg stared straight ahead; her mind was somewhere else. Isobel's grip tightened, and the sensation of magic that flowed between the two women stung her fingers, but she refused to let go. Meg blinked and pulled away from Isobel's grasp.

"I am worried about you going in there alone," Isobel said, as her hands covered Meg's around the goblet.

"I can do this, Isobel. Besides, if you enter, he will have no need to drink from this cup, and our plan will fail. If that happens, our lives—all three of us, and likely Gavan too—will be in jeopardy."

Isobel knew Meg was right, but regardless, she felt helpless. Meg's reaction to the closeness of Diarmic Abbey had alarmed her.

"Isobel, thank you. If it weren't for your knowledge, I would be chained to Cristian for as long as he let me live. And besides, you have your daughter to protect, and I am most certain Cristian has no concern over her. He is quite reactive and truly only thinks of himself. She would not survive an attack, Isobel."

She could not lose her daughter. Nodding, she sighed. "I am going to be in the shadows of the pines directly behind us."

Isobel looked back and pointed, but when she turned around, Meg had already made her way up the embankment and stood at what once served as the entrance to the monastery.

Moving downhill, Isobel hid underneath the branches as

she said she would and waited for any indication that signaled trouble as she looked for the magpie.

Fara, however, was far from Diarmid Abbey. Instead, she sat perched atop an awning over the local tavern and listened to a few of the regulars answer Dario's questions about Cristian.

"He's here most nights. Strange fella he is. Usually sits back there," one of the men explained, motioning to the back of the bar. Dario nodded and excused himself. Then stepping between the men, he moved indoors and sat at the vampire's table.

The conniving smile that spread across his face told Fara all she needed to know. Dario had returned to seek vengeance on Cristian once again. Luckily, for her one true love, Dario's wrath would never come to fruition. She had seen to that a long time ago. The magpie lifted from the canopy, spread her wings, and headed back to Elden Castle.

Chapter 33

Stepping across the crumbled threshold, Meg slipped past the old, weathered door and made her way down the narrow corridor toward the sanctuary. Despite the openings riddled randomly throughout the stone structure, the air inside was thick and pungent and filled Meg's head with reminders of that deadly night a few weeks before Isobel had arrived.

Diarmad Abbey once thrived as an entity of holiness that granted peace and acceptance with open arms to anyone who came looking for solace, but today Meg only felt suffocation. Anxious to escape and return to the freedom of the open air, she moved through the building in search of her sister.

The light that poured through the cracks and crevices of the dilapidated sacred walls guided her steps while reminders of the terror she'd recently experienced here chased through her mind. Her hurried footsteps stirred and shifted along the layers of dust from the earthen floor, and her nostrils flared at the intrusion. She needed to sneeze, but she didn't dare.

She wanted to call to Elspeth but was afraid to make a sound. Meg knew it wasn't the cry of her voice that drew Cristian to attack, but she questioned that he may not be the one holding her sister captive. Silently she begged for Elspeth to be unharmed. Holding her breath, she stepped around the corner and into the sanctuary where she expected them to be waiting.

Hunched into the farthest corner was Elspeth, and Meg's knees gave way. Her sister was still and her eyes were closed, but the rosiness of her cheeks and the slight rise and fall of her chest told Meg that she was alive.

"Elspeth!" she whispered. Quickly glancing around the room, Meg made her way toward her sister, careful not to spill the goblet she held onto so dearly.

Elspeth looked up, but her wide, tear-filled eyes that looked past her younger sister told Meg that they were not alone.

"Meg, my darling!" Cristian called out from behind her.

Meg froze. She had not seen him, but when had she ever seen Cristian coming?

Slumping into the wall, Elspeth fell unconscious, but Meg was grateful; she hoped to protect her sister from seeing what was about to take place. Turning, Meg met the eyes of her hunter.

"Cristian." She studied his lazy pose as he leaned against the wall. His arm was outstretched, and dangling from his finger was her ring, the one her mother had left for her, the one that allowed her inside the minds of others. The goblet in her hands tilted, and she nearly spilled Isobel's blood. "Where did you get that!" she demanded. "It is mine, and I'd like it back."

Pulling away from the wall, he laughed. "I don't believe so. The ring is mine. I gave it to your mother over a century ago when we became betrothed."

"You gave it to my mother?" she gasped, wide-eyed. She had always assumed the ring had come from her father.

Cristian smiled.

Behind her, Elspeth whimpered. Meg needed to remember why she was here and what she needed to do. She looked away from his hand as if the ring meant nothing to her. She would take it back the second the poison rendered him motionless.

Meg released her breath. "P-perhaps I am mistaken." Her words stumbled as she quickly gathered her thoughts. "I have brought you what you asked for. Now please, let Elspeth go. She has nothing to do with us." And with that, Meg stretched her arms forward and offered him the chalice mixed with Isobel's blood and the deadly herb they had picked. Her gaze flittered back and forth from her mother's ring to the vampire.

Strings of venom dripped hungrily from the corners of his mouth when he caught the scent of the goblet's contents.

"No one is going anywhere, Meg. You don't make the demands," he hissed, wiping his mouth with the back of a hand. "Besides, I don't believe that you have. I asked you to bring me the witch. I just see you and a goblet. Am I mistaken?"

"It is filled with her blood. It is what you want—"

"You do not tell me what I want!" Cristian stepped forward. "What I want is the witch!"

Meg watched as his eyes rolled back and transformed from the rich blue that could hold her enchanted to a hungry crimson red before disappearing into their sockets. Instinct was setting in, and he would not be able to deny Isobel's blood regardless of what he wanted. This was what Meg had been counting on. He had to drink what was in the goblet; it was her only chance for freedom.

"Please," she said softly, forcing herself to ignore the anger that reddened his face. "I brought this for you." Meg stepped forward and met him in the middle of the room.

A low growl formed in Cristian's throat, and he grabbed the cup from her hands. Her fingers released the goblet, and she watched as he swallowed the contents in one long gulp. She had hoped he would relish in the taste and take his time, but when had the vampire ever waited?

Turning the cup upside down, he threw the pewter goblet across the room, leaving tiny splatters of blood in the hallway where Meg had entered. The sun had begun its descent, slowly dimming the light that minutes ago had shone brightly through the cracks.

"Do you remember the first night we spoke?" he asked.

How could she have forgotten? The look on his face was as if he was seeing a ghost. "Yes," she answered. "You called me by my mother's name."

Cristian took a step forward and closed the gap between them. He bent forward, and the rich scent of cloves filled her nostrils so heavily that she thought she might get ill. "Yes. Well, I failed to answer your question as to how I knew her. However, I'd like to tell you a little story now," he whispered. "Your mother and I met more than a hundred years ago when I was human and she was— well, she was who she was. We were barely older than you but fell in love immediately. We were to wed soon, but our nuptials had to wait as I had been called to court in honor of my country." His stare, once again, looked distant and lost to another place in time. Meg took a step back.

"If only I had known—" Again his body shifted off balance.

Meg had never given any consideration to Cristian's age. She had believed him to be much older than herself, but certainly not greater than one hundred years. She wondered how long a vampire could live? What if Mariam was wrong and the tainted blood would not kill him? Maybe that was why Isobel's mother had not been successful in destroying him all those years ago. This new revelation was frightening. She could not let him leave the abbey; she absolutely would not. Cristian had to die.

He jerked upright, and his movement startled her. A blackness had filled his iris' so dark that they blended in with his pupils. Strings of venom oozed uncontrollably from his mouth and dripped to the floor.

"Did you have my mother killed?" Meg stammered. Her voice gained strength as a cold sweat broke out across her body. Gavan had told her that their mother had been accused of witchcraft. Had Cristian become angry that she had married their father and had her killed?

Cristian grabbed her by the upper arms, "Of course not! I loved her!" Both trembled as he spoke.

"That day I spotted you walking along the path, I thought I was seeing a ghost. Your hair, the way you carried yourself, even the scent that wafts from your skin—honeysuckle—was identical to hers. I had just found my way back to the Highlands after being gone for nearly sixteen years. I had heard rumors of her death about five years after I fled, but I didn't want to believe them. I swore I would never return to Dunkinshire, but the Highlands are my home and eventually I made my way back once again. Seeing you, I thought that somehow your mother had also returned. She had ways about her that were unique, so for a brief moment I thought it could be possible."

His eyes drifted from her, and she took another step back. The color of his skin no longer held its normal icy white, tinged with a slight hue of blue; instead, Meg thought it looked more ashen. Perhaps Isobel's tainted blood was working.

"I was wrong that day!" he snapped.

Meg frowned, unsure what he was referring to.

"You are nothing like your mother, and now, my darling, it is time that I teach you a lesson. I have been patient, but it's as if you have no respect for my wants. I warned you this day could come, and I do apologize, but Meg, you have failed to obey me yet again, something your mother would have never done."

"Maybe you didn't kill her, but if you loved her so much, why didn't you come back for her? You could have protected her, kept her secret of witchcraft safe. That is, if you really loved her. Maybe all of this is just a lie. Just another reason to justify attacking me. After all, how could my mother live to be one hundred years, or older? You, I think, are a liar."

Opening his mouth wide, Cristian hissed.

Meg had crossed a line. She stepped back until her heels pressed into the wall and she had nowhere else to go. Cristian spoke—a proclamation of how much he loved her mother—but his words were slurred.

"Your mother was born in 1403, and if it weren't for my maker, she would still be alive today." They were Cristian's last words before he sprang forward, grabbed Meg, and they collapsed to the ground.

Meg, however, was prepared for this to happen. As she entered the abbey, she had worried that the poisoned blood in the cup wouldn't be enough. If he bit her now, there would be no question that he would die; Meg had made sure. But as his anger mounted she now doubted she would survive his attack. At least her family would be safe from harm though, as would Isobel and her daughter.

Cristian's bite moved unevenly and painfully across her flesh. A faint ringing sounded in her ears, and her surroundings tumbled. Seeing death before her eyes, Meg thought it most strange the moments of time that came forth in her mind; the gentle touch of her mother and their whispered words in the garden, the swooshing sound of her pendulum, the bagpipes that played at market, and the odd arrangement of steps in the tower that led to her room. And Isobel. Sweet, knowledgeable Isobel. The first witch Meg had ever considered a true sister. She had been sent from the future to save Meg's life. If only she could have been successful.

Cristian had vowed to protect her, to keep her safe. Forever. But Meg knew all about making and breaking promises. After all, she had done them both most of her life. Perhaps, this was fate holding her accountable for all the trouble she had put her family through.

Please let him die.

They were her final words before his weight stilled and everything dissolved in a sea of black.

~~~~~~~~~~

The sound of his teeth puncturing Meg's soft flesh pushed Cristian into oblivion. Unable to recognize the pain he was inflicting, he devoured her just like he had the bar maid.

Meg's moments of defiance were unacceptable, but that wasn't what drove his violence against her. He was lost and sensed himself drifting away from Diarmid Abbey. He was desperate to immerse himself into his life before he had become this monster.

Images of his parents and brother flipped through his thoughts like they had this morning. They were smiling and waving their arms as though they were directing him to come to them, toward the bright circle of light that sat as a backdrop behind where they stood.

Catarine's voice called out, pulling him away from the light. He couldn't see her, but her tone was not soft and alluring as it always was. No, Catarine was angry, and Cristian sensed her detest for what he had done to her daughter. Clumsily, he reached out toward the faint image of his family, but the movement of his hand erased them in a single swipe.

Catarine. He was too weak to speak her name aloud but hoped she would hear it in his thoughts and reappear. Something was terribly wrong, and tonight, more than any other night, he needed her. The lavender scent he had detected on Meg's skin now filled his veins and wafted from his skin along with a trace of vervain; the blood in the cup had been tainted. Dizzy, Cristian bit down hard and inhaled. But as he drew long and hard against Meg's flesh, he also tasted the toxic herb that mingled in her blood. No magical hallucinations, no super immortal strength, no honeysuckle sweetness. No, her blood only made him feel one way, no matter how hard or often he punctured her flesh, ill. The two witches had poisoned him.

The sound of footsteps tapped in his ear. Someone else was

near. Cristian didn't have the strength or desire to separate himself from Meg, so he turned into her and continued leaving his marks down her arm until his body became so heavy that he could no longer move.

Reaching out, his blood-stained fingers slid down Meg's arm in search of her hand. Lacing his fingers with hers, he pulled her wrist to his mouth and latched on one last time.

Chapter 34

"This is taking too long," Isobel whispered. "Meg should have come out by now. I can't wait any longer."

Moving from under the branches, Isobel grabbed her skirt and climbed the grassy landing the ancient priory stood on. The earlier feeling of danger that had weighed heavy in her bones had lifted, and she no longer sensed the vampire's coldness like she had when she and Meg had arrived.

As she reached the flattened land, a sudden awareness of death overcame her. Her magic buzzed and then snapped back in her veins, and the bottoms of her feet prickled. Looking down, she knew that although their bones had long ago turned to ash and been absorbed into the earth, she was walking on the tombs of the dead. The innocent victims of the unholy rituals of war that had brought the religious entity of Diarmid Abbey to an end. Their torturous deaths had come without warning, and Isobel hoped that none of them suffered. But as she was reminded of the violence that history retold, she knew better and her lips quivered. Stepping lightly, she made the Sign of the Cross and prayed for peace for their souls.

Isobel's movements were quick, as always, and no sooner had she left the safety of the trees, she found herself staring into an eerie curtain of darkness that draped behind the decayed main doorway of the crumbled entry. The door sat ajar and was the only barrier between her and the other side. A layer of lichen covered the outer wall around the entrance, and as far as she could reach, Isobel dragged her fingertips along the mortar that rested between the stones. Metal bars were affixed to window openings to her left and right, making the abbey look more like a prison cell than a house of God.

Fear fell upon her shoulders like a weighted cloak as she prepared herself for what she might see. She pushed the door open, and the single hinge it hung from creaked loudly against the hammering pulse that filled her ears. Isobel wouldn't forgive herself if Meg or Elspeth were injured, or worse. Resting her hand against the cool rock wall that remained mostly intact in what was once the foyer, she listened to a rustling noise that came from the end of the corridor. She wanted to call Meg's name, but for their safety she remained quiet.

Piles of rubble littered the old monastery floor and forced Isobel to step with caution. The sound she had heard came from the opening to her left, about twenty feet from where she now stood. Moving alongside the jagged edge of the wall, she noticed the pewter goblet turned over at the end of the hall and the tiny drops of dried blood that surrounded it. Bending down, she traced Gavan's family crest that was etched across. It was the cup she had taken from Elden Castle and filled with her blood and crushed verbena. And now it was empty.

Isobel sighed. "He drank it." The feeling of danger that had lifted now made sense; the vampire was dead.

Peering around the corner, Isobel saw Elspeth slumped in a corner across the room. Her eyes were closed and her body lay motionless as Isobel studied her from head to toe. The royal blue gown that she had left the castle wearing yesterday hung below the edge of her cloak. Her feet were bare and her skin dirty, but Isobel saw no noticeable wounds. She exhaled, relieved that Elspeth appeared to be unharmed.

"Elspeth!" she called out.

The sanctuary was taller than it was wide. Its design was simple with a lone wooden alter, earthen floor, and three windows along the far wall: the only direct sources for light. Years of dust layered across the remaining jagged panes of stained glass that had once formed a barrier from the outside world, now only to give way to the spiders and their intricate webs that wove from corner to corner, filling in the gaps.

Isobel stepped forward, ready to run to Elspeth's rescue, but she stopped as suddenly as she had started for she had not, in any way, prepared herself for what lay in a heap to her left. His back was to her, but even in the hazy light of the afternoon sun that filtered into the sanctuary, his poise was one Isobel both recognized and feared.

Meg lay beside him. Her eyes were closed, and the pulse of her magic was faint but detectable; praise God she, too, was alive. But for how much longer? Her cape was tossed to one side, and

Isobel saw her torn sleeve and the bite marks that had been inflicted along her flesh. Her bare arm was pressed against his lips, but he was still. Until he captured Isobel's scent and whipped around, meeting her stare.

Isobel gasped and clamped a hand over her mouth as her eyes widened. Her body trembled and she wanted to speak, but her words were trapped in her throat behind her shaky palm. A cold sweat beaded along her spine and formed on her palms as she leaned into the half-wall beside her. *Impossible!*

Meg's blood dripped from the corners of the vampire's lips, and the look in his eyes became lost the longer he stared in Isobel's direction. He blinked and his eyes rolled back before returning and squinting; he was unable to focus.

Meg's arm fell from his bite and landed on the floor with a soft thump. Pushing up, his body swayed with the same uncontrolled motion of his eyes, and then he collapsed. Face first, he hit the floor with a sickening crash. The force of his weight shook the building, his body forming a crater where it landed. Isobel couldn't take her eyes off of him.

Three hundred years in the future there existed a man who called himself her father. He had forced himself into her mind and shared his most treasured moments of her existence, but it was his sincerity, the desperation in his voice when he cried out as she escaped through the portal, that had haunted her the most over the last three weeks. Isobel hadn't believed his confession until

Mariam admitted that Isobel's father was not the man she had been led to believe. Rather, he was a ruthless, selfish vampire her mother had kept nameless. That was, until now.

With mixed emotions, Isobel looked at the unmoving form that lay collapsed in front of her. His long blond hair lay across his broad and muscle riddled shoulders, and his profile—chiseled jawline, high cheek bone, and square chin—were carved to perfection. Isobel remembered thinking how beautiful, how angelic he had looked the moment he stepped out of the woods, sandwiching her between Dario and himself.

His cheek rested on the floor. One eye was pressed into the dingy surface, while the other—leeched of its rich blue color and framed by an open lid and long golden lashes—stared ahead, unmoving and void of life. Small, sharp teeth stained red sat in two perfect rows as far as Isobel could see behind his pale, opened lips. His arms and legs no longer twitched, and the warmth from Meg's magic that had briefly radiated across his skin had rapidly faded to a sickly shade of gray; the vampire had reached his final stage of death. His maker had initiated the process years ago, but it was Isobel who brought it to an end. And now she knew the truth and could give her father a name: Cristian.

Her stomach tumbled and the walls of the abbey appeared to sway as the tale that Mariam wove about Isobel's father being a vampire unfolded before her eyes. Her mother's vampire, Isobel's true birth father, was Meg's vampire. Three hundred years had separated the living, but the undead had existed without the restraints of time, wreaking havoc down the magical bloodline that she and Meg shared. But if Meg's hunch that the three of them were connected was true, then something still remained amiss. And Cristian—the last person who possibly could have had the answer—now lay dead at her feet.

"I will never forgive you for not protecting my family." It was the first thing that came to her mind. "Your family," she added. He had vowed to keep her mother and Meg safe but had failed.

"Meg! Isobel!" Elspeth's cry came from the darkest corner of the room. Her voice was weak but loud enough to break the trance Isobel had on Cristian.

Elspeth stumbled to her feet and quickly made her way to Meg. Falling to the floor, she threw her arms around her younger sister. "Are you all right? He tore your clothing, and you're bleeding." Terrified sobs broke free between Elspeth's words as her eyes darted back and forth across Meg's punctured body that she clung to.

"I am fine, Elspeth; let me sit please." Pushing up, Elspeth loosened her grip and gave her sister some room.

Meg squinted, her vision swimming in front of her. She was weak from the herb she had ingested as well as the loss of blood. She only needed a few minutes though and her mind would begin to clear. Her body had become quite accustomed to

Cristian's feedings and could recover quickly. She pulled her cape tightly around her body in an effort to keep Elspeth from staring at the marks and losing consciousness again.

"Who is that? What did he want?" Elspeth's eyes shifted towards his body that lay lifeless at their feet as she leaned into Meg.

"Elspeth, were you harmed?" Isobel asked, drawing attention away from Meg.

"I don't think so. The horses screamed, and when Huxley reared back, I was snatched off his back. I never saw anyone approaching. Someone covered my head with a sack and bound my wrists until we got here. Once I was freed from the ropes, I crawled into the corner. I was so afraid I must have swooned. The last thing I remember was burying my face in my hands and begging for them not to kill me." Tears streamed down Elspeth cheeks as she recalled the moment. "It happened so fast. Ian didn't come with me. Do you think he was able to escape?"

Isobel was certain she knew the answer but was afraid to share it. She didn't know how much more Elspeth could handle. She wasn't weak, but the last two days had taken quite a toll on her.

"I'm sure Gavan will search for Ian," Isobel answered as she bent down and squeezed the older sister's hand for reassurance.

"Meg?" Isobel raised a brow and the two shared a look.

"I'm fine. A little weak, but I'll regain my strength in no time." She would have to be cautious around Elspeth and not draw any attention to how fast she could move or how strong she could be. Even though it was poisoned, Cristian's venom still flowed in her veins. Meg could feel the effects taking place already.

"Meg, did he not drink from the goblet?" Isobel asked, feeling confused about him still being alive when she entered and the empty cup in the hallway.

"Yes, but he was angry that I didn't bring you here. I was afraid of that, so when we were picking the flowers I hid some in my pocket. Before I entered, I ate them. I knew if he got angry, he would punish me, and I wanted to make sure there would be enough poisoned blood to kill him." Isobel closed her eyes and sighed in reaction. Meg could have been killed.

"Meg, I don't understand what you are saying. What flowers did you eat? And what did you mean about drinking poisoned blood?"

Meg had hoped Elspeth hadn't caught on to her explanation. "I will explain it all to you when we get home."

"Is—is he dead?" Elspeth asked, glancing in Cristian's direction.

Isobel and Meg nodded, and the remaining color drained from Elspeth's face.

"Come on," Isobel said, worried that Elspeth would swoon

again. "We need to get you two home before your brother discovers that Meg and I aren't there."

Already on her feet, Isobel extended a hand and helped Meg and Elspeth up. The trio moved around the dead vampire and out of the sanctuary, careful not to step on anything as they proceeded toward the opening that led outside. Isobel followed behind with slow steps.

"Are you coming?" Meg asked as she stood in the entryway.

"Get Elspeth some fresh air; I'll be right there."

Isobel turned, walked back to the sanctuary, and took in the moment. She would never have a reason to return to this place or time again. She and Cristian shared no obvious similarities except for the depth of color that filled their eyes. Her looks—her emerald green irises and dark brown hair—had been given to her by her mother. However, what lay mostly beneath her skin was all him. It was the reason he had been so fascinated watching her grow.

A pain formed in her stomach, and Isobel wished she had known Cristian when she was a child. If she had, their lives might have been different. Maybe her mother would be alive. Maybe they could have found a way to become a family, but then again, maybe Isobel would have become just like him—a violent, dangerous killer.

Emotion overtook her and a wretched sob that formed in her chest forced her to double over. Three weeks ago, the vampire that lay in front of her was a villain, one that for all she knew had participated in the brutal killing of her mother and husband. How could she mourn for this man? Or better yet, this animal. He had taken nearly everything away from her, and she hated him for it.

"It doesn't even matter," she mumbled. "He's gone."

Outside, the sun had begun its descent behind the tree line and diminished the light that once spilled into the priory. As Isobel stood in the shadows, an aura of death emerged and she shivered. It was time.

"Goodbye, Father." The words tumbled through her, and she left Diarmad Abbey without another glance.

Chapter 35

Isobel shielded her eyes and looked for Meg and Elspeth as Fara came into view, ascending high above the tree line. The magpie's ebony wings whipped as she soared over Meg and her sister's head, and Isobel released a sigh; her familiar was unharmed. Walking across the grassy landing, she lifted an arm for Fara to join her, but instead, her familiar flew past and straight inside the highest window of the abbey bell tower.

"Isobel!" Elspeth called out. "It will be dark soon."

Staring at the sisters who stood arm in arm, Isobel knew Elspeth was right. Fara had made her choice going to the vampire, and now everything Isobel had learned while she was in Dunkinshire came together. Meg's idea that they were connected was true.

Remaining quiet as she worked out the details in her head, Isobel joined Meg and Elspeth, and the three women made their way in silence towards Elden Castle. The sisters walked together and leaned on one another for support while Isobel distanced herself a few steps behind. The wind was at their back, and with nighttime approaching, the gusts had lessened and thankfully blew more like a breeze.

Isobel's mood was somber and her mind distracted. Knowing who her father was gave her an odd sense of relief, but with both her parents gone, she may never learn the answers to all her questions. She had, however, learned enough to move forward, return to her home and prepare a future with her daughter. She thought of the times in her life when she had wished there had been someone who was stronger. Someone who would have helped ease the burden of difficult times and let her be weak for once. But that lifestyle wasn't meant for Isobel. Rather, she was bred to be strong and capable and independent.

The thundering sound of hooves racing toward them broke Isobel from her thoughts, and she looked ahead. Gavan and Kenneth were riding in their direction. With his boots safely anchored in his stallion's stirrups, Gavan stood, leaned over Ahearn, and shouted at him to go faster. His loose, blond hair blew off his shoulders as the snug fit of his plaid against his bare chest and his sword by his side solidified Gavan's commanding position; he was ready to battle.

If it weren't for the deadly outrage that was etched across his face, Isobel would have been relieved that Gavan had found them. They may have been freed from the vampire's wrath, but until she returned home, she would never escape the disdain this Highlander had for her. Jerking the reins, Gavan brought Ahearn to a halt. As the stallion's legs braced and his hooves slid across the ground, dust and tiny pebbles sprayed into the air. Throwing a leg over, Gavan dismounted in one fluid motion and gathered Meg and Elspeth in his arms.

Isobel looked away from their emotional reunion, but not before catching the tick in his jaw as he glared over Meg's head and directly at her. The look of disgust that she was not only alive, but that she also accompanied his sisters, was easy to read. Last night, after allowing her to stay at the castle for one more night, he had made her a promise; if she interfered with his family again, he would have her head.

Releasing his sisters, Gavan stepped with an over-exaggerated swagger toward her. Pulling his sword from its sheath, he raised it high, but as he lowered into a full swing meant to take off her head, his movement was stopped.

"No!" Meg shouted as she stood between Gavan and Isobel, her hand wrapped around her brother's wrist, bringing his arm to a stop. The muscles in her arm burned as she held Gavan at bay. The poisoned venom in her system gave her the strength, but just barely; she wasn't going to be able to hold him off for long. Gavan's eyes went wide and shifted between her face and her arm, which began to shake.

"Brother, not here," Kenneth said. Moving between Meg and Gavan, the stable master shielded the women's bodies while his hand gripped the sword. Meg let go and moved back to Elspeth's side.

"Move!" Gavan commanded.

"No." The two warriors stood in a stand-off, their eyes locked with one another and their bodies rigid.

"Gavan, stop. The man is dead. Go see for yourself; he lies lifeless on the floor of the abbey behind us. Isobel saved my life, brother. She is to thank, not to kill," Meg said as she held on to Elspeth's hand.

"Please, Gavan, let's go home." It was Elspeth's quiet, trembling voice that called out this time.

Shifting his weight, Gavan exhaled and lowered his sword. Kenneth stood in place until the weapon was secure at the Highlander's side and then stepped beside Isobel. Looking at the stablemaster, Gavan motioned his head towards the abbey.

"I will help you get the women to the castle, and I'll return," Kenneth said.

After a moment, Gavan nodded. Kenneth helped Elspeth mount his steed and then seated himself behind her, pulling her back to rest against his chest. Ahearn moved towards his master, bucking his head and pawing at the ground.

"Meg!" Gavan called out as he grabbed the stallion's reins.

Meg refused to look at her brother and, instead, linked arms with Isobel. They followed Kenneth as he turned and lead his horse south, Gavan and Ahearn at their heels.

The last rays of sunlight had slipped into nothingness as they reached the border of their land. The shadow of Elden Castle was now in view and not too far away. They arrived at the stables just as darkness had set in. As Kenneth and Elspeth dismounted, he held onto her for a few more minutes than necessary.

"You are alright, lass," he spoke before cupping her face and kissing her softly on the lips.

Gavan took a sharp breath in, the sound filling all their ears. Meg looked at her brother from the corner of her eye and smiled. Blushing, Elspeth nodded. Stepping around the horses, she stood between Gavan and Meg, and linked fingers with her siblings.

"I will let you know what I find," Kenneth told Gavan before placing Ahearn in his stall and returning to his own steed.

Gavan nodded, and the four turned and made their way to the castle's main doors. The racing of hooves across the hardened dirt path behind them caused Elspeth to look over her shoulder. She watched until Kenneth and the sound of his horse disappeared in the darkness.

As they reached the wooden cathedral-style doors, Isobel, who had been silent since they began making their way home, made an announcement.

"It is time for me to go home." Relief washed over her as she said the words.

"Now? What about the mid-wife? It isn't safe to leave after dark, Isobel. Please stay one more night," Meg pleaded and grabbed Isobel's hands. "Gavan? Just one more night so she can be rested for her journey in the morning?" A sadness filled Meg, knowing that she wouldn't see Isobel, the one true person who understood her, again.

"If it is all right with your brother, I will leave in the morning so that I can give a proper good-bye. But if not, I can leave now," Isobel answered.

She was desperate for sleep and sensed an unusual weakness in her blood and bones. She feared it was Mariam's words coming true, her body not feeding itself properly during times of physical exertion. Isobel was not ready for that to happen, for her life to begin its ending before she ever got started. She had to take care of herself, live effortlessly, so that she could give birth. She and Charlotte were all that they each had.

"First thing in the morning." They were Gavan's only words as he swung open the oversized wooden doors that Isobel had first stepped through three long weeks ago. "Before the cock's crow and not a minute later." Isobel met his stare and nodded that she understood.

"Thank you," she said and followed Meg and Elspeth indoors.

She climbed the stairs alone to her room as the others made their way toward the Great Hall. Isobel was surprised that Gavan hadn't trailed after her, but she knew the three had a lot to discuss.

Closing the door behind her, Isobel was thankful to be alone. She moved to the window, pushed aside the plaid covering, slid the iron bar from its latches and looked out for the last time. Emerging from the darkness, Fara landed on the ledge. She raced across the cold stone and stood next to Isobel.

"It is time to return home, Fara." The magpie hopped on top of Isobel's hand and was silent. "I don't know what our time has in store for us, but I have a sense of peace that hasn't existed in weeks. Years, if I really think about it."

Scooping Fara in her hand, she pulled the shutters closed. "We are going to make a new home for ourselves, far away from Massachusetts. I am hoping that Dario won't find us as we make a new start on the west coast, and that with Cristian—" Isobel stopped and corrected herself. "With my father gone, Dario will forget all about us."

Daytime thoughts and overnight dreams mixed in Isobel's consciousness. The characters—witches, vampires, a lone familiar, and a magical bloodline—were all present. Catarine's diary, the storybook of their lives, held the answers. Isobel was certain. Unfortunately, she would never get the chance to read it.

"Maybe some things are better left unknown," she said as she bent down and lit the still smoldering coals from this morning. The fire quickly cast competing flames as the wood crackled and popped and gave the room some much needed heat. Isobel stood, stretched out her arms, and warmed her hands.

Looking around the room, she took everything in for the last time—the smooth slab walls, the family plaid that blanketed the window, the nearly empty stack of wood on the hearth, the pile of furs covering the bed and the basin filled with water from the day before. The north tower had been her home the last three weeks, and now that it was finally time to leave, Isobel felt a sense of sadness. She would deeply miss the companionship of Meg and Elspeth and the sisterhood they had created. Ironically, she had found comfort at Elden Castle despite all that had gone wrong. There would be no more trickery, no more deceitfulness on her part, nor would she be saying goodbye in the morning. Isobel's time to return home was now, and she was grateful to have the freedom to walk out the door once the castle was quiet.

"Elden Castle holds many secrets, Fara," Isobel said. "But I'm guessing you already know that." Isobel thought about Mariam's discovery of Catarine's diary hidden in one of these walls. "Perhaps you were the one to start them." She looked at Fara and smiled. "I hope that you will return home with me, but if not, I do understand."

Tears filled Isobel's eyes at the thought of leaving Fara behind. She would miss the magpie more than she could ever express, but if given the chance, she too would choose to remain with her family.

Stripping off her gown, Isobel pulled out her black dress, the one she had worn the night she arrived, and slipped it over her head.

"Charlotte, you are growing," she said with a smile, and gently patted and shifted the snug woolen fabric that now pulled across her waist.

A slight rap on the door interrupted her dressing. Isobel jumped, but her fear passed quickly as she detected Meg's energy and nothing else; the girl stood in the hallway alone.

Isobel walked to the door, and let the young witch in. It was time to say goodbye.

Chapter 36

"I wish you didn't have to leave. I understand why, but you have become family. A sister to me," Meg said to Isobel as she stroked Fara's back. "Will you return to Dunkinshire? After your daughter is born, that is. I cannot stand the idea that I may never see you again." Meg lowered her gaze and her voice and looked like a frightened child—innocent and incapable.

However, despite her look of vulnerability, Isobel had no plans of visiting Meg and her family anytime soon. It was just too dangerous.

"I'm not sure," she replied, unable to look Meg in the eye as she spoke.

"You can't lie to me either, remember?" Meg said to her as she lifted Fara from her lap and stood. "I can sense that this is a final goodbye."

Isobel grabbed Meg's hands and held them tightly. "You are like a sister to me too, Meg. Please take care of yourself and stay out of trouble." Dropping hands, the two embraced until Meg let go and stepped back, her eyes filled with tears.

"I have agreed to go to England with Elspeth to stay with our cousins. Not that Gavan gave me much choice. Our family there is from my father's side, and as children, Gavan, Elspeth, and I were very close to them. After my father was killed, I was sent to live with them. It was a terrible time for me to be separated from my brother and sister, but as I have told you before, I was quite mischievous as a child, and Gavan and Elspeth needed some time to get our household in order. At least this time I won't be going alone. Kenneth will ride with us as well. He made it clear he was all in favor of Elspeth's safety, but I'm wondering if it will be easy for him to return to Dunkinshire without her. It is easy to see how much he's in love with her. And Mariam did say that they end up marrying." The tears pooled in Meg's eyes remained, but a small smile pulled at her lips.

"I don't think anyone was more surprised than our brother when Kenneth kissed Elspeth in the stables. Gavan grumbled about it more than half of the time we were in the hall tonight. Poor Elspeth couldn't stop blushing and begged our brother to stop." A soft laugh escaped from both women.

"Meg, I think going to England is a wonderful idea," Isobel said. Fara patted her feet across the stone ledge; she, too, agreed.

"It's just for a short time. Gavan wants to make sure we are both safe and hopes the persecutions and the violent attacks will quickly move away from the Highlands. He and Elspeth also promised to tell me about our mother along the way."

Isobel nodded. "Meg, it is going to take more than a few months for the witch hunts to cease, but I am pleased you agreed to leave the Highlands for now. I will pray for your safety and for Gavan, Elspeth, and Kenneth's as well."

"Thank you, as I will for you and your daughter." Both women sat quietly for a few minutes. Unable to stand the silence, Meg decided to tell Isobel about Kenneth returning to the abbey.

"Isobel, I told Gavan what happened at the abbey today. Well, maybe not everything, but almost. I also showed him the marks on my arm. Elspeth had already seen them and I was worried that I would never be able to keep them from him. I think he had started to believe me about Cristian, but then Kenneth returned. Elspeth and I were sent out of the Hall, but I pressed my ear against the door and listened. Isobel, Kenneth told Gavan that there was no body. He said he searched Diarmad Abbey in its entirety and found nothing. The only thing he said he could confirm was a rotting smell that hung so heavy in the sanctuary that it nearly suffocated him."

It must have been the same smell Isobel had detected just before she walked out of the abbey; death. She couldn't imagine the thoughts that must be running through Gavan's head. Meg had shown him the bite marks, told him that they had killed someone, and Elspeth must have confessed that someone took her against her will. Yet there was no body to be found. Gavan would not think his sisters were daft, but if he could find a way to blame any of this on her, she knew he would.

"Isobel, we killed him, right? Cristian was there, lying dead on the floor when we left?" Meg asked, interrupting Isobel's thoughts.

"Yes, Meg, we killed him," she answered softly.

"Then what could have happened? The dead don't just get up and walk away."

No they don't, thought Isobel. *At least not on their own.*

"Someone must have found his body and removed it," Isobel said. "Perhaps for a proper burial." Isobel shuddered at the thought. There were only two people, Cristian's maker or his one true love, Catarine, that she imagined doing so.

Meg nodded but didn't look any more convinced than Isobel sounded.

"It is late, and we all need some rest. Good night, Meg. I will see you early in the morning. Before the cock's crow, if we are to follow Gavan's orders, and I think that it is best if I obey at least one thing he has asked of me before I leave." A warm smile spread across Isobel's face.

Meg lifted a fur strap from her shoulder and over her head. "This is for you," she said. Connected at the other end was a rectangular fur pouch. After winding the strap around the bag, she set it on the foot of the bed.

"What is it?" Isobel asked, pulling her brows together as she stared at it.

"Just a little something for you to remember me by. It is something that I made for you, and I want you to take it when you leave here."

"Meg, I will always remember you, but thank you for the

gift; it is lovely. I thought you couldn't sew?"

"I never said I couldn't; I said that I was terrible at it. But this was important to me." Meg seemed hesitant, as if there was something more she wanted to say.

"Meg?" Isobel asked, her brows furrowing, again.

Meg sighed, and the corners of her mouth drooped.

"What is it?"

"It's just something Cristian said before he collapsed. It didn't make much sense, and perhaps it was the poison speaking, but he claimed that he met my mother in the year 1418 when she was my age, fifteen years old. That is also the same year that is inscribed on the first page of her diary."

Meg had made fair progress reading her mother's diary. She had trouble with many of the words but had been able to pick up on enough to understand that her mother was a very powerful witch, and that she and Cristian shared a past.

"My mother died thirteen years ago. If what Cristian said was true, that would have made her one hundred eighty-one years old. How is that even possible?"

"What exactly did he say?" Isobel lowered herself into the chair near the hearth.

"Just that he knew her when he was human. They were betrothed, but he was called to court and never returned. He didn't explain why he never returned but stated that the first day he spotted me walking along the dirt path, he thought he was seeing the ghost of my mother. He was so taken aback he had no choice but to show himself and speak."

Isobel looked at Fara. The magpie had moved to the top spindle of the chair, her gaze only on Meg.

"Isobel, do you think that's true? Her age, I mean? And if it is, what does that mean for me? Will I live to be one hundred years old or older? And again, how is that even possible?" Meg's tone teetered on the edge of hysteria.

Isobel stood and gathered the girl's hands in her own.

"Meg, I remember my mother telling stories about powerful witches who did indeed live for hundreds of years, some even thousands. I don't believe it is all that common, but they do exist. When I was very young, I believed her, and then I went through a time where I didn't."

"And now?" Meg asked, her eyes wide and pleading.

"My father was a vampire. I am half witch-half vampire. Meg, I think that many things are possible. You are a special and powerful woman. I believe great things will come for you if you channel yourself in the right way and keep out of trouble. Go to England and rest. There will be plenty of time to learn of your heritage, and it will be easier with a clear head. If you are able, take your mother's diary. Perhaps with Gavan and Elspeth's stories and your mother's written words, some sense and a true timeline can be made. Now please, get to your room before Gavan comes looking for you. I don't know that I have the strength to endure another confrontation." Truthfully, Isobel was having an equally difficult time saying goodbye. She needed her strength to get her and Charlotte home, and the longer Meg hung on, the more drained Isobel became.

"You are right. Thank you, sister." Meg smiled, this time much bigger and more convincing as she embraced Isobel tightly. "Sleep well. I will see you in the morning."

Meg left, closing the door softly behind her. Isobel sat down and stared into the fire, wondering if she should call the portal from within her room. She was certain it would be safer and quicker. However, she had one last obstacle she wanted to face before returning to her own time, and this would be the only chance she would have.

Isobel leaned back, closed her eyes and waited for the siblings below her to settle. Hours passed, and the flames that once held her mesmerized diminished to ash. The magic in her blood prickled with unease, and the weight of her bones remained heavy. She was exhausted but couldn't have slept if she tried, so instead she rested. Pattering across the slab floor, Fara moved toward her and settled in her lap.

"Only one more trip," Isobel murmured as she stroked the feathers of her familiar's head.

A few hours later, the movements within the castle silenced. Isobel looked down at Fara, who sat puffed in her lap, and motioned that it was time to leave. The magpie flew to the window ledge, turned, and watched as Isobel put on her shoes and cloak and stepped to the door.

Drawing in a breath, Isobel clasped her fingers around the lever and pulled it gently. The knob moved with ease, and the cracked door that hung uneven sprung open. Isobel half-expected to see Gavan sitting on guard, but the platform outside of her room was empty and the stairwell dim.

She turned back and grabbed the keepsake from the top of the mattress and, like Meg, slipped the strap over her head and let the fur bag rest at her hip.

"I am ready," she whispered to Fara. "I will meet you outside." The magpie bobbed her head and, without making a sound, dove into the darkness.

Unexpected energy filled Isobel as she made her way down the stairs and toward the back of the kitchen. She opened the door—the same one Meg had fallen through on Isobel's first morning at the castle—and a burst of cold air slapped her in the face. Before she had time to reconsider or feel guilty for not saying a proper goodbye, she stepped over the threshold and crept along the castle walls until she reached the cobblestone path that led away from Elden Castle. Racing downward, her heart beat in tandem with her steps as she made her way toward the forest as she had seen Meg do so many nights before.

Chapter 37

The open sea stretched to the horizon in a sheet of glistening silver, and the brilliant light cast by the full moon filled Isobel's vision. Through lowered lashes, she watched as the swells moved in purposeful patterns of silver and black before crashing into the jagged rocks and dispersing in all directions. One path of the salty mist sprayed upwards and dampened Isobel's face. Her breath caught in her throat, and her lungs tightened; she felt exposed.

"Fara, if it were daylight, everyone could see us," she whispered. Her eyes darted toward the glittering stars above. "But this is the right place."

Over the last few days, one by one, the hesitations that had kept Isobel anchored in the Highlands had been freed, except for one. It is why she stood, out in the open, where she could easily and safely be found. Relaxing her arms at her sides, she drew in a breath and beckoned her next move.

Heed my words, the time has come
To replace us in the time we came from.
Old fears lie dead, yet new ones will exist.
We stand ready, the three of us. Come forth and assist.

The words effortlessly flowed from her tongue, the mouth of the gateway taking form before she finished reciting the last line. Its circular motion stirred the waves, and the foam that layered the top ceased its collisions with the jagged rock edge. Changing course, the water below the portal began to follow the same churning movements.

Fara clung to Isobel's gown, the tips of her familiar's claws piercing her skin. Entranced by the swirling waters below, and the notion that they would all soon be home, Isobel felt no pain. Her thoughts shifted to her father and her existence on the other side.

"Fara, do you think we will make it?" Isobel asked, gazing into the portal. "What if we get lost in time? Or disappear altogether?" Instinctively, she cradled her belly and her mother's warning, which Isobel now fully understood thanks to Mariam's explanation, sounded in her head.

"Daughter, your powers will weaken with every jump you make. After a while, it will become harder to pass through time, your magic words will become jumbled and then finally, the portal door will close, never to reopen. Isobel, you don't want to be on the wrong side of time when that happens. Always pay attention and never take your powers for granted."

The magpie leaned her silky feathers against Isobel, and her familiar's silent request forced Isobel's memory back into hiding.

"We could stay here, Fara, but I don't know how long we would be safe. And I would be afraid for Charlotte's birth, not to mention where we would live or how we would survive. We wouldn't be able to remain at Elden Castle, Gavan would never agree to that. Besides, this is not a safe time."

Vampires and witch hunters roamed as they pleased from village to village, each inflicting whatever justice they deemed fit when a situation against their liking or logic arose. Death—by fire, or hanging, or mutilation—took place regularly. No, any way Isobel looked at it, staying in Dunkinshire was not a safe option.

She was certain she knew who had discovered Cristian's body and removed it, but whether it was the vampire she suspected or the townspeople, the witches would be blamed. A shiver trickled down her spine, and she slipped her hand inside the fur bag that hung at her side in search of comfort. The bag, however, was not empty and took Isobel by surprise.

Her fingers curled around its contents: a leather-bound stack of papers. Why would Meg give her a book? Isobel's blood pulsed excitedly. A knot formed in her gut as something grew deep inside of her; there was magic in this book! Had Meg given her Catarine's diary!

As she pulled her hand from the bag, a well-known coldness wrapped around Isobel and Fara's claws sank deeper into her flesh; they were no longer alone. Shoving the book back into the pouch, Isobel turned around and scanned the wall of trees along the edge of the densely wooded area. No sign of human life. Only that of a vampire lurking in the shadows. Isobel could only presume that it was where he felt the most comfortable.

He wasn't visible, but his sharp intake of air as he breathed in her scent told Isobel all she needed to know. He had come. She could only assume now that her theory of how Dario fit in with Cristian had been correct; he had turned her father into a vampire.

"Dario," she whispered into the cold, clear air in front of her. His icy eyes bore a recognizable burn into her flesh, but this time she expected it, and the pressure was manageable.

He stepped out from under the shadows and Isobel found herself staring at the same man she had fearfully fled from three hundred years in the future, three weeks ago. Tonight, a shadow of dark hair stubbled his face between the sharp angles of his nose and jawline and framed the most perfect set of full lips Isobel had ever seen. His olive complexion was as smooth as marble and equally flawless, unblemished of any battle he may have ever incurred. His coloring was the exact opposite of her bright-eyed, light-haired father, but just as magnificent. Just as breathtaking. Returning three hundred years in the past had not changed the inhuman perfection of Dario's features nor the monster that lived behind the sinister black eyes embedded in his skull.

Isobel dropped her gaze to the clear, round buttons on his shirt. She followed them one by one until she reached his arms that folded across his chest. They, too, were dusted in the same dark hair that shaded his face, and she watched as the muscle beneath his forearms flexed. She lifted her chin and met his menacing dark stare, refusing to be intimidated.

Dropping his arms, he took a deliberate step forward, his look more hungry than evil, and a cautionary dread spread inside Isobel.

"Have we met before?" he asked in an accent Isobel couldn't fully make out. It sounded mostly Italian, but something cold and calculating heightened its scope as it filled her ears. The corners of his soulless eyes narrowed, and he tilted his head. Without waiting for Isobel to respond, he answered, "Well, of course not. I would never forget such a delicious scent." His voiced vibrated in the back of his throat, the sound soothing against Isobel's eardrums.

He closed his eyes and inhaled again, his long, dark lashes closing against his olive complexion. The smooth, warm coloring told her that he had recently fed, not that that would keep him from indulging himself again.

"Oh, but we have, Dario," she answered as she gathered her thoughts. "In another place and time." Isobel's voice was strong and her tone unwavering. Dario's lids flipped open, his irises now an inviting golden brown that swirled around each small, dark pupil. Isobel held her ground and stared through his glamour, refusing to fall victim to his powers.

"Please forgive me for not remembering. You can rest assured that won't happen again." An evil smile parted his lips as he spoke, and a drop of venom dripped to the ground.

"I trust that you found my father's body in the abbey?"

Standing over her father this afternoon, Isobel had realized that if Cristian, the vampire, was present in 1597, then Dario would be too. After all, their past had to begin somewhere.

She stepped back until her heels neared the edge of the cliff. She sensed Dario's appreciation for patience, his desire to come at her at his own pace. Quite the opposite of how Meg described Cristian. Dario delighted in the hunt and the terror he could inflict in his prey, but Isobel would be ready if he changed his approach and rushed for her.

"Your fa-father? My dear, you must be mistaken. Cristian was n-no father." His chuckle, as he stumbled over his words, was patronizing, and he shook his head before jerking it upright, the color of his eyes returning to black. "I am the one who gave him life. And since your scent filled him, you must be the one responsible for taking him from me." Dario's anger had returned, and he took another step forward.

Isobel knew this would be her one opportunity to speak her mind, face to face, so she continued. "I would love to tell you the full story about your beloved vampire mate, Cristian. How he manipulated my mother, consumed her magical powers for his own selfishness, took advantage of her fear and vulnerability, and finally, when she tried to rid him from her life, impregnated her with a daughter. A daughter who is half witch and half vampire. Who can call forth magic while maintaining unrelenting strength and stamina much like, well, like yourself."

Opening her hand, Isobel presented the rock that sat tucked away in her palm. Dario kept a watchful eye as she closed her fingers and squeezed until the stone dissolved into sand and spilled between her fingers to the ground.

His eyes widened, his nostrils flared, and the slight tick of his jaw as he ground his teeth alerted Isobel she had his attention. The magic within her blood prickled, and a warning formed in her gut. *This is dangerous.*

Feeling strong and sure of herself, Isobel ignored the internal caution and focused on the silent vampire, whose mind stood questioning but considering some truth to her words.

"You may have sired Cristian and believe that the only way he could create a child would be to turn them as you did him, but rest assured that I speak the truth when I say that Cristian was indeed my father. For just a moment, put aside your own selfish thirst and desire to kill and listen."

Dario's eyes locked with hers. Years ago, he had conceded to the idea that the leech had created one offspring, given the witch he chose to bed, but two! *Impossible!*

"That's right. Inhale deeper, and you will find his immortal scent that flows in my blood. And our eyes, although different in color, are shaped identical and bear the same rich intensity. I have my mother's coloring, the warmth of her skin, and a small amount of her magic, but to the core, I am my father's daughter."

A coldness weighed heavily on top of Isobel's head as tiny

ice crystals from the sea mist formed and drifted in sync with Dario's gaze, blanketing her cheeks, her neck and then spidering throughout her body, her toes and fingertips burning in reaction. A dusting of snow gathered at her feet as Dario's head dropped and he stared into the ground, silent and unmoving. He was doing exactly as Isobel asked, processing her claim to Cristian.

It was only seconds before his head snapped upwards and his eyes filled with fury; he believed her. A guttural growl vibrated against his throat, and then oddly enough, he smiled, clapped twice with slow deliberation, and froze.

"You think you know everything, is that right?" He paused. "You know nothing!" Dario's shout shook the ground beneath them and startled Isobel. She took a step forward and regained her balance.

"I know my father must have loathed you. You took so much from him; his humanity, those he loved, everything that he once had, all for your own selfish needs. But Dario, one must always be stronger, smarter, and one step ahead of their immortal brethren."

Dario tilted his head. For a moment, he stared at her, his features unreadable. Isobel kept her eyes on him, but her focus was on the sound of the portal that churned below. They stood that way for minutes, neither moving, then a thoughtful look softened his face. He raised his brows and unclenched his jaw. Cupping an elbow in one hand, he took a theatrical pose and drummed his fingers against his lips with the other.

"Let me tell you a story; after all, nothing is more telling than a story, especially after one's rebirth, wouldn't you agree?"

Chapter 38

With great animation, Dario wove a tale. One of love found and love lost. One of friendship and revenge. One of devotion and hatred. His words were haunting and his tone so mesmerizing that for a moment Isobel forgot herself.

"Cristian and I were childhood friends. His family owned a sheep farm, and their house was not far from mine. We had responsibilities, but there was also plenty of time to be mischievous. That was until my mother married and we moved away from Burna. Cristian and I were only ten years old, but we vowed that no matter what, we would always consider ourselves brothers. But as it turned out, Cristian's promise was a lie. At the age of eighteen, he betrayed me. Betrayed our brotherhood in the worst way." A gentleness still splayed across his face, but his harsh tone warned Isobel that it was just a mask.

"I don't believe you, Dario," she replied. "I see the menace in your eyes, feel it in your presence. And didn't you just confess that it was you who took his life? Stole his humanity from him?"

"Yes!" Dario spat. "But that was only after he had taken my everything away from me."

Isobel's brows furrowed; she hadn't thought of her father being turned into a vampire as an act of revenge. Rather, she had assumed it was out of jealousy, Cristian's refusal of Dario's companionship within the immortal world, and instead, created his own family.

"Cristian stole the very thing that made me want to keep living. The only thing I ever wanted. The only thing I ever loved. My betrothed, Catarine."

"Meg's mother." Isobel's words were barely audible, and her legs weakened. "How? When was this?" Unblinking, she waited for Dario to answer.

"We first met in 1415."

Isobel saw a storm building behind his eyes as the haunting memories came forth. Her own thoughts about Catarine, as well as Meg's distress over her mother's mortality, and what that meant for her, tumbled through Isobel's mind. She pressed the bag against her hip and remembered what Mariam had said before they left. *Everything you need to know is told in here.*

"Catarine had rescued me from the wretched hands of the man who was left to raise me after my mother—" His words silenced for a moment. "He killed her," Dario said softly. "With his bare hands. I wanted revenge, but I was just a boy of twelve years and no match to a grown man, so I ran. Catarine found me in the woods crying like a bairn. We were the same age, but Catarine seemed older. Wiser. That first night, she hid me in her family's stables. I had been so afraid I would be found and returned home, but as soon as she could, she slipped out and stayed with me through the night. The next morning, she convinced her family to take me in. I lived there for six years. We were inseparable and in love. I had even asked her father for her hand. After that, it all fell apart. By happenstance, she met Cristian when she and her mother traveled to visit a dying relative. They stopped at a market in Burna to purchase a few items, and Cristian was there."

Dario balled his hands into fists, the bones in his fingers cracking just as they had before she escaped through the portal.

"He was shocked the first time he came to the house and saw that I was there. He said he had wondered what had happened to me all those years after I moved. But after that, he barely acknowledged me; soon afterwards, Catarine also ignored me. It was like I no longer existed. I wanted him dead, but as luck would have it, the fool thought he was man enough to appear in court and pledge his allegiance to defend his country. He left for Fort Canon within weeks. I was never so thankful and thought this would be the chance for Catarine and me to be one again. I had even prayed for him to be killed in battle, or at least so disfigured that she wouldn't be able to stand the sight of him. But after he left, she became more distant, so I decided to go after him. I had planned to confront him and demand that he stay away from her. Maybe even write her a letter explaining that he had met another woman. And if he didn't, I was going to rip him apart with my bare hands. Unfortunately, I had witnessed how volatile a man's hands can be. The taste of hatred lay so thick on my tongue that I vowed Cristian would pay. It was while I was on my journey after him, as I circled

Loch Lomond, that I was brutally attacked. My mortality was ripped from me so painfully that it was I who was begging to die."

Dario stopped for a moment and took in a deep, unnecessary breath. "Perhaps for a brief period I did, but when I finally awakened—" straightening, he anchored himself to the ground and clasped his hands behind his back—"I was this. And I was thirsty."

Isobel remained still and silent, unsure if she should speak. If she did, what would she say? Dario's confession of his past, his human life, and the connection he shared with Catarine and Cristian was not something she had prepared herself for.

"With my newfound abilities, I picked up his scent and moved with such incredible speed that I found him within minutes, propped against a tree, just as the sun went down. He never saw me coming. As soon as I buried my teeth into his flesh and felt his blood soothe my thirst, I decided I wouldn't stop until I drank him dry. I walked away that night believing he was dead, that I had killed him and no one would ever know. I was elated with the idea that he would never have Catarine again. I didn't find out until more than a decade later that Catarine had discovered almost immediately what I had done; she had ways about her that were inexplicable.

"You see, our paths crossed a few years ago as I was passing through Dunkinshire. She and the red-headed witch, who was just a wee one at the time, were together, walking alone in these woods. Catarine asked me if I knew anything about the leech's whereabouts. I was taken back at first. I had killed him so long ago and told her that I couldn't believe she still longed for him. It was then that she revealed she had placed a protection spell over Cristian the day he left for court so that if he did ever go into battle, he would return to her. She went on to explain that he had shown up at Elden Castle three years earlier and disappeared after some time without saying a word. I looked down at the wee girl who clung to her mother's hand, and I couldn't help but notice that her glaring blue eyes were hauntingly familiar. I looked back at Catarine and saw the sadness reflecting in her face, and suddenly, I was as livid as the first day I saw her and Cristian together. He didn't die after my attack. Instead, he became an immortal just like me. For a moment, I was speechless. But as I looked from mother to daughter, I realized that this time she and Cristian had gone too far. I had to put an end to any possibility of them ever reuniting again, and to my own suffering. So, six days after we spoke in the woods, I stood and watched her burn at the stake."

Isobel took a step back, her heals now teetering on the edge of the cliff. Had he just confessed that he was responsible for Meg's mother's death? And what did he mean that they had gone too far this time?

"I know what you're thinking—that it doesn't make much sense for me to have her killed, loving her so much. But I wanted her to feel the finality of never getting to be with those she loved again—her children, her husband, her family, but especially him."

Silence filled the space between them, and then, clearly agitated by the memory that unfolded in his mind, Dario shouted, "She deserved it! And so did he. Cristian was never my mate, you see; I never chased after him for companionship, but rather in an act of revenge, slowly stealing everything that he treasured the most."

"Then why are you so angry that I killed him?" Isobel asked, regaining her confidence.

"Because he is now at peace and no longer suffering. They are once again together, and I am here, alone, awaiting the curse Catarine also confessed that day that would punish me for my actions against him. However, I am beginning to think that was a lie. It's been more than a decade, and as you can see, I am perfectly fine." Spreading his arms wide, Dario turned in a slow circle.

"So you didn't remove Cristian's body from the abbey this evening?" Isobel asked. Kenneth had said there was no body in the sanctuary, only the smell of death. "And what was the curse?"

Dario tilted his head and squinted, giving Isobel an odd look. "No. I may have been a bit angry and moved him around as I kicked his body into the wall a few times, but I walked out of there alone." Raising an eyebrow, he asked, "Why would you ask me that?"

"What was the curse, Dario? The one Catarine claimed she

cast on you," she asked again.

A drop of venom fell from one corner of his mouth as a growl rumbled in his chest. "Of course, that is all you care about learning from me. Why should I be surprised? Actually, I wonder why the red-headed witch didn't tell you, for she is well aware. If she were here right now, we could both ask her, for I don't know."

"Meg?" Isobel thought about the book that remained pressed at her side. "She was just a child when her mother died; how could she know?"

Ignoring her question, Dario stepped forward. "Enough about me and that half-breed witch," he stated. "What about you?"

Dario's face had turned hard and unforgiving as he spoke. "I told you my story, my reasoning behind wanting him dead. What's your excuse? If you are who you claim to be, then I want to know, what daughter kills her own father?" Dario drew out his accent with a particular boldness as he crouched, looking ready to pounce.

Isobel had seconds to decide her next move when a glimpse of white moved in the darkness behind Dario. She gasped and nearly slipped off the cliff.

Chapter 39

"I can tell you about the curse," Meg said as she stepped out of the shadows of the trees, her words sizzling in the icy cold air.

Cloaked in confusion, Dario spun around, his cheeks warmed and eyes widened. Clearly, he hadn't expected Meg's arrival.

"It came from my mother as an act of retribution for taking her one true love's life, or rather, his mortality. Dario, my mother has cursed you to a life of solidarity and loneliness. You will never achieve the companionship you desire, and as I am sure you have realized by now that every time you try, you will only experience heartbreak and disappointment."

"Meg, you were just a child when—" Isobel was going to say when she and her mother spoke with Dario in the woods, but Meg cut her off.

"Wait, Isobel, there is more." A rustle overhead forced the three to look up just as a cluster of leaves followed by a magpie swooped from the thickly woven branches above.

Fara, be careful! Isobel silently called to her familiar. The magpie squawked loudly as she flew past Dario and landed on an uprooted tree nearby.

Unaffected by Fara's presence, Meg resumed her story.

"My mother has also claimed that a divine presence came to her and spoke of how a great prophecy will unfold. I wasn't able to make out much of the details, but what was clear was that Dario will experience a great loss of power at the hands of one of my mother's descendants. This successor will overcome many misfortunes, all of which will prove her strength and resiliency, and in the end, she will be rewarded by a greatness well beyond her imagination. There is no day or hour given as to when the prophecy will be fulfilled, but fate will know when the time has come. It cannot be stopped or altered, and there is no escaping The future for us all has been put in place."

Meg's eyes lifted and met Dario's. "In the end, there will be Dario's death, executed at the hands of his greatest enemy, Cristian."

But Cristian was dead.

Moving her arms tighter around her abdomen, Isobel felt the fur pouch that sat at her hip and the bulk of the papers inside. She grasped the opening and clamped it shut.

Meg's eyes dropped to the bag at Isobel's hip. "You will see," she said with a smile. "Thank you for teaching me how to read and taking me to the future to meet my niece, Mariam. Without doing so, I'm not so sure I would have learned the truth about my mother and the great legacy of our family that began with her."

Isobel stood still. It was true! Catarine's diary was in her possession! Meg was sending her to the future with greater knowledge of this prophecy that she had just explained! Could her unborn daughter be the fulfillment of the prophecy that Meg just spoke of? The idea made her knees buckle, and she shuffled her feet forward to keep from falling.

"Preposterous! Look around me," Dario said, breaking the silence.

Meg and Isobel looked away from one another and at the vampire between them. For a brief moment, they had forgotten he was there.

"Do I look like I have great power? Am I sitting on a throne?" he asked. "And as for Cristian causing me any sort of harm, much less my death, well, did we both not just discuss the death that you felled upon him?" Annoyance sounded in his voice, and Isobel stood tall and took a step back toward the cliff. She couldn't believe that she had left herself unguarded.

Her heart tapped rapidly at the realization, and the sensation of it blinded Dario for an instant. Throwing his head back, he dropped his arms and inhaled the rush of lavender that saturated the air around them.

"Tragedy corrects everything, Dario," Meg said as she looked away from him and toward the sea behind Isobel. "Those were the last words my mother wrote."

Disorientation gripped Isobel, and she sucked in a breath. Pins and needles pricked at her hands, and her legs quivered. Meg's blood sizzled with so much heat that it seared Isobel's insides and pushed her thoughts away from her own life and toward Meg's. The expression in the girl's eyes was identical to the one Isobel had witnessed when they reached the abbey to rescue Elspeth. At the time, Isobel had feared that the empty look was somehow related to the evil that once lurked within the abbey, but once Meg had confessed about ingesting the vervain, Isobel understood. And now she had done it again; poisoned herself to kill a vampire. This was too dangerous. Dario was not Cristian. He had no reason to keep Meg alive. If she didn't have enough of the herb in her blood, Dario might only suffer some mild hallucinations, but Meg, the girl Isobel had come to love, and even called sister, could be killed.

"Meg—" The rest of her words died in her throat as Meg's hand slipped into the pouch of her cloak. *The pendulum!* A desperate and violent hope rippled throughout Isobel's body. If Meg could channel into the charm, maybe she could hear Isobel's thoughts, just like she had the night Isobel had arrived in Dunkinshire and begged her not to go into the woods. Instead of speaking, which she couldn't have done without alerting Dario, Isobel silently willed Meg to move behind the trees and return to Elden Castle as fast as she could.

"I know you must be wondering what I'm doing out here," Meg said. Isobel heard her, but she wasn't really listening. Rather, her attention was drawn to Meg's hand that had suddenly stilled underneath the woolen fabric of her cape. Over and over, Isobel wordlessly commanded Meg to race home, but if Meg was aware of Isobel's unspoken message, she showed no signs of it and continued explaining her unexpected presence in the woods.

"I couldn't sleep, so I went to the north tower. There were many things I wanted to tell you earlier but at the risk of Gavan barging in on us, I didn't. But when I got to your room, you weren't inside and the door and window were open. I was worried Gavan had gone back on his word, so I pulled back the loose tapestry and looked out to see if he was dragging you into the woods again. That's when I saw you running, Isobel, followed by Fara flying overhead. You were going to leave without saying goodbye, weren't you?" Meg asked softly, her voice tinged with sadness.

She took another step closer to Dario and Isobel, and the shards of light from the moon shifted from her face to her arm, illuminating the bite marks that Cristian had inflicted upon her earlier. The wounds had sealed, and their redness had begun to fade. By tomorrow, her magic would see that they had healed completely, just as it had before, except for the pair of hardened white circles that pocked her left wrist. The thin, fragile skin there had endured too much damage and the best that her magic could do was keep the wound sealed.

"I planned to keep my distance and wait, but when I saw your reaction to Dario's appearance, I couldn't leave." Meg's tone was now cold and direct, and Isobel listened carefully. "I had no idea you had planned to meet him; your knowledge of him was a bit of a surprise to me. Why didn't you tell me that you knew the vampire who created Cristian was here? We could have come to meet him together just as we did before."

"I didn't tell you because my plans are different than they were in the abbey. What you are doing is much too dangerous," Isobel said.

Fara, who had not moved from the stone since she'd come down from the trees suddenly flew toward Isobel and landed on her shoulder. The sleek feathers of her head rubbed against her neck, and Isobel began to calm.

Another snarl vibrated against Dario's throat. He stood in reverie between the two witches: Meg in the trees and Isobel teetering at the edge of the cliff with her familiar. Desire consumed him, and Isobel knew he wanted them both, but for very different reasons. However, she also guessed that he yearned to hear more about Catarine and Cristian, or maybe himself. Otherwise, why would he have allowed the conversation to go on for this long without advancing on one of them?

"Isobel, there is one more thing. Something that I think will be of interest to you too, Dario."

"I sincerely doubt it," he responded with feigned interest. "All I'm interested in is silencing the both of you." He looked back and forth between the two witches, calculating who he would devour first. "However, benevolence has suited me from time to time, so if continuing this ridiculous conversation is how you'd like to spend your final moments of life, then please, carry on."

"Remember when I told you that I believed that the three of us—you, me, and Cristian—were somehow connected?" Meg asked, appearing not the least bit concerned with Dario's declaration of their impending deaths.

"Yes." Isobel's eyebrows arched along her forehead.

"Well, I was right. There is a reason that you and I bonded so quickly, and it has nothing to do with magic." Meg took a deep breath. "We are sisters, Isobel. Half-sisters actually. Three hundred years and two different mothers separate us, but we share the same father. Cristian."

Isobel wasn't sure she heard Meg correctly. "Cristian—"

"Yes, it is true. I overheard the story Dario was telling you before I announced myself. In her writings, my mother confesses that she succumbed to weakness that afternoon and found herself in Cristian's arms within minutes after he arrived. Too many years had kept them apart, so they spent most of the afternoon in the stables trying to make up for lost time. The following winter, I was born." Meg pulled the magical charm from the woolen pouch, and Dario's eyes widened.

"It is why she left me this ring. Cristian gave her this band before he went to court. It was his promise that he would be back and they would be together forever. But from that day in the stables until her persecution, my mother never saw him again. She was never given the chance to tell Cristian that they had a child. All those months he spent feeding from me—sharing his immortal abilities and revisiting his past life—we were father and daughter, and neither of us knew." Fara bounded off Isobel's shoulders and in the direction of Meg.

"Enough! I have heard enough!" Dario shouted. He swiped at the magpie who dived in front of him before landing on Meg. Agitation consumed him, and he thought he would explode if any more was said about the man he regretted never killing when they were both human. Turning, he faced Isobel.

"Now, where were we before the red-headed witch appeared? Oh yes, I remember. I was going to kill you." His nostrils flared, and he flashed a wicked smile as he tilted his head toward Meg. "She is begging for me to bite into her flesh, but that will not happen until you are destroyed." Then, like a pair of polished daggers, his eyes grew dark and his pupils swallowed the charming golden irises that had encircled them just seconds ago.

The moon ducked behind a passing cloud, and without its light, Meg's and Dario's figures were swallowed in the darkness. This vampire projected no images into Isobel's mind, nor did he speak any more words aloud; he didn't have to. The coldness that enveloped her and the feelings he emitted were enough; he was tired of hearing all that cursed him. The magic within his body had thinned, and the blood had turned to ice. Dario had returned, limb by limb, to his cold, hard state of the undead.

The time had come for Isobel to make her final move.

Chapter 40

Three weeks earlier, Isobel had believed that her journey to the Highlands was about saving her and her unborn daughter's life. It was true that traveling to the past had allowed her to escape her possible death and find a brief solace from the vampires that had murdered her family, but tonight, as she stood on the edge of the cliff, just a few feet away from the predator who emitted the most danger, Isobel realized that her call to the past had been for a greater purpose.

Dario and Cristian had been chosen to chase her into another realm, just as her one hundred year time jump discrepancy had been no mistake on her part. Rather, the prophecy had commanded the distortion of the portal route against her initial request, manipulating the invisible passageway through twists and turns until it reformed its destination to where she was needed first. Landing in the year 1597 had been Isobel's fate from the beginning.

She stared at the vampire's silhouette as he stepped toward her, his movements pulling her from her thoughts. His clothing clung to him like a second skin, and he hunched forward, allowing his shoulders to lead the way. Isobel kept her gaze locked on him, sensing his anger intensify with each step that brought him closer to her. He had waited long enough, and the sparkle that reflected off his eyes from the moonlight told Isobel that the demon in him was delighted; he believed her to be trapped.

Isobel thought of her own time and Dario's continual pursuit of her father. She would never forgive either of them for Dario's attack on her mother, but at least it now made sense; he had killed her out of revenge toward her father. He hadn't cared about the power her magic temporarily gave to him or even filling himself with her blood. No, draining her mother of life and removing her from Cristian's world had been Dario's only intent. She imagined Dario stuck, living a life devoid of clarity and satisfaction, year after year, decade after decade, century after century. No wonder he was so angry, so full of hate and revenge.

Like the first time their paths crossed, the vampire was unaware of the gateway that lay churning beyond Isobel's reach. Fara, who had seemed confused, flying back and forth from Meg to Isobel, now clung to the front of Isobel's dress. Isobel knew her familiar was having a difficult time saying goodbye.

"It is fine, Fara. Meg needs you now. She needs her mother." The magpie cocked her head, and within her tiny black irises, Isobel saw the spinning blue flecks that had surfaced in the portal on their way to the Highlands three weeks ago. A tear slid from the corner of the magpie's eye. Isobel cupped Fara in her hands and held her close one final time; breathing her in and brushing the silky feathers of her head against her palm. *I will miss you.*

Before she could change her mind, Isobel opened her hands and released the magpie into the air. Grabbing the pentacle at the base of her neck, she squeezed the five pointed star between her thumb and index finger. Her sudden movement along with the sound of Fara's mournful caws caused Dario's composure to snap. His jaw unhinged, and as his ivory canines gleamed in the moonlight, drops of venom wet their tips. An evil burst of laughter poured around her like a thick glass of ale, and he lunged toward Isobel, but she was ready and let herself fall into the raging waters and the center of the spinning portal below. Dario skidded to a stop at the edge of the cliff, fury pooling in his chest. The rocky ledge crumbled under the impact of his weight, his arms frantically reaching for her.

Isobel fell with ease and once again left the deranged and demonic vampire empty-handed. His roar of anger chased after her but silenced as the gateway sealed shut and swallowed her whole.

Unlike her journey to the Highlands, Isobel experienced no feelings of being sucked in or jerked recklessly about. There was no struggle for breath nor feelings of entrapment. Her abdomen, which had become hard with Charlotte's rapid growth, softened, and her daughter, too, relaxed as they drifted effortlessly through time.

Isobel's mind recalled the past and present, and all the events that had happened between; her mother and Thomas's death, her travel to the Highlands, and meeting Meg. Taking Meg to the future and confirming from Mariam that her father was a vampire. Assisting Meg to commit murder and then watching her father, whom she never thought would be living in this time, die on the floor of Diarmad Abbey and turn to stone before her very own eyes. Discovering that she and Meg were not only blood related, but sisters fathered by the same man; the vampire they together had plotted against and poisoned.

She thought of the book at her hip and hoped that the pages inside would fill in the gaps of Meg's story. The idea that she had a sister born three hundred years before her was not only a shock, but also a sadness as she knew she would never see Meg again. She had no plans to return to Dunkinshire, or anywhere, for that matter. She would save her energy and take care of herself so that she could live a long life beside her daughter. Isobel did worry about Meg, Elspeth, Gavan, and Kenneth. Closing her eyes, she prayed for their safety not only as they made their way to England, but also for the remainder of their lives.

Isobel had once believed that the loss of her mother and husband would weigh her down forever. But to her surprise, as she moved through the portal and felt her daughter's strong pulse beat within her, she realized that gone were the shadows of gloominess. The heaviness of devastation. And in their place, Isobel had developed the strength to move forward.

An uncertainty remained as to her purpose and who she was supposed to be; learning the truth about her father hadn't lessened that. If anything, it had made her more cautious. More aware. She thought of herself as someone who straddled life between two worlds: the mortal and immortal. One thing she was certain of, though, was that her existence was important to the prophecy. The telling tale was the date of her birth; December twenty-first, the shortest day of the year, the winter solstice. She rested a hand upon her swollen abdomen. Charlotte's birth wasn't expected until after the new year, but the child inside of her already felt full term.

A spark of excitement stirred for the new life that she and her daughter would begin. One far from Dario and where she could raise Charlotte free of secrets. Isobel's whole life had been built on a lie, and she had no plans to repeat her mother's doings.

"I will share only the truth with you, my daughter," she said. "I will tell you everything. Prepare you. Make sure that you know how to take care of yourself, no matter what traits you are born with; my otherworldly or your father's ordinary."

Isobel would always hold dear the precious memories she, and Thomas and her mother shared. And she knew that one day they would all be reunited. Until that time came, she would make them proud.

Releasing the pentacle, Isobel thanked the ancient elements of fire, water, wind, and earth, and let the spirit lead her and Charlotte into the next chapter. Their lives were bound together in the center of a storm that churned wildly but with purpose. Isobel's only hope was that her daughter was not the child the prophecy spoke of. She prayed Charlotte's life would never intersect with Dario's, not even in his downfall.

Isobel understood that she had been sent to find the origin of her ancestry. Her mother had once said that time was a never ending circle. "History repeats itself, Isobel. You must always be aware. And you must always remember. Everything is connected. As is everyone."

History repeats itself; the words echoed in Isobel's head as she landed on the hard ground. Looking around, she smiled at her surroundings. She closed her eyes, drew in a long breath, and filled her lungs with the salty air that blew off the ocean. The breeze that moved through her hair was warm, and the call of the birds as they flocked overhead was calming; her new surroundings were as peaceful as she had expected.

Isobel placed her hand on her abdomen, and her daughter pushed against her touch. Rolling to her side, she slid the fur pouch beneath her head; the weight of sleep barreling down on her. Before slipping into a deep slumber, she grasped the pentacle at her throat and accepted the task she had been called upon to carry out when she fled to the Scottish Highlands—preserve Catarine's legacy and prepare her descendants for the future.

Epilogue

Cristian awakened, the right side of his face pressed into the cold slab of the sanctuary's floor. His eyelid fluttered as it struggled open and he squinted to focus: Where was he? What had happened?

He lifted his head, but a searing pain exploded down his spine and throughout his broken body, forcing him to collapse. His legs bucked fiercely against the pain, sending dozens of tiny cracks scattering across the earthen floor. Cristian grimaced. His eyelids closed, but they couldn't hide the agony behind his bright blue eyes and pale white skin.

How many times had he evaded death? How many more chances would he be given? It seemed impossible, as though he had been cursed not to die.

Cristian? Catarine's voice sounded in his ears, and his heart gave a single loud thud, his long golden lashes quivering against his cheek. The promise of unconsciousness that weighed him down wasted no more time and consumed him whole.

The magic from the blood he had devoured raced through his veins and conjured Catarine's image so clearly that when she called out his name again, it was if she was lying beside him.

"If only you were really here—" he mumbled.

"Darling, I know you are in there and can hear me,"

Catarine said as she slid one hand beneath him and cupped Cristian's face, her thumbs brushing his hair from his eyes. "Rest, and don't be afraid. Your body will heal just as it has all the other times. I made sure of that a long time ago. I know that you believe I am a vision brought on by drinking magical blood, but my darling, Cristian, I am real. And I am here. We have had some dark days, too many years torn apart, but I am alive, and I vow never to lose you again. There is so much that I have to tell you as soon as the time is right, but for now all I ask is that you trust me and believe what I'm about to say."

Cristian lay motionless, lost in a dream too good to ever wake up from. Perhaps he had been wrong earlier. Maybe he was dead and had somehow been granted a second chance to spend eternity with Catarine. Maybe his soul hadn't been damned after all! Could it be possible?

He tried to make sense of her words, but they jumbled in his mind as the darkness and the pain that engulfed him demanded a greater presence. And then, suddenly, he stilled. Her whispers silenced, and he felt the gentle pressure of her lips on his. The scent of honeysuckle consumed him so intensely that his surroundings began to swirl. Never before had his visions seemed as real as they did now. He wanted to move against her and kiss her back, to reach out and pull her into him, but his unconsciousness anchored him to the floor and wouldn't allow it. Then, all too soon, her weight lifted, and his dizziness came to a halt.

"Good bye for now. I love you."

Cristian strained to hear more, but only the whipping sound of wings, frantic at first and then slowly fading into the distance followed Catarine's declaration of love.

The sun moved across the sky and towards the horizon, its rays of light shifting through the cracks of Diarmid Abbey until they shined down on Cristian's now flawless and perfectly healed form. It had taken longer than normal due to the herb Meg and Isobel had tainted themselves with, but as always, his injuries had healed perfectly. His eyelids flipped open and revealed tiny red flecks spinning in his bright blue irises; the blood he had ingested earlier still circulated throughout his system. He took in the smells around him, the intoxicating scent of blood teasing his nostrils and making them flare while the absence of noise, quieter than silence, vibrated in his ears. A stream of wetness seeped from the corner of his lips and pooled between his cheek and the sanctuary floor.

How long had he been unconscious?

An empty pewter goblet turned on its side caught Cristian's attention, and he eyed the dried dark red droplets that lay scattered, causing his venom to release uncontrollably. Beside the cup lay the single black feather of a magpie. Cristian's heart gave a second thud and then a third. He wasn't dead, nor had he been dreaming. Catarine had been here! And her final words before she went silent now made sense: Catarine had the ability to change her form. She was alive! A frosty breath of air burst from his lips, and without warning, Cristian sprang to life. He stood tall. Strong. Ready.

His head snapped upright, and his fists clenched, the bones throughout his body cracking with the abrupt, sudden movements. The distant sound of hooves pounding across the glen hammered in his ears, and lifting his nose in the air, he stilled; others were on their way. Humans.

His heart gave a fourth thud. His lips parted, and his venom now streamed in a soundless motion. The energy within the abbey turned feral, and the air filled with bloodlust. Instinct had surfaced, and Cristian was hungry.

Wide-eyed, he scanned the room. His mind was a tangle of thoughts, none of them as clear as he remembered while he lay unaware. Images flashed before him—Meg and the mysterious familial witch he had been drawn to protect. She had uttered the words *'Goodbye, Father'* just as the blood, thick and laced with his own scent and heavily tainted with deadly herbs, subdued his body. A distinct bitterness formed on his tongue.

He had known as the chalice touched his lips that demise would fall upon him, but he couldn't deny its contents. His one weakness as an immortal was the absence of self-control, even in his own best interest. And Catarine had known this. He bit back a growl as her whispered words came back to him as he lay lifeless—*It is true, I am alive— you have to keep Meg safe,*

Cristian, just as any father would do—she is proof of our love—cursing you not to die was the only way I could protect you—when the time is right, we will be a family— I love you.

His eyes widened as it all came together. The first time he saw Meg, he thought he was seeing a ghost and had even called her Catarine.

"No, I am Meg," she had corrected. "But Catarine was my mother. Did you know her?"

As he had looked at her, ready to answer that indeed he knew her mother quite intimately, her eyes held him captive, their shape and bright blue color a true reflection of his own. That should have told him all he ever needed to know. He could have asked her more questions; at the least, discovered her age and counted back the years to that day in the stables, but maybe he hadn't wanted to believe it to be true. Or even possible, for that matter. Until now. Catarine was Meg's mother, and he was—

The weight of Cristian's burdens reflected in his glassy eyes as the transformation from bright, mesmerizing blue to hungry, crimson red completed. He threw back his head, unhinged his jaw and fled from the sanctuary, his thundering footfalls echoing off the stone walls with each fervent step he took. He would bring Catarine back to him. He needed more answers.

"Meg!" he roared as he reached the abbey entrance, and then he took off in search of his daughter.

Made in the USA
Coppell, TX
18 February 2026

72291433R00229